INVITATION TO THE MARRIED LIFE

INVITATION TO THE MARRIED LIFE

Angela Huth

GROVE PRESS
New York

Published by Grove Press
A division of Grove Press, Inc.
841 Broadway
New York, NY 10003-4793

First published in Great Britain in 1991 by
Sinclair-Stevenson Limited, London

Library of Congress Cataloging-in-Publication Data

Huth, Angela, 1938–
    Invitation to the married life / Angela Huth.—1st American ed.
        p.   cm.
    ISBN 0-8021-1465-2
    I. Title.
PR6058.U8515   1992   91-31446
823'.914—dc20   CIP

Manufactured in the United States of America

Printed on acid-free paper

First American Edition 1992

3   5   7   9   10   8   6   4   2

For
Simone
and
Fred

Contents

'Marriage ought to be the object of universal respect . . .'
                                                    Balzac

PART ONE
THE
INVITATIONS

THE POWER of Rachel Arkwright to annoy her husband Thomas, always active, was particularly strong at eight in the morning. For her, breakfast was the most dangerous time of day. It was then, unwittingly, several times a week, she would find herself making the first mistake. Sometimes she would determine to keep silent. But even silence was no armour against his irritation.

'What's the matter now?' he would demand. 'Bad night again? No, don't tell me about it.'

And Rachel would sigh, trying to weigh up whether it was worth answering the question, or whether to keep her vow of not speaking until it was time to say her daily, lustreless goodbye.

It had not been as bad when the children were at home, although Thomas had still dominated breakfast, ensuring his general air of displeasure made its effect. Jeremy, who had never been afraid to stand up to his father, would occasionally goad him with some left-wing view of whatever was in the news. They would shout at each other, bang down mugs, slopping coffee over the sides to make rings on the beeswaxed wood of the table. But at least it was *their* row, not Rachel's responsibility. She and Helen would exchange minimal looks, nothing so unsubtle as a raised eyebrow – they had learned that lesson many years ago. To Thomas, a raised eyebrow was an indication of ganging up against him, betrayal. He would become further enraged, shout abuse which – possibly – he did not mean. So mother and daughter had pared their solidarity down to a look of recognition invisible to the outside eye, and indeed to Thomas, who in many ways was not an observant man.

Nowadays, Rachel desperately missed the protection of the children. The daily tension of trying not to do the wrong thing made her clumsy. She would burn toast, break fried eggs, spill salt. The bones of her hands were bleached ridges shining through the skin. In the mornings she felt old.

Today, a Tuesday in early summer, was one of the silent mornings – an irascible silence on Thomas's part. This he made clear by breaking it with noisy pecks at his coffee, and impatient slashing at the newspaper as he turned its pages. Last night he had been at a business dinner. He had returned home after midnight complaining of a headache. Mornings after business dinners were particularly fraught with danger.

Rachel pushed away her finished grapefruit and looked at the familiar sight opposite her. There he was, a caricature of a husband, almost completely hidden – guarded against her – by the *Daily Telegraph* (he had recently switched from *The Times*). Two pinkish blobs of fuzzy-backed hands held the pages wide open. Rachel could visualise the equally familiar sight of Thomas's lower half beneath the table: plump pin-striped knees and calves, solid ankles in socks of wrinkled grey wool, feet trussed up in expensive leather shoes. She often marvelled at the heaviness of Thomas: he had been almost bony as an undergraduate. On the rare occasions she had to experience his weight, she would shut her eyes against the bulge of his stomach and think of him by day. Dressed, his bulk (which was well proportioned) was enhanced by the tightness of his clothes. His tailors had orders to take in seams as far as they would go, streamlining his suits in a way that was appropriate to far thinner men. Thomas's vanity screened him from reality. He did not think of himself as a fat man.

Rachel laid her hand over the small pile of letters on the table beside her. The slight anticipation they afforded her

4

every morning was a small, secret comfort. She had always enjoyed both writing and receiving letters, though it seemed to be a dying art these days, and not many came her way. Jeremy's only communication in term was a reverse charge call from Cambridge once a week to absolve himself of guilt. Helen wrote quite often – warm, funny letters that made life at Durham sound more entertaining than it really was. Rachel looked forward to hearing from Helen. She would read the new letter several times, when Thomas had gone, and store it with the collection of others in her desk. Mostly, though, the pile was disappointing: bills, reminders from the dentist, witless duty postcards from friends abroad.

This morning Rachel observed, with an excitement out of all proportion to the event, an expensive white envelope at the bottom of the brown ones. She pulled it out, examining it carefully. Black ink, large arrogant handwriting. Postmark: Northampton. The Farthingoes, obviously. . . . Rachel slit open the envelope. In her exhilarated state she forgot that the noise of tearing paper would be bound to annoy Thomas; and suddenly she didn't care.

The thick white card, beautifully engraved, was indeed from the Farthingoes.

'Thomas,' said Rachel, fingering the card with all the reverence of a woman who once used to love parties and cannot quite discard the habit, 'Frances and Toby have asked us to a ball.'

There was a moment's terrible silence. Rachel could imagine her husband's eyes blazing to the end of a sentence. She could hear her own heart thumping very fast. Once again, in her foolish excitement, she had made an irretrievable mistake and would now have to bear the consequence.

'When?' asked Thomas at last.

The question, a chip of ice in the warmth of Rachel's expectancy, was devoid of all interest. Its single, tiny sound managed brilliantly to convey the uprising of his annoyance.

'September.'

Thomas put down the paper at last, folding it untidily. His

reddish eyebrows, raised, scratched at the furrows on his brow
– incredulous, scathing, bored.

'That's in four months' time, for heaven's sake.'

'You have to ask people very early if you want to be sure of
their coming.'

'Ridiculous system.'

Their eyes met. As usual, Thomas's lower lashes were
divided into three pointed clumps. They made his pale eyes
look startled as a starfish, rather silly. Years ago, when they
were first married, Rachel had laughed at them. Thomas,
willing in those days to please her, had allowed her to brush
them apart with a small mascara brush bought especially for
the purpose. But the practice had been given up long
ago. Rachel had grown accustomed to the look of silliness
that fronted his sharp, agitated mind, so that it only struck
her at bad moments. And possibly, to be fair, it was something she alone saw. Many women mentioned his handsomeness.

'Shall I accept?'

Thomas sighed. It occurred to Rachel he was attempting to
exercise self-control. For her part, she tried to dim the light
she knew must be fulminating in her own eyes. That would
be bound to go against her.

'I suppose so. *You* obviously want to go. Though what the
middle-aged want to give balls for I can't imagine. A more
ridiculous way of spending money –'

'Thank you.'

Rachel's heart increased its pace, making her careless
again. Anticipation (of a far higher order, of course, than the
actual party would be) suffused her in an amorphous golden
cloud that she would not attempt to describe. But could
not resist blurting out some trivial thought to indicate its
presence.

'We'll have to get your dinner jacket cleaned,' she said,
knowing even as she uttered the words she had gone too far
this time.

Thomas stood up. A purple flush enlivened his jowls.

'For God's sake, Rachel, do we really have to think about the cleaning of my dinner jacket four months ahead?'

Thomas took in the shape of Rachel: grubby towelling dressing gown pulled tightly in at the waist so that the (once flat) stomach protruded. Why would she never dress for breakfast? Her hair, unbrushed, more grey than auburn now, was backlit from a pale light from the window. Two-dimensional London trees outside, still the piercing green of mid-May, slightly moved their fretwork of leaves. Small shadows jiggled on the table. Butter on a dish shone so fiercely yellow that it hurt Thomas's eyes: he transferred his gaze to the cloudy ambers of marmalade in a glass jar, and then to the jug of bluebells slumped over the pottery sides of their jug. Rachel had picked them in the country last weekend and should have thrown them away two days ago, but she was disinclined to throw away flowers until they had reached the papery state of their death, no matter how often Thomas objected.

Had Bonnard been present, thought Thomas, and approached his canvas with half-shut eyes, he could have painted the kind of *Still Life with Breakfast and Wife* that would have made people dread middle age.

Rachel blinked, dryly. Once her eyes had been gold. She had been introduced to Thomas as the only girl at Oxford with genuinely gold eyes. That had been 1961. In London, nearly thirty years later, she was now the only woman he knew with eyes the colour of washing-up water. That was it, a sort of creamy dun. Colourless as oatmeal, flecked with faded saffron. The mean thoughts made him smile.

'Late again tonight,' he said. 'Nottingham all day, blast it.' He abandoned the hypocrisy of kissing his wife on the cheek, and left in a hurry.

Rachel, standing breast-high in her invisible cloud, was glad to see him go. She had her own life and this morning, as every morning, she was eager to get back to it.

7

For Thomas, driving slowly up the crowded M1, the prospect of the day ahead was not a happy one: a meeting with some French importers in the morning, board meeting in the afternoon. He had agreed to meet Gillian at The Wine Bar for lunch, and it was this plan he dreaded most of all. For today, Thomas had decided last week, would be the one he would *take the bull by the horns* (Gillian's language) and tell her it was all over – *curtains, finito*. If he used her own favourite expressions, perhaps she would understand and not make too much fuss, though this was unlikely. Gillian was a determined young feminist; any man who stepped out of line with her paid for it. Thomas had experienced many a thwack of her clichéd verbal abuse. He was often puzzled, considering how *short he fell of the mark* in her eyes, why she should wish to go on seeing him. All men were bastards, including Thomas. What she did not seem to realise was that he had no interest in proving her wrong. She also seemed to have no inkling that their association, as it had been from the beginning, was a disaster. *Wiping the slate* (heavens, it was catching) would be a relief. Normally, Thomas would not have baulked at the thought of a rough termination (he had weathered many in the past), but today the wretched headache was a hindrance. His mind was staggering uncertainly about, when it should have been braced, ready to fire accurately. Maybe, by late morning, things would have improved. He dabbed his temples with a handkerchief. A few years ago it would have been a cologne-scented handkerchief. Now, Rachel had given up buying him cologne. He missed it, along with the small surprises of Glenmorangie, cashmere socks, Bendicks Bittermints and gravad lax that she used frequently to arrange. But it was impossible to mention that he had even noticed the disappearance of such things, let alone minded that they were no longer part of his married life.

By five-past-twelve, when the two Frenchmen left his office, Thomas felt no better. The last of his energies had been exhausted by speaking French for half-an-hour, which had greatly held up the proceedings, and had not been necessary. The French clients were proficient in English, but to speak to

8

them in their own language was a matter of pride to Thomas. He abhorred the general British lack of talent at foreign languages, and was determined to prove that not all English businessmen were uneducated. Besides which, meetings conducted in a foreign language deterred the arrogant Doug, managing director of the firm, from interrupting as often as normal. Doug's talents – and Thomas had to concede he was an able man – did not include speaking French, though he kept up the pretence that he was absolutely *au fait* with everything that was going on. I may not be much of a linguist when it comes to the spoken word, he had once explained to Thomas, but as for understanding, I'm right there with the best of them.

'Everything understood, then?' Thomas asked him, aware of his meanness for the second time that morning, when the Frenchmen had gone.

'Of course, Tom. All be in hand by the end of the month.'

On Doug's notepad were several long, unknown words (phonetically spelled) which he would be obliged to look up in the dictionary at home this evening.

'Good,' said Thomas, getting up from his leather armchair, a fat hand splayed over his aching forehead. 'I'm off for an early bite. Wouldn't mind a breath of air before the session this afternoon.'

As he left the office he was aware of Doug's disapproval. Hell, it was his firm. Why shouldn't he come and go when he liked? Doug knew perfectly well that most of Thomas's thinking and planning, concerning the business, was not done in the office. Profits showed there were no flaws in this method. All the same, he could never be totally impervious to Doug's silent disapprobation. It annoyed him.

Out in the street a small wind touched his stricken temples. An idea came to him: he would slip along to The Gallery. There had to be some joy in a man's day, and he had promised himself to take another look at the beachscape he fancied. It would do no harm to keep Gillian waiting. On the one occasion he had been punctual her delight had been so extravagant he determined never to be on time again. Her chiding was easier to stomach.

In the silent gallery, with its soft carpets, white walls and gentle spotlights, Thomas felt peace at last. The girl at the table, writing, head bowed, took no notice of him. He had not seen her before. She had long amber hair. A small, dead white hand protruded from an over-long woollen sleeve, a translucent perspex ring on the middle finger. Funny, Thomas thought, how the young these days are so addicted to clothes that are much too big for them. Did they represent some sort of refuge, some sort of necessary camouflage against hard eyes? Or were they merely the innocent uniform of youth? Thomas had once ventured to ask his daughter why she was so attached to a grubby Viyella shirt that reached to her knees, billowing over a vast ethnic skirt. 'Oh, Dad, really, what d'you think?' had been Helen's inadequate reply.

Thomas turned his attention to the pictures, a collection of watercolours by an artist unknown to him. By jingo, he thought – just as he had on the previous occasion – the man can paint. Jealousy seared his heart. He would have given anything to have such talent, the skill to edge the paint to so perfect a hard line, to smudge the colours together in a way that made their moment of fusion almost imperceptible. Dammit. A lifetime in his studio at home, and he'd never achieve a tenth of the effect of this R. Cotterman. Thing to do, of course, would be to take a picture home, study the technique with a magnifying glass, have yet another try. . . . He found the one he had remembered, stood in front of it for a long time. Such simplicity! A pallid beach, a flat sea (amazingly, it seemed to have been painted with a single stroke: how could that be? what manner of brush, for heaven's sake?). A luminous grey sky. A single moment, caught by just one man.

Thomas made up his mind. He strode over to the table.

The amber hair parted. A shining white face, to match the hand, tilted up at him. Grey, unexpectant eyes met his. There was a strange, almost tangible tranquillity about the girl. Or perhaps, thought Thomas, she was just bored stiff working all

10

day in a gallery that almost no one visited. Inured by rare customers who hardly ever bought a picture, she seemed drained of all anticipation. Her pale face revealed nothing but nonchalance.

'I'll take the seascape, if I may,' said Thomas. 'The one in the corner. *Norfolk: Early Morning.*'

The grey eyes flickered, surprised, disappointed. 'It's three hundred and fifty pounds,' she said, so softly Thomas could scarcely hear.

'Worth every penny,' he said, and wrote out the cheque.

The girl wrapped the picture in several sheets of new brown paper. Thomas watched, fascinated, as she tied string into several small, efficient knots. He was surprised at her expertise, considering that the navy lambswool sleeves fell right over her thin fingers, but she made no attempt to push them back. Finally the parcel was finished. Thomas, glancing at his watch, realised it had taken ten minutes, for all her skill. It had been a very fast ten minutes. His headache, he realised, had quite gone.

'That be all right?'

'Fine. Thanks.'

'I'm sad to see it go, to be honest. It was my favourite.' She gave Thomas the merest smile, then glanced towards the empty corner.

'Oh dear, I am sorry if I've deprived you.'

The girl shrugged. 'Can't be helped. If I was a real pro, I'd be pleased we've made a sale. My trouble is, I fall in love with pictures much too easily, can't bear to see them go.'

Thomas smiled, sympathetic. 'What's your name?' He hadn't known he was going to ask any such impertinent question.

'Serena.'

Thomas was relieved she answered with the swiftness of a girl who did not mind such irrelevancies. Apt, her name, too.

'Very hard, feeling like that,' he said. 'I'd feel just the same myself.'

Serena gave him an incredulous look. 'Are you a painter?'

Thomas hesitated. 'Sort of. That is, I try.' Her incredulity

11

lingered. 'I've had my eye on this R. Cotterman for some time,' he added. 'In fact, I daresay I shall be back for another in the not-too-distant future.'

Serena sat down. She pulled her sleeves right down over clenched hands, defensive. 'Will you,' she said, but it was not a question.

Parcel firmly under his arm, Thomas hurried across the silent carpet to the door. Late for Gillian, he determined not to hurry. Confused by this girl, Serena, a mental picture of her luminous face accompanied him from The Gallery to The Wine Bar.

The designers of The Wine Bar were not innovators in their field. They had converted the small Nottingham premises in precisely the same genre as thousands of wine bars in other cities: high-backed chairs, inadequate tables, posters on the walls, the inevitable potted plants whose dull leaves claimed all vitality had been drained from them by the shadowed, smoky air. But for all its lack of charm, The Wine Bar was always crowded, noisy, popular. Thomas, who had been coming here for five months to meet Gillian, increasingly disliked it and had often suggested an alternative. But she felt at home in the place – Thomas could see why, having come to know her own flat – and resisted. So they continued to conduct the daytime part of their affair at a small table in the window, which Gillian had recently taken to calling 'our table', and was much annoyed if it was ever occupied by others.

She had secured it today, probably by arriving at noon: the graphics studio in which she worked seemed not to mind the flexibility of her hours. The familiar sight of her – indignant shoulders hunched up, spiky fingers riffling through peanuts as if they were worry beads – filled Thomas with gloom. Her total lack of joy in life had struck him within moments of meeting her, in this very place. The only thing that had intrigued him – mildly – ever since, was that any human soul could remain so bleak. She had had a happy childhood, friends, lovers, a job she enjoyed, and yet everything, most especially

Thomas, seemed to cause her offence. As he approached her, Thomas relished the thought of her ignorance: she could not guess, sitting there sipping at her large glass of thick tomato juice, that in half-an-hour he would be gone for ever from her life.

'Hello,' he said, arriving at the table.

'Hello, Tom.'

Thomas sat down and propped the parcel up, on the floor. The seat of the ridiculously small chair cut into his thighs, making them splay and bulge. The table top was too small to hide them.

Preoccupied with her own reasons for indignation, Gillian never noticed his discomfort.

'You're late,' she said, 'so I went ahead and ordered.'

Thomas had no intention of apologising. 'Time was against me,' he said.

'Don't I get a kiss, at least?'

They both leaned forward, brushed mouths. Thomas could smell sardine. A picture of her last night's solitary supper flashed into his mind. She had a terrible passion for sardines, which she ate from the tin with raw onions and some kind of dark gritty bread.

An overweight girl in jeans and a T-shirt dumped scampi in the basket in front of Gillian, accompanied by a knife and fork wrapped in a paper napkin.

'Yummy.' Gillian picked up a piece of scampi in her fingers, unable to contain herself. 'I'm ravenous. I didn't order one for you. Didn't think you'd like it.'

'Quite right,' said Thomas. Food was another of their incompatibilities. He ordered himself a gin and tonic and a tuna sandwich. 'Any news?' he asked.

'Not a pussycat.'

'Oh, dear. I am sorry.'

'You know me. Nothing ever happens.'

Thomas scrutinised her small, whey-coloured face. He could never quite remember it when she wasn't there – except for the eyes, the translucent gull's eyes, so sparse of eyelash there would have been no point in attempting to enliven them with mascara. They were the most intense eyes he had ever known, with a mean, accusatory glitter he had grown to dread. Gillian was altogether bird-like, he thought – beaky little nose, the bleached bone shining through transparent skin: claw-like fingers and toes, cocky strut of a walk. How on earth . . . ? he often asked himself.

Many times he had reflected upon the unfortunate mistake which had resulted in this paltry affair, and could never quite explain it, even to himself. The initial meeting – yes. Any man, bored and lonely, might have succumbed, had he chanced upon an available girl that December night.

Thomas had arranged to meet a colleague, in this then unknown wine bar, for a drink after work. The colleague had not turned up. Gillian, at the next table, eked out a sullen-looking tomato juice, alone. She pretended to be engaged in a crossword puzzle. After four glasses of inferior wine, depressed at the thought of the evening alone in his hotel, Thomas introduced himself and suggested they share a further bottle. She had agreed, surprisingly eager. They talked, for some reason Thomas failed to remember, about biorhythms. Then Gillian supplied a crisp little word portrait of herself: health freak, militant socialist, the sort of girl who would march in the name of many a cause. Yes, she had spent a month at Greenham – the most meaningful experience of her life so far. Irritated from the start by her ghastly vocabulary, Thomas had told himself to be tolerant. This could be interesting, he remembered thinking. He had never met anyone like her before. And that first evening, in retrospect, was the only good one. Being with her felt like a slightly wicked adventure, a new experience. By midnight they were in her studio flat drinking herbal tea. Events after that were not entirely clear in his mind. He had had nothing to eat since lunch, and too much to drink. As the sludge-green walls of her flat swirled treacherously before his eyes, and Gillian's head bobbed up and down like a juggler's orange, it was all he could do to comport himself with some dignity. In fact, he was forced later to remember,

14

pulling off her jeans was a process he could never have accomplished without her help. His hands had been as useless as frozen gloves: his normal skill with buttons and zips had quite deserted him.

But he can't have been that maladroit because he then noticed Gillian's cheeks were now blotched with scarlet – ugly, hard-edged shapes that R. Cotterman, watercolourist, would have abhorred. Also, she mewled like a chained dog straining for freedom. Thomas was amazed by her stick-like thighs. She had the figure of a girl of twelve, which was faintly disturbing. But she was surprisingly strong. She interrupted his gaze with an impatient push. He found himself sprawled on the hideous duvet, where he encountered the first whiff of sardine, a smell which was to become all too familiar. Definitely in charge by now, she scrabbled all over him like an eager squirrel.

Next morning Gillian offered Thomas carrot juice and muesli and berated him for being tired, clumsy, and generally inadequate. But when he left, breakfastless, an hour later, she suggested they should meet for another drink next time he came to Nottingham. Somehow, the arrangement became a habit, and by now they had lumbered on for five months. Why? That was the enigma.

'As a matter of fact, not quite nothing,' Gillian was saying as she plunged a piece of scampi into a pool of tomato ketchup. 'Jenny came round to my place for supper last night.'

'That was nice,' said Thomas.

Jenny was her colleague at work. He had met her once: a scraggy little thing in a shrunken jersey and etiolated jeans. She had looked critically at Thomas and had hardly spoken. Plainly, he *had not come up to the mark*.

'Yes. We had a hot meal and, guess what? This'll surprise you – we shared a bottle or two of wine.'

'Good heavens, that does surprise me indeed,' said Thomas, who was never offered anything but herbal tea. 'Were you celebrating something?'

'Might have been.' Gillian looked down almost coyly.

Thomas could not bring himself to ask what: his interest

15

was rarely flared by her snippets of news. He drank his gin and tonic in silence, watching Gillian's odd, huffy movements as she dipped her bread in the rest of the tomato ketchup and sucked at it, making a smudged scarlet web round her mouth. He vowed that never again would he associate with a girl whose manner of speech, as much as her table manners, were likely to drive him mad.

Her head suddenly snapped back. A flycatcher tongue darted briefly at the red mess. She caught his eye, braced herself.

'Why don't you ever call me Gilly?' she hissed. 'You know how much that would mean to me.'

Thomas sighed. God knows how many times she had asked him that question. God knows how many times he had given her his 'unreasonable' answer.

'Don't let's go into all that again, please. You know I can't, I don't want to, I never shall. Why can't you just accept that?'

'The trouble with you, Tom, is that you're afraid of intimacy. Aren't you?' The gull's eyes scoffed over him.

'I dare say I was brought up to believe that a certain formality between people has its advantages.'

'Huh. Between lovers?'

'In the case of this ridiculous Gilly business, it's not that I stick to your real name for the sake of formality, but just because I detest the word *Gilly*. I find it aesthetically unpleasing to the ear, if you really want to know.' There, he was away. Here was his chance, sooner than anticipated. Now all he had to say was that none of it mattered a damn anyway because tonight it was to be goodbye, *curtains*, *finito* –

'I just wanted to try one last time,' Gillian interrupted, 'to make quite sure that you had no intention, ever, of making the smallest concession to my wants. And I *am* sure.'

'I don't know what you're talking about –'

'You're a bastard, Tom: a selfish, unthinking, fat, pompous, conceited, unfeeling boor – and I'm here to tell you, that as far as I'm concerned it's goodbye, curtains, finito, for ever.'

She wiped her furious mouth with the back of her claw; straightened herself up, triumphant.

16

'And just in case you're interested, which I don't suppose for a moment you are, Tom, Jenny's moving in.'

There was a silence between them. A horrible picture, involving the sardine duvet, came into Thomas's mind.

'You mean . . . ?'

'I mean she's moving in. Think what you like.'

Gillian pushed back her chair and stood up. She hoisted a very old school satchel onto her shoulder, pulling the stuff of her T-shirt taut so that Thomas could see the bones of her mean little chest beneath it.

'So, bye then, Tom. Cheers. I can hardly say thanks for the memory.'

She strutted off, bird's head eagerly forward, bony shoulders hunched in their usual, off-ended position, gull's eyes darting about for some new prey to arouse her indignation.

Thomas watched her walk past the window. She gave a brief wave, no smile. Thomas did not wave back. It occurred to him it was the first time he had seen her look cheerful.

When she was out of sight, he glanced at his watch: time for another drink. Then, to Doug's surprise, he would turn up early for the board meeting. He would also get his secretary to ring Rachel and say plans had changed: he would be home for dinner after all.

Every morning the ritual of Rachel's secret life began in the same way. She would stand at the bedroom window, watch Thomas fling his expensive briefcase on to the passenger seat of the Mercedes, then hoist himself into the driving seat. He never looked up.

When the car was out of sight, Rachel returned to the vast double bed. She added Thomas's two pillows to her own. The pillows were huge, old-fashioned squares, inherited from her grandmother (you could not buy them today), encased in fine linen, hand-embroidered with swirling initials in the corners. The letters were so delicate in design that Rachel often wondered if they were inspired by an illuminated manuscript. The

17

flourishing 'A', she liked to think, with its honeysuckle tendrils, was the work of a fifteenth-century monk.

The barely creased top sheet and blankets had been turned back, as if by an efficient maid preparing for her employers' night: this Rachel had done herself before going down to breakfast. On the large round bedside table, among the clutter of photographs, flowers, pens, notepads, engagement diary and piles of books, was a cup (white porcelain splattered with violets) of fresh coffee. Its smell fused with that of winter jasmine.

Rachel took off her slippers. For a moment she felt the pleasure of soft thick carpet beneath bare toes: then, between the sheets, the delicious contrast of chilled linen with its random whirlpool of creases which the toes could sensuously explore. She shifted herself into a position of maximum comfort, searched for her reading glasses and put them on. Beside her lay the *Telegraph*, battered by Thomas's rough handling, and her own neat copy of the *Independent*. They would take her half-an-hour to read. She would begin at nine o'clock. For the moment she cast her eyes up to the intricate ceiling of the four-poster bed, marvelling as usual at the fine geometry of the chintz pleats, the exquisitely central rose made of the same stuff. The building of four-poster beds was no mean art, and this one had cost Thomas several thousand pounds. It was a wild purchase she would never regret.

There was silence in the room. Rachel closed her eyes, waiting for the guilt, the daily guilt, to ebb away: then she picked up the first paper, and took the first sip of coffee.

She often wondered if, had it not been for the unfortunate combination of events one day eighteen months ago, she would ever have discovered her addiction.

It had begun as a perfectly normal day: letters at her desk in the morning, taking Thomas's clothes to the cleaners, shopping for something for dinner. It was a particularly cold January, and she returned from her small expedition to the local supermarket with stinging cheeks and frozen hands. To warm herself, she heated the remains of last night's carrot soup, and sat at the kitchen table cradling the hot earthenware mug. It was a functional rather than cosy kitchen: not a place where the family normally sat or ate. The silence, that bitter day, only punctured by erratic ticks from the fridge, made her shiver. Unwanted thoughts came to her mind, concerning the void in her life now that Helen had gone. Her duties as a magistrate, and her work for several charities, and the occasional business dinner party, took up a certain amount of time, but there were still many hours to spare. In the past, she remembered longing for the time when she would have hours to herself during the day, to read or listen to music undisturbed. Now that she had them, they were less wanted. In the three months since Helen had been away (thereby shattering the former discipline of arriving home at four after school, needing tea and encouragement with homework) Rachel had read most of the books she had been postponing for years, and had listened to hours of concerts on the radio. But the enjoyment of such luxury was beginning to pall. The shadow of a strange, unnameable guilt had crept up on her: she should be doing something, surely, instead of wasting her days, her life, her once competent and curious mind. At Oxford, she had read Law: perhaps she should resuscitate her skills and try, even at this late stage, to get some sort of legal job. But enthusiasm for this idea did not flourish, as it had in the days before marriage. Enthusiasm for any sort of job, in truth, was unavailable. And so the conflict grew: guilt at the pointless life on the one hand, lack of inspiration as to what she could do on the other. She did not discuss any of these matters with Thomas, but they became a preoccupation.

As one who had always abhorred the disturbances of introspection, Rachel made a great effort, that cold afternoon, to deflect her wearisome thoughts. She rose and washed-up her mug, dried it slowly and put it away. Outside a nasty yellow sky was broken into shifting flakes by a strong wind. The geriatric tree in the small back garden, all knuckles and fists and scraggy arms, tore at this chipped sky in terminal frenzy. Rachel found herself smiling at its anger. Deeply rooted in life between the paving stones, it knew its fate all too well: another spring, another flowering, another interminable year just standing. Their conditions were similar.

It was exactly the sort of afternoon on which Rachel would most have liked to stay at home, lit the fire and retired to an armchair with Turgenev's short stories. But, in fear of further disagreeable thoughts, and to prove to herself she had some strength of will, she decided to go out. She had recently spent a morning exploring the contents of her linen cupboard and had discovered that, after twenty years of neglect, many sheets were beyond repair. This afternoon, then, she would take a bus to Oxford Street and become cocooned in the linen sale at John Lewis. Quickly, before she could change her mind, she put on her thickest coat, scarf and gloves, and made her way to the bus.

The outward journey she rather enjoyed. Wedged warmly beside an old lady in a fur coat, she looked through the steamy windows at the passing flotsam of humanity, cold faces blasted by the wind. As always, she wondered what each one of them had had for breakfast, where they were coming from, where they were going, why, at that precise moment, they happened to be in her vision, innocent of her interest. She wondered how many thousands of people each of us merely sees, a most provocative connection, before they vanish for ever. She wondered if all her companions shared her hopeless curiosity about every passing human being, or if this was some worrying kind of mental disturbance which, in the end, would drive her mad.

In the linen department of John Lewis, she did her best to concentrate on the matter in hand: sheets. She studied her list, looked at tickets with their sale prices screaming in red ink, took off a glove to run a warm finger along flanks of percale, sea island cotton and, most desirable of all, real linen. Where should she begin? It was uncomfortably hot. A needle of sweat ran down her spine. The bland overhead lighting made the piles of white sheets reflect like snow. Curiously, she seemed to be the only customer. Had no one else in London run out of sheets? There was something unnerving in the emptiness of the place. Perhaps it was all a mistake. Perhaps she was not meant to be here, and the bargain sheets, arranged merely to tempt her, could not be sold. When she had made her choice, the saleswoman, if ever she could find one, would laugh at her and say it was all a trick. . . .

A man was suddenly at her side. Cheap suit, wall eye, chunks of hair slammed down with grease.

'Would Madam like any assistance?'

Yorkshire accent. Old-time courtesy. How many years since anyone had addressed her as Madam? Rachel stared at him, amazed. But, dizzied by the unaskable queries that fizzed in her head, she was unable to answer his question. At what point in his life had this man said to himself, That's it, then: the linen department of John Lewis? What, in his frugal Northern childhood, had made him aspire to the alien world of Oxford Street? On his wages, where did he live? Was he one of the millions of commuters thrust daily into the city, their tedious working days beginning and ending with tedious train journeys? What had *he* eaten for breakfast? She felt instinctively he was a Ready Brek man. Had a wife cooked it? Was he a happy man? From his helpful eyes, she could not tell.

'Oh yes, please,' she said eventually, and decided to return one old-fashioned courtesy with another. 'I would be most grateful.' The man took her list.

Any lack of customers in the linen department that afternoon was made up for by Rachel's purchases. The obliging York-shireman at her side, sifting easily through prices, sizes and textures, inspired her to buy extravagantly. The whole process, having magically turned from a chore to a mad kind of pleasure, she prolonged for as much time as possible. In two hours she had completely restocked her cupboard not only with sheets, but with a dozen towels and a dozen blankets besides. Her eyes grew accustomed to the flat lighting: she began to understand the structure of the place, the order among the stock, and the secure pleasure in maintaining that order that her helper must feel. She began to comprehend the anticipation

21

he must feel each morning, returning to his flocks of linens, being in charge. She envied him the purpose of his life, the usefulness.

'It will all be delivered tomorrow,' he assured her, when finally the large bill was paid. The tower blocks of stuff she had bought stood impressively on the counter, nicely balanced. Rachel, who had never experienced the adrenalin brought about by shopping, familiar to many women, stood looking at her purchases with a strange new excitement.

'Would you mind,' she asked, 'if I took just a few of them home with me now, in a couple of bags?'

The man did not hesitate. As if he silently understood her need for proof of her acquisitions, he quickly put a few pairs of sheets into strong bags.

'Not too heavy?'

'Not at all, thank you.' There was no possible reason to stay longer.

'Then I'll see to these others right away. They'll be on the delivery van tomorrow. You can rely on me, Madam.'

'Oh, I can.' Rachel realised she was smiling. She hoped she did not sound frivolous, insincere. 'Thank you again.'

With great reluctance she left the store and made her way back to the bus stop. By now the sky had darkened, congealed. The wind was fierce and icy, sharpened with occasional blades of rain. She took her place at the back of a long queue, shivered. The bags were sudden dead weights. She wondered how long she could bear standing there. A fragment of dialogue splattered in her mind.

'I went to a linen sale at John Lewis this afternoon.'

'Did you?'

'Completely restocked everything.'

'Marvellous.'

'I was lucky enough to find a very helpful man.'

'Good, good. Now, what about a drink?'

It was a dialogue that would never take place because, being the mere introduction, it was pointless. The nub of the matter, were she ever able to explain it, would be of no interest to

Thomas. She had learned long ago not to ruffle his evenings by accounts of her own mundane day. As the wind slashed her cheeks and bit into her breastbone – with both hands occupied with bags there was no hope of adjusting her scarf – she felt hot ribbons of tears fleeing from her eyes, mingling with the rain.

The bus came at last. Somehow she survived the journey, complications of reaching purse and money, wedging the bags of linen between tottery feet, tears obscuring her eyes. Millions of women, with much bleaker lives than mine, have to survive such experiences every day, she told herself. But they don't cry. Why am I crying?

It was then the enticing thought of *bed* came to her. Sleep. The privacy of her room. Refuge.

Later, she realised that this strange vision had given her strength to walk the short distance from the bus stop to the house, hunched against the wind, shaking, crying. Once through the front door, she dropped coat, bags, gloves and scarf randomly on the floor, ran up the stairs as if pursued. Reaching the bedroom, she slammed the door behind her, drew the curtains across the vile sky, and threw herself on the bed. Immediately the cover was dampened with her tears. She had no idea for how long she sobbed, but eventually she fell asleep.

When Rachel awoke, some three hours later, she felt re-freshed, calm. She lay for a while, looking round the dull room – walls, once cream, now the colour of old teeth, herbaceous curtains with flowers the unreal colours of illustrations on seed packets; kidney-shaped dressing-table, from her childhood bedroom, with a limp skirt of indeterminate green. The thought came to her that, having replenished the linen cupboard, her next job would be the bedroom. The ideas for its transformation began to dance in her mind.

An hour later, face carefully repaired, she put the matter to Thomas over their dinner of oxtail stew.

'Why ever not?' he said, after a few moments of the kind of huffing and puffing which indicated co-operative thought. (At times of disagreement, he answered swiftly.) 'In fact, while you're about it, why not do something to the whole house? It hasn't been touched since we moved, has it? Could do with a lick of paint, I should say.'

Rachel followed his look towards the lugubrious walls of the dining room, paper stained and cracked in the corners, damask curtains bleached by years of sun at their edges, symbols of uncared-for middle age. Never having been interested in interior decoration, she had organised the refurbishments, when they bought the house, without enthusiasm. A friend had brought to her notice wallpaper that looked like drag paint, ubiquitously popular in the mid-1960s. Rachel had used it in many different colours. She had noticed at first that this paper gave the rooms a stiff, prim air, but familiarity soon dulled the impact. Elsewhere she resorted to cream or white paint – hopelessly impractical with young children – while for curtains and sofas she chose fabrics of a sub William Morris design. Subsequently she discovered her liking for this material was shared by an unusual number of doctors and dentists, in whose waiting rooms she spent many hours. But the idea of change did not occur to her. Rather, she was pleased to observe that so many others shared her taste.

While Thomas's reaction to doing up the bedroom was pleasing, his suggestion about the rest of the house alarmed. Rachel knew her interest and energy would never extend that far, but murmured her agreement – this was not the time to convey her fears. Instead, a budget for the bedroom was discussed. Thomas suggested a figure far in excess of anything Rachel had imagined. He was not mean when it came to material things.

For the next month, wholly preoccupied by the confusion of choosing things for the room, Rachel did not cry again. The Afternoon of the Linen Sale was a dream she did not dwell upon. The only proof it had ever happened were the new sheets, wool blankets and luxurious towels that now occupied the shelves. She spent recklessly, for the first time in her life enjoying the unnerving exhilaration that comes from parting

24

with large sums of money on things that are not strictly necessary. Thomas did not seem to mind, and was pleased with the end result.

'Meant to be an aphrodisiac, what?' he joked, tugging at the curtains of the four-poster, the first night it was ready for use.

He fell asleep as usual, conceding it was money well spent, and Rachel fell in love with the bed, the room. The next morning she began her new ritual: the return to bed after Thomas's departure. That afternoon she was compelled to go up to the room again, gaze in pleasure at the ruffled chintz wild with hollyhocks, the dressing-table transformed to look like a debutante in a lace balldress, the walls demurely pink as old roses. She found herself pulling back the quilted bedcover, returning to the linen sheets, scarcely creased by a single night, and sleeping.

Thereafter, the pattern was established. Bed in the morning, bed for a couple of hours every afternoon. She became a secret sleeper, addicted to her room. At moments of stress, or melancholy, the thought of the silent private life in that room gave her strength. No matter how surly Thomas appeared before his morning departure, by the time Rachel had had her afternoon sleep, she felt the better able to face him again with cheerful countenance.

She spoke to no one of her habit. It was a secret closer than any lover. Thomas never enquired how she had spent her day, so there was no need to lie. But she found, as she knew she would, all passion was spent on the bedroom – the rest of the house remained as it had always been. She was grateful to Thomas for not chiding her: one day she would do something about it, but her time was now pleasantly structured. There was no need to look for further occupation.

On the afternoon of the day Thomas bought the picture in Nottingham, Rachel slept as usual, having read a Chekhov short story to speed the heaviness of her eyes. She was woken prematurely by the telephone – some amorphous feeling of guilt determined she should not switch it off. What if she was needed in an emergency? (What emergency, for heaven's sake, she had asked herself impatiently.) It was Thomas's secretary, and certainly not an emergency. Simply, she said, he was on his way back and would be home for dinner after all.

Rachel forced herself from the warm nest of her pillows, reluctant and annoyed. She had planned her own supper of poached eggs; now she would have to search for something in the deep freeze, peel carrots, arrange cheese on a plate with several kinds of biscuit. But, restored by her sleep, her ill humour did not last long. She set about preparing dinner, listening to the radio as she chopped things for salad, quite happy. She did not wonder what sort of plans had changed in Thomas's day. As she had never been able to envisage his life at the office or the brewery, she had never bothered to find out precisely the nature of his working days.

Thomas arrived home at seven, the wrapped picture under his arm. He aimed a perfunctory kiss at Rachel's cheek. She turned her head at the same moment, so that it landed, a damp click, on the lobe of her ear.

'I was in luck. Missed the worst of the traffic.'

'That was lucky.'

'Couple of French chappies in. But the evening meeting was cut, thank God.'

'Bought another picture?'

'Good one. Norfolk man I was telling you about. Makes the paint billow, somehow, rather like Turner.' He was pouring himself a drink, awkwardly, the picture still under his arm, impatience to study it again making him clumsy. 'When's dinner?'

'An hour.'

'I'm famished.'

'Less, if you like.'

'I'll be down.'

Thomas hurried out and upstairs, as he did every evening, moments after his return home, to his studio at the top of the house. There, with shaking fingers, he tore the paper from the picture and put it on an easel.

The studio was originally an attic bedroom. A large window had been inset into the sloping roof, giving good light. If Thomas looked up through it, with half-shut eyes, he could pretend he was under a naked sky, clouds scudding about his head. From the ordinary casement window, the only view was of treetops. Their leaves were a searing green, this May evening – the colour peculiar to the foliage of early summer, a green so intense that it burns itself out in a couple of weeks: darkens, loses its initial shine. The treetops were very familiar to Thomas, by now: gossipy, restless, city trees, anxious in wind, prematurely wizened by sun and fumes, pathetic – in a way that country trees never are – in their winter nakedness. Thomas was quite fond of them, despite the longing they caused him for an eventual life in Herefordshire, county of his birth. One day, not too far off now when the children were grown-up, he planned to move to some remote hill there, keep a few cows, convert a barn into a decent studio. . . . But to achieve this dream would mean many a dreary confrontation with Rachel. He had little heart for such events at the moment. At some point he would have *to take the bull by the horns* (heavens, was he still afflicted with Gillian's dreadful expressions?) and broach the subject. He hoped there would be no need to threaten: but she was such a stubborn old thing, sometimes, Rachel.

Thomas swerved his eyes from the chortling leaves of the trees outside to the calm spaces of sky and sea in his new picture. He sipped at the icy gin and tonic, hearing gulls somewhere in the back of his mind, feeling the cold hardness of slatted sand beneath his feet, smelling the shell scent of sea. . . . As a small boy, he had asked his mother (blistered shoulders, sand in her eyebrows) to catch the smell and trap it in a box so he could take it home. She had pretended to do just that, snapping shut an empty chocolate box. Home, he had opened it to find nothing but the papery smell of the extinct soft centres. Thomas had raged at his mother, and registered her first betrayal.

This R. Cotterman fellow brought it all back, God how he

brought it back. How could he, Thomas, ever hope to paint a picture that would ever bring anything back to anyone? Wearily, he looked at some of his own efforts, propped randomly against the walls: stiff, dry little landscapes, heartless husks of paintings, the product of so many talentless hours, the cause of his most profound grieving.

'Thomas, you wanted it early!' The voice came up from the kitchen as it did most evenings, martyred, accusing, hard-done-by. 'It's ready. Or shall I put it back?'

On his depressed journey downstairs, Thomas decided not to talk about the picture. When he had had his private fill, he would hang it in the drawing room: Rachel's comments could be postponed till that far-off time, What, then, should they talk about tonight? As it had not been one of her days in court, there would be no case to discuss. But, ah, inspiration, the party: the Farthingoes' party. She would like to speculate on that. Pleased with himself for remembering something his wife would find an irresistible topic of conversation, he helped himself to the delicious veal stew. When they were both sitting down, passing each other salt and pepper, pouring Sancerre into glasses, Thomas took the plunge.

'Tell you what I was thinking,' he said, 'it probably *would* be a good idea to get my dinner jacket cleaned sooner rather than later. I mean, there may be occasions it's needed before the Farthingoes. And what sort of thing *is* it, exactly, that they're lashing out on this time?'

He was rewarded by Rachel's incredulous smile. But even as he studied the familiar pattern of her greying teeth, and prepared to take an interest in her answer, a vision of a young girl filled his eyes. She had long amber hair, and white knuckles small as bone thimbles, and skeletal fingers that tied knots of string faster than anything he'd ever seen.

*   *   *

A wind from the sea had battered the east coast all night. Rain had fallen heavily, waking Eric Yacksley, renowned postman and churchwarden of these parts for thirty years, well before dawn. He had rolled quickly from the bed and kissed his sleeping wife (she would scold him later for not waking her to get his tea) taking care to avoid the mass of curling pins that covered her head like a hedgehog's prickles. After a quick breakfast he had pushed his heavy scarlet bicycle out to face the dark and wind-torn sky. Now, hours later, he pushed the bicycle – much heavier, with its sackload of letters – along the lane by the marsh.

Puddles, glinting from verge to verge, would make riding too perilous. For it was all a matter of balance, in Mr Yacksley's experience, when it came to a heavily laden bike. There could be no question of taking risks when responsible for a valuable cargo of Her Majesty's mail. So, walking it was, this morning, which meant deliveries would be on the late side. And occasional late deliveries, caused by the weather, were not a good enough reason (people round here being of an understanding nature) to give in and accept that the time had come for a van. It wasn't that offers had not been made, more times than Mr Yacksley would remember. But, despite the tiresome pressure from head office, he had continued to refuse one. He and his bicycle had been in happy partnership for his entire working life, and he was determined it should remain that way until the day he retired. (In just two years' time, God forbid.)

The division of opinion between head office and himself, Mr Yacksley realised, was insurmountable. And, as far as he was concerned, there was no point in wasting time trying to make them see sense. While they thought his arguments for sticking to his bike quite daft, he considered them very reasonable. Thus it would remain.

'I like to be out in the open air,' he had patiently explained to head office.

'What, these days?'

Head office was a catarrhal young man who worked in a sealed office in King's Lynn. Radiators blasted their stuffy air so thickly that Mr Yacksley, choking, realised his good reasons emerged less convincingly than he had intended. Head office had smiled in a pitying sort of way, didn't so much as offer a glass of water, and said the situation would be kept under review.

Head office would never understand. No hope of that. How could so shrimpish a chitling of a man ever comprehend the width of sky, the cut of wind, rain on the face, the snarl of sea? How could head office be expected to experience the inexplicable difference of every single day, outdoors? Or the blessing of pure air? How could head office ever understand why any sane man, given the choice, would not wish to spend a morning like this exposed to the elements rather than enclosed at the wheel of a van?

Mr Yacksley stopped, and looked over the marsh. The wind had quietened, but still bent the reeds. Beyond them a dun beach reached to invisible sea. A single, distant figure stood small as a peg in the landscape. Mr Yacksley could just see a flash of yellow oilskin, no larger than a goldfinch's wing. An arm was stretched out towards something the discerning postman supposed to be an easel. He smiled. There was another one head office would no doubt consider daft. He lifted his nose into the sky, breathing deeply, feeling the chill of ozone gush through his lungs. A kestrel hovered high above him, hustled by the wind, struggling to maintain its normal stillness. Then it swooped to earth, swift as a robber's knife. A marsh mouse for breakfast, no doubt. One day Mr Yacksley would like to take head office by the scruff of its pathetic little neck, bring it out here on a round. Force it to see life. Feel it. Smell it. Mr Yacksley smiled again, at the unlikely thought.

With a swish of heavy tyres through puddles, he set off on his way once more, turning left up the inland lane. His destination was the grey stone rectory, long abandoned by any vicar. Beside it was a matching church, long abandoned by any congregation. The two buildings, half-a-mile away, stood blackly against the sky at the top of a mild hill – the highest point for miles in these flat lands. From here, they looked in good order. Nearer, you could see the fine church tower was crumbling. Not many years from now, it would be a complete ruin. Pity, thought Mr Yacksley, each morning. He had climbed that tower every Sunday of his remembered childhood. Terrible pity. But as far as he could see, there was nothing to be done. The Lutchins shared his distress, but the Lutchins could never afford to repair the tower on their own.

Mr Yacksley stood, as he did every morning, at the Lutchins' kitchen window. He liked it best when he saw Mrs Lutchins before she became aware of him, so that he could enjoy a moment looking at the scene as if it was a picture. It was like that this morning. Mrs Lutchins had her back to him, rolling pastry at the kitchen table. Mr Yacksley watched her pink little hands fly back and forth on the rolling pin. Behind her was a huge dresser crowded with pale jugs and plates and mugs, gathered from country markets over the years, none of them matching. It was a scene that gave Mr Yacksley daily pleasure, made the journey in all weathers worth it. Mrs Lutchins was not much older than his own wife, Nancy. They shared the same skills – cooking, knitting, gardening. They exuded the same magical air of tranquillity, joy in life. Never lacking for occupation, never seeming to dash about in the frantic modern way Mr Yacksley so abhorred. They understood the weather, the rhythms of the earth. They were his kind of women.

'Morning, Mrs Lutchins.'

She turned. She was, as the postman had often remarked to his wife, by far the most beautiful woman on his round: white hair, eyes soft as pansies, a smile that made dimples in both cheeks. She always wore pretty jumpers covered in flowered or Fair Isle patterns, muted colours, that she knitted herself on winter evenings. And Mr Yacksley had never seen her without her pearls: three strings of pink, shell-coloured pearls that caught the meagrest sun and dappled her chin with tiny pink reflections. They looked, these pearls, as if they had come straight from the oyster. Mr Yacksley could swear they had never lain on the sterile velvet of a jeweller's box, artificial lighting draining them of their colour. Extraordinary, their pinkness: a colour they shared, come to think of it, with many things from shore and sea.

31

'Oh, Mr Yacksley. I didn't hear you.' Mrs Lutchins smiled. Deafness was her only concession to old age.

'That's a rough night we had, then.'

'Terrible. The big balsam poplar's down, the one my father planted. Bill's out there now.'

'I remember the day that tree went in.'

The postman passed a single envelope through the window. 'Just the one, this morning.'

Mrs Lutchins took the thick envelope.

'It seems dreadful, your coming all this way just for one letter,' she said. 'Time for a cup of coffee?'

'Thank you, but I'm running late. Water across the lanes. Let's hope that's going to clear up later.'

The postman moved away from the window, his fine, weather-grained face crinkling into a half-smile of farewell. They waved to each other, then Mary Lutchins watched his back view till he disappeared round the corner of the drive. Upright as ever, he was a little stiff these days, she thought. She hoped that, unlike Bill, Mr Yacksley would be spared arthritis.

Her mind on the fallen balsam poplar, and the dejection it had caused her husband, she slit the pristine envelope without interest. The invitation from the Farthingoes struck her as very curious: it would be their second large party in two years. What on earth made them so keen to spend their money on such transitory events? Would Bill want to go all that way just for an arthritic little waltz? Would her old ruby velvet do? Or would . . . ? Not liking to imagine the thought of a trip to London to search for a new dress, Mary left the invitation on the window ledge, and returned to rolling her pastry.

Half-an-hour later, her husband, Bill, came in, stepping out of muddy boots at the door. He sniffed at the smell of chicken pie coming from the Aga, and took off his battered oilskin jacket. Every day he spent several hours outside, attending to his trees, partly to be out of Mary's way, partly the better to appreciate the habitual returns at mid-morning, lunch, and tea, to the apple dumpling warmth of the kitchen.

'Miracle how it missed falling across a couple of others,' he said. 'Blasted nuisance. Miserable things. Smell this.'

He held a muddy finger and thumb to his wife's nose. A few minutes earlier, he had been pinching the leaves of the fallen tree. On warm still evenings, its scent had filled the whole garden.

Bill and Mary Lutchins sat side by side at the kitchen table drinking their coffee. Mary could read her husband's distress in the slight shaking of his head, the nervous scratching at his ear. It was no easy matter encouraging a woodland area on this exposed coast, and in the past ten years Bill's trees had suffered several calamities. But he continued to plant, to nurture, to learn: he intended to leave a thriving wood by the time he died so that future generations – perhaps his grandchildren – to whom places where wild plants and creatures thrive were becoming rare, would be sure of this small corner. Also, he sometimes thought, it might in part make up for the ruined church tower, a matter much on his conscience.

Mary pushed a plate of homemade shortbread towards him, deeming it a wise moment to deflect his thoughts.

'The Farthingoes,' she said, 'have invited us to another ball. September.'

It took Bill a few moments to switch his mind from the picture of the sprawling tree, its thin trunk snapped to a raw point, to the merriness of a ball. But he made an effort to help his wife in her own effort to cheer him. Turning to her, he smiled. Mary rather enjoyed parties, even at her age.

'You'd like that, wouldn't you, darling? Let's say yes. We'll go to London in a month or two, get you something nice to wear. Shall we?'

'You know I'm not very good at that sort of thing. I've got my old velvet.'

'Nonsense. You wore that last time. You looked tiptop. But you'd better have something new for this.'

Mary decided to hold out against the whole project a moment longer. If he pushed her to the point of agreement, she would know he wanted to go, not just for her sake, but because he reckoned he might enjoy the evening too.

'It's such a long way, just for an evening,' she said.

'Only an hour from Ursula. We can spend the night there.'

'Well, if you're sure. It might be fun.'

'You write and say yes.' Bill finished his coffee, rose from the table and returned to his boots. 'I'm not sure what to do with the thing. Start sawing, I suppose. No idea what sort of logs it'd make. I'll ring around this evening. Find out.'

As he went through the door, he glanced at his watch. An ex-naval man, punctuality was the mast in his life. The measuring of time was all-important to him. Ten minutes precisely for coffee: no more, no less, despite the crisis of a fallen tree. In exactly one-and-a-half hours he would be back for lunch. Mary looked forward to that. In their old age she looked forward to his many, small returns, with as much eagerness as, in his days in the Navy, she had longed for his shore leave after months away at sea.

The Lutchins had moved to Norfolk ten years ago. Before that, when Bill left the Navy, they had lived in York, where they ran a private museum inherited from Bill's father. The museum had been a place of some charm and considerable interest to the serious local historian. Housed in a converted warehouse, it contained an impressive collection of local artefacts, to which the Lutchins were able to add a few newly discovered treasures from time to time. They loved the place, and cared for it assiduously. Faded labels were replaced. Mary supervised copious dusting and polishing. The soft wood floors, which muted visitors' footsteps, were polished with beeswax, whose smell permeated the whole building.

But in the early 1970s, visitors began to decline. The Lutchins's quiet collection lost out to more vulgar productions, and they found they could not bring themselves to compete with the modern world of tourist attractions. Kindly advisors, wanting to save the museum, suggested waxworks in period costume, explanations taped soullessly on to earphones, all the tatty paraphernalia of history brought to 'life' for those devoid of imagination. The Lutchins abhorred the thought: they would rather sell the place, leave. So, when an offer was made by a property development company, they accepted the impressive sum immediately, and tried not to think of the ruination after their departure.

The problem of where to live then was solved by the timely death of Mary's sister, who had lived at the Church House, in Norfolk, since their parents had died. It was the house in which Mary and her sister had spent their childhood. Their father had been vicar of the parish. He conducted the wedding service of Mary and Bill in his church, on a temperate June day in 1935. After it was over, the newly married couple had insisted on climbing the tower for one last look at the marshes. Mary's view had been half-obscured by her veil, blown across her face by the breeze, so that what she mostly remembered was a blurring of lace and scudding cloud. The glorious peal of bells, up on the tower, enveloped them. There was no use in trying to speak – the sea-thrash of the reverberating bells drowned all other sound. The Lutchins clutched at each other with nervous, excited hands, and looked over the edge of the tower – quite firm, then. Below them waved the wedding guests, herbaceous points of colour in their pre-War clothes. Their shouts were smothered by the vast crashes of campanological music. On the way back down the circular stairs, stone dust from the steep steps dulling the satin hem of her dress, Mary felt a single private sting of regret among the happiness: she did not want to leave this place for a rented house in Portsmouth.

So when, many years later, the house unexpectedly became available again, she and Bill returned with joy, and set about the huge task of refurbishing the place. House and garden had fallen into a state of neglect in the years Mary's ailing sister had lived there: there was much to be done.

The Lutchins' retirement was a lively and busy one. Once the house was renovated, they set about rescuing the garden, and Bill had the idea of planting his trees. They managed to do many of the things they had always intended to do when they had the time – read, listen to music in the evenings – they still had no television and did not want one – apply themselves to local affairs (Bill, with Mr Yacksley, was a church warden). They lived an orderly, quiet life, full of interest to themselves, though they appreciated the small scale of their activities might not seem the stuff of fulfilment to others. Once a year they went abroad, with increasing reluctance, often returning disillusioned by the unhappy change in places they had previously enjoyed. Every few months they visited their married daughter, Ursula, in Oxford: Ursula and her family came to Norfolk each summer. Occasionally they went to London, hoping to enjoy it, to see a play or exhibition – an attempt to keep slightly in touch with the world of arts they both loved. But they were increasingly disillusioned by the physical frustrations of London, the proliferation of alien crowds. Whenever they returned from one of these exhibitions, Mary's love of Church House was renewed. She would go around opening windows, watering plants, even (stupid, she knew) touching things – dishes, walls, books, papers on her desk, to make sure of their unchanging solidity. The pleasure of being home she never took for granted. It was an active, daily thing, shared, though never discussed, with her husband.

There was a cosiness that was almost tangible, Mary often thought, in Church House. It had crept in, indiscernibly as a devious cat – taken over the hearths, the rooms. Sometimes such cosiness, such self-satisfied tranquillity (complacency, could it be called?) was frightening. It was frightening because time was running out and one day, in some unthinkable form, it would be destroyed. The greater the sense of present near-perfection, the greater the disaster of its end would be.

Mary did not relish such morbid thoughts. But, being of a practical nature, she was frequently assailed by them. The evening after the balsam poplar had been struck down, sitting by the log fire engaged in *The Times* crossword, Schumann's *Piano Quintet* on a record, a nameless dread scuttled through her, plucking at her innards with its deadly incisors. Bill, on the other side of the fire, put down his book, *The Art of the Arboretum*.

'Be all right,' he said.

Mary sighed. Her husband's instinctive awareness of her shifts of mood never ceased to fill her with awe. How could he have known the unwelcome turn her thoughts had taken? Sometimes, when he seemed to read her mind, she longed to explain. But she kept her silence, in the firm belief that spouses should protect each other from their amorphous feelings. The modern school of better understanding through total, exhausting revelation, so often discussed on the wireless, was a habit she could never imagine herself adopting. The nuances of communication are fragile enough, she thought. In over-taxing them, there is danger of further misunderstandings. She had seen couples – friends – drained by the practice of mutual baring of their souls. And in their hunt for explanations, they had lost the art of judgement – judgement of when best to keep silent. They had lost much of their dignity, and often their humour.

Mary smiled. 'I think I'll ring Ursula,' she said.

'But you rang her last night.'

'I know. But she'll have read about the gales here. She'll want to know if the trees are all right.'

Bill smiled, then, too. The closeness of his wife and daughter always touched him. The restlessness he had sensed in Mary, all evening, would be quelled by a conversation with Ursula.

'Tell her the storm's quite over,' he said, 'and we can't really complain – a single poplar.'

He threw a new log on the fire. The crouching flames rose instantly to attention, straight-backed, emitting new warmth to reinvigorate the old. Bill waited until Mary had left the room to telephone – a kind of marital politeness he could never quite discard – before picking up his book. There was a whole section on the balsam poplar. If that didn't tell him all he wanted to know, he would ring Ralph Cotterman in the morning. Ralph was extraordinarily well informed on trees. Mean-

time, there was an hour in which to read before bed, at
10.30 p.m. precisely.

*   *   *

Ralph Cotterman was in love with a married woman.

At the age of forty he was still unmarried, still wishing to
find a wife. But, apart from the one woman, who happened to
be the wife of his oldest friend, there was no one he had
encountered so far with whom he could contemplate spending
the rest of his life. As a man of energy and – to some –
considerable attraction, he had not been short of available
women eager with suggestions of permanency. And, indeed,
he had spent considerable time (though never quite a year)
being faithful to some of them. Fifteen years ago, he had
dallied with Frances Rudge (before she married Toby Farthingoe) who had, she declared at the time, loved him passion-
ately. That passion, as Ralph knew in his heart, had not been
fully requited. She was not wife material, in his view – though
he had to admit she had succeeded in cheering up the once
mournful Toby Farthingoe, mostly by the liberal use of his
money, previously hoarded for lack of imagination as how to
spend it. Frances was an uncomplicated girl of straight ambition, teasing eyes and good legs. She and Ralph had remained
friends, despite her irritating tendency to flirt when Toby was
upstairs communing with his computers. For Ralph's part,
there were no regrets concerning Frances. For her part. . . .
He had a slight suspicion, which he would not allow himself
often to reflect upon, that she felt differently. However, she
was mostly decent enough to keep her feelings to herself. Only
occasionally did she give the tiniest clue that the old passion
was not quite dead, and on such occasions Ralph pretended
not to notice.

Ralph had left Cambridge – where he became friends with
Martin Knox, husband of the desired woman – with a good
degree in science. But, after some years of working in a large,
unlively firm, he had decided to abandon his career for politics.

He fought and lost several Liberal seats, but worked hard for the Party. To support himself, he wrote a couple of scientific books for children which, to his surprise, sold thousands of copies. After the 1988 split of the Liberals, confused about where his loyalties lay, he abandoned politics as spontaneously as he had previously abandoned the world of science. Now, content in his work at last, he made writing scientific books his chief occupation. He was fired by an overwhelming belief that introduction to the subject at an early age was imperative. (The success of his books may have had something to do with the inclusion of jokes and witticisms not normally part of scientific texts.) He cared very much about Britain's technological future and liked to think that his small contribution, snaring the enthusiasm of children, might be of some value.

His friend Martin Knox, always reticent about girls, had not introduced Ralph to Ursula until a few weeks before their marriage. The meeting took place on Oxford station. They had gone together to meet her off the London train. Ralph would for ever remember his first, fatal sight of her: irrepressible pale hair and a heavenly smile, struggling with suitcase, papers, trilby hat, umbrella, and beautiful pink suede gloves, quite out of keeping with the rest of her high-spirited clothes. Ralph's heart positively stopped for a moment, in the manner of a thousand corny love songs. The scientific part of his mind then zoomed in to wonder what it was, in human chemistry, that could make a man on first sight of a girl, who had not spoken a word, want to throw himself at her feet, declaring extraordinary love? He knew that first instant, as recognition dizzied his head and weakened his legs, that she was the only girl for him. But she was Martin's.

She had stretched out her hand, the exquisite Ursula. Ralph briefly felt her warm fingers: this was the changing point in his life.

'Hello. Heard so much about you,' she said.

Then her trilby fell off, papers splattered to the ground. Martin was at once helpful, protective, bending, carrying, taking her arm, laughing, kissing her cheek several times.

Ralph stood watching the small loving scene, unable to speak.

Often, over the years that followed, Ralph wondered why neither Martin nor Ursula had guessed at his curious love. Naturally, he had never said a word, being a man of honour towards his friends, or even indulged in the sort of sly hint that Frances sometimes let forth. But he spent much time with the Knoxes, in their house or his: they went on holidays together, he was godfather to their daughter, Sarah. Frequently, when Martin was working, he entrusted Ursula to Ralph's care. They would go for walks, see a film, have dinner. In Ralph Ursula confided all the searing hatred she felt for the City of Oxford, and in return listened to his stories about his slight, always unsatisfactory, affairs. In public their fondness was revealed in bear hugs of greeting (deeply disturbing to Ralph) which plainly meant nothing more than affection to Ursula: never once had she indicated that, to her, their relationship might overstep the boundaries of friendship. In private, Ursula's air of vague distance was a bridge Ralph was helpless to cross. His silent suffering, undiminished, responded to no antidote. It remained the most secret fact of his life.

This evening he drove from his cottage near Oxford to the Knoxes' house. Beside him, on the passenger seat, a short-haired, blue-grey cat lay sleeping. It was not his cat. He had found it on his doorstep one evening a month ago, crouching tensely. Ralph remembered cat-loving friends declaring cats 'found' people. Ralph was no cat lover. He had no wish to be found by a cat. But an hour later, it was still there: impassive. Ralph gave it a bowl of milk and was rewarded with a grateful look in its elongated, opal eyes. But still it made no signs of leaving. Later that night, it mewed so pitifully that Ralph, knowing such a move was unwise, let it in to spend the night in the kitchen.

He had made enquiries in the village, but no one knew who the cat belonged to, or where it came from. Its strength of character showed in its determination to make Ralph's cottage its home. Apart from that, it was a docile creature though the

40

pale eyes, staring, staring, sometimes caused Ralph a nameless feeling of unease.

When, after a month, no owner had come to claim the orphan cat, he decided it was time to act. His first idea was to give it to Ursula. The second, better idea, swiftly followed. He would give it to Sarah, his enchanting goddaughter. At the age of nine, she had never had an animal and frequently requested one, to no avail. Here, then, was her chance. Ralph was excited by his inspiration. Sarah would get her cat, and he would have a good excuse for a midweek visit to the Knox household.

His day's writing at an end, he had shared his tea with the cat, stroked it, held it, been unusually friendly. The cat, wise thing, was suspicious. When Ralph lifted it into the car, it had arched its back and lashed a suddenly indignant tail. But the motion of the car seemed to soothe, and it appeared to doze quite happily.

Ralph drove slowly through the lanes. He had not telephoned to say he was coming – the Knoxes were used to his dropping in at all times. He was always welcome.

It was warm in the car, stuffy, with a slight smell of peppermint. The thrill Ralph always felt on going to see Ursula sharpened his senses. The May green of trees and hedgerows, sequinned still with rain from an earlier shower, dazzled his eyes. He thought of Ursula. In ten minutes he would be with her. Ridiculously happy, he patted the sleeping cat. He could feel the brittle geography of its bones beneath the blue-grey fur, and was glad he had decided to give it away.

* * *

Ursula Knox, who spent much of her time planning how to get out of Oxford, had had the kind of busy day she most enjoyed. Having dropped the children at school, she had driven to Somerset to deliver plants to a client. On the way back, in her eternal quest to find someone who could make her romantic shoes, she had stopped in Gloucestershire to visit a local cobbler. Then she had lost her way trying to find a remote house in which lived a dealer in antique paste jewellery, a woman she had recently met at a rural antiques fair. The journey had been worth it: she bought a rare and beautiful French paste brooch in the shape of a lyre. There would be few occasions on which she could wear such a thing in Oxford, where any sartorial effort upon the part of a don's wife was considered frivolous. But, as she would explain to Martin later, the brooch was not only a bargain, but an investment. Bargains and investments of this kind were the stuff of Ursula's private life. The pleasure she had in tracking down, and often finding, pretty but inexpensive jewellery, was not something she ever tried to explain to Martin or the children. Martin proudly admitted she had 'an eye', and admired her growing collection. But stories of her small adventures among eccentric antique dealers in the West Country would mean nothing to him. Ralph was the only person in whom she could confide her observations of the intriguing worlds in which she found herself. Ralph was always interested.

Ursula had planned to make up for her lost day (lost in business terms only, that is) by working all evening. It was to be an unusual evening, alone. The children were at a local circus with friends, returning after supper. Martin was dining in College.

In the chaos of a North Oxford kitchen (murmurous fridge, Hockney prints, clumps of unwashed saucepans awaiting attention in the sink), she sat at the table absorbed in horticultural catalogues. She had cleared a space for her drawing pad and pencils. They were enclosed by a hedge of the sort of things that for ever seemed to gather on the table – two pots of sweet geraniums, one jug of lilac, a bottle of homemade apple juice, three novels, a jar of sugarless marmalade, a toy dolphin, a school scarf, and the paste lyre, sparkling in its open box. Ursula, glancing at this exotic barrier between herself and the rest of the clutter, smiled to herself: it revealed a good deal about the inhabitants of the house, she thought, in the way that all our possessions portray us. Or did she mean betray?

Such silence! Even the fridge was quiet for a moment.

Ursula stretched, revelling. Solitude was infinitely precious to her, all the more valuable for its rarity. Had she not married Martin and had the children, she would – she liked to think – have been happy spending her life alone, in some remote part of the country. Family life had uncovered the charms of solitude for her. Small, innocent but private spaces were essential to the sanity of all married couples, she had soon discovered, and she made sure that these parts of her life were as much a priority as her duties to Martin and the children.

Ursula bent her head over the pristine graph paper, drew a confident line with the lethally sharp lead of her pencil. She always loved such beginnings. It was later, changing details to accommodate the whim of an ignorant customer, that things became tedious. Mrs Robbins, whose Iffley garden she was presently designing, had been insistent about the inclusion of a great deal of York stone. She wanted a curving path that led to a hideous statue. She wanted terraces on various levels; she wanted steps leading to nowhere, rockeries, goldfish ponds, and stone troughs with plants that would survive with no care. Such suburban taste was abhorrent to Ursula, but she was in no position, just yet, to turn down valuable commissions. And at least the plants had been left entirely to her choice. Mrs Robbins's only knowledge of flowers came from cellophaned bunches from Interflora. Ursula planned to surprise her. The amount of bulbs she would find between the stones next spring. . . . Ursula drew a second, parallel curving line – a nice fat path for Mrs Robbins. It would be a path wide enough for all her fat cocktail friends. Ursula pictured them: cigarettes lolling in red mouths, puffy hands pecking at the avocado dip, patio people, stilettos firm on stone, haters of grass. One day perhaps she would be asked to design a wild garden.

Ursula concentrated. The thin rasp of her pencil was the only sound. Late sun flared on the protruding saucepan handles at the sink, but the rest of the room was in shadow. It was never filled with light. North Oxford was a dark place. Its glowering ruddy houses soaked up any sun that managed to penetrate its sullen trees. Martin had always promised they would leave, eventually. Eventually. . . . How imprecise a word. The waiting to leave, starved of light, of sun, of abundant proof of changing seasons, of earth, might one day drive her mad. This was Ursula's greatest fear. But this evening, blissfully alone, she was determined not to allow herself melancholy thoughts. To finish Mrs Robbins's stony garden was her only aim.

The bang of the front door broke the happy silence. Ralph's hurrying footsteps. I can't bear it, Ursula thought. Not tonight. Not Ralph. She heard him fling open the door behind her. She heard his usual cry of delight.

'You're in! Wonderful!'

Ralph's eyes quickly attuned to the husky light. The funny greenish colours of Ursula's tousled hair matched the leaves of protective geraniums crowded round her. For an agonising moment her bent head did not move.

'Oh Lord, you're seriously at work,' he observed. 'I didn't mean to disturb you.'

Ursula swung round, furious angelic face taking him in. He loomed above her, cat in arms, hooded eyes flinging out messages of appeal.

Ursula threw down her pencil, stood up.

'What's that cat?'

Ralph licked his lips, tried a small smile. 'I've come to explain. . . .'

'You know I don't like cats.'

She saw that his top lip, unfortunately designed prissily to overhang the bottom one, gleamed with a speck of saliva. She held up her cheek. On occasions she did not do this he sought it with undignified haste, sometimes bending down, even pushing back her hair to reach it. Now, as he kissed her, she felt the tiny damp smudge of his saliva.

'You know I'd never have one,' she said.

'It's not for you. It's for Sarah.'

'For Sarah?'

'She's gone on so long about wanting an animal. I thought I'd better do something about it. I knew you never would.'

44

'I see. And who do you think will have to look after Sarah's cat? Pay the vet's bills, have it put down when it's been run over by a cyclist?'

'I wouldn't have gone out and bought it, Urse,' Ralph interrupted. 'You know I would never have done that. But this creature just appeared on the doorstep last month, and wouldn't go.'

'Very good reason for keeping it. It's obviously chosen you, as those daft cat people would say.' She heard the sneer in her voice, knew that any minute she would relent.

'Don't be cross.'

'I'm not cross. At least, not very.'

Ralph's smile was such an improvement on his serious mouth that it often won her over.

'It's a nice enough cat. No trouble.'

'Cats are always trouble.'

'Nonsense. You'll see.' Ralph lifted the animal onto the table, disliking its thinness once more. It sat very upright, like a china cat, tail curled neatly round its feet. Translucent eyes looked only at Ralph. 'Where is Sarah?' he asked.

'At the circus. She'll be back about nine.'

'Sorry to have missed her. Look, if you're really put out, I'll take it away again. Find someone else.'

Ursula shrugged. 'It could stay for a while,' she said. 'See how it behaves. See if I can stand it. Drink?'

'You having one?'

Ursula shook her head. Ralph went to the fridge and took out an opened bottle of white wine. Then he found a wine glass in a cupboard. His knowledge of their kitchen, Ursula thought, was strangely irritating. Guilty at her curtness to him, she tried to sound more mellow.

'You all right?' she asked, noticing his paleness.

'Fine.'

Ursula detected despair in his single, flat response. The cat did not blink, did not move.

'Martin's dining in College,' she said, 'but I don't mind cooking something if you'd like to stay.'

45

Ralph's mind accelerated with wild, impolite alternatives to plans already made. He could always put the Farthingoes off. . . .

'I thought you were working?'

'I am.'

But he was determined to be strong. 'Thanks very much, but I'm dining with Frances and Toby. I'm on the way.'

'You'll be able to ask them why they're giving their second ball in two years.'

'We all know the answer to that. Frances has to be occupied. Organising a huge party, she tells me, takes an enormous amount of work. Not a moment left to think.'

'Poor Frances. I don't know what she'd do with a moment to think.'

Ralph finished his wine. Ursula picked up the invitation from a pile of opened letters on the dresser.

'Years ago, it would have been something to look forward to,' she said.

'Don't you like parties any more?' He felt he sounded like a stranger.

'Oh, sometimes. Not this huge, elaborate kind, chuntering around with other people's husbands.'

'I'll dance with you. I'm not a husband.'

'No.'

Faint smile. No hope of the idea thrilling her, thought Ralph.

'It just might be fun.'

'Doubt it.'

Ursula sat down again. She wanted to return to her drawing. The way to get rid of Ralph was to tease him about Frances.

'You know why I think Frances plans these parties? Apart from something to do? Her real reason is so that she has a chance to dance with you.'

'Don't be daft,' said Ralph crossly. He hated to hear such truths, even from Ursula.

'You know perfectly well she's been dotty about you for years.'

'That's something I don't ever want to think about. It may not even be true any more. People come to their senses eventually.'

'I don't know about that. Unrequited love takes a tremendous hold on people. Sometimes, they don't even *want* to shake it off.'

They looked at each other. Ralph licked his lips again. The cat's eyes were still upon him.

'What will it need?' asked Ursula, after a while.

'A basket, I should think. I'll bring you one.'

'No, Ralph. You're always bringing me things.'

How could he help it?

'I'll bring it for Sarah. Look, you must get back to work. Sorry I disturbed you. I must go.'

Ursula picked up her pencil, sighed. He was easy to offend. She did not want to offend him.

'I met a cobbler in Gloucestershire today,' she said quietly. Ralph was also easy to pacify, with small fragments of the life no others would find interesting. 'His workshop was by a millpond – you could hear the water all day. He had shelves and shelves of different leathers. I left him some designs. You know, the kind of silly shoes I'm always looking for. He had the most amazing eyes.'

Ralph smiled at last. He picked up the paste lyre from its box. The cat, barely moving, shifted its glance to watch him.

'And this?'

'A bargain. From a rabbit breeder in Somerset. I tracked her down, as well as the cobbler.'

'You're so clever. You do have a funny life.'

'It's fun.'

'Bye.' Ralph kissed the top of her head. Left.

Returned to silence, Ursula felt the sadness she often experienced on Ralph's going. She had disappointed him. She nearly always disappointed him. But what could she give, apart from friendship? To be loved by someone whom you did not love in the same way was full of awkwardness, she found. It was a

47

responsibility from which she longed to be released, but did not know how to set about it.

She tried to return to her work. But the previous mood of the evening, fragile as eggshell, had been cracked beyond repair. And the weird cat still had not moved. It stared ahead at the door from which Ralph had left.

'Cat?' she said.

But it would not look at her.

*　　*　　*

The early evening sun had given no warmth to the Farthingoes' vicarage. Sumptuously Victorian, it was a cold house. Always cold. Draughts brushed in small tides across dark polished floors. Mean wood fires, on the occasions they were lighted, were apathetic in their struggle against the chill. Unhungry flames kneaded damp logs for many hours before releasing an ineffectual warmth.

The house was also dark. Majestic Pugin wallpapers rose to high ceilings. Elaborate cornices of deep-stained wood lent the rooms an ecclesiastical air. Tall windows, shaped like shields looked onto vast cedars of Lebanon, in the garden, that had taken root three centuries ago. Their snarled branches were pale as pith, as if skinned by the years: their needles so dark a green they seemed quite black. The cedars protected the house from sunlight, cast their magnificent gloom through the windows in all seasons.

Toby Farthingoe liked all these things; 'small defects', as the estate agent had put it, which had deterred many a potential buyer. He had secured the house very cheaply. He loved the dark, the chill, the rich austerity, the orchestration of sounds denied to a carpeted house. He had given firm orders to his wife that, here, nothing should be prettified: only in the bedroom could she have her way. For this house, as he had instantly felt on finding it, and the feeling had grown ever since, was definitely *his*. In return, he gave the London flat to Frances – a place that meant no more to him than a hotel –

and had enjoyed watching her spend money on it. He marvelled how the purchase of elaborate curtains and finickity lamps could give a woman so much pleasure.

His order of no carpets meant that the vicarage was full of noises that gave constant delight. Toby revelled in the changing timbre of footsteps as people moved from wooden floors – muffled taps, as of gentle dancers, to the flagstone floor of the hall – harsher, chipping sounds. Climbing the stairs slowly, as he did now, he heard the familiar, distinct note of every step. His hand trailed up the handsome bannister, supported by its 'black, purgatorial rails', enjoying the slide of polished wood beneath his arched palm. At the half landing there were more reminders of *St Agnes' Eve*:

A casement high and triple arched there was,
All garlanded with fruits and flowers, and bunches of knot
  grass.
And diamonded with panes of quaint device . . .

Lines from Keats, learned in childhood, often came back to Toby Farthingoe as he made his dark journeys through the house.

He continued on his way, slowly, for once he opened the door of the bedroom the sweet, melancholic dusk of the stairs and landing would be shattered. He disliked the artificial peach, the pale blues, the plush carpets and satin lampshades that were Frances's choice in the one place she had been allowed to indulge her decorating talents. He tried never to go into the bedroom in daylight. But this evening there was the matter of wine to be discussed. A visit could not be avoided.

Toby did not much mind that Ralph Cotterman was coming to dinner. He was a very frequent guest, as he had been for years. And these days Toby was impervious to Ralph. He could at last trust him – indeed, he had been wrong, in the past, ever to have had his suspicions. Ralph was an honourable man. What Toby felt for him now was, primarily, pity. It was rotten luck on a man to love another man's wife. Frances had confessed to Toby long ago, before their marriage, to her affair with Ralph, and the concern she felt about the enduring love – unrequited, of course – Ralph felt for her. 'He'll grow out of it,' she often said. Toby had no idea whether Ralph had grown out of it or not; it was not a subject he cared to discuss – particularly since the drama, the disaster, eleven years ago. (Eleven years ago this month, he remembered.) It was odd, Toby sometimes thought, that Ralph still had not married – but that must be some reflection on the type of women available to a man in his early forties. Presumably he *had* recovered from Frances, for ever since that terrible evening he had behaved impeccably. Perhaps, even that night, Ralph had not actually done anything . . . *this* suspicion did not dull with time. Certainly, these days, there was no gesture for which Toby could reproach Ralph. Whatever the man currently felt for Frances, he was a magician in disguising it. Sometimes, in fact, he was so distant as to be almost rude. Frances, curiously, was the one who constantly conveyed warmth, affection, the kind of love made easy by old habit. Occasionally Toby would catch her smiling at Ralph, teasing him, putting her arms round him, all to no avail – signs, surely, that Ralph's passion *was* dead and that Frances's gestures were permissible because they ceased to affect him. Toby was not an analyser of human relations (computers and badgers being his greater interests). The only thing he could be sure of was that, these days, he shared his wife's affection for Ralph, thought of him as a friend.

Toby crossed the shadowed landing, swung open the heavy wooden door of the bedroom. A peached light instantly confused his eyes. It rose in dull haloes from many fringed lamps, unnecessarily on, considering the luminous evening sky outside. More Keatsian adjectives flamed in his mind: 'silken, hush'd, chaste'. This was more a bed*chamber*, than a room, Toby often thought. As his eyes grew calmer, he approached his wife. She was sitting at the dressing-table, wearing a carelessly wrapped white dressing gown. Her crossed legs were swung to one side of the stool – an uncomfortable position, it appeared, but a habitual one. The skirt of her dressing gown parted over fragile knees.

'Hello, darling,' Frances said. Very briefly her eyes shimmied away from her own reflection in the looking glass, to Toby's. 'Have you been shut up with the computers since lunch?'

Toby ignored the small undertone of accusation.

'I have,' he said.

Frances's mouth, still only visible to him in reflection, widened as she pulled on the shining brown lipstick. Or maybe it was a smile.

'People have been ringing up all day saying their invitations have arrived, and they're coming.'

'That's good,' said Toby, who had been living with party news, party ideas, party speculation, for many weeks now. Were he not to keep his (not very great) interest in reserve, The Party would dominate all their conversations. 'I just wondered what we're eating tonight so that I can think about the wine.' (Wine was another thing he had little natural interest in thinking about.)

'Lamb fillet with ginger and spring onions,' said Frances. 'And – guess what?'

'Chocolate soufflé?'

'Right.'

Toby smiled. Frances, equipped with a talented Italian cook, took a great deal of trouble to choose all the food she knew her husband liked best. It was one of the things he loved her for. She turned a little: Toby could see her profile. She pushed a long strand of hair behind her ear, the side Toby was standing. His eyes were drawn magnetically to the small, pearly lobe. A tiny vertical scar, silvery as a snail's trail, shone on the white skin. Frances picked up a gold earring, tilted her head the better to find the pierced hole. It was a ritual, repeated innumerable times in the years of their marriage, that Toby dreaded witnessing and tried to avoid. He cursed himself for his mistiming this evening.

'Damn this thing,' said Frances, jabbing the point of the earring about the lobe. 'You going back up till dinner?'

'Think I will.'

'Ralphie's coming about eight.'

'Give me a shout when he arrives.'

'Right.'

The earring was in place. Frances was now securing it with its small gold butterfly. Toby turned away, went swiftly to the door. He felt quite sick. Some guilts, he had discovered, do not diminish. Frances's scar – reminding, reminding – would it never fade? – fed his regret, haunted his life in a way that was increasingly frightening. It may have been for this reason he spent so many hours designing complex computer programmes (brilliance in this field had made his fortune). It was possibly for this reason, too, that he agreed to Frances's extravagant plans for parties: thus there was always something to be talked about, worked upon with her, a project in hand. Deflection of the mind was essential to Toby Farthingoe. If he allowed himself time in which to reflect upon the darkness of his soul, he dreaded to think what might happen.

The May evening that had caused Toby eleven years of remorse had been very similar to today: all the brightness of young leaves washed by a light shower of rain, rough parts of the garden hazy with forget-me-nots and bluebells. They had gone to a supper party given by Martin and Ursula Knox in North Oxford. The Knoxes lived in a smaller house in those days, and had paid little attention to its shabby aspects, knowing it would be a temporary measure before finding somewhere larger. A previous owner had invested only in an elaborate conservatory attached to the kitchen which led to a long, narrow back garden.

As the evening was unusually warm for early summer, guests took their food and drink out into the garden. They sat on coats and rugs and terminable cane chairs. Ralph Cotterman was the only one who would not allow himself to relax. He chivvied about helping Ursula, collecting plates or refilling drinks, acting in a more host-like manner than Martin himself. As the sky darkened, someone lit a garden candle. Coats were gathered round shoulders. There seemed to be a mutual, unspoken reluctance to go inside. But by ten o'clock, the illusion of summer had evaporated. The air had become sharp. Toby, who drank very little himself, noticed that others emptied their glasses faster, at Ralph's insistence, to keep out the cold. He also noticed that Ralph paid no more attention to Frances than he did to any of the other guests. His only concern seemed to be to help Ursula. This disguise, for the love Frances had claimed Ralph felt for her, was indeed impeccable.

Toby had sat on a bench at the far end of the garden, happy that no-one felt obliged to seek him out and make conversation. It was his habit, on occasions he was forced to join such a gathering, to detach himself at the earliest possible moment: to observe rather than join in. His own feeling was that parties of any kind were not the places for proper communication. He was bored by small talk and idle chatter, though entertained by his observations from afar. His wife, for instance, assumed a special way of standing at parties: hips thrust slightly forward, head tilted to one side in the traditional guise of a good listener, long hair tumbling over one shoulder, sparkling with blond lights. Was she conscious of what the professional observers of such things now called body language? At this very moment she was making herself agreeable to an elderly professor. Frances was indiscriminate in her attentions. It mattered to her very much that she should be liked and, if possible, remembered, by everyone.

Someone – Ralph, at Ursula's request, Toby supposed – turned on some music. The melancholy voice of Ruth Etting singing *Harvest Moon* trailed down the garden. Through the conservatory windows, Toby could just make out two people, partly obscured by pots of geraniums and summer jasmine, move in a preoccupied dance: Ralph and Ursula. Then Ursula shouted to the others to join them. One or two couples rose obediently from the grass.

The music deflected Frances's concentration from the professor. Toby saw her look wildly round in anticipation of a partner. She was a passionate dancer, scathing of many

53

inadequate men who fell short of her waltzing standards. Her gaze swivelled to the far end of the garden. She saw her husband, smiled. Then she bunched up the gauzy red stuff of her skirt in one hand – quite unnecessary, considering its shortness – and pranced towards him. As she approached, Toby recognised the almost imperceptible glitter that always came to her eyes after several glasses of wine. She stopped a yard short of him, tilted her head to one side.

'What are you doing here, Tobes? Come and dance.'

'You know perfectly well I never dance.'

If Frances had been completely sober she might have been more insistent. She might have taken his hand, pulled him up, forced him on to the improvised dance floor, as she had succeeded in doing on rare occasions in the past. As it was, she merely gave him another small smile, indicating that she had no intention of wasting her allure on a husband who was not interested. Toby's reaction was further determination not to move. He hated any form of flirtation directed towards him, particularly by his wife.

'Oh, Tobes. . . .'

'I'm sorry.'

'Very well. I dare say I'll find *someone* who won't mind.'

She turned and moved away, her back view sprightly with offence. Had Toby conceded to her wishes, he reflected a thousand times since, the rest of the events of the evening might never have occurred.

He had continued to sit in his dark corner of the garden, watching the flame of the fat candle splay over the wax, and shadow figures of the dancers moving awkwardly through the crowded plants. After a while he looked at his watch and saw that it was past midnight: time to go home. Dreading the argument which would doubtless ensue with Frances, whose stamina for late nights far outreached his own, he made his way to the conservatory.

He stood at the French windows, looking in. Despite the high-pitched scents of lilies and jasmine, the place smelt as musty as a potting shed. Hot, cloying air from within em-

54

balmed his face while his back, exposed to the garden, felt cold. The dancers, their feet gritty on the quarry-tiled floor, were joyless, tired, uncomfortably cramped by the jungle of trailing leaves. Ursula and Martin, dancing together, seemed the only ones to be enjoying themselves. Martin had one hand round his wife's waist; they swayed, a little apart, talking with animation. Toby peered beyond them. Where was Frances?

As his eyes grew accustomed to the moon-slatted light, slanting through the glass roof, Toby saw her. She stood at the far end of the conservatory, by the kitchen window. Ralph was her partner, but they made no attempt to dance. Ralph loosely held her waist. Frances's hands were on his shoulders. They stared at each other. From Ralph's expression – slight frown – it seemed to Toby he was reflecting on something Frances had just said. Then, without smiling, Ralph took a hand from her waist and pushed a stray lock of hair from her eyes. Frances tossed her head, completing the process. She raised one hand from its position on Ralph's shoulder, pointed her long-nailed finger at him accusingly. Then she gently brushed it across a few inches of Ralph's aggressively striped shirt, and whispered.

Even as Toby scythed towards them, he saw Ralph push Frances back – alarm, guilt, on his face. Toby slashed at Frances's shoulder, spinning her round to face him. Her eyes, too, were bright with fear.

'Home,' said Toby.

They did not say goodbye to their hosts. It was no occasion for the niceties of convention. Frances followed him without protest to the car. Toby slammed the doors, but then drove more slowly than usual, bending over the steering wheel to ease the lacerating pain in his insides.

They did not speak for some incalculable time. Then Frances embarked on her explanation.

'I don't know what's come over you, Tobes. Really. Are you off your head? What on earth did you imagine Ralph and I were up to? We were completely innocent, I swear it.

Completely innocent. All right, he pushed a bit of hair out of my eyes, but that's something any friend would do. I mean, you'd do it to Ursula or someone –'

'I wouldn't –'

'– and anyhow, you know, feeling as he does about me, Ralph would never make a move. He's a gentleman, for heaven's sake. Don't you trust him? Don't you trust me?' Her voice rose. 'Tobes: answer, for heaven's sake. I can't bear your ridiculous silence. If you're angry, then bloody well shout at me, even though there's nothing in the world to be angry about. Oh, for heaven's sake. You silly old thing . . . you can't be jealous, can you? I've never known you jealous. You never warned me that talking to an old friend would make you jealous. I don't know. . . . But do say something, accuse me so that I can defend myself of whatever crime you think I've committed.' She paused for a while, then sighed. 'Very well. Keep your silence. If you feel like that. I'd never guessed you could be such a fool.'

Toby, his eyes meticulously on the silver road, still said nothing.

Home, they entered the house in silence. Frances walked huffily upstairs without switching on lights. Toby heard the slam of the bedroom door. He paced the darkness of the hall for a while. Moonlight, obstructed by the cedars without, splintered through the landing window, silvering the braided wood of the bannisters. The grandfather clock chimed one. Married just three years, Toby thought, and it's over. He dug his nails into his palms and felt a blade of cold sweat split his spine. He felt murderous, terrified.

At last, he climbed the stairs, bent as an old man, still trying to ease the pain in his guts. He knew he was about to do something inconceivable, and had no power to control himself. Quietly, he opened the bedroom door.

Frances's scarlet dress lay like a pool of rumpled blood on the peach carpet. She herself sat at the dressing-table, in the white satin dressing gown she had bought on their honeymoon, brushing her hair.

'Come on, Tobes,' she said. So innocent. 'Don't be silly.'

Toby walked to the dressing-table, put out his hand to feel its cold glass top, hoping to steady himself. Frances went on brushing her hair, seductive, pushing it behind her ears. From the ear just inches away from Toby swung one of the dangling pearl and diamond earrings which he had given her last Christmas, and which she loved. Mesmerised by the glinting rhythm of its swinging, Toby heard himself suddenly cry out, fighting for breath. A web of computer-like coloured dots clouded his eyes. The next thing he knew the earring was between his finger and thumb. He was pulling, pulling downwards. Frances's head was sinking beneath his force. She screamed as the point of the earring tore down through the rubbery skin of her small lobe. Toby stepped back, bloodied earring in his hand. Frances was on the floor. Blood spurted from the split lobe, reddening strands of hair, and splattering her white satin shoulders.

The physical manifestations of Toby's mania fled within seconds. It was replaced by a feeling of great strength, great calm. His hands did not shake as he carried Frances to the bed, put towels beneath her head, telephoned the doctor. Timeless moments later, he sat holding her hand while the doctor gave her a local anaesthetic, stitched up the lobe and insisted she take a sedative.

'As for you,' the doctor said, 'perhaps you would come round to my surgery in the morning and do some explaining. Your wife will be all right. I think we should sort out what's the matter with you.'

'Very well,' answered Toby.

Alone with Frances again, he continued to sit on the side of the bed, stroking her arm. She said nothing, just looked at him with bewildered eyes. The other earring still hung from her unharmed ear, at rest against her cheek. Soon she fell asleep.

In bed beside her, Toby was aware of the lightness of his body, the relief after explosion. But as the hours interminably passed, he sensed the first savage ticking of remorse, a thump as regular as his heartbeat. In the silence of that night he wept internally – the kind of weeping that brings no tears, no sound, and no relief.

The sun had been up several hours when he moved over to Frances and laid his head on her chest. She woke at once. She said her ear was painful, but nothing too serious. She ruffled her hand through Toby's hair.

'I understand,' she said at last, 'and I'm sorry. You misunderstood, but that's not the point.' Toby had never heard her speak so quietly. 'The important thing, now, is no recriminations on either side. No – please don't say anything, anything. Except to make me one promise: promise never, ever to speak about last night again, the whole of our married lives. Will you?'

Toby, who had been expecting her to suggest arrangements for divorce, promised. And they both kept their word.

Over the ensuing years, Toby often wondered, and indeed marvelled, at the nature of his wife's extraordinary forgiveness. Frances, for her part, was fractionally subdued for some months, as if seeking a quest, a mission. Then suddenly inspired, she asked Toby if they could give a party. He agreed eagerly, and watched her spirits recover as she made her elaborate plans. For the next nine years there were many Farthingoe parties: their daughter Fiona was born an hour after a dance one New Year's Eve. Once her torn ear had healed, Frances continued to wear the earrings, saying she would always love them. This seemed to Toby most extraordinary of all, a gesture he had long since given up trying to understand. But the unanswerable questions would not go away. Was it all part of her strategy of forgiveness? Or was she determined he should never forget?

*   *   *

In truth, the matter of the earring troubled Frances less than Toby imagined. Once the first shock of his violence had subsided, and the ear had healed, she did not find it hard to cast the event from her mind. She could understand the force of Toby's jealousy and even such rough flattery eased forgiveness for his one, uncharacteristic outburst. Thoughts of vengeance did not occur to Frances, nor did the grip of bitterness take a hold. And the fact that her love for Ralph grew stronger did not impair her love for Toby. The feelings ran easily in harness: it was just a question of responding to them differently. So, if anything, she was more demonstratively loving to her husband than she had been before he split her ear, and less flirtatious with Ralph. But still, in occasional moments of weakness, when she and Ralph were alone together, she would sometimes signal violently – to no avail. For years now Ralph, friendly as ever, seemed not to notice her messages. He appeared deliberately to misunderstand her overt gestures, or to ignore them as politely as possible. Such immunity to her powers of charm exasperated Frances. The challenge of re-seducing Ralph was far greater than the challenge of winning him in the first place.

On the summer evening that he was coming to dinner – as he so often did, alone – Frances found herself unexpectedly re-inspired. By now Ralph was such a part of the household – the ear incident long forgotten, and relations between him and Toby as affectionate as ever – that opportunities to entice were frequently there. Toby, to assuage his guilt at so often deserting Frances for his computers, positively encouraged her to invite Ralph to keep her company on long evenings. They would all dine together: Ralph and Frances would later watch television, or talk, while Toby returned upstairs.

Ralph, as Frances knew, felt at home at the vicarage. While he would not go so far as to open a bottle of Toby's precious wine without permission, if he arrived early (which he always did) he would not hesitate to go up to the bedroom and chatter to Frances while she completed the niceties of her make-up and hair. Toby knew of these innocent visitations and often joined them. Many an evening had begun with the three of them in the bedroom, wine and glasses on the dressing-table. By now, Frances would be surprised only if Ralph had *not* come bounding up the stairs, tapped on the door, and rewarded her careful dressing with a smile of approbation.

Her new inspiration was, on brief reflection, tempered by impatience. It was time, she thought, to make some kind of a stand at last, present an ultimatum. She realised such an act was rash: there was risk of losing Ralph completely, though it was unlikely. For she could never believe her feelings were unreciprocated – it was just that Ralph was too much a gentleman to reveal them.

Firm of purpose, Frances spent longer than usual in the bath. The first part of her plan depended on accurate timing.

*   *   *

Ralph Cotterman could never happily accustom himself to the permanent dusk of the Farthingoes' house. Having let himself in through the open front door, he hurried noiselessly up the stairs, determined to avoid the Italian butler, whose suspicious smile he had no wish to bump into. He opened the bedroom door. There were a few seconds in which he was able to contemplate Frances before she realised he was there. Back to him, she was easing a narrow dress up over her hips, regarding the essential wiggling with some satisfaction in the mirror.

Then she saw Ralph's reflection, turned. The dress had only reached her waist. Ralph was faced by a very white bra bulging with suntanned breasts. The picture merged with one from the past: Frances standing Biblically in summer corn, an identical white bra thrown away before the same suntanned body crashed to the earth, flattening the corn into a haphazard nest. Ralph had eagerly joined her. Fifteen years ago, was it, that afternoon? How swiftly changing are the objects of our desires, he thought. Frances, this evening, for all her provocation, was wholly unalluring. After the incident in the corn field, wild, spiky, slippery with sweat, he had never fancied her again, although their affair had continued for a few months.

'Pull it up,' he said, annoyed.

'Oh, Ralphie, I'm sorry,' Frances giggled.

She dragged the dress over the offending breasts, slid her arms into tight sleeves. Its stuff was covered in splodgy flowers: flowers that had been bashed by storms, crushed, and turned to the colour of bruises. Not Ralph's sort of thing at all.

'It isn't as if. . . .' Frances giggled.

'That's not the point.'

'Tobes is engrossed in his computers. We're quite safe.'

'That's not the point, either.'

Frances, seeing his seriousness, changed her tone.

'Would it be in order to ask you to do up my zip?'

She shimmied over to him, turned so that he was challenged by the deep bronzed V of her back. He pulled up the long zip, businesslike.

'Thank you.' Frances swivelled round again, hair tumbling. 'And am I allowed a kiss?' She arranged her lips into a kissable pout.

Ralph scarcely touched her cheek with his mouth. Her silly mood, her baby voice – which she used only when they were alone – irritated him profoundly. He went to sit on the bed, thinking about Ursula and the cat. Frances returned to the dressing-table. She began sifting through handfuls of pearls, amethysts, moonstones, in search of the right necklace.

'Coming to the party?' she asked.

'Course.'

'A lot of people have rung up already. It should be fun.'

'I'm sure it will. Your parties always are.'

'I hope Ursi and Mart will be able to make it.'

'Ursula and Martin will definitely be coming,' said Ralph. 'I've just seen them. At least, Ursula. Martin was out.'

Frances was running a necklace from hand to hand, letting the pearls trickle through her fingers.

'You seem to see so much of Ursi,' she said, 'always calling in. Lucky old her, living so near you.'

'I gave her a cat,' said Ralph, wondering why he should bother with an explanation. 'I'm pretty sure that was a mistake, even though it was meant to be for Sarah.'

'Is that what's put you in such a jumpy mood?'

'Could be.'

'I know you so well.'

'You don't, actually.'

Ralph got up, went to the window. The shadows under the cedars were very dark, the shaven lawn a strong yellow-green.

'I know this: you're only nice to me, you only flirt with me, when you're in a good mood.' Frances was petulant.

'I don't ever flirt with you.'

'That's a matter of interpretation.'

'Indeed.'

'I agree you keep your distance in front of Tobes. Quite rightly.'

'I always keep my distance.'

'No: sometimes when we're alone, I get the distinct impression that this . . . ridiculous thing I feel for you isn't entirely one-sided. You just repress things. There's no need for that.'

Frances's voice had risen. Ralph watched her. He stood with arms folded, leaning against the window sill. It was crowded with pots of African violets and small silver photograph frames filled with miniature pictures of her wedding to Toby. He dragged his thoughts from Ursula and the cat.

'I've told you a thousand times, you misinterpret my feelings. Since our short affair came to an end – fifteen years ago, Frances – I've never given the slightest indication of feeling anything for you other than friendship. Friendship is what I feel. That's what I'd like to go on feeling. We're old friends. But if that's not good enough for you, then the friendship will have to come to an end, because it's all I can offer.'

'I wouldn't want that.'

'Nor would I. In which case, don't let's have any more of these tiresome conversations. They don't get us anywhere. They make me jumpy, reluctant to come here.'

'We don't have them very often.'

'Too often, lately. And if you really feel for me as you say you do, then you should try to believe me. I love your company, your gaiety, your energy, your generosity – all sorts of things about you. You know that. But we're never going to be lovers again. You should have given up all such hopes years ago. If you were more practical, less romantic, you'd have realised ages ago. . . . Apart from anything else, Toby's my friend.'

There was a moment's silence. Then Frances smiled brightly up at Ralph.

'What a speech, Ralphie!' Tears glittered halfway up her eyes. She blinked them back again before they could brim over.

'Sorry.'

'I'm all right most of the time.'

'I know. I was being too harsh.'

'No: just honest. It's just that sometimes I get caught unawares. I get weak. I get stabbed, thinking what might have been, and seeing you.'

She sniffed, and reached for a peach paper handkerchief. This she took a long time to fold into a small neat square before employing it to dab each glistening nostril.

'I suppose the truth of the matter is . . . you don't fancy me any more.'

She began to unfold the handkerchief, now creased into symmetrical squares, two of which were darkened with a tiny spot of damp. Fascinated by the precision of her movements, Ralph thought again of Ursula and the cat.

'No,' he said. Gently.

Frances gave a small, resigned sigh, and let the handkerchief flutter into the wastepaper basket.

'That must be a terribly hard thing to tell someone. My own fault for asking. Still, it's cleared things up for once and for all. I suppose I was silly to have supposed, all these years. . . . Anyway, with this new party, there won't be much time for sad reflections.'

'Exactly. You've always had an instinct for deflection. It's one of your many skills. And apart from that there's Toby. You should never underrate the good things in your marriage.'

'Oh, I don't, I don't. I adore Tobes, you know perfectly well. He's a most marvellous husband.'

She gave a small laugh and finally fastened the clasp of the pearl necklace behind her neck.

'Much better than you could ever have been. In fact, I chose the right man.'

'You certainly did.'

Ralph refrained from observing that there had never been a choice. Sometimes he wondered if Frances had actually forgotten the truth: the evening she had proposed marriage, and he had turned her down. But allowing a woman her conceits was the kind of generosity he believed in.

'There should be some Pimm's down on the terrace,' said Frances, apparently in control now. 'Go down and help yourself.'

As Ralph left the room he saw that she was fingering the bruised flowers of her dress, tight over the bosom, completely absorbed in locating the ideal place for a diamond brooch.

Later, at dinner in the melancholy dining room – windows darkened by the vast trunks of two cedars outside – Frances toyed unhungrily with her food. She contemplated her husband and her old lover – her old friend – either side of her. They were engaged in a technical conversation concerning the Rusisans' space programme versus the Americans'. Frances scarcely listened. Such subjects were so far beyond her understanding or, indeed, interest, that it would have been pointless to make any attempts towards enlightenment.

Instead, she weighed up the relative attractions of a yellow and white striped marquee versus pink and white. On the whole, she thought, marquee makers dealt in more handsome yellows than pinks. On the other hand, there would be so many pink flowers in the garden in September. . . . And how thin Ralph's hair was becoming, she observed. Curious she had not noticed this before. Perhaps she was too used to him to take in slow changes. Absence spurs the shock of change. In middle age, if you do not see a friend for three months, you are surprised by new lines, more grey hairs, the swift progress of decay. To perpetuate the illusion of youth among contemporaries, it is necessary to see them constantly, thought Frances. As she saw Ralph. Why, then, suddenly tonight, did the sadness of his thinning hair strike her? She glanced quickly at her husband. Had she missed anything about him, too, knowing him so well? No: Toby's hair was still as thick and dark as when she had first known him, though his eyebrows, curiously, had turned an independent silvery grey. But his hand. . . . As he pushed a bottle of claret towards Ralph, Frances saw the veins standing high, a complicated pattern of blue-green streams, and the pale fingers trembled slightly. This was something recent, some new intimation of the ageing process. Frances shivered and purposefully turned her thoughts to a less haunting worry – the size of the dance floor.

After dinner, coffee on the terrace. The three of them sat on an iron bench. Behind them, wisteria dangled in a thousand fading earrings from the wall of the house. Toby put an arm round his wife.

'Think I'll be off to the woods, if you'll forgive me, Ralph. Breath of air before bed.'

'But it's not dark enough,' protested Frances.

They all stood.

'It will be by the time I get there. You two go in. It's getting cold. Bye, Ralph.' Toby was off across the lawn, soon lost in the deep shadows.

'Tobes goes badger watching almost every night we're here now,' Frances said. 'Think he's becoming obsessed. Shall we go in?'

'Think I'll be on my way. Have an early night for once.'

'Very well,' Frances replied lightly, for she did not mind.

'Thanks for a lovely dinner. Delicious food as usual.'

Frances was still looking at the place where her husband had disappeared into the shadows.

'If your life isn't engaged in some major pursuit, then it's not very difficult to organise good food,' she said.

Ralph turned to her, cut by the bleakness of her voice.

'I suppose not.' He kissed her on the forehead.

'Come again soon.'

'I will.'

When he had gone, Frances remained for a while outside, quite cold. Clouds moved across the moon, but it was dark enough for badgers, now. A curious lightness of heart seemed to possess her, an indefinable sense of relief. This was the evening, she realised, that she had conceded defeat, released the fantasy she had lived with for so long. Ralph with his thinning hair was never going to be won, and she no longer had any desire to fight for him. She would not embarrass him again. Very quickly he would realise that she, too, was offering nothing more than friendship.

Meantime, unusually, she felt impatient for Toby's return. He had been preoccupied, these last few months, too much by the badgers. They had kept him from her at night. Now it was time to woo him away from them, back to bed at a reasonable hour. Funny, the fluctuations in marriage, she thought, and decided to make a list headed *Suggestions for Food* while she waited for Toby to return.

Later, propped up in her decorative bed, wearing satin pyjamas Toby had once said he liked, she concentrated on possibilities for the party supper. At midnight, perplexed by her own disappointment when Toby still had not returned, she put out the light and continued to wait, thinking, in the dark.

But for Toby, sitting on his jacket beneath an oak tree in the woods, the night had scarcely begun. There had been no sign of a badger so far, but the two hours of waiting had been full of pleasures: the snuffling of unseen creatures, an exuberant song of nightingales, moonlight like shattered glass splintered over bramble and leaf, the smell of wild honeysuckle. One night, Toby thought, he would sleep out here. He had loved sleeping in the open, as a boy. He would find his old sleeping bag, build a small fire and grill himself sausages at dawn. . . . Enjoying such plans, he patiently waited, unmoving.

When eventually Toby returned home the birds were singing and the sky was pale as a young pigeon. He found Frances asleep under a confetti of lists. Her face, even in sleep, was animated: dreams of the party, Toby supposed. He sat down, scattering the lists, undressed quickly. About to get into bed, he noticed his wife's pyjamas – satiny things she had not produced for years. Unease fluttered within him. The calm induced by the solitary, untroubled night, was instantly destroyed by an old and nameless anxiety. Sleep, he knew, would be impossible. He decided to take his chance – go through the paraphernalia in the attic, and find his old tent.

Toby put on his dressing gown quietly as a figure in a silent film. He gave one last, puzzled glance at the seductive position of his sleeping wife, and left the room.

* * *

In Oxford, Ursula and Martin Knox were awake in bed. Both lay on their backs, opened books on their chests. Martin was thinking about the lecture he had to give tomorrow, Ursula was thinking about the cat.

'It was so stupid of Ralph,' she said eventually.

'Oh, I don't know. Sarah's over the moon. She'll look after it.'

'Sarah's not here all day. She doesn't have to be alone in the house with it spooking around. I shall hate coming back not knowing where it is, not knowing where it's going to jump out from.'

'If it haunts you too much, we'll give it back to Ralph.'

'We bloody well will.'

Martin turned towards Ursula, pulled her towards him.

'Stop thinking about the wretched cat.'

Ursula bent her head into the familiar crook between Martin's neck and shoulder. He smelt faintly of ginger. She shut her eyes, suddenly drowsy.

'Do you remember those long mornings, before the children were born?' she asked.

'Course.'

'I wish they still existed, sometimes.' Because since they had had Ben and Sarah, days would go by when Martin was no more than a presence, morning and evening, whose mind was elsewhere. Their marriage ticked over agreeably enough but time, now, was against them – time to wonder, to explore, to keep in touch with the other's days and thoughts, as they had done in the beginning.

Martin kissed her closed eyes, tickled her jaw with one finger. 'Don't go to sleep,' he said.

Ursula opened her eyes. Her vision was completely filled with the close-up of the fine, familiar face she loved so much. His eyes were wholly concentrated upon her, loving. So often they were preoccupied.

'I'm not going to sleep,' she smiled.

Then the telephone rang.

'Who the hell, at this time of night?'

Crossly, Martin sprang away from the shell position with his wife, turned over and hunched the bedclothes over his shoulders.

'It can only be your mother.'

Ursula sighed, picked up the receiver on her side of the bed. It was her mother.

Mary apologised for ringing so late, but felt she had to report the sad news about the balsam poplar. Although she expressed no particular anxiety, Ursula could tell from her voice that her mother was in one of her faintly stricken moods. These could often be cured by a soliloquy about anything that came to mind. So Ursula let her talk uninterrupted for twenty minutes, before trying to assure her that the freak storms were over and there was nothing further to worry about.

When at last the conversation came to an end, Ursula thumped Martin's shoulder.

'Sorry. But I had to let her go on. She was in one of her dithers about nothing. Come back here, now.' Martin did not stir. 'Martin, please.'

She pressed herself into his back, ruffling his hair with an impatient hand. But Martin was asleep. Imagining the hard day he had ahead, she could not bring herself to wake him.

Ursula returned to her own side of the bed, turned out the light. She wondered if the cat, downstairs somewhere, was asleep too.

*   *   *

The Sundays when Jeremy came home for his dutiful visits were always an ordeal for Rachel. They meant that she had to spend the entire morning cooking a very large lunch, the real reward for his presence, after which maternal guilt forced her to iron at least some of the clothes he had brought home to wash. While she was engaged in this task, Jeremy and Thomas would shut themselves in the study, curtains drawn, no matter what the weather, and watch whatever sport happened to be on television. Then, after a perfunctory cup of tea, Thomas would magnanimously offer his son a lift to the station. Jeremy would accept the bag of clean clothes with gruff thanks, and hug his mother with considerably more enthusiasm than on his arrival. Relief, she supposed, that it was time to be on his way.

When the two of them had gone, Rachel would set about clearing up the lunch. Tired, bad-tempered and inefficient by now, this was never finished by the time Thomas returned. Therefore, it was safe for him to make his weekly proposal, his weekly gesture towards the wife.

'Like to see a film?'

'Not really, thanks. I've still got all this to do.'

'Fine. I'll go back to the studio till supper.'

'I'll give you a call.'

The yearning Rachel felt, late on Sunday afternoons, to go to her room, almost overcame her. But she dared not risk it. In the two hours free to her, she might fall asleep, be late in the preparation of supper, find herself woken by a shocked husband. What? Asleep at this time of day? Are you ill? She could hear his incredulous voice. With a weekly sense of deprivation mixed with resentment, she would therefore set about sorting out the crumpled mess of the Sunday papers that her husband and son had left on the floor. She read them without interest, fortified by a strong drink. God, how she hated Sunday evenings.

This particular Sunday morning, for all its ironic brightness, was little different from many others when Jeremy came down from Cambridge. A taciturn Thomas had bashed the papers with particular ferocity at breakfast. But Rachel felt, suddenly, equally bloody-minded. She determined not to let him off the hook completely.

'Would you have a moment to lay the table, later?'

'Probably not. I've got to get something finished, then I'll have to go and get Jeremy a can of that disgusting beer, or there'll be trouble.'

He did not meet his wife's despairing eye, but stomped out of the room trailing the *Sunday Times* behind him. Its cumbersome pages were as plumped up and creased as a bustle. Rachel picked up a pottery jar full of liquid honey. She considered throwing it at Thomas's back. Instead, she slammed it down on the table. The jar cracked in three places. Topaz beads of honey quickly oozed forth. It was past repair. Rachel carried it, gently as a small dead animal, to the rubbish bin, threw it away. Then, washing the stickiness from her fingers under the cold tap, she felt tears on her cheeks. She realised that, if she was going to be able to cook the lunch, she would need a stint in her room, just lying on the unmade bed, eyes shut, to regain her composure.

Within half-an-hour she had recovered her equilibrium, found herself slightly enjoying, even, the routine process of peeling potatoes and carrots, chopping courgettes, spreading the leg of lamb with honey from a new pot, and whizzing homemade strawberry jam into brown breadcrumbs for Jeremy's favourite Guards' Pudding. At twelve o'clock, she heard Thomas bang out of the house: his mission to buy a single can of beer. Rachel had long since given up suggesting he bought a decent supply, thus sparing himself the irritation of a short walk to the off-licence on the Sundays Jeremy came home. But Thomas's one area of irrational meanness concerned drinks for his children: he never offered them more than a single glass of wine, and was annoyed when they helped themselves to more. He refused to stock any of the innocuous drinks they liked – lager, ginger beer, coke – on the grounds that there was no room for such commonplace drinks, and stocking them would only further encourage the children's pedestrian tastes. Rachel laid the table.

Jeremy arrived punctually at one. He trailed into the kitchen reminding her of a latter-day Dick Whittington, in ragged jeans and ghastly tartan shirt. He carried a large pouch-shaped bag which would have looked appropriate at the end of a stick. He also held a small bunch of flowers. Their cheap brown wrapping paper indicated they came from a stall in the station.

Jeremy kissed his mother on the cheek, gave her the flowers. 'So, how's things?'

Rachel looked inside the paper cone, dreading peonies. They were peonies, thunderous colours.

'Fine. And you?'

'Bout the same.'

To please him, Rachel took the flowers from the paper. Their sooty stems smudged her fingers, an intense black. She hated peonies. She wondered why Jeremy didn't know by now how much she hated peonies.

'Thank you, darling. They're lovely.'

Jeremy hitched his bag off his shoulder. A dirty shirt sprouted, cauliflower-like, from its opening.

'Shall I put these in?' He made it sound like a generous offer.

'Why not? And don't forget the powder this time.'

'For heaven's sake, Mum.'

Jeremy shambled off to the downstairs cloakroom to the washing machine. While he was gone, Rachel took the opportunity to rinse the flower dust from her fingers. She dumped the loathsome peonies in a jar, and put them on the window sill. A sensitive and observant son, she reflected, would notice

71

his offering had not been put in the sort of place it could be admired. Jeremy loped back.

'Darling, I don't mean to sound perverse,' said Rachel, who had every intention of sounding just that, as her earlier exasperation returned, 'but are there no launderettes in Cambridge?'

The question brought Jeremy to a complete halt in the middle of the kitchen floor. He stood, unmoving, bemused for a moment, a shambolic, familiar stance. Then half a charming smile rearranged his mouth (a smile that had been so winning as a child) as comprehension came to him.

'No need for the sarcasm, Ma. Of course there are launderettes in Cambridge. Millions of them. Let me tell you I spend hours and bloody hours in launderettes.'

'Then why do you always find yourself with so much unwashed stuff to bring home? Not that I mind, really. . . .'

From his great height Jeremy looked down on his mother as if she was pathetic, or insane, or both.

'You know how it is. I'm not into ironing. It's not my thing. How many more times do I have to explain?'

Rachel sighed. It was useless ever to reproach her son, and the matter of the laundry, a universal one among mothers of children who do not live at home, was of no great importance. She could not think why she had bothered to say anything, really. She had been spurred by a nameless irritation which would not subside.

'And you're so thin, Jay. Don't you eat in Cambridge?'

'Course I eat. I eat tons. The College like feeds us. You know?' He was gentle, this time, as if dealing with the mentally disabled. 'Is there a beer, by any slim chance?'

Jeremy slopped over to the fridge and pulled open the door with a bonelesss hand. He stood before the brightly lit shelves, arms folded, enjoying his act of acute concern and puzzlement. His expression – for her benefit, Rachel knew – made her, at last, want to laugh. Jeremy's ways of love were private and uncommon, but Rachel had always recognised them.

'Wow, Mum! Zap! Found it!' He swivelled round, smiling

completely now, holding up a very small can of beer. 'Dad's really gone to town this week, I'll say.'

Rachel laughed, blushed. Shame fused with loyalty. Jeremy's lack of malice, concerning his father's peculiarities, always increased her love. She resorted to harmless conspiracy, something she and Jeremy had enjoyed ever since he was very young.

'One day, I'll get a whole case of beer and hide it for you under my side of the bed. . . .'

'Brilliant, Mum.' He opened the can. Precious froth pierced out. 'The madness of possibility. Quick, a glass!'

Rachel rushed to a cupboard, thrust a glass under the spilling liquid. She felt full of energy, lightness: she had the absurd impression her movements were swift and graceful, as if part of a ballet.

'Of course, I couldn't really do that.'

'Of course you couldn't.' Jeremy took his first swig. Just half the glass remained. 'Tell you what, though. I'll eke out this wonderful drink, shall I? Agonising sip by agonising sip all through lunch. Bet you Dad won't notice, nose stuck into his claret.'

'Bet you anything you like.'

Suddenly, they were both laughing.

But later, at lunch, unease returned. Thomas could scarcely conceal his distraction. Jeremy sat hunch-shouldered eking out the beer in attention-seeking sips, as promised. Rachel threw rhythmic glances between husband and son, ready to lob some defusing practicality, should the slow burn of tension threaten to flare.

'Work eased up, second year, has it?' Thomas asked Jeremy, eventually.

'Yeah. Sort of. You could say.'

'In my day, we were warned of the dangers of slacking off in the second year.'

'Were you.' It wasn't a question.

'Suppose you're involved in a lot of other activities, as usual?'

Thomas was always trying to discover the precise habits of

73

Jeremy's life at Cambridge, and to compare them with his own.

'That's right.'

'Footlights, still?'

'Yeah. They're good.' He glanced at his father who was cutting into several roast potatoes with the tip of his knife, as if for surgery. 'And the Labour Club. That takes quite a bit of time.' Jeremy was firm of purpose.

There was a long silence. Even the sloshing of Thomas's severed potatoes in a pool of gravy made no noise.

'I'm sure it does,' said Thomas at last. He paused to finish a mouthful, then looked squarely at his son. 'Now, don't take this question wrong, but can you tell me what, exactly, a band of undergraduate Socialists thinks it can do, effectively, for the benefit of the nation? Or, indeed, for the Labour Party itself? I take it you're a kind of unofficial think-tank?'

Jeremy sighed, patient.

'Thomas, please,' said Rachel.

Thomas shrugged. 'Very well. I was only attempting some kind of conversation. It seems to me pretty odd that Jeremy comes home for the day and we sit round the table in near silence.'

Jeremy finished his beer, held up the empty glass.

'But your idea of conversation, Dad, is to ask me a lot of questions. Some of which I've no intention of answering. I never ask you and Ma questions –'

'– ask what you like.'

Rachel flinched. Neither of the men noticed.

'I'm not much interested in asking you questions, as a matter of fact. I mean, no offence. The answers wouldn't be exactly riveting. You lead quite dull lives.'

'Dull?' Rachel's loyalty swung towards Thomas. She rose and began gathering the empty plates.

'Seems to me.'

'I don't know about that,' said Thomas, suddenly huffy. He wiped his mouth and most of his face with a huge damask napkin.'We lead quite an active life,' he said, conscious that

74

he spoke for himself. 'We're pretty busy. We don't sit at home in front of the television every night, you'll be amazed to hear. Next week, for instance, we've been asked to dine in an Oxford College, no less. I forgot to tell you that, Rachel. St Crispin's. Wednesday. Patrick Pruddle. Suddenly rang up and said would we like to, after all these years.'

'That's great,' said Jeremy.

Rachel spooned out two large helpings of Guards' Pudding, and pushed a jug of Jersey cream towards her son.

'Oxford, midweek?' she said. The thought of being sixty miles from her bedroom filled her with dread.

'You sound raring to go, Ma,' Jeremy smiled. 'Jesus, what a pudding.'

While he and Thomas returned to their silent eating, Rachel observed how alike were their downcast eyes – same starfish lashes making small pointed shadows on flat cheeks. But Jeremy's nose was blade-thin, like her own, and in his rare charming smile, she recognised a strong look of herself thirty years ago. His wild long hair (strangely, Thomas had made no comment about it this week) bore no resemblance to Thomas's dry stuff – again it was hers – at least, her hair as it had been in lustrous youth. But oh, the worry about the etiolated state of his limbs, his cadaverous chest and concave stomach. Did he never eat in Cambridge? She'd asked him that, hadn't she, today? Mustn't ask him again. Questions pestered, though. What did he do? What was his life? Where was he this time yesterday? Where would he be this time tomorrow? Was there a girl? Rachel sighed as she peeled a small, early, expensive peach: she knew so little about the daily hum of his days, and Jeremy was not one generous with clues. But unlike Thomas she had learned to control her curiosity. Jeremy's reaction to questions was to clamp up altogether. Why could Thomas never understand that?

Meanly, Rachel longed for lunch to finish, for Jeremy to go, for the day to be over, for the security of normal weekdays, luxurious in their solitude.

When, three long hours later, Thomas and Jeremy did

eventually leave for the station, she took the unusual risk of going to her room, drawing the curtains and lying down. Relief, calm, came swiftly. She did not think, was only aware of the heaviness of her limbs and the sweet drowning sensation as sleep overcame her.

She woke at six with a start. Thomas must have returned some time ago. Had he looked for her? Crept in and found her asleep in the dark? The idea made her shudder. She quickly got up, snapped back the heavy curtains. The evening sun made a buttery gleam on the hollyhock chintz. He would have wondered why the lunch had not been cleared away, what had happened to delay the usual pristine state of a Sunday evening. In her panic, Rachel paused for a moment to plan some explanation for her absence. It was then she heard, overhead in the studio, troubled footsteps pacing to and fro. Thomas was a great pacer, while thinking: she had heard him travelling many miles in his studio. But there was something about the unevenness, the resonance of these steps, that alarmed her. What was the matter? Where was Thomas, as always so far from her?

Rachel ran downstairs, flung open the kitchen door. There, to her amazement, she found everything cleared away, washing-up machine humming, cling-film over a dish of remaining vegetables. Implications of this sight were so extraordinary, Rachel heard herself gasp out loud. In their entire married life, she could not recall a single occasion on which Thomas had made any such gesture, unasked. On the rare occasion she begged him for help, he would reluctantly and inefficiently make some futile contribution. But never, never had he taken on so large a job and accomplished it so faultlessly. There could only be one explanation. Something must be dreadfully wrong. . . . Rachel sat down at the kitchen table, laid her head in folded arms, and let the dizzying possibilities swirl confusingly about her.

While his wife sat in her stunned condition downstairs, Thomas continued to pace and agonise in his studio three floors above her. As one who for the last decade had always felt the necessity of extramarital stimulation in the romantic area of the heart, he knew quite well what the nature of the problem was: the girl with the amber hair. The wretched girl had loomed ever larger in his mind since their brief meeting last week, a sort of amorphous beauty – to be honest, he could not quite remember the exact details of her face – with very long sleeves. By Saturday, his desire for her was almost overwhelming, and this had been the longest Sunday of his life.

He had, he was quite aware, been a less than perfect husband and father today, as on many occasions. But Rachel and Jeremy were accustomed to his artistic temperament by now. They believed his distracted states were caused by the creative process within him. Over the years, he had dropped many a hint that therein lay the explanation for lapses in his attention. They had no notion that in truth his mind was far from sublime thoughts of painting a good picture. Had they known that it flurried, instead, in basest areas of the flesh, they would have been incredulous, shocked. For if he paused and contemplated the barnacles of sin encrusting his soul – a practice he avoided as much as possible – Thomas was confronted by a shameful truth. It was, simply, that he was almost constantly agitated by a state of lust. So upright in his pinstripes to the outside world, Thomas was a man positively besieged with lust within. Age did nothing to dispel this weakness. In fact he was more mercilessly taunted than ever. And his reaction was to give up the fight, believing that his inconvenient appetites, eventually surfeited, would die. So far there had been little sign of any such progress. Over and over again, the sight of some distant, strange girl caused him such anguished yearnings that he found himself forced to make a clumsy approach. Often, this led to disaster.

Gillian was the most recent in a history of terrible mistakes – though for her, Thomas realised even at the time, drink and boredom had spurred him more than any real attraction. There was a back catalogue of cringe-making rebuffs. Once, on an aeroplane to Paris, he had bought a girl in the next seat to him

77

several glasses of champagne. Having discovered their mutual liking for the Norwich School of watercolourists, it soon became plain she was willing to join him for the weekend. Thus encouraged, Thomas had not thought it untoward to put a gentle hand on her knee, by way of confirming the unspoken understanding. Unwittingly, he had pressed some alarm bell within her. In an instant, the stupid girl became a hysterical tiger, screaming at the air hostess, clawing at his face, demanding he should be reported to the captain and removed. ('By parachute?' he remembered asking, as she was dragged away from him.) Much embarrassment all round, though in the event he came out of the whole crisis quite well. The air hostess joined him in Paris instead.

For all his good intentions, Thomas never learned from his mistakes, and his mistakes exhausted him. The nervous energy consumed by his fantasies left him physically drained, nervous, ill-tempered, detached. These days there were few occasions when he experienced an untroubled mind, a body devoid of craving. When this did happen he meant to make up to Rachel, a tolerant creature on the whole, for his past misdemeanours. But he was so out of practice in the art of humouring a wife that whatever suggestion he made came out grudgingly: it was no wonder Rachel turned it down. The cycle had become too complex, now, to break: he was forced to find some solace in good claret and malt whisky.

This particular Sunday evening Thomas was suffering irritating guilt about his churlish behaviour towards his wife and son. On his way back from the station – a desultory farewell, as usual, that no doubt Jeremy took to be lack of interest and paternal love – he determined to make amends. Some distant childhood habit reminded him Sunday was the Lord's day, and it was appropriate to try loving one's wife as well as one's neighbour. But as he drove through the slow traffic he knew his heart could not be in any suggestion of an evening at a film or, worse, dinner, just the two of them, in some restaurant. His mind was desiccated from six days' thinking about the girl with the amber hair. His body was sluggish from the large lunch and several nights' lost sleep. So, once again, his good intentions failed him.

When Thomas arrived home he found, surprisingly, nothing had been touched, and Rachel was not about. He was too tired to imagine, or care, where she might be. In fact, her surprising absence was something of a relief. He stared at the mess of things on the dining-room table and at the further chaos in the kitchen beyond. He waited for the rage, the irritation at such incompetence, to come. Instead, he was aware of a strange inspiration: he would clear it all up as an act of contrition – a thing he had never so much as thought about in his life before.

Indeed, the thought was so peculiar that Thomas continued to stand looking at the detritus for several moments, unmoving, while he reflected on the brainstorm that had accosted him. A vision of Rachel's incredulity and pleasure produced a curious excitement. A moment later it occurred to him that the whole idea was mad: if he undertook such a thing once, it might well become incumbent upon him to repeat the process. Rachel might grow to expect such help from him regularly. And that . . . oh no. The *habit* of domestic help was something too awful to contemplate.

All the same, he began to move slowly, clumsily, gathering up plates, putting away clean silver, struggling with the dreadful problem of how to deal with cold vegetables stuck in their wax of hardened butter.

Two hours later, hands puffy from the long session of scrubbing pans in hot water, he looked round in some triumph. There was nothing further to be done. It was all, he thought, just as Rachel would have left it. He flung open the kitchen window, victorious.

But the task over, elation fled. Back in his studio, he contemplated the Cotterman picture for a while, depressed. The taunting memory of the girl with the amber hair returned to him. There were still eighteen hours until he would see her again. And then? Plans were smudged in his mind. Buy another Cotterman? Or two, or three, if necessary. Of course, to ease the way. Then, well – caution. Above all, he must be very careful. Take things slowly. Not frighten her. Win her confidence, her respect. Which one day might grow into equal desire. . . .

Thomas began to pace. Backwards and forwards, backwards and forwards past the seascape. He longed magically just to be there, walking, this Sunday evening. Far from London. With her. Not talking much. Just sniffing the sea, feeling the breeze. If the place was as deserted as in the picture, then he would suggest they sat for a while in the dunes. He would put an arm round her shoulders, perhaps. See how she reacted to that. The thought made him shudder. Ridiculous idea, that he should ever get as far as the Cotterman dunes with her. What a fool he was. But if he did . . . he must bloody well restrain himself. Oh God, he said out loud, slow me down. Let me take the girl with the amber hair very slowly.

*   *   *

That Sunday afternoon Mary and Bill and their dog Trust walked on Brancaster beach. It was fine, but cool. They wore gumboots and thick jumpers against an edgy breeze. Mary had tied a scarf over her head so that only a fringe of grey hair was free to skitter about her forehead.

They had been coming to the beach for years, in all weathers. High summer was the only time they avoided. Then, crowds – people had discovered the empty stretches of dune and sand in the last decade – penetrated further and further along. Although by normal seaside standards the place was still thinly populated, they liked it best when it appeared as they had first known it, long ago, empty but for a lone distant figure looking for mussels, watching the birds or walking a dog.

Over the years they had observed the gradual disintegration of the wreck. Once a sturdy shell of a ship blown up in the last War, it had slowly succumbed to barnacles, seaweed, lashing storms and strong currents. Now, when the tide was out, just a few posts of blackened steel remained – too few even to indicate the former shape of the ship's bones. At high tide the two or three small posts protruding from the water could be missed by all those unfamiliar with the disappearing skeleton.

There was a high tide this afternoon: sea dull as an elephant's shank in moments when cloud obscured the sun. Then, when the sun passed, herbaceous blues and greys and greens of a sophisticated garden border.

Mary loved the beach, its ankle-high gusts of sand stinging her boots, its ribbed distances scrunchy with shells, its wind-wrinkled pools blinking fast as troubled eyes. But she did not like the sea. It made her think of death, endings, the remorseless indifference of Nature.

She threw a piece of driftwood a long way for Trust. The dog bounded off, mindlessly pleased to fetch the wood for the thousandth time. Mary stood watching him, shielding her eyes against the glare, legs firmly parted, small face pale as a bird's egg in the momentary sun.

'If I should die . . .' she said.

Bill, a yard away, could scarcely hear her voice against the brush of sea.

'What's that, darling one?'

'If I should die first, you must keep bringing Trust here for his walks.'

Bill moved nearer his wife, tightened the knot of her scarf beneath her chin.

'Such silly thoughts,' he said.

'But if I should,' persisted Mary.

'You won't. But if you do, don't worry about Trust. Death shouldn't break old plans and habits.' He smiled at her.

The breezes stung Mary's eyes. Bill saw them fill with pink, child's tears, that do not dull the whites. Mary sighed, unable to say more. The sigh ended in a small shudder that contained her immeasurable fears of the future combined with a sad nostalgia for the past. Bill took her hand. They began to walk to meet the returning Trust. The dog, so constantly easy to please, bounded towards them. Its fat golden body reverberated from the powerful wagging of its tail. The piece of driftwood dropped from its mouth at Bill's feet. He threw it again, much further than Mary. Trust jumped and swerved fatly into the air, then thudded off after it once more.

'Ursula said of course we could stay with them for the Farthingoes' ball,' Mary said, omitting to add *If I'm still around.*

'Good, good,' said Bill, not interested in such matters, but pleased his wife's more lugubrious Sunday afternoon thoughts had been deflected. 'We must get back. I must get cracking with the saw. Poor old tree. It was that one lonely poplar, planted by your father – God knows why, mad decision in such an exposed position – that inspired me with the whole idea of the arboretum. If it'd been one of our young ones down, don't suppose I would have made half so much fuss.'

Mary sighed. She had long since discovered the best way to rescue Bill from a trough of regretful thought was to increase her deafness.

'They're such an energetic couple, Toby and Frances.'

'We were full of life at their age.'

Bill took Mary's arm, steered her round the way they had come. The wind was now in their faces, the brightness puckering their eyes.

'We're still pretty energetic, aren't we?' Mary put an exaggerated springiness into her step.

'I should say so. Not too bad.'

'We've weathered quite well.'

Bill smiled again and stroked the back of his wife's neck.

'You've kept your looks and your spirits. That's the secret.'

'Haven't exactly managed to fend off the arthritis, have I?' Mary held up a small white hand, fingers swollen at the joints, but the nails were still perfect, luminescent; they had somehow defied the ribbed look of elderly nails. 'People are always asking me -- how have you and Bill managed to be happy for so long?'

Bill laughed. 'Huh! Bloody hard work, I hope you tell them. Bloody hard work keeping up the impetus. Almost impossible, fighting off the monster of familiarity. Devours everything.'

'After all these years – I never knew you thought that.' Mary laughed. 'It's the familiarity I love. Anyway, my answer is usually something about our trying to adjust now the exhilaration of youth has turned to the slower waters of old age.'

'Good heavens! Very grand phrasing. I wasn't aware of doing any such thing.'

'Of course you weren't. You're a purely instinctive creature. You never work out anything.'

'But I nearly always agree with you when you've worked it out.'

'Well, in this case I'm right –'

'– as nearly always. Course you are,' Bill reflected. 'Half the divorces must have something to do with the fact that no-one is taught what to do when the passion goes. Perhaps we should drop a few hints to Ursula and Martin.'

'They're perfectly happy.'

'Who knows? Who knows anything about other people's marriages?'

'Passion doesn't have to die.' Mary looked out to sea.

'The death – or indeed the keeping alive – of passion is not at all the sort of conversation I'd be keen on having with the children.'

'I can see that, with your upbringing. But it's a hard thing to make people believe these days. This world of fast food, fast travel, fast passion. Dizzying ephemerality.'

'Balzac asked a jolly good question: "Can a man always desire his wife?" he asked.'

'And what was his answer?'

'"Yes." Definitely yes.' Bill kissed Mary on the nose. 'I'll always remember that. Encouraged me no end when I was thinking of marrying you. He was most emphatic, old Balzac, on that point. He said it's as absurd to deny it's possible for a man always to love the same woman, as it would be to think a famous musician needed several violins to execute a piece of music. I haven't needed any other violins, I suppose you could say.'

They both laughed, moved on. Trust bounded up behind them once more, making brief fans of sand in the air. Bill threw the driftwood. They watched the dog run after it again.

Trust's game gave a rhythm to their walks on the beach.

'By the time I've finished chopping up the poplar,' said Bill, 'we'll have enough logs for five winters.'

'You can start after tea,' said Mary. She could feel the warmth of the sun through her jersey, and, at the same time, the distance of winter.

*　　*　　*

The air of efficiency Frances Farthingoe frequently exuded was in some measure due to the tools of business with which she surrounded herself. On Sunday evening she had arranged herself in a comfortable chaise longue in the shade of one of the cedars. It was an old 1930s piece of outdoor furniture, of cumbersome wicker frame and comfortable cushions re-covered (efficient forethought) last autumn. The newness of the striped linen stuff smelt faintly of mothballs. A few days in the air, and the more familiar smell of the original stuffing of the cushions would predominate again.

By her side, a garden table was equipped with everything she could possibly need for her party working session: full glass of Pimm's, Filofax, tape recorder, file of acceptances, file of refusals, various incomplete lists, felt-tipped pens with very fine points of black, red and green.

Frances was skimming through a cookery book seeking further inspiration for the buffet. Should this book fail her, there was on the grass a pile of others to turn to. Her positive thought was that Coronation Chicken was absolutely out. She would never stand accused of such a cliché. Delicious though it could be, the Farthingoes could do better than that. Coronation Chicken – her actively critical mind whirled on – was as laughable among a certain class of people as festoon blinds. Twenty-five years after its invention, it had become the dis-covery of the nouveau entertainers, the excitement of the petits bourgeois at their outdoor lunches on the patio. Not suitable for a Farthingoe ball, Frances's mind hummed on. Koulibiac, on the other hand. . . . Koulibiac was a real possibility. Koulibiac, up and coming in popularity, still had a few years to go before it, too, became a caterer's cliché. Perhaps – just – they could get away with it. On the other hand, as a well-known perfectionist, an innovator in the transitory world of beautiful parties, Frances felt disinclined to take any risk. . . .

Even as these dilemmas fully occupied her concentration, inspiration came to her blindingly. Excitingly. Her hand trembled on the glass of Pimm's. The inspiration, it happened, was not about the food, but about the marquee. The matter of pink or yellow had been tormenting her for several days, now. Still unresolved this morning, she had determined to put it on ice. Often, Frances had found in the past, putting problems on ice meant that the ice broke of its accord, in its own time, and revelation came. Well, once again, her method had worked. The solution was wonderfully obvious – grey! A dove-grey and white striped marquee. Thus there would be no fear of imperfect yellow or pink, and anyhow those colours were too popular. Grey would be unusual, original, subtle. There was a slight doubt in Frances's mind that marquee contractors would stock grey and white striped tent lining, but that could be overcome. Once bent on an idea, Frances could rely on herself to triumph over any problem that might stand in its way.

Oh, the happiness of having resolved that! Real achievement. She lay back, cookery book a redundant thing in her limp hand, looking up at the thunderous branches of the cedar, its black-green needles shredding the sky. Images of September flowers against grey and white stripes crowded upon her. The brilliance of the idea! The only pity of it was that there was no-one with whom she could share her joy. Frances knew from experience that few people in the world are genuinely interested in others' ideas unless passion for the same subject is shared. All most people judged was the finished product. They did not have the imagination to conceive of the trouble and ingeniousness that went into its making; nor did they really care. In a decade of party giving, Frances had received much praise and many congratulations – transitory rewards, which never

85

quite made up for the loneliness in the months of struggling with practicalities that precede a party on a grand scale.

She shifted her gaze. At the end of the garden was the figure of a man in sunglasses. Dazed by her imagining, she thought for a moment it was Ralph. Ralph! Curiously, she had not given him a thought since his departure last night. Now, she would have been glad to see him bound over, throw himself on top of her (something he had never done, of course, since her marriage), kiss her, and above all share her happiness at having found the solution to the problem of the marquee. Then she remembered she wanted no such thing. Her passion for Ralph had finally died. Genuinely, thank God, she was free of him. The old habitual thoughts of him, natural wake to a long one-sided involvement, would soon fade away.

As her eyes focused, she saw that the man was Toby, not Ralph. The brightness of his blue shirt and white trousers dulled as he stepped into the shade. He stood at her feet, eyes invisible behind the impenetrable dark glasses.

'I've been doing well,' Frances said at last. 'Lots of ideas.' She could tell by the rigidity of her husband's mouth that there was no point in elaborating further.

'Good,' he said.

'There's some Pimm's left . . .'

'No thanks.'

Toby sat at the bottom of the chaise longue. Frances swung her bare feet to one side so that he should have more room. Toby kneaded one of them with his hand. Frances felt a prickle of alarm down her spine. She knew from his face he had come with an announcement. A cut in the party budget, perhaps. . . . She had been as economical as possible: any further cutting would make things impossible. He must see. . . .

'I want to ask you something,' said Toby. 'It may seem a bit strange.' He fell silent, rubbing just the big toe now, staring at its accurately polished scarlet nail.

'Go on.'

'I want to spend a few nights in the woods, badger watching. You need the whole night, really.'

'I suppose you do.' Relief flared through Frances. Unasked, she would do what she could, after all, about further economies.

'I found my old tent and sleeping bag in the attic. Thought I'd have a go tonight. It's so warm. Would you mind?'

'Mind? Why should I mind?'

'I didn't think you would.'

'Course not. You'll love it. Back to boyhood.'

'Perhaps. You should come one night.' He knew he was safe, there.

'Me?' Frances laughed. 'Not on your life, all those midges.'

Toby stood up. He, too, felt strong with relief.

'I'll try tonight, then. I won't be off till after you've gone to bed. It won't interrupt our evenings.'

'Fine.' Funny old thing, Toby, sometimes.

'I'll get the sleeping bag off the line. It's been airing all day.' Extraordinarily co-operative, Frances could be on occasions. Often when he least expected it.

Toby walked back over the lawn, which was almost completely white with daisies. Frances, after a sip of Pimm's to celebrate her relief, took up a black pen and flipped her file open to a new page. Ring tent people re GREY and white, she wrote, and underlined the GREY in red.

* * *

When Thomas came downstairs that evening, he found Rachel at the kitchen table, her head in folded arms.

'What's the matter?' he asked, puzzled. 'I thought you'd be pleased.'

Rachel stood up at once, ashamed to have been caught out by Thomas. She wiped her eyes, though they showed no sparkle of tears. Thomas could tell she had been crying only by the dark spots on her sleeve.

'Nothing's the matter,' she smiled, always good at the gallant lie, 'except that I'm completely overcome.'

Thomas patted her shoulder, smiling too, pleased with himself. He had not had such an effect on his wife for years.

'Even I can be surprising sometimes,' he chortled, 'but you mustn't expect –'

'– of course not.'

'Drink?'

Rachel nodded. She needed one. And in a moment they were back to their normal rhythm, their normal places. Rachel began to prepare the supper.

Thomas stood by, watching her. Occasionally, evenings like this, he felt curiously at peace in his own house, glad of Rachel's detached, familiar company. He could never have told her this. Perhaps she knew. She was an intuitive old thing in many ways. Also, she caused no agitation, for which she earned Thomas's unspoken gratitude. No: she just bumbled on, seemingly happy, accepting life as it was. She was jolly good, actually, at accepting the fact that most marriages sloped into a kind of passivity after a few years. She didn't complain. She was almost touchingly pleased by small gestures – her reaction to this clearing up this evening, for instance, was out of all proportion to the act itself. Good old Rachel. She was a blessing, really. Without knowing him, she seemed to understand him. He'd probably never leave her in the end.

*   *   *

When Ursula came down on Monday morning, she found the cat had moved from the kitchen table to the dresser. With its impeccable deportment, it sat in its china-cat position in a small space between mugs, plants, racks of eggs and piles of school books. Its dish of milk on the floor was empty. At Ursula's appearance, it shifted its gaze from its neatly placed paws to her face. In the morning light, she fancied its look was scathing, threatening, superior. Again she dreaded the thought of returning to the house, later in the day, and being alone with the cat. She was glad of the usual breakfast noise from the children.

Ben and Sarah were squabbling over the free gift from the Cornflakes packet, a small plastic clip whose ubiquitous usefulness was heavily advertised. Ursula could never understand why children, who did not lack in toys and entertainments of every kind, were so acquisitive when it came to 'free gifts' of minimal interest.

'Well, anyway, if you have it I'm going to feed the cat this morning and this evening, so there,' Sarah shouted to her brother, long hair swinging furiously about.

'You're jolly well not. That's not fair. That's not fair, Mama, is it? Here, have the stupid thing.' Ben dropped the plastic clip into his sister's cereal.

'Don't you dare!' Sarah picked it out, small milky fingers flailing, flicked it at her brother's head.

'Shut up, both of you,' bellowed Martin, putting down the *Independent*, 'and hurry or we'll be late.'

Lateness was a daily threat which left the children unmoved, but their father's tone of voice reduced them to a moment's silence. Ursula remained at the table, back purposefully to the cat, with her mug of coffee. Sarah got up, went over to the animal and picked it up. For a moment, its legs stuck out at all angles in rigid protest, then it relaxed into her arms.

'I'm going to name it,' she said to Ben, 'whatever you think.'

'Oh no you're not,' retorted Ben. 'It's going to be a democratic decision. We'll put suggestions in a hat and get someone to pull one out.'

'No, we won't. That's a really stupid idea.'

'We'll sort it out after tea,' contributed Ursula. 'Now, come on. Hurry. Got your homework? Ben, where's your jacket?'

Sarah, sulking, returned the cat to the dresser. She took up her empty cereal bowl, filled it with milk, and put it within the cat's reach. It looked at her with supreme ingratitude.

'I think it's a pretty horrible cat anyway,' snarled Ben. 'All bony.' He swung his long blue and yellow scarf round his neck.

'Don't you dare say that. You know how many years and years and years and years I've longed for an animal. . . .' Tears animated Sarah's eyes, dividing her long, dark lashes.

'Crybaby –'

Martin took hold of his son's collar, pushed him from the room and kissed his wife on the head in passing, all in one long, efficient movement.

'You can't want a scarf on a day like this, Ben,' Ursula yelled after him.

'Oh yes I can,' was the determined shout from the front door. Ursula, her melancholy daughter in her arms, gave up the idea of trying to defeat her son.

'There's nothing to cry about, darling,' she said. 'Cheer up, and remember whatever-its-name-is will be here waiting for you when you get back.' She smiled, encouraging.

'But it's my cat. I should name it.'

'We'll sort it all out when you come home, I promise.'

'All right.'

Ursula kissed Sarah's pink cheeks, pushed her fringe from her eyes. Often so extraordinarily grown-up, now, at eight, in rare moments of despair intimations of babyhood returned to remind. They hugged. Ursula could feel the wild beating of her daughter's heart.

'There's Papa hooting. Run. See you at half-past-three.'

'Love you, Mama.'

Sarah was gone.

After he had dropped the children at school, Martin drove to his College. He collected a package of dreary-looking letters from the lodge, and walked across the quad. The sixteenth-century buildings, of sand-coloured stone, were pale in the still opal light. In flowerbeds beneath the ground floor windows, yellow tulips shone lantern-like through the dusk of forget-me-nots gathered round them. There was not a morning on which Martin was not affected by the beauty of the place, or failed to realise his good fortune in working in such a building.

In his room, wood-panelled, book-crowded, but curiously tidy for a don, he sat at his large desk in the window, reluctant to open his post. Instead he picked up the latest copy of the *Economic Journal* and flicked through its pages. He had an agreeable, easy day to look forward to: only one pupil, at midday, a long afternoon in the Bodleian to start making notes for his Thursday lecture. The thought of Ursula, left at home with the detritus of breakfast and unmade beds to deal with before she started on her work made him, as always, guilty. He did what he could in the evenings, took the children off her hands at weekends. But he really could not be expected to return home, after the school run, to share domestic duties on the day that the cleaning lady did not come. Ursula rarely complained, but he knew that the undertaking of two jobs ('a woman's lot − best to get on with it without whingeing,' as Ursula sometimes said) was both frustrating and exhausting.

Today Martin was aware of an especial unease. After a moment's reflection, having cast away the *Journal* and picked up the *Spectator*, he was able to pinpoint its source: something to do with the cat. That bloody cat. In Ursula's quietness, and distracted eyes, last night, Martin had begun to understand the depths of her antipathy to the animal. He had not realised until then that she did not merely dislike cats, and had refused to have one over the years because of all the nuisance of looking after it − they obviously unnerved her on some more profound level. She wouldn't like to be alone in the house with it 'spooking around', she had said last night. She was alone in the house with it now. What was she feeling?

The question made Martin even more restless. He could not bear the thought of his wife's unhappiness in any measure. Should he go back home right now, see how she was doing? No: probably not. She would think that most peculiar. Rather, he decided he would ring her in half-an-hour before she went off to see about some garden (he could not remember which one, where) and apologise for his hurried departure. Not mention the cat. See if she said anything.

Consoled by this idea, Martin switched on the kettle and

made himself the first of many cups of coffee he would drink during the day. Once he had talked to her, been reassured she was all right, he would put his mind to his books, the mental lego of economics, which absorbed him so completely most days of his life. Sometimes, he thought, the sterility of figures, percentages, the fluctuations of world prices, cut him off too far from what was left of the romance of life. But Ursula seemed to understand his passion, was proud of his achievement, even managed to assume a curiosity in a subject that was far from her natural interests.

The only thing, sadly, she could not understand (*would* not understand, it seemed) was the old and tiresome question of *place*. His life was in Oxford. Ursula did not like Oxford. Too bad. As his wife, she must put up with it, though he supposed that some far-off, inconceivable day when the children had grown up, he might contemplate moving somewhere nearby. Ursula's dislike seemed to him so curiously stubborn – endless complaints about horrible shops and lack of sky. Were she to make more effort, rather than preoccupy herself thinking up almost daily escapes, she could come to like the city better, if not to love it as he did– well, used to. (Did he *really* love it anymore? That was a question he might dwell on when he had a moment.) At any rate, Ursula's dogged, vociferous dislike of a place most people regarded as exceptionally beautiful and agreeable, was one of the few things about her that made Martin angry. After some violent quarrels he swore to rise no more to her provocative jibes. So now her grumbles were met by silence. Sometimes he caught a look of disturbing anguish in her eyes, and knew that, ridiculously, *Oxford* was the only reason – everything else was fine, wasn't it? – or was he, in some unthinking way, an unreasonable husband in other respects? Perhaps he did not acknowledge her talents fully, or take enough interest in her work – well, she was the first to admit that gardening wasn't much up his street.

Heavens, though, he was the first to appreciate her great energy, her efficiency, her good humour and loving nature: so many qualities all in one wife. One day Martin intended to tell

Ursula how inconceivable his life would be without her. Not that she had ever requested any such assurances. She was not, thank God, the sort of woman who needed declarations. She read the messages in actions. At least, he thought she did. But he could never quite tell. Even after some sixteen years of marriage to a woman you loved profoundly, sharing children, house, daily proximity, you had no real idea of ninety per cent of what was going on in her mind. (Ninety per cent of the gross, as it were. Martin smiled to himself.) You just had to hope all was internally well.

As light from hesitant sun began to brighten the room, he sipped his black coffee. Why wait half-an-hour? Ursula might be pleased to hear from him now. He picked up the receiver and dialled their number.

When they had all gone, and the kitchen had switched into the silence which was as familiar as the noise, Ursula opened the window and went upstairs. She had long ago worked out that the best way to deal with domestic matters was to give herself a time limit. This limit varied according to the pattern of her day. This morning, as she had to be at the concrete garden at half-past ten, it would be half-an-hour. That would mean time to make the beds, throw the dirty washing in the machine and do something to the kitchen. Anything that had not been accomplished by ten o'clock would be left till later, much though she detested arriving home to a disorderly house. But half-an-hour, she found, was always necessary for the process of transference – from housewife to artist, as it were. Even so minor a job as the dreadful garden in Iffley required some reflection: arguments had to be mustered, ideas (frustratingly inadequate ideas, in this case) had to be marshalled. She had to clear her mind, completely, of perennially nagging lists of food needed for supper or things to be taken to the cleaners, and pretend for a while that she was as free as any man to concentrate wholly on her job.

Having dealt with things upstairs, and put on the washing machine, Ursula returned to the kitchen. The cat had disappeared. She glanced under the table and sink, and behind the sofa, but had no intention of looking elsewhere. Relieved that her movements were not to be scrutinised, she hurried to stack the dishwasher, fold the newspapers and wipe the splatterings of milk and Cornflakes from the table. Then she went to the sink to wash a couple of pans that Martin had intended to do last night, before he had been deflected by an essential programme on television.

She looked out of the window. There was no sun, as yet. The narrow strip of lawn, and what could be seen between a fair sample of North Oxford trees, were silvery as moonstones: strange to think that within the hour they would turn to definite blue and green. The white lilac tree drooped from last night's heavy rain: cornflowers were rampant in the beds. Ursula had planted them to remind herself of fields of corn surging towards a horizon of Wiltshire downs, where one day she would return. Poppies, which would appear later in the summer, had been planted for the same reason.

Two pigeons, almost camouflaged by the grey of the grass, were strutting and fretting over a metre of earth engaged in some territorial argument. Fat and slow in their movements, they did not seem to be much aggrieved: rather, they were going through the rituals of an old battle they enjoyed, puffing up their feathers for the benefit of their partners hidden in the trees. They ducked and swayed and muttered encouragement to themselves with all the expertise of two old hands who have been fighting for many a season, and are fully acquainted with the other's every mood.

Suddenly, there was a sharp squawk, a clap of wings. One of the birds volleyed into the air, claws scrunched up to its chest, flightpath all askew, uncontrolled. The other was trapped in the mouth of the cat. Pinkish breast feathers fell like rose petals as the cat sloped skilfully across the grass. One splayed wing dragged, fluttering behind the bird, making a noise like the shuffling of old cards. For a second, Ursula saw its terrified eye cast up to heaven in search of its old enemy and friend. Then hunter and prey disappeared under a bush.

Ursula ran shouting into the garden. She scoured the bushes and shrubs, lifting the skirts of soft new leaves and hunting through the shadows. She shook the branches of trees, causing several birds to fly away screaming with alarm. She glanced along every part of the walls that divided their garden from their neighbours. But there was no sign of the cat and pigeon. In the moment she had run from the house, it had probably slipped through the wrought-iron gates at the end of the garden. God knows where it was now: mashing the struggling feathers and palpitating heart in some safe hideaway. . . . Hopeless to go after it. Too late, too late.

Ursula walked back over the lawn, desolate, avoiding the trail of small white feathers, startling as first snowflakes of the year. Back in the kitchen, heart beating audibly, she sat at the table in a state of shock, running the short violent scene over and over again in her mind. This evening she would ring Ralph and ask him to fetch the cat, find it another home. The practicalities of this idea ran like a sub-title beneath the horrible pictures. She knew cats chased birds, killed them. But never again did she want to witness such a scene in her own garden.

The telephone rang. Dully, Ursula stood, went to the dresser, picked up the receiver. It was Martin. Alarm further shook her.

'What's happened?'

'Nothing. Why?' He sounded reassuringly calm.

'You never ring in the mornings.'

'I do sometimes.'

'Hardly ever.' Heavens, it was good to hear his voice.

'I just wanted to say sorry for the dreadful rush to school: didn't say goodbye properly or have time to tell you I'd be back for tea.'

'For tea?' Delight in the idea gave her strength.

'What are you up today, anyway? I stupidly can't remember.'

'Just the boring Iffley garden.'

'Of course.' His mind struggled with some story Ursula had been telling about the woman's love of concrete slabs. There was a long silence. 'Are you all right?' he asked at last.

'Absolutely. Why?'

'Cat not spooking you?'

'It's out in the garden. It's just caught a pigeon, probably killed it.'

'That's the trouble with bloody cats. We ought to get rid of it before Sarah gets too attached.'

'That's exactly what I was thinking.'

'Anyway, I'll be home by five.'

'Goody,' said Ursula.

When she had put down the telephone, she went to the window and closed it. Then, quite calm now, she gathered things for her briefcase and imagined the cat's return. When it found the place barred, it might have the intelligence to understand it was not wanted, and would seek some other home of its own volition. That way, although Sarah would still suffer anguish and disappointment, at least she would not blame her parents for the cat's dismissal.

But Ursula was fed up with thinking about the animal, now. She would not give it a moment's more time. Hurrying, late, she set off for Iffley, pleased with herself for so skilfully concealing from Martin the piercing drama of the pigeon.

*   *   *

On Monday, after breakfast, Frances went straight to her desk in the morning room. It was a large piece of dark oak furniture whose familiar landscape gave her unaccountable pleasure. An agreeable clutter of things furnished its top: photographs in leather frames, a wonky clay mug for pens made by Fiona, a brass inkwell of Indian design on whose sides, later on, the sun would make small flames. High piles of papers, concerning the business of the party, were reassuring evidence of all there was to do.

Much earlier, Frances had woken to find Toby had not slept in the bed at all. He had spent the whole night in the woods, badger watching. Tonight, he had said at breakfast, he would be taking a flask of coffee.

'Tonight?'

'Well, the thing is, they'll soon get used to me. Are you complaining?'

'No. Just imagining.'

'You know there's an open invitation any night you like to join me.'

'Thanks, Tobes. Sweet of you.'

He had gone off to his computers as if nothing whatever was amiss. After a single flat moment, Frances had hurried to her desk where there would be no more time for imagining. She had to ring the marquee man at once. She lifted the receiver.

'Mr Bush? Mrs Farthingoe speaking. The Old Rectory, Sulworth –'

'I'll just get him for you, Mrs Farthingoe.'

Unstinted sharing is the way to happy marriage, Frances's mother had said. It had worked for her. Not an entirely sound theory, married to Toby. I tried in the beginning, didn't I? Hid nothing from him. Result? He was bored out of his mind by my entirety. All he wanted was selected parts. There was that day, not a year after the wedding, he actually said I had a trivial mind and he would be grateful if I would spare him its workings. I sobbed and sulked for several days, I remember –

'Ah, Mrs Farthingoe. Mr Bush of Cockerell and Bush here. On the subject of the marquee for the September ball, no doubt?'

'That's right. Colour.'

– And then he gave me a scarlet sports car but never actually apologised. After that I tried to keep my thoughts to myself –

'Since we last spoke, you'll be pleased to hear we've made up our minds exactly what we want.'

'You mentioned it was a pink and white stripe you might be after, and I think I've managed to locate one. Just the job. It would be a question of sub-contraction, of course.'

'Pink and white? Oh dear, I hope you haven't taken too much trouble. Because what we actually want is dove-grey and white.'

97

– I tried to win his approbation through the smooth running of the house, being a good wife and lover, a conscientious mother, wearing the clothes he liked, giving parties, going on his kind of holidays without complaint –

'A *grey* and white?' Mr Bush cleared his throat. 'I don't think we could come up with a grey and white, in all honesty, Mrs Farthingoe.'

– I could never understand how, on the one hand, the slightest attention I paid to another man caused such searing jealousy, while on the other, he was so resistant to my giving of myself, sharing everything as I had believed –

'I mean, put it like this, it's not a regular request, a grey and white. People like, more, a splash of colour on their party walls, as it were. As I was telling you last week, the red and white is our most popular, though some people are partial to the blue. But I have to admit, there's an increasing call for our yellow – canary, we call it. But grey – no. No requests at all for grey, I'm afraid.'

– Still, it's an irregular thing, married love, and how dull if it wasn't. After all, besides all the wonderful obvious advantages of being married to Toby, I do love him profoundly. Always have. Probably always will. Pro-foundly –

'Well, it's grey we want, and grey we must somehow find.'

'Put it like this, Mrs Farthingoe. . . .'

– Put it like this: the fact that I was in love with Ralph Cotterman every day of my marriage (right up to last night) made no difference whatsoever to the profundity of my love for Toby –

' . . . I wouldn't advise a grey. Grey's not – what shall I say? A life-enhancing colour. Take it from me. I deal with a lot of stylish clients, and none of them in all my experience has ever asked for a grey and white. It's my belief you'd be better off with a red or a blue or a canary, and if I can't persuade you there, then, as I said, I can probably locate this pink – a salmon, I'm told – sub-contraction. But not a grey, Mrs Farthingoe.'

– My insane love for Ralph was the only secret, I suppose, I never confessed to Toby –

'Mr Bush, it's grey or nothing.'

– Guilt is the only thing you should not share, Mother said, and I never did. Though there was little to be guilty about, once I was married. Before: oh, those afternoons, those 'picnics' as Ralph called them. Rain, snow, wind, sand. We were creatures of the earth, he said – or perhaps I said. Yes, he would have scoffed at anything so sentimental, he never touched me again –

'Then I'm not sure I could satisfy you there, Mrs Farthingoe.'

– Despite all my . . . encouragement –

'I mean, you appreciate, I couldn't go and get a whole lot of lining stuff specially striped up in a grey for you just for the one occasion, now, could I? Then have it, like, on my hands?'

– Ralph never knew my passion for him did nothing to deter my constant desire for Toby. The night before last – Ralph gone, leaving me quite free of him, at last – where was Toby when I wanted him? Off with his badgers –

'However, here's an idea just come. Let me put it to you: green, Mrs Farthingoe. It's fairly new to us, the green, but very popular, I must say, in a short space of time. We used it for a Rotary Club dance not three months ago. Comments were very favourable, concerning the green. In fact, I would go so far as to say that I myself, above all others, *prefer* the green.'

– Do you, Mr Bush? You prefer the green. Toby prefers sleeping out in the woods with the badgers –

'We don't like green, actually, thank you, Mr Bush.'

– Well, I don't like it. Toby's always had a thing about green socks –

'To tell the truth, it is more of an aqua.'

– He was wearing his green socks in the woods last night, all night. He'll be wearing green socks out there again tonight. All night –

'Look here, Mr Bush. I don't think there's any point in beating any further about the . . . wasting your time and mine.

99

If you can't supply grey and white stripes, that's fine, I quite understand. But I must get on to someone else.'

'Ah: there I think you'll run into a bit of difficulty, Mrs Farthingoe. You'll be bound to come across the same problem. No one in marquees goes in for grey. You can take my word for it.'

'I tell you what: *I'll* order the lining.'

– What will happen to Ralph now? To Toby? To me, once the lining has come down and the party's over? –

'*You* order the lining?'

'Leave it to me. I've friends in the theatre. It'd be the sort of thing that wouldn't faze them at all. You just let me know precisely how much we need, and I'll provide it.'

'That's putting you to a lot of trouble, Mrs Farthingoe. . . .'

– Is it worth it, the trouble I take? –

'. . . and I look forward to hearing from you as soon as possible. Goodbye.'

Instinctively, she longed, then, to ring Toby's room, to tell him about the unco-operative Mr Bush and her inspiration about the lining. Perhaps to make him laugh. But then she remembered Toby would hate any such interruption, so she dialled her friend in the theatre instead. The sad thing was, by dinner her story of the battle with Mr Bush would have died. It would no longer be worth telling. Toby would return to the woods for his night with the badgers, innocent of a small triumph in his wife's day, and she would spend another night fighting the resentment caused by that innocence.

'Eliza? It's Frances. Can you help? This ball we're giving. I need hundreds of yards of grey and white striped muslin.'

'That shouldn't be too hard,' said Eliza.

Toby and the badgers were mercifully obliterated for the space of another telephone call.

*　　*　　*

After a sleepless night, Thomas left London at dawn and found himself in Nottingham long before The Gallery was due to

100

open. He had no intention of going to the office until later, but was keen to hide his conspicuous car so that the nosey interfering Doug would not be inspired to ask awkward questions. He drove to a safe place a mile from the Centre, walked slowly back, collar chafing his prickling neck. His plan, once he had mopped his brow and generally calmed down, was quietly to enter The Gallery and come upon Miss Amber Hair, his beloved girl, wonderfully unawares. She would be sitting at the desk, curled into her ridiculous cardigan, just as before. Once he had slipped inside the door, he would make a grand gesture with one arm, indicating every single Cotterman left on the walls, and announce that he would take the lot.

That, Thomas reckoned, would be the sort of unlikely gesture early on a Monday morning that any girl worth her salt would respond to. He would be rewarded by a smile of sheer disbelief, and then at least two hours' delight while she carefully wrapped up each picture. Next would be the writing of the astonishingly large cheque, which would earn him another smile of appreciation. Following that, the most normal thing in the world, Thomas would suggest a celebration lunch. After all, he would explain, there would be nothing to hurry back for in the afternoon, would there? Nothing but bare walls left. As a precaution, Thomas had booked a double room in his usual hotel in the unlikely (likely?) event of Miss Amber Hair being so fascinated by his conversation about the Norwich School at lunch that she would urge him to continue. In truth, Thomas's vision of the latter part of the afternoon was wavy in his mind. He didn't really care to think about it, for fear of disappointment. The first part of the plan, though, was *sure fire* (oh Lord, Gillian again) *flawless*, *top ho*. Thomas felt himself bouncing, heard himself humming: '*But the pavement's always been beneath my feet before.*'

He checked his watch. Five-past ten precisely. Perfect. *Absolutely bang on.* Miss A.H. would have had time to take off her coat, settle herself at the desk. Unknown to her, she was now experiencing the last few seconds before her life was to be radically changed, seized by a passion she could never

101

have envisaged, a desire that Thomas, with all the weight of his maturity, could –

– He stepped out of hiding in a nearby doorway, made a dash, despite himself, for the doorway of The Gallery. In a timeless flash he found himself pressed up against the locked glass door. The vision of Miss Amber Hair, pressed equally close on the other side, flamed in his astonished vision. For a moment, they were as one – flattened shapes, with only the wretched plate glass dividing them – eye to eye, mouth to mouth (she was a tallish girl) bent arm to bent arm. Oh no! She was late opening up, the plan was dashed. Bliss it was to be alive, for that second, so near and yet so cruelly divided – and not at all what he had planned. Now it was goggle eye to goggle eye, open mouth to open mouth, still the chilly glass between them, flattening his nose (making his face ridiculous?). *'Bold Lover, never, never canst thou kiss* (through this bloody glass) *Though winning near the goal –'* But ah! The door was backing away, the girl was fading, the picture lurched. Thomas was stumbling in, dignity all awry, while the object of his desire was laughing. Laughing!

'Oh, my God, was I pushing? I'm sorry. Good morning.' His breath was coming so damn fast, a rhythmic owlish noise above the silent carpet.

'Sorry. I was a bit late, then that ruddy lock, so stiff. I can never do it.'

'No. No, I don't suppose you can.'

Thomas could not move, marooned on the acres of haircord, shoulders jibbering, chest heaving, sweat running down the backs of his legs. Would it had been a film they could have cut – gone straight to Take Two, Man Walks in to Surprise Girl at Desk, got it right. But it was no bloody film, just a right old cockup if ever there was one. . . . And what now?

Miss Amber Hair was sliding into her place behind the desk, incident over as far as she was concerned: no big item as the children would say. Nothing for it but to carry on with part two of the grand plan. With a great effort, Thomas raised his arm, cast his eyes round the walls . . . to see a collection of

102

abstract paintings, garish things hurtful to the eye, incomprehensible rubbish that had the effrontery to call itself Art. . . . Not a Cotterman in sight.

'The Cottermans?' he asked weakly. His arm flapped down at his side.

'The exhibition finished Friday.'

'Really.'

'Sorry.'

'I'd come to buy the lot. . . .'

'Sorry. Not one left.'

Thomas moved nearer the desk. *The Times* was folded in front of his beautiful keeper of The Gallery, crossword puzzle the object of her attention. She had no pity.

'I love Cotterman,' he said.

'They're good.'

'It's a disappointment, I must say.'

'Must be.'

'Still. . . .' He watched the small mouse of her hand peer from a long sleeve of the cardigan, snuffle at the paper with a pencil as she quickly filled in a word. 'I wonder. . . .' He wondered if she could hear the wail of his breathing. 'I wonder . . . I mean, if by any chance you happen to know the artist? Know where I could track him down?'

Another word was added to the puzzle, then the girl looked up.

'I do, as a matter of fact.' Pause. 'She's my mum.'

'Your . . . er . . . mum?' It was a word Thomas could hardly bring himself to say. 'Your mother?'

'That's right. Rosie Cotterman.'

The girl looked at him squarely now. Impatient, defensive. She wanted the old crasher to leave so that she could get on with her puzzle in peace.

'I'd always thought . . . I'd always imagined, R. Cotterman as an oldish man, beard, pipe perhaps. . . .'

'Well, it's Rosie Cotterman. My mum.'

'The idea takes getting used to.'

'Tell you what. I'll give you her card. She lives in Norfolk.

You could buzz on down there, couldn't you? She's got a lot of stuff in her cottage. Daresay you could persuade her to sell it. She wouldn't say no to the money.'

'Eh, quite.'

Rosie Cotterman's daughter handed him a small card. His hand touched the mouse nose of her fingers for half a second. It was icy.

'Thanks most awfully,' he said. 'I'll have to see if I can get down there sometime.' Tomorrow, for instance.

'I could give her a call, warn her you were coming, if you like.'

For a transient moment, the girl's face flared with a sort of kindness. His heart pounded. Stage three of his plan might still. . . .

'Thanks very much. And well, this tracking down of my favourite artist at last. . . . I can't help feeling it calls for some kind of celebration.'

'How do you mean?'

'Would you like to have lunch with me?'

'No thanks. I can't leave. I have my apple here.'

'Just a drink, then. Champagne.'

'No thanks. I don't drink.'

'How about dinner? I don't go back to London till after dinner.' (Surely that would reassure her.) 'You must be hungry by dinner time? Anywhere you like. . . .'

'Look, thanks very much, but I don't want anything with you, so you might as well stop your invitations and get on down to see my mother.'

Thomas took a step backwards. 'Well. Yes. I quite see your point. Strange man and all that. I'm sorry.'

'That's all right.' She was bent over the puzzle again. 'Any good on quotes, are you? *We look before and after and blank for what is not.*'

Thomas was back at the door. The small card bearing R. Cotterman's address cut into his palm.

'I think *pine* might be the word you're looking for,' he said.

'What a daft idea,' she said.

How right she was, Thomas thought, gently closing the door on the scene of his defeat. What a daft idea.

*   *   *

Ursula sat in a traffic jam in the road that ran past the College of Further Education. She wondered, as she always did when contemplating the desecration of Oxford, who were the anonymous men who had been inspired to design such terrible buildings? Where was the man who had woken up one morning and decreed that blocks of vile red brick should be trimmed with eye-scorching blue? Had the man no sensibilities, no love of pleasing colour and fine proportion? Was he immune to the offence of ugliness? The preposterous new city buildings now far outnumbered the old and beautiful ones – a disaster that no-one had managed to stop in time and, even as lovers of the old city protested, more and more monsters rose to shatter the dreams of the original spires. It was outrageous, tragic. Why should contemporary architecture, for the most part (and oh, what a pleasure were the exceptions), mean ugly? The shocking answer must be that the population is either unobservant or so used to ugliness that it has become impervious. The mass threshold of the pain of ugliness must have lowered. How much farther would it go? In the next decade it might well be that ugliness is the norm, beauty so unusual that future generations may rarely witness it.

Ursula lurched forward a few feet. She had worked herself up into one of her Oxford furies. The place made her angry every day. Martin's insistence that they had to stay added terrible unhappiness to that anger. She was afraid any longer to speak of her feelings – his customary reaction of bewildered incomprehension further exacerbated her frustration. The trouble was, as she now kept all such blackness to herself, he probably thought she had *come round* at last – seen sense, grown fond of bloody Oxford. Little did he know! What blindness stopped him from recognising her daily longing to leave? His work – the priority, of course, above everything –

meant they could not do so. The complications would be impractical, impossible. But still, Ursula reflected as the heat of her fury began to wane, they were lucky to have only *one* major chasm in an otherwise pretty good marriage. Somehow, one day, it would be resolved, bridged, whatever. And what was Martin doing now? Ursula imagined him in his room, reading in the old armchair by the window, utterly absorbed in a world of figures which meant nothing to her. There would be silence. If he looked up, through the window he would see tulips in a sixteenth-century quad of dun-coloured stone. In his privileged position as a member of the university, he was, naturally, protected from the realities of the city. It was no wonder he found Ursula's multiple complaints hard to understand. The mental picture of him in a place so different from the ugly road calmed Ursula, and the traffic at last began to move.

Half-an-hour later, she sat in the open-plan sitting room in Mrs Robbins's semi-detached Georgian-type house in Iffley. Mrs Robbins had urged her to be seated on the Dralon sofa placed at an angle beside the French windows so that she would have a full view of the bald 'garden area', as she called it, which Ursula was to transform with slabs of mock York stone.

'I was thinking about plants,' Mrs Robbins was saying, pecking at her third Craven A in ten minutes. 'You know I'm not much up on plants, as I explained, and, as I told you, you can be at liberty to do what you like.' She inhaled, exhaled. 'But I do have one or two little preferences. Perhaps they could be accommodated in your general plan?'

'Of course.' Ursula wrote *Preferences* in her notebook.

'I love red, and I love a mauvey blue. So? You can guess.' Ursula nodded, expressionless. 'Salvia and aubretia. I know that's not very original, but it's what you like that counts, don't you think? Put in whatever else you like, Ursula, but make sure you include plenty of salvia and aubretia, or I'll be a disappointed woman.'

'Right.'

Ursula picked up her briefcase to dissipate a new fury that

106

was rising within her. Her entire plan would be ruined by salvia and aubretia. On the other hand, the plan was so grim in the first place, to satisfy Mrs Robbins's wishes, that perhaps two more nasty additions would not matter.

'Would you like to see my drawings?' she asked.

'Can't wait,' said Mrs Robbins, her tone of voice in direct opposition to her words.

She pushed away a tray that stood on the low table between them. The tray held a bottle of medium sweet sherry which was surrounded by six matching glasses rimmed with gold. On their sides was stamped a matching gold cathedral and the word 'Durham' in Gothic print. Mrs Robbins, unable to resist drawing these new acquisitions to Ursula's attention, picked one up and ran her little finger round the rim. (Salvia-red nail.)

'Just look at these! Such detailing. I got them up in Durham only last week in a gift shop. I thought they were a lovely find.'

'Lovely.'

Ursula unrolled her sheets of paper, spread them out. Mrs Robbins fiddled with the silk bow of her blouse, embroidered with machine-stitched forget-me-nots – another masterpiece of detailing.

'As a matter of fact,' she said, lighting her fourth cigarette but not looking at the drawings, 'I think detailing is the secret of my life. I'm a real one for detail, as you may have gathered from our first meeting. It makes all the difference, don't you think?'

'Quite,' said Ursula. She tapped at the paper with a pen. 'Now, this is possibility number one. . . .'

Mrs Robbins raised the pencilled arcs of her eyebrows: they shot up into her hair like miniature skipping ropes. She glanced at the drawing for a scant moment.

'Very nice,' she said. 'Would there be room for my little suggestions?'

'Of course.'

'Where?'

'Well, anywhere.'

'That's a relief. I was quite nervous of getting in a landscape gardener, you know. I thought I might be pushed into having one of those bleached-out gardens that aren't me at all. All silver and white: that kind of thing gives me the shivers.'

'My job's to do what the customer wants.'

Ursula forced a smile and placed possibility number two on top of the first drawing. Her client seemed in no hurry to study it. She was staring out of the window, cigarette twitching at the corner of her mouth.

'You know something, Ursula? I've never admitted this to anyone before, but I suppose my tastes are what might be called municipal. I love bright colours. I love those bright orange flowers the Council men put in year after year at the Pear Tree roundabout. I love pansies and marigolds – and salvia, of course. Splashes of colour, nothing subtle. I don't know why we should be made to feel so guilty these days if we're not supporters of subtlety, if our tastes don't happen to coincide with those hoity-toity people who write about gardening in the press. I like . . . brightness. . . .' Her glutinous blue eyes were staring at some colourless point out of the window.

Ursula rustled the papers. 'Would you like to see drawing number two?' she asked.

'Oh yes. Though I don't see how it can improve on your first idea, really.' The eyes moved, jelly-like, to Ursula's sketch, but plainly did not focus.

'It's probably all because I grew up in – well, a poor northern city, and the only beautiful place I saw as a child was the park. It had a huge flower clock, I remember, that changed colours with the seasons. I used to stand for hours and hours looking at that clock.' She smiled, squashed the tiny stub of her cigarette into a brass ashtray, braced herself to concentrate on Ursula's second drawing.

'Very nice, again,' she said. 'Could we have the clump of aubretia there? And perhaps my dear old salvia there? What do you think?'

I think that somewhere under a tangled bush a bloody-breasted pigeon lies dying. Or perhaps it's dead, already cold, chewed: feather and flesh and bone, that once clapped through the sky, now a tangled mess on the earth.

I think that by the time I tell Martin about having to include Mrs Robbins's little preferences, even in this unsatisfactory plan, the pain will be over.

'I think that's a pretty good idea,' she said. 'Let's try.'

Ursula took a red pen from her case and, to the delight of her client, drew a line of small red flowers each side of a path which, contrary to Mrs Robbins's instructions, she had made to curve. The fact that Mrs Robbins, high on the thought of her salvia, did not notice the curve, was, for Ursula, the small single triumph of a bad morning.

*   *   *

That evening, to Rachel's surprise, Thomas arrived home at six. She had not been expecting him till the following day: his plan had been to spend the night away.

Her immediate reaction was one of annoyance. Her own idea had been to watch a play on television and go to bed at half-past-nine. Now, suddenly, she would have to think of food, laying the table, something to talk about. But Thomas was in such unusually good humour that her irritation evaporated within moments. He even suggested they went out. Out, Thomas? What can be the matter? Rachel, it was decided, should book a restaurant while he had a bath and changed.

She duly telephoned eleven restaurants, all of which had no tables, and eventually settled for an expensive place in the Fulham Road. In the end, there was no time for her to change. Instead she hurriedly brushed her hair and fastened an elaborate suede belt – Thomas's last birthday present – round her waist. The novelty of the unexpected events of the evening put her in high spirits. She found herself laughing as Thomas opened the door of the car, took her arm in the restaurant, and showed extraordinary concern that she should choose exactly the right things to eat. She had always appreciated his good manners.

Over smoked salmon and *farafalle*, Thomas admitted to Rachel the most significant event of his day: the tracking down of R. Cotterman. He told her of his plan to visit the artist to buy more pictures.

'Where does she live, this Cotterman lady?' asked Rachel.

'Norfolk. On the coast. I'll go very early Wednesday morning, be back in time for dinner in Oxford.'

'You do dash about so.' She said it admiringly. 'Why don't you wait till the weekend?'

'Can't wait.'

'I haven't seen you in such a state of excitement for years.'

'No.' He paused. 'I'm a silly old fool, sometimes.'

Rachel shook her head. They both smiled.

'And what sort of generation do you suppose your artist is?'

'Her daughter must be somewhere in her late twenties, so I suppose she's quite old.'

'My age, roughly?'

'Older, I expect. Now I know Cotterman's not a man – and I'm still not used to the idea – I imagine she's an old lady. All I care about is snapping up a lot of her pictures. . . .'

Thomas pressed his wife to a zabaglione, and made her laugh with the latest stories of his managing director's attempts to speak French. Incredulous at such treatment, enjoying herself, Rachel became a little drunk. Back in the car, she found herself putting her hand on Thomas's thigh, and thanking him for such an unexpected dinner. He leaned over and kissed her on the cheek. She wondered if . . . possibly. He removed her hand to put the car in gear, and they drove home in amiable silence.

Thomas helped himself to a large glass of whisky. On the way upstairs, arm round his wife's shoulder, he said he would go up to the studio for a few moments, then come to bed. He was pretty tired, he added. Outside the bedroom door, they stopped, leaned spontaneously towards one another. Rachel, head spinning a little, laid her head against his shoulder.

Thomas patted it awkwardly with his whisky-free hand.

'I'm a rotten old husband,' he said.

'Rubbish.'

'Still, sometimes a man finds himself at a crossroads.'

He disengaged himself from Rachel without further explanation and went slowly up to his studio. There, he switched on a single light, sat on a high stool and contemplated the Cotterman seascape. He felt slightly drunk, very calm, and warm with good intentions. After the disastrous beginning of the long day, he had been surprised to discover how quickly he had recovered from so disagreeable a rebuff. The disintegration of a fantasy can be less painful than that of a reality, he concluded. And on the way down the motorway, he had had a long think.

It had occurred to him that the time had come to stop gadding about after unlikely young girls, making a fool of himself, and to pay more attention to his wife. After all, they had acquired a useful kind of compatibility over the years, and that was no mean quality. She didn't grumble, much, and, although she had let herself go, she could still rise to an occasion and look pretty good when she made the effort. This evening, in the dim light of the restaurant, she had looked quite handsome, and her pleasure in the whole thing had been touching. Perhaps he ought thus to treat her more often. Be generally nicer to her, show more concern, more interest in her life and thoughts. Well, it wasn't too late. He'd start tomorrow. Make some extraordinary gesture like taking her a cup of coffee in bed, to show he was serious about the crossroads. Better still, he would start tonight. Carry on where they had left off.

Thomas stood up, finished his drink. Trouble was, after his lack of sleep last night, the driving, the emotional turmoil caused by the vile Miss Amber Hair, more driving, and then the effort needed at dinner to launch his new plan, he was so bloody tired. He yawned. Also, he was not exactly overwhelmed with desire. That was the problem with good intentions. You could successfully apply them in most areas, but not all. The one thing that could not be resuscitated at will was physical desire. In the last five years, between girlfriends, Thomas had dutifully made love to his wife for a single, nefarious reason: that she should not wonder at his total abstention. As Rachel never questioned him, even those perfunctory occasions had become almost non-existent. . . . It must be almost a year, come to think of it. Perhaps, then, tonight, he really should make an effort. Treat the whole thing as a symbolic act.

Rachel was sitting up in bed, reading. She always managed to make any bed look comfortable, even the impersonal beds of hotel rooms. She had a way of enticing pillows to curl round her, cloud-like.

When Thomas returned from the bathroom Rachel had taken off her glasses, put aside her book. He saw she was wearing a lacy jacket, the sort of thing his mother, as an old lady, wore for breakfast in bed every morning. Beneath it, he couldn't help noticing, Rachel was naked. A nipple protruded through one of the lacy holes. Very unusual. It signified, he realised through the fuzziness of his head, something he was unable to imagine very sharply.

Rachel smiled. Thomas began to undress. He was a clumsy undresser, and didn't like to be watched. Tonight, Rachel's eyes never left him. Most disconcerting. But he refrained from asking her to look away for fear she should ask why. He hung up his suit, put his shirt and tie neatly over a chair, drawing out the process in the hope that Rachel would get bored of looking. No such luck. He pulled off his socks, before his pants, as she had trained him to do many years ago. In their rapturous youth, when they would say anything, *anything* to one another and understand, she had told him the one way for a man to kill all desire in a woman was to approach her naked but for his socks. Thomas had never forgotten this. In all his escapades, he had remained faithful to his wife's rule, thereby astounding many a young lady, less discerning than her, and in a hurry. Now, still playing for time, he rolled his blue and green Argyll wool socks into a ball, tossed it up to the ceiling and caught it. Rachel laughed. Plainly there was going to be no way of deflecting her intentions. But it was worth one last try. Thomas finally stood up in his underpants. He patted his large stomach. That might put her off. She had not had much chance to notice, of late, how much weight he had gained.

'Why don't you not put your pyjamas on?' she asked.

A multitude of answers came to Thomas's mind, but none of them from his lips. He gave a mock shiver, but could hardly pretend to feel cold in the almost tangible heat of the room. He stood for a while, speechless still, then slid off his underpants. This seemed to be a cue for Rachel. She rose from her cloudy pillows and took off her jacket. Her heavy breasts lay on the sheet. Thomas found himself staring at them in some fascination. He hadn't seen them for a very long time.

'Come on,' she said.

Thomas padded to the bed, stifled a yawn. He clambered in, switched out the light on the table beside him. Before there was a moment to plan his next move, Rachel had sidled up beside him. Their naked shoulders met. She put her hand under the bedclothes, touched him. Even as she did so, Thomas pictured the hand as he so often saw it, emerging bubbly from a sink of washing-up water, or laying knives and forks on the table. Her grasp was more peaceful than erotic. A wave of sleepiness crept through his veins like warm treacle, and he knew that just to keep awake would be an almighty struggle.

But his good manners, coupled with his good intentions, combined to make one last effort. He shunted himself into Rachel's arms, kissed her gently. Their legs intertwined. He could feel hers stiffen. He could feel her hope. He stroked her breast. It filled his hand. She squirmed. He ran the hand on down to her ribs, well-covered in flesh – so strange after Gillian's brittle bones. Altogether a larger landscape, his wife, with whom he would have to reacquaint himself. . . . Close to her, like this, he was reminded of curling up on the nursery sofa as a child. There was the same sense of peace, lack of

113

urgency. . . . His hand, he realised, had come to a stop on Rachel's stomach. All the good intentions in the world, then, could not inspire him to go farther. Drowsiness warmed him like fur. He felt Rachel's lips on his closed eyelids, urging him not to worry, to sleep, to sleep. How kind she was.

He did not hear her put out the light, or move away from him, or wipe away the silent tears that poured down her cheeks in the dark.

At breakfast next morning, from behind his paper, Thomas said, 'Sorry about that, old thing,' and returned to his usual silence. He left early, kissing Rachel on both cheeks rather than the customary one – perhaps an indication that there would be another attempt at the crossroads.

Rachel, back in bed, smiled inwardly to herself. Eventual sleep had quelled frustration. In fact, this morning she felt not the slightest desire for Thomas – should he return at this moment and attempt to seduce her, his vitality restored, she would beg him to refrain. Instead, she was conscious of a weary old affection, a comfortable feeling of ease, security: far preferable to the bleakness, the tension, the irritation which were her normal companions. Thomas, she thought, whatever happened in the future, would never leave her. He was a man of some honour and deep habit, and in the end the practicalities of staying with his wife would seem preferable to the palaver of settling elsewhere.

So, in a way, it was a happy morning.

In a way. But. But, what?

Rachel struggled to decipher the thin mist of amorphous thought that came to her. Something to do with restlessness, a vague idea of compensation that was very different from secret, solitary sleep. All very unclear, and perhaps dangerous to grapple with. In no mood to clarify her faintly disturbing thoughts, she put aside her unread newspaper and returned to sleep.

She awoke two hours later, irritated at the thought that she would now have to hurry to prepare lunch for her sister.

Her sister, Anne, was younger than Rachel, an efficient feminist, wife and mother, and director of an employment agency. Rachel found her wearisome. They had little in common, but out of some sort of sibling convention met a few times a year for lunch, sent presents at Christmas.

'You're so pale, Rachel,' Anne observed, immediately annoying, as she swept into the kitchen. Her blowlamp eyes scorched round the comfortable muddle of the kitchen so unlike her own arrangements at home.

'I'm perfectly all right,' said Rachel.

'I didn't mean anything was wrong.'

'Well, there isn't anything wrong. Everything's fine.'

'I never suggested. . . .'

They often got off to a bad start. Things would ease after the vegetarian salad – Anne's recent exaggerated vegetarianism was another of her annoying features – and a couple of glasses of wine. Anne settled into a long monologue about her new exercise routine and her plan to join the Greens. Rachel picked at grated carrot, disliking Anne: she disliked the gold-rimmed spectacles, the frizzy hair, the pale grey tracksuit, the aggressive attempt not to look attractive. She was irritated by the self-congratulation of the voice, the implied criticism of Rachel's lesser life.

With the herb tea ('You know I never touch coffee, God if only people would give up drinking so much coffee, we'd be a healthier nation') Anne at last turned her attention to Rachel.

'And how's everything with you?'

'Fine, as I said. All much as usual. Jeremy likes Cambridge, Helen loves Durham, all much as – '

'Thomas?'

'Thomas?'

'How's he?'

'He's fine, too.' This was ridiculous. Anne had no interest in how any of them were. 'Painting away at weekends. Buying watercolours.'

'Ah.' The tip of a grey tongue explored Anne's precise,

115

colourless lips. 'Look,' she said, 'for once I'm going to say something. About you.'

'Oh?'

Anne fiddled with a gold chain round her neck. Even her sudden embarrassment was glazed with an air of efficiency. 'Right. This is it. Here goes.' She coughed. 'Rachel, I think you ought to take a lover.'

In the split second afforded to her, Rachel calculated she must extract all feeling from her answer.

'Why?'

Anne looked her sister in the eye, gave a pained sigh.

'It would change your life,' she said.

Rachel had always thought that to take offence is a waste of both time and energy, and when necessary fought hard against that particular reaction. But she felt herself stiffen at her sister's words, and drew herself up very straight.

'What an incredible, impertinent idea,' she said at last. 'I've never had a lover, and I don't want one now. From all I've heard, they're a terrible complication and not worth all the deceit. Besides, what makes you think I've any need for a lover? You know nothing about my life. Thomas and I are perfectly happy, thank you.'

'You're right. I don't know much about your life, and I'm sure you and Thomas are fine if you say so. But I have this instinct – I don't know – that you could be happier.'

'Don't be so absurd. Everyone could be happier. I wouldn't have thought calculated infidelity was a way to ensure marital bliss.'

Anne sighed again, a touch impatient. 'Perhaps the word I'm looking for is *livelier*. More like you used to be.'

'Livelier? Thomas said I was the liveliest girl he had ever met.'

'That was a long time ago.'

Rachel reflected in a moment's silence, determined to appear unperturbed by such cheek.

'Youthful skittishness would look pretty silly in middle age. I agree I haven't your energy, of course. I'd never manage all the swimming, exercise, dashing about, that you manage so well. I'd hate all that.' She paused, then added quietly, 'But I think I'm still reasonably lively.'

'Well, you're not.' Anne thumped the table. 'You're fading, Rachel, if you really want to know. You're retreating into some private place where you're inaccessible.'

'How can you say that?'

'I've noticed.'

'You've hardly seen me.'

'I've noticed all the same.'

'It's not true.'

'Look, this isn't an attack.'

'It sounds like one.'

'It's meant to be a help.'

'Very peculiar help from you, recommending adultery, I must say. You, the greatest upholder of monogamy –'

'One can change.'

'Change?' Rachel was mildly curious.

'I'll tell you, if only to support my suggestion. Since we last met – what, six months ago? – I've begun looking into myself. Really looking, to see if I can discover what's going on behind all the frenetic dashing about. Begun finding out who I am.'

'Oh Lord, not all that,' answered Rachel with distaste.

'Despise me if you like,' said Anne, huffily. 'I know your aversion to any real kind of truth, so I won't bore you with my discoveries. But I'll just tell you this. The people I turn to – and, yes, they'd be the sort of people you'd love to scorn – recognised there was a part of me longing to be liberated, a part that was struggling to be fulfilled.'

Rachel flinched. 'Look, I'm sure you find all that sort of stuff rewarding,' she said tightly, 'and I'm glad. But I really don't want to hear about it. I think expensive ego trips are for the humourless and the self-indulgent. They're one of the really ill-conceived practices of this age – far worse for the population than coffee,' she added, with a smile which Anne did not return. 'If only perfectly able people would stop agitating about their every feeling, and get on with their lives. . . .'

117

'You're not exactly getting on with your life,' said Anne.

There was a long silence.

'If you think about it,' Rachel continued at last, more gently, 'all the most interesting people in history, the great men and women we aspire to, didn't spend their lives boring themselves and everyone else with their introspective findings. It was Nietzsche, wasn't it, who said: "Find myself? I'd run away." Of course I'm not against soul-searching. It's been a preoccupation through the ages. But on the whole its finest discoveries have been used in the cause of art. It's only in the last twenty years or so the whole business of looking into yourself has descended to such a trivial, commercial level, mostly indulged in by people who have nothing more vital to occupy them –'

'Please don't go on,' shouted Anne. 'Such short-sighted nonsense makes me angry. And besides, I insist on telling you about me before I go.'

'You. Yes.'

Anne took a deep, magnanimous breath. Efficient control against blighted prejudice.

'As you know, I've a good marriage, I love my children, I like my work, I'm blessed with energy and friends and enough money. All wonderful, super, fine.'

'So?'

'So that wasn't enough, I found.'

'Good God. What more do you expect?'

'A touch of – outside adventure, you could call it, to complete the happy picture. It was all too good.'

'I can't believe it,' said Rachel. 'You.'

'The . . . people I consult about these things believe a touch of nefarious pleasure is in fact an asset to a marriage. The adrenalin it engenders cancels out the resentment. That can't be bad. You must do your own thing, if that's going to enrich your life. Applied selfishness can be beneficial.'

'I think it's appalling, an immoral recommendation,' said Rachel. 'Who are these people who make such ghastly suggestions?'

'You wouldn't understand about them: I've no intention of

telling you. And it's all right if you stick to certain rules. No-one need be hurt, if that's what you're thinking. Andrew's fully aware of what's going on. He has his own meaningless flutters here and there.'

'It wouldn't work for us,' said Rachel.

'It might. I bet Thomas allows himself the occasional diversion.'

'Of course he doesn't.'

'All I'm suggesting is: it works for some. It works for us. I've never felt better. The new regime suits me. It might be worth trying. It might put some colour in your cheeks.'

Rachel shook her head. She felt sick. She stood up, wanting Anne to go now. It was time this horrible lunch came to an end. Anne stood, too. She put a hand on her sister's shoulder.

'Sorry if I've shocked you. But there are times when one suddenly realises one has come to a crossroads.' Rachel winced. 'And times it's worth trying a new direction. If that direction doesn't work for you, well, you won't have lost anything. But it's worth experimenting. Honestly. Better to experiment than to fade altogether. Thanks for the lunch.'

Anne left the kitchen silent as a ghost in her hideous trainers. Rachel watched her through the window, bouncing down the steps, so cocky, confident, smug, unattractive. Suddenly, the shock and effrontery Anne had caused lifted. She wanted to laugh. The thought of her wiry, frizzy-headed sister with her loathsome tracksuits, cramped teeth and onion-smelling fingers acquiring queues of eager lovers was completely absurd, darkly comic. How on earth . . . ?

Rachel flew down the path.

Anne was already in the driving seat of her Fiesta, pursing her washed-out lips. She wound down the window.

'Yes?' Suspicious eyes crinkled into tiny slits.

'Where do you find these men?' Rachel asked.

At last, Anne laughed. It was a long, frilly laugh that set the crooked teeth jiggling on the blanched lips, and spit bulleting from their corners.

'Oh, that!' she finally managed to splutter. 'That's the least

of the problems. Signal your availability and they flock, believe
me.' She shut the window and drove off, waving.

Signal your availability, indeed, Rachel snarled to herself.

She returned indoors. The routine of her afternoon was by
now shattered irreparably. There was only one thing she could
contemplate: bed.

Five minutes later, curled between cool sheets, head cradled
in her huge, soft pillow, she shut her eyes. Among the indeterminate scarves of sleepy thought an unexpected idea came to
her: to signal availability might not be a bad idea before fading
altogether, she thought, before the darkness of sleep released
her from any clear plan.

*　　*　　*

Mary's private rule was not to think about death in the house.
It was a superstition she had first put into practice years ago,
when thoughts of dying had begun to accumulate.

On Monday morning she drove the few miles to the beach,
parked at the golf course. Two old ladies were putting on a
brilliant green, the only visible players. They wore shapeless,
colourless anoraks, but gaudy socks enlivened their stick legs.
Their identical angora berets, brushed by a small breeze, made
scarlet spume of their hair. My generation, thought Mary. Do
they think of dying as they position the ball, aim for the hole,
wipe the wind from their eyes with blue-veined hands?

Mary crossed the golf course, unobserved by these contemporaries. She climbed the dunes, making her way along paths
scratchy with marram grass and sea gorse. At the top she
stopped to survey the high tide, the empty sweep of beach.
Through the thickness of her jersey she felt the sun. She made
her way down on to the sands. There, in the sharp morning
light, each small stone and shell made its particular shadow.
A single seagull kited above her, rising and falling, pulled by
an invisible string. How many more times can I have all this,
she wondered? She was glad she could not know.

Mary's purpose in coming here this morning was to reflect

upon the practicalities of Bill's life once he was alone. It was a subject which she knew would both repel and appal him, and which she would never dream of talking about. To Bill, any speculation about death was the epitome of bad taste, something he was not prepared to consider. Did other couples, Mary wondered, discuss what would happen when one of them died? Or was the topic unmentionable in the majority of elderly households? Did millions of husbands and wives, like her, keep their private fears to themselves?

As she wondered about these things, Mary saw a large, uncomfortable-looking man shuffling and slipping down the dunes, waving. When he came closer she saw that she did not know him. Overweight, inappropriately dressed in a tight tweed suit, he was red in the face and shining. Mary glanced about her. Not another person in sight. What ailed this troubled stranger? (She liked the word ailed, not often used these days.) She smiled, more at herself than at him, still not moving.

A few feet from her, the man returned her smile.

'Lovely morning.' He looked at his watch. 'I'm a bit early. Thought I'd fill in time with a breath of fresh air on the beach. Didn't realise how far it was, across the golf course, over the dunes.'

'No. It's deceptive.'

'Heading for Marsh Cottage, actually. Would I be on the right road?'

Mary laughed. 'It's back up the road you've come on, then first left up a small lane leading to the marsh –'

'Thanks, thanks. I missed the lane. I'll be all right once I'm there.' He panted, still out of breath. 'Visiting the painter, R. Cotterman, as a matter of fact.' He looked at his watch again.

'She's an old friend of ours,' said Mary, 'and our favourite painter. We've been collecting her pictures for years.'

'Really? Coincidence, coincidence. I'm about to become a collector, I hope. Well, I must be off. Thanks for the directions.'

He loped back off across the beach, anxiety in every step. Mary wondered where he had come from, and what was the

121

cause of his trouble? In the brief crossing of strange paths it is ignorance that makes us helpless: there is rarely either the time or the possibility of discovering what the other person has come from – what state of life, what state of mind. Meetings are conducted in a fog of signals whose significance is often missed or misunderstood. Thus the act of communicating, even on the most superficial level, is full of mysteries. Many of them can never be solved but can only become the grist of speculation.

Engaged in such thoughts, Mary followed the deep footsteps made by the man. He had curiously aroused her pity, her curiosity. Who was he? Bill might know if Cotterman was expecting a rich buyer. . . . She would ask. Or perhaps they would invite her round for a drink this evening, find out.

Mary reached the car park to see the man driving swiftly away in a Mercedes. She waved. He did not appear to notice her. She unlocked the door of her own small car, lowered herself into her capsule of familiar, dog-smelling warmth. The problem of Bill's life after her own death had been blasted from her mind. In the quiet pattern of her life, the idea of Cotterman's strange visitor gave rise to a small, unexpected *frisson*. She looked forward to questioning Bill as they ate their lunch of cottage pie, sprouts and rice pudding. What she would keep from him, of course, was the timeliness of the stranger's arrival – the happy dissipation of her thoughts it had caused, and this agreeable feeling of curiosity.

*   *   *

Thomas drove down the lane to the marsh. It was so narrow that hedges scratched the sides of his car. He was generally unnerved, both by the prospect of the meeting, and his brief visit to the beach. There, he had seen in a glance that all the elements of the place, familiar to him from R. Cotterman's paintings, were precisely, searingly conveyed in her simple and melancholy watercolours. He felt weak with awe.

The cottage was a small Norfolk building of brick and

122

flintstone. A smattering of careless gravel edged the forlorn grass, hovered round the front door. Thomas spent a long time parking; whatever angle he tried seemed to take up too much room. When he had finally determined on a corner and locked the door – unbreakable habit of a Londoner – he was dismayed to see how vulgar the car looked in this hidden place. He wished he had borrowed Rachel's old Fiesta.

There was neither bell nor knocker on the door – a door whose brown paint was so bleached, blistered and uncared for that it put Thomas in mind of a back door. He thumped on it with his fist. Two flakes of brittle paint fell to the ground. He tried again. Silence. Nothing. Long silence.

Clumsy with impatience, Thomas turned the handle. The door opened directly into a room which extended the entire length of the cottage. For several moments he stood where he was, arms limp at his sides, taking in the muddle of objects and smells that assailed him. He did not feel the awkwardness of an intruder but, rather, the intense relief of one who has arrived somewhere he always has wanted to find, though he has not been able precisely to envisage that place. With a strange and wonderful sense of ownership, Thomas banged the door behind him, and made his way further into the room.

He moved with caution into the dense jungle of tables, chairs, easels, pictures, books, newspapers, magazines, plants, gumboots rimed with pale dry mud, jerseys, teapots, candles, bottles of wine huddled randomly in groups, unopened letters, jars of paint brushes and countless boxes of well-used paints. At one end of the room was an ancient Aga, the colour of old teeth. A fat tin coffee pot sprawled on its top. The muffled bubbling that came from it was the only sound in the silence. Two smells – distinct and yet merging, like distant railway tracks – filled the room: burnt toast and turpentine. Tears blurred Thomas's eyes. He could not account for the emotion he felt: it was a kind of recognition that left him both weak and strong.

He reached the window, which stretched almost the length of the room. Outside, in contrast to the chaos within, stretched the supreme simplicity of marsh, distant dunes, vast sky. Thomas found himself puzzling how to paint such a scene: raw umber, yellow ochre, cadmium yellow, windsor yellow, burnt sienna, cerulean blue, sap green – the names in his paint box fumbled through his mind, none of them the pale, hay colours lit from behind 'by heaven's light' that were actually there, before him. How, in paint, could a man convey the tautness of May sky, so surprisingly edged with frivolous cloud? At the hem of this particular sky shirred clouds ruffled the horizon, evocative as petticoats. . . . How could I ever? thought Thomas. He glanced down, wondering.

There, on a path of beaten mud – a towpath, a right of way, perhaps – he saw a small figure in a yellow fisherman's mackintosh and sou'wester, dazzling in the sun. She carried a sketchbook under one arm. Brushes stuck out from a pocket. Very upright, she moved slowly, as if the weight of each footstep was of some private significance. She came to a halt just at the place where Thomas stood behind the glass. She turned, waved, smiled, as if she had expected him to be there. Her hat, fallen forward on to her forehead, concealed her eyes. But Thomas saw her hand was small and brown, speckled as an egg. Having taken in the sight of him at her window, she then moved on at the same pace, giving no indication the rhythm of her progress should be interrupted by a stranger who had let himself into her empty house.

Moments later there was a shuffling behind Thomas, and a voice that sounded rusty from lack of use, yet full of possible laughter.

'Mr Arkwright, I presume?'

Thomas turned to see what could have been a miniature lifeboat man, almost swamped by the yellow (Indian? Cadmium?) waterproof and matching sou'wester, still concealing her eyes.

'I'm so sorry . . . I . . . hope you didn't mind –'

'– glad you came in. I always leave the door open, hoping.'

Hoping what?

In a brisk movement, R. Cotterman tipped back the hat. It

124

fell to the ground behind her. A small pointed chin rested on the high, stiff collar of the waterproof, reflecting its colour on her skin like childhood buttercups. The cheeks were the colour of sand, and grained with a million tiny lines – lines so fine that when she moved her head from the sun into shadow, they became invisible.

The eyes were the palest rims of topaz round huge black pupils – so pale as to be almost transparent, like the sky.

With the speed of light, Thomas sifted through several observations, designed to convey something of his feelings. They all seemed inadequate. Besides, it was not the time.

'I was early, trying not to be late,' he said.

'What's that, Mr Arkwright?'

R. Cotterman was pulling at the zip of the waterproof. It sliced down through the shining yellow stuff like a wire through cheese.

'I'm afraid that due to a certain little error in the past, I'm slightly deaf. You'll have to speak up.'

At that moment, Thomas fell in love with Rosie Cotterman – irretrievably, ecstatically, and with a strange sense of humility – a feeling so unknown, so curious, so tangible, that he felt physically stiff, and found himself kneading his hands to soften the sensation of wearing new gloves.

'Would you like some coffee, Mr Arkwright? I keep it ready, in case.'

'Please.'

'And for when I come back. I like to come back to the smell of coffee.'

She was moving towards the stove, expertly avoiding all hazardous objects, a tiny figure swamped by a very large black jersey. On her way, without stopping, she picked up mugs from the muddle of things on the table, slid a packet of cigarettes from the pocket of her jeans, and pushed away a wisp of lively hair with the backs of both occupied hands. Thomas watched every movement, entranced. 'But this new smell – smell it? Good, don't you think? The finest turps you can get on the east coast, I'll tell you that. However, it's not

125

for me. I tried an experiment this weekend – oils. Portrait of my daughter, Serena. You met her at The Gallery. Hopeless, though. Can't do it. Won't try again. Do you paint at all, by chance, Mr Arkwright? Sugar? Milk?'

The soft lilt in her voice, Thomas realised, was from Southern Ireland.

'Yes, well, a little. Sugar, I mean. No milk. I paint, but I'm not a painter.'

'Sit down, won't you? Push things off a chair. Here: there's room at the table. Make sure you face the window, now, if you've only come for a while. I'll show you some pictures if that's what you really want, is it? And we'll give ourselves a glass of wine and some brown shrimps on toast. You must be hungry, all that way you've travelled, Mr Arkwright.'

Still as if not quite sure of his movements, Thomas sat down at the table, facing the window as instructed. Rosie Cotterman sat to one side of him.

'So many still-lives, aren't there?' She indicated the clutter of things on the table. 'They seem to arrange themselves unconsciously, but I never paint them. I don't ever paint indoors.'

Thomas looked again and saw what she meant: the division of things, the many possibilities of composition. Then he turned his eyes to her face. The sun was bright on its beauty and its flaws.

'Now, what is it you can be thinking of, I wonder? You don't have the demeanour of a businessman about you at all, despite the strict suit, Mr Arkwright.'

Rosie Cotterman laughed, her face crumpling so prettily, her smile so enchanting, that Thomas's heart doubled its pounding. He laughed, too.

'My thoughts, I must admit, were quite irrelevant to my reason for this visit. I've come to buy all your pictures.'

'All?'

'Whatever you'll let me take.'

'And what were you thinking? Your eyes so far away?'

Thomas felt himself blush. 'As a matter of fact, I was

thinking about beauty,' he said. 'The simplicity of it. The simple conjunctions between eye, mouth, nose, cheek. So obvious when you see it, you can't think why it's so rare.'

'Ah, that. I don't look at faces much myself. I listen to voices and look at the land.' It was plain Rosie Cotterman had no idea Thomas's thoughts had been prompted by her own face. 'Now, you won't say no to brown shrimps if I put in a piece of toast, Mr Arkwright, will you?' She was away at the stove again. 'You'll need something in you against the journey back.'

Thomas's hands were no longer stiff as new gloves. He was warm, flushed from the awed beating of his heart, as happy as he could remember in his entire life. With a strange feeling of being home, he took off his strict jacket, unbuttoned his waistcoat, loosened his tie. Rosie Cotterman gave him an approving smile.

'That's better, now. More undone. Here, open this, will you?'

She handed him a bottle of dusty claret, her fingerprints on its sides. And two glasses. The sky curved in miniature in their sides. Thomas shuffled among the things on the table until he found a corkscrew, and set about opening the bottle with the imprecise movements of one in a dream.

'We'll be needing a drink to get us through the business side of things. I'm no good at business at all. You'll have to guide me, Mr Arkwright. I'll be putting my trust in you.'

'How about calling me Thomas, then? No more of this Mr Arkwright, if we're to do serious business.'

'Very well, Thomas.' She gave the name some thought, her head tipped to one side. 'Thomas. I had a friend once, a Thomas. A good blunt name.'

She took two burnt pieces of toast from the Aga, and a bowl of brown shrimps from an ancient fridge. 'But let's have our lunch, don't you think? Before we get down to the business. There's all the time in the world, is there not?'

Thomas smiled with the barest shake of his head. He could not bring himself to tell her he had to leave in a couple of hours. The prospect was unbearable. He took a sip of wine, determined not to think of his departure, but to resort to his childhood habit of pretending to himself that good moments will last for ever.

Two hours and ten minutes later (his instinctive sense of punctuality having agonisingly hounded him) Thomas was on his way back to London. On the back seat of the car lay three of Rosie Cotterman's paintings. He had insisted on paying more than the Nottingham gallery prices, having persuaded her that anything less would be taking advantage of her innocence. He would have liked to have bought many more, but feared such desire might appear greedy. Besides, a gradual acquiring of her works would mean many future visits to Norfolk.

As he drove, more slowly than usual, Thomas replayed the extraordinary visit in his mind. They had talked, over the prolonged shrimps and wine, about painting, about colour, about the quixotic skies of Norfolk so fleet of pattern and temperate of mood. Lunch over – at what exact point it had ended was unclear in Thomas's mind – Rosie had held up picture after picture for his inspection. He had made the almost impossible choice as quickly as possible, and scribbled a quick cheque which he left folded in a mug. They drank more coffee and ate chocolate biscuits. Thomas did up his waistcoat, he remembered, at twenty-past-two. What else, he asked, did the cottage consist of?

He then immediately regretted so impertinent a question, fearing it sounded intrusive, or akin to an impatient overture. But apparently no such thought came to Rosie's mind. She led him up a spiral staircase to the room above, the bedroom, which echoed the length of the studio beneath it. The double bed, unmade, faced the marsh and stood beneath a skylight in the sloping roof – 'to see the stars'. Books were piled everywhere on the floor. There was no dressing-table, no sign of make-up, mirror, twinkling slippers, the sort of things usually to be found in a woman's bedroom. A pair of man's striped pyjamas and a small hairbrush were among the rubble on the floor.

Thomas, warm from the excellent claret, was much affected by the scene. The thought briefly flamed that he should take Rosie into the unmade bed and change his life from this day forth. But that was not what he wanted – yet. He had known the moment he saw her that seduction was not his priority. The rarity of this situation left him confused. But in the mists of his confusion one beacon burned very clearly: love. This, Thomas recognised, was the proper thing, and should be treated with the care due to such a pure sensation. Besides, he felt no torturing physical desire– only a longing, more powerful, more awful: an amorphous and indescribable yearning to give himself entirely to this strange woman.

Rosie, her back to Thomas, was looking out of the window. She said something about the funny contrast she had always lived with: the physical muddle all round her, and the absolute clarity of what she was trying to paint. Thomas put a hand on her shoulder. He hoped she would see the gesture as one of understanding, nothing more indelicate. She did. With a firmness of purpose, she patted the hand in motherly fashion before removing it. Then she suggested they should return downstairs for tea. But Thomas, whose sense of duty to his wife had ensured that his nefarious ways over the years were never discovered, admitted it was time to leave. Rosie Cotterman did not try to detain him. In contrast to her daughter's careful packing, she thrust the three pictures into a plastic bag and carried them to the car. There was no mention of any further meeting: just a brief, polite kiss on the cheek. As he drove away Thomas had looked back, waving. But Rosie was not standing there, in the manner of most women he knew, silently grimacing. She was gone, the door shut behind her. Perhaps she had found that one of the rules of a solitary life was to put brief visitors out of mind as soon as they had gone. Visitors? Who did Rosie see?

Thomas realised, in his slow passage back along the motorway, that for all their animated talk they had exchanged no information. Rosie had made no enquiries about his wife, children, job, life. He had been equally restrained, asked only about painters and paintings. But, on reflection, Rosie had not appeared to stifle other questions: as far as Thomas could judge, they had not come to her mind. Perhaps this was another wise move on the part of the solitary: when people do arrive, to learn of their passions is of more interest than to learn of their lives.

All the same, Thomas now regretted he had lost his chance to find out more. He was filled with a sudden longing just for a few basic facts. Who was the father of Serena and what had happened to him? Were there other children? A current lover? Roots in Ireland? On reaching the outskirts of London, Thomas found himself in a frenzy of anxiety. Questions swarmed uncomfortably over him. What a fool he had been. And yet he would not have had their hours together otherwise. The very lack of curiosity about each other, their talk only of things that concerned them both, had constituted the charm of the meeting. All too often, Thomas thought, beginnings with new women were identical: a swapping of autobiographical facts (in his case, much edited) followed by a long summary of the girl's emotional curriculum vitae. A very dull way to begin, really. The more rewarding way for two people to begin to know each other was surely to pick up clues slowly, gradually building a picture, as in the reading of a good book. But most women these days, Thomas found, were desperate for instant affection and swift commitment. They were impatient for a man, and once they found one they were then impatient for development. They had no notion that the essence of romance is to take time. And that's how it would be with Rosie, whom he loved. . . . Slow.

Thomas looked at the car clock. He realised that if he did not hurry he would be late, and he never wanted to be late for his wife. Even overwhelmed by his feelings for Rosie, to be punctual for Rachel was a rule. He would not want to break it. Though he might, one day. He accelerated, conscious he was smiling, conscious he would have to make considerable effort, this evening, to conceal his distraction.

*   *   *

Ralph Cotterman had come to the end of his day's writing. He took a mug of tea into the garden and sat on a deckchair, back to the neglected herbaceous border. Ursula had begged him to let her replant it, but he had always resisted her offers. When eventually he came around to analysing his curious stubbornness over this matter, he decided it must be because he could not bear the idea of looking daily upon something she had made him: the poignancy of her absence would be even more unbearable. The reasoning was not watertight: there was a large photograph of Ursula (with children) on the bathroom wall, a constant reminder. But the illogicality persisted in his mind, and the border remained uncared for, seldom even weeded, not a thing to please the eye. Ralph was no gardener.

Mug in one hand, pen in the other, sun agreeable upon him, Ralph contemplated the block of paper on his knee. When he was not at work, or visiting the Knoxes or the Farthingoes – enjoyable interludes that needed no accounting for – he relied on his lists of instructions to himself to provide the necessary discipline of a solitary life. He wrote now, without enthusiasm:

Ring Mother
Ring Ida

Ida was a girl he had met buying postcards in the Ashmolean last week. He was unsure just how he had found himself in the position of asking her to the cinema – it was not his custom to pick up girls at random. But she, like him, was obviously alone for the evening. Kindness, nothing more, had prevailed. They had gone to *Dead Poets Society*, and then to supper in an Indian restaurant – kindness again. Ralph felt it would have been churlish to deliver her to her College unfed. And the evening had not been too bad. Ida, quite pretty, spurred by the film, had talked seriously about education, then moved on to her thesis about Wagner. She suffered, like many of her generation, from over-earnestness. Ralph found earnestness tiring. Ida's views had been unrelieved by humour; it was hard

131

to pay full attention to all she said, an effort to respond with courteous interest. So it was a great surprise to himself when he heard his own suggestion, at the lodge gates of her College, that they might go to another film next week. He would ring her, he said. She seemed pleased.

But now the time had come for the call Ralph felt an onrush of reluctance. He would leave a message with the porter – some convincing excuse, and not ring again. There was no point.

> *Ring Ursula*, he wrote next.
> *Cat?*
> *Ring Frances*

After a moment, he scratched out this last piece of advice.

He updated the list fast: things he must shop for, a train to be looked up, an American professor's paper to be read. He finished his tea, put the mug on the grass and ran his hand through the profusion of daisies. Their petals were closing, dimming the whiteness of the lawn. Ralph realised it was quite cool now the sun had disappeared behind the mulberry tree. He hurried in to ring his mother.

'Oh Ralphie, I've had such a nice afternoon,' said Rosie Cotterman, which was a surprising start. Usually, she was economical with information about her life. 'Such a sweet man came. Businessman, I should say. To buy a few. When are you coming down? Soon?'

'Soon, I promise.'

Ralph rather enjoyed an occasional weekend with his mother. He chose to stay in a bed-and-breakfast place rather than sleep on the sofa in her studio, and would keep out of her way all morning while she worked. They would lunch in a pub, go for a long walk on the beach, then return to Marsh Cottage for fish stew and claret. (Years ago, she had been given five dozen cases as a farewell present from some French wine-growing lover.)

'And how are things with you?'

'Fine,' said Ralph.

'You don't elaborate much, darling.'

132

'Maybe something I've inherited from you.'

Rosie laughed. 'Have you found yourself a wife yet?'

This was a regular question. She was careful to phrase it slightly differently each week, to give variety. Today there was laughter in her enquiry. Sometimes she was serious.

'Not yet, Mother.' Ralph had been disappointing her for so many years he was used to the dying fall in her response.

'I hope you're out there looking about, Ralphie.'

'I am, I am.'

'There must be plenty of women in Oxford.'

'There are.'

'But they don't come your way?'

'Not the right ones, no.'

'They will. Surely to God, they will.' This she believed. Her son could not be so different from her in that respect, handsome and genial and altogether desirable as he was. 'But otherwise things are swimmingly, are they?'

'Busy. I had an invitation to the Farthingoes' ball. Frances said they'd asked you.'

'Ah! I tore it up. Serena will be going.'

'You should come. You might enjoy it.'

'I doubt it. Besides, I couldn't make my way across the country.'

'I'd fetch you, or Bill and Mary could bring you. You can stay here. We could go together.'

'You may have a woman by then, Ralphie. I'd not be surprised.'

'Unlikely.'

'I'll think on it.' There was a long pause. 'This man, a Mr Arkwright, paid me very handsomely, I'd say. Three pictures. He's coming back for more.'

'Good. You've done well. All those sales at The Gallery, too.'

'That's where he saw them in the first place. He was a sad man, I thought. The pictures seemed to cheer him up. I must be going, darling. Things to do.'

'I'll ring as usual. Bye, Mother.'

Next, Ursula. Ralph settled into an armchair, hoping for a long talk. He always calculated Ursula's movements carefully to avoid ringing her at an inconvenient time. The children should be at their homework, now: with any luck, he would not be interrupting her domestic life.

Ursula answered after an unusually long time.

'How's the cat?' Ralph asked. 'I've been feeling reasonably guilty.'

'The cat? Oh, the cat.' Pause. 'There was a bit of a drama, I'm afraid. I took against it the first morning when I saw it killing a pigeon. I chased it, tried to rescue the bird, but it ran away. It hasn't come back yet. . . . I'm sorry. Sarah loved it. Perhaps it will.'

'Perhaps it's trying to find its way back to you.' Ralph chewed his pen. 'How did Sarah take it all? The quick disappearance?'

'Desolate, as you can imagine. Cries herself to sleep. Bloody cats. I don't know how to console her.'

'Look, give it a day or two, and if it still hasn't come back, I'll –'

'Please don't bring us another one.'

'No.' Ralph sighed. 'All right. I am sorry. Any other news?'

'None. And listen. I'm in a desperate hurry. We're meant to be at St Crispin's at seven-fifteen, and I haven't made the children's supper. I'll ring you as soon as there's any cat news.'

'Thanks.'

I'll ring you as soon as there's any cat news. The words were repeated so clearly Ursula might have been in the room. Again Ralph sighed. There were times that bachelorhood and the solitary life were far from a pleasure. Perhaps his mother was right. Perhaps he should, seriously, put aside his wasted feelings for Ursula and look for a wife.

He rose from the chair, went heavily to the kitchen wondering if there was anything frozen he could tempt himself with for dinner. It was then he remembered it was his birthday. (Why had his mother forgotten? She always did.) He was forty-two. Middle-aged. He picked up a glass. It was an occasion to open the bottle of fine malt whisky Ursula had given him last Christmas. He remembered her pink cheeks from unaccustomed champagne at lunch, an orange paper hat on her head. She had hugged him extravagantly by the Christmas tree, making the children laugh. For a split second, they had been so tightly packed together that Ralph, stabbed by cruel fantasy, had had to dismantle her arms quite brusquely so that she should not feel his reaction.

He opened the bottle, poured the whisky, and because it was his birthday he allowed himself to continue his remembering.

*   *   *

Mary walked across the field to the place where the balsam poplar lay. It was evening. The anxiety that had accosted her that morning, deflected by Rosie Cotterman's strange visitor, had not returned. Thanks to the visitor, the morbid thoughts of Bill's life after her own death had been scattered. She had returned home eager to ring Rosie, whom she had not seen for some time, to find out if she had made a successful sale. At lunch, she and Bill had talked only of their curious neighbour: the odd, solitary life she led, the little they knew of her after so many years, her extraordinary single-mindedness. When Bill returned to continue sawing up the tree in the afternoon, Mary refrained from ringing Rosie immediately for fear of interrupting negotiations, although she was impatient to find out what was going on. Never having experienced the precarious state of supporting herself, she had always taken vicarious delight when commercial success came to her friends. She restrained herself till after tea. Rosie, in one of her more forthcoming moods, accepted the invitation to a drink. It would be by way of celebration, she said. The strange man from London had bought three pictures for ludicrous money.

Halfway across the field, Mary became conscious of the lightness of heart and freedom of mind that often came sudden from heaven between bouts of anxiety. She reflected – as she was always able to do at such moments – on the life-diminishing effects of her doom-filled spells. 'Is the life we do not know worth all the tormenting thoughts that corrode our brain?' she asked herself. For nearly fifty years she had listened to Bill talking about Balzac, but Chekhov was her man: Chekhov had asked that very question. What had his answer been, she wondered. No, surely. All reasonable people must consider corrosion of the brain through tormenting thoughts of death a foolishness we should not allow ourselves, an unhealthy indulgence that should be controlled. And yet . . . how? At moments like this, unfettered, Mary felt the usual determination not to succumb next time. But the attacks took her unawares. They crept up from nowhere, gripped before she could muster the strength to repel them. And once in their stranglehold, she was helpless. Relief would only come with time (sometimes hours, sometimes days) or surprising interruption, such as the incident of the man on the beach this morning. Calculated deflection – cooking, reading, gardening – were of no avail, though she continued in her customary way of doing all these things, no matter how savage the attack.

Her ability to carry on as normal, during the black times, was, she liked to think, a disguise Bill could not see beyond. He had only the faintest knowledge, Mary was certain, judging from his observations, of her plight. Very occasionally she had considered trying to explain, but it was too late now. Besides, she always thought the subject too amorphous, too silly, too shaming, even, to describe, even to the man who would best understand. It was the only secret she kept from him. By keeping it, she believed she had spared him many years of worry on her behalf. As it was, they had had a married life that was rare in its continuing happiness.

Mary turned the corner. A few yards ahead, back to her, Bill was waving his electric saw over a small branch. Beside him was a pile of meticulously neat logs. Mary smiled at this characteristic show of orderliness: the logs would have to be carted by trailer to the shed, but to Bill this was no reason to throw them carelessly on the ground in the first place. He was a man of strong habit in matters of time and symmetry.

136

The pile of logs was also small. Mary, still smiling to herself, considered how many hours Bill had been working on the tree by now. Fast sawing was not one of his skills, or perhaps his enjoyment of the job slowed him down. Mary continued to watch him. The back of his head was unruly with thick grey hair that overlapped the neck of a sweater she had knitted many winters ago. His powerful shoulders moved with a rhythmic thrust and rise: his knees, in slumped corduroys, were slightly bent for better balance. How potent is the familiar, she thought. And then she knew, quite suddenly, he would be all right without her. Was it the neatness of the logs that convinced her? She saw them as a symbol of the discipline that would rule his life, a discipline the death of his wife could not corrode. Bill was a man strong enough not only to survive after her death, but to continue to enjoy his life. The thought, in the cool evening air, gave her comfort.

Mary knew he had no idea she stood behind him. The snarl of the electric saw meant he could not have heard her. She felt a slight intrusive guilt, having crept up on one of his pleasures unobserved. Before she could step into his vision, he turned. Surprised, he held the buzzing saw high in the air, then switched it off. The sudden silence was infinite.

'Look at that.' He grinned, pointing to the pile of logs.

'Wonderful.'

'Slow work, though. Poor old tree.' He kicked the trunk, looked at his watch. 'Haven't come for me, have you? Six-thirty I said I'd be in.' His self-appointed hour.

'Rosie's coming at six. She won't stay long. Says she's busy. Missed a whole afternoon's work because some man came and bought three pictures.'

'Ah.'

Bill picked up a log, looked at the pithy whiteness of its wood in its thin skin of mottled bark. He added it to the pile, shuffling it about with all the precision of a bricklayer squaring up the next brick in a wall. When it was placed to his satisfaction, he looked at his watch again.

'I'd better come back with you, then.'

He said it lightly. The decision bore no trace of sacrifice. Self-appointed hours were for his own benefit. He was always happy to change them for his wife's convenience.

'I'll make an early start tomorrow,' he said. 'Hope Rosie got a good price.'

He offered Mary an arm. She took it. They returned to the house in the bright silence of the evening.

* * *

Everything had conspired against Ursula's plan to give herself a long time in which to change. Ben had sulked over his piano practice; she had had to add five minutes in order to fit in his reluctant scales. At supper, Sarah had cried suddenly, yet again, into her Heinz vegetable soup.

'Where's the cat now? Dead, I expect, and none of you care.'

Finally, Ralph, intent on one of his languid conversations, had rung just as she had escaped upstairs.

She now sat at her dressing-table looking critically into the mirror. She had wanted to make a particular effort, as she always did, for dining in College. The fact that no other dons' wives, as far as she could tell, were interested in making a similar effort, spurred her on. The dress she had chosen was jade silk, very simple. She would be overdressed, of course, because any silk dress in a gathering of academics' wives was overdressed, and she did not care. Make-up completed – she would probably be the only one to indulge in anything so frivolous as mascara – and hair brushed into as wild a halo as she could manage, to contrast with the scrunched-up perms that would be meeting in solidarity – there was only jewellery to be chosen. Ursula's fingers ruffled through a pile of paste stones with a sense of wicked defiance. She chose long earrings, and the brooch shaped like a lyre. No-one but Martin would notice, because the average Fellow was as sartorially unobservant as his wife. But at least the wearing of such things gave her pleasure.

She pinned the brooch on her shoulder, checked its position

in the mirror. Then she saw the reflection of Sarah, standing at the doorway.

The cat was in her arms.

'She's come back,' the child said. 'She suddenly just jumped up at the kitchen window. I let her in. She was famished, I think. I gave her some milk. Isn't she good?'

Sarah moved towards her mother, stopped beside her. The cat seemed uncomfortable in her arms, rigid. It stared at the floor.

'Isn't she good, I said, Mama?'

'Very,' said Ursula.

'Aren't you pleased? Weren't you worried? We won't let her run away again.'

'No. We'll do our best.'

Martin then appeared in the mirror's reflection. Ursula saw him observe her own anguished expression, and Sarah's smiling face.

'What's the matter?' he asked.

'The cat's come back,' said Ursula.

She set about putting on her earrings. Their small glare made dancing reflections, pale as moonstones, on her neck. The opposite of shadows, she thought, mind gliding hectically about.

Martin came up to his daughter and kissed her on the head.

'Great relief for you,' he said, thus loyal to both wife and daughter. 'But I'm late and I must hurry. You take the cat back to the kitchen and – I don't know – settle it down.'

'The basket's still there,' said Ursula.

'Okay.' Sarah moved away. 'But anyhow, as I was the one who found her, I'm going to name her. She's going to be Catt. C A T T.'

'Very good name,' said Martin, shutting the door behind her.

Ursula sighed. 'Oh Lord,' she said.

'Damned cat.'

'I hate it.'

'With any luck it'll be off again.'

'Ralph's a fool.'

'Poor old Ralph. He's so bent on pleasing.'

Ursula stood up. She turned to Martin who was undoing his tie. His eyes washed up and down her in humorous rather than earnest appraisal.

'If more of the wives looked like you,' he said, 'there'd be an overwhelming vote for them to dine in more than once a term.'

Ursula laughed. Martin took her in his arms, kissed her eyes, trailed a hand through her shining hair. The cat was forgotten again.

*   *   *

Thomas drove down the M40, uncomfortable in the dinner jacket that was destined to be cleaned for the Farthingoes' ball. At home he had had to change fast. There had been no time to show Rachel the pictures, or tell her the few things he proposed to tell her about the day. A state of blissful detachment had slowed him down, made his fingers clumsy as on an ungloved frosty day. Even as Rachel had urged him to hurry down the front path, he had been doing up his black tie. Concentrating on this, and dizzied by the glowing state of his heart, he was in no condition to observe details. However, through the mists of his euphoria something – something rather unusual – had struck him. About Rachel.

Now, to check his suspicion – the road being almost empty – he glanced sideways. Indeed, he was right. She was looking very peculiar.

'You've done yourself up a bit, haven't you?' he asked.

Rachel patted her hair. A flash of scarlet nails bit into Thomas's astonished eyes.

First step in her plan to signal availability had been to go to the hairdresser. She had not been to Giorgio for years, and rather enjoyed her pampered afternoon in his salon of brown and gold leather. After three hours she emerged with hair in a charming Edwardian bun on top of her head, wispy curls about her ears. Oh, so seductive, Giorgio had said.

'Just went to the hairdresser, for once.'

But it wasn't just the hair. Thomas gave her another glance. Her skirt seemed to be flashing gold stuff – Christmas stuff, he would judge it – while the black velvet top had a low V-neck that revealed a deep groove of cleavage.

'I mean, women in Oxford don't dress up much,' he said, confused.

'So? I'm not an Oxford woman. You used to like it when I dressed up. You were always encouraging me to spend more money on clothes.'

'Not used to you taking up my suggestions, I suppose. Have I seen that before?'

'No. New this afternoon.'

Rachel patted the gold skirt. The movement caused savage rays to shoot up into Thomas's eyes, even though they were firmly on the road. He desperately wished she was wearing her usual old black dress. All this gold stuff was completely inappropriate for an Oxford College.

'And, you may have noticed,' Rachel went on, 'I took out the earrings.'

The earrings, he remembered, were the only ones he had ever given her. Wedding present. Socking great rubies set in gold and diamonds. She had not retrieved them from the bank for years.

'Good heavens,' he said. 'Where do you think we're going? The Mansion House?'

Rachel's small silence indicated he had offended her.

'But a good idea,' he added quickly. 'You might as well wear them when you can.'

Rachel moved huffily in her seat. Nails, gold skirt, earrings all sent out their clashing rays, dazzling in the evening sun that blazed through the windscreen. Whatever would old Pruddle think?

'And your afternoon? Successful?' When Rachel had

digested Thomas's implicit criticism, she was calm and cheerful again.

'Very. Three pictures. Marvellous.'

'What was this Rosie Cotterman like?'

Thomas allowed himself a long time. 'Rather odd,' he said eventually. 'Eccentric, I suppose you might call her. Lives alone on the marsh.'

'Young?'

'Oh no. Quite old.'

'How old?'

'Hard to say.'

'Roughly?'

Why was she so interested in Rosie's age? The matter had not occurred to Thomas.

'Mid fifties, perhaps. Or even sixty.'

Peculiar thought, that. He had never looked at anyone over thirty. Rachel was the oldest woman in his life.

'Not that old, then. Though, even at forty-five, I can't imagine being sixty.'

They re-entered their silence. Thanks to Rachel's general indifference about anything to do with his paintings, the subject of Rosie was now obviously over. Thomas's thoughts returned to his short, ineradicable hours with her: her voice, her hands, her topaz eyes, all such an enchanting confusion in his mind that it was a wonder his body was able to continue the automatic driving of the car.

Beside him, Rachel smiled to herself. She thought how funny it was that Thomas's anticipation should be entirely connected with good wine – which, judging from the flare in his eyes, it undoubtedly was – while her own danced in quite different areas. The possibility of a don was what occupied her own imaginings. An available don with whom sometimes there could be lunches on a punt on the Cherwell, talks of books and poetry and university politics, just as when she was an undergraduate – but calmer. She asked nothing else. She did not crave emotional involvement, sex, passion, romance. She abhorred the idea of complication. No: all she desired, she told herself quite convincingly, was companionship. At one dinner in St Crispin's, would she find it?

To be realistic, it was unlikely. But as Thomas accelerated over Magdalen bridge, a salute to his youthful way of driving, perhaps, and the late sun drenched the tower with gold to match her skirt, Rachel noticed her hopes were rising.

The Senior Common Room, in which High Table guests gathered for drinks, was architecturally a fine room: barrel ceiling, handsome cornice, deep windows. But some years ago even the most myopic of the Fellows had noticed that it could do with refurbishing. This decision caused almost as much heightened feeling as the one concerning the provision of contraceptives in the undergraduates' cloakrooms – a subject which had forced Fellows for many weeks to scour rusty areas of moral philosophy deep within them. Outsiders, who like to believe the minds of learned Fellows grapple with more serious issues than the colour of paint, would have been amazed by the furore in the Governing Body once the Motion to Redecorate had been passed. Their approach to so unfamiliar an area as interior decoration was naturally cautious. It was agreed the whole thing had to be decided upon by committee: no such undemocratic act as appointing one competent professional, to present alternative schemes, could be considered.

And so the Fellows, of disparate tastes, struggled with this new and perplexing subject. It soon became clear that it would be hard to achieve any unanimous agreement, except on one point: no wives, absolutely no wives, should be allowed to interfere. When this suggestion was made, it was received with much nodding of wise heads and concealed smiles, as the Fellows thought of each other's North Oxford houses, all that sponging and dragging and pretentious rubbish. Definitely none of that for the Common Room. No wives. Jolly good idea.

Left, then, to themselves, they tried to be practical. As was natural to them, they took an academic approach to the problem. One Fellow brought in a Sandersons chart with a thousand choices of colour, each one illustrated by a tiny chip. This was solemnly passed round. Small random crosses were made by each Fellow against shades of yellow, cream, rust, blue, green, grey and brown. Reference numbers were solemnly taken down. It was agreed further research would be undertaken – what research, and by whom, was not specified. Not a single member of the Governing Body suggested their method of solving the problem was impractical and once more they left the meeting dizzied from studying such myriad specks of colour, their eyes tired and confused.

Some three months later a speck of 'apricot' was finally voted for, though not unanimously. A few of the younger, more revolutionary members, sick of the whole mind-numbing matter and hoping the Governing Body meetings might no longer be preoccupied by discussions of Sun Yellow versus Moon Blue, suggested inoffensive white would be a compromise no-one could quarrel with, and the matter would be settled. White! The Warden jumped to his feet, and roared his disapprobation. They had not, he snarled, spent so many hours' valuable discussion about the colour of the Senior Common Room's walls to come up with the pathetic suggestion of white, had they? He thought the idea insulting to their intelligence. The fire of his feelings rallied enthusiasm among the older, wearier members. And so Apricot Queen, ref.no. 12/4M won the day.

What had not been taken into account by the troubled Fellows is that a snippet of colour on a chart bears no relation to swathes of paint slapped on to walls. When the College painter had finished, they were surprised to find something unexpected, and nothing like the apricot they imagined they had chosen. What colour . . . exactly . . . had emerged? It was hard for any of them to say. The Latin tutor called it Sub Rosa. The gay Bursar saw it as Blush. Others swore it was Autumn Copper, Creamy Beige, Pink Sand, Magnolia, Chocolat au Lait (the French tutor) – Sandersons' language had had its influence. Amazingly, though no agreement could be reached as to what it was, there was unanimous feeling that it

144

was not offensive. It was safe, uncontroversial. It could stay. No-one could face further research and more voting.

Having settled, then, for the no-colour walls, the next thing on the agenda was curtains. By now, the academics' long struggle with mundane matters had begun to pall. Tempers and patience were both wearing thin. There was a tetchy meeting when the Motion for Contrasting or Matching was thrashed out. Finally, the distinguished members of the Governing Body, en bloc, made an outing to a small curtain shop in Summertown. There, they found their ability to find the right book in a glance was of no help whatsoever when it came to choosing between hundreds of cottons, chintzes, damasks, velvets and easy-to-wash satins. So another safe decision was made by the three Fellows who had not escaped for a reviving drink in the nearest pub: rust corduroy.

This was made into thin little curtains, not quite to the ground (despite the size of the budget) and hung from modern pine poles quite out of keeping with the room's grand proportions. They turned out, triumphantly, to cost hundreds of pounds less than the estimated budget, which made up for any visual disappointment.

There was but furniture and lighting left to choose. Exhausted by now, they agreed that one of the more artistic Fellows, who had had shares in an art gallery in the 1960s, and who knew where he could get black leather and steel sofas at a good price, could do what he liked. . . .

This story had been told to Martin by a Fellow of St Crispin's, Timothy Lovat, their host tonight. Martin had relayed it in great detail to Ursula, knowing what enjoyment it would give her. Now, a glass of minor champagne in hand, evening sun agreeable through the windows, she looked round at the beautiful bones of the room and thought: what a waste.

Her attention then turned to the Fellows and their guests. The men were mostly distinguished-looking in their fine gowns of gathered black stuff – oblivious, probably, of the snow of dandruff that uniformly settled on their shoulders. Many of them seemed to suffer imperfections beyond their years – faulty

145

eyes, hair dry as hay, mulberry cheeks and noses. Such things, Ursula supposed, were the price of the learned life, crouched indoors over books by day, gorging four-course dinners and quantities of wine most nights. But she had nothing against the dons. Their unworldliness, their innocence about insignificant afflictions such as scurf, she found rather endearing. Their minds you could not but admire, even if some of them were unable to convey with any infectious spirit the amazing thoughts that went on within them. Ursula had spent many a stimulating evening sitting between Metaphysics and Ancient Greek, Philosophy and Medieval History, Anglo-Saxon and Mathematics. She had discovered that once a Fellow diner had found out her husband's subject, and which College he belonged to, he felt at ease. Then, it was not difficult happily to engage him in conversation about his own subject.

Martin was at her side, smiling. 'The usual,' he said.

'The usual.'

The usual were the wives.

The merest glance at them gave understanding to the decision, in many Colleges, to invite them to dine as infrequently as could be considered courteous. They were not, at first sight, a spirited or attractive crowd – indeed, many gave the appearance that being an academic's wife was no easy matter. Years of silent suffering from their husbands' selfish and single-minded dispositions had caused them to languish, fade, give up. All most of them were left with was the automatic duties of wife and mother: children, children's schools (a favourite competitive conversation among them) and charity work. The teachers and academics among them were less cowed, but inclined towards militancy and aggressiveness. Both groups were united in their sartorial indifference. With few exceptions, their clothes were either dull or ugly. (At one Christmas dinner, Ursula remembered, a St Crispin's wife had chosen an aertex shirt, grey flannel skirt and walking shoes as suitable clothes to accompany candles, magnificent silver and rare wines in the sixteenth-century Hall.) The fashion among them was unkempt hair, no make-up, and hairy legs glowering

146

through flesh-coloured tights. It was as if to make any effort with appearance would be an admission of frivolity: attraction proclaimed lack of seriousness, effort was not worth it. Ursula found herself enraged by such attitudes. She often asked Martin why dons chose such women. He thought it was because most of them were so ensconced in their work that they did not notice – just as they did not notice stale rolls, or lack of salt, pepper, candles and flowers at High Tables. Total preoccupation with one subject, he said, can preclude aestheticism in others.

Ursula's eyes journeyed through the women, colourless as female birds by their husbands' sides, looking for an exception. There was just one. She stood by the window, talking to Professor Pruddle, Warden of St Crispin's. Ursula quickly realised that the woman was not a university wife, but a guest, and in her innocence had made some effort.

The results were endearingly eccentric: a wintry dress of gold and black, wonderful earrings, Edwardian hair of tawny grey streaks. She was a handsome woman past her prime – solid, bulging, soft, with aristocratic nose, good cheekbones, tawny eyes to match her hair. As she smiled at the Professor, a childlike dimple appeared at one side of her mouth. Ursula wondered about her, a rare sort of creature not often found in Senior Common Rooms.

The man beside her, dinner jacket straining over a solid paunch, stared into some middle distance, not even pretending to listen to the conversation. Thick eyelashes gave him an incongruous, youthful look, belied by the plumpness of jowl, and a fine, but anxious, forehead. Ursula wondered about him, too.

'Stop looking,' Martin said, and took her elbow.

Guests began moving towards the door. In the crowd, Ursula found herself beside the man with the staring eyes. Their glance met, as did their simultaneous polite smiles. Then he stood back, indicating Ursula should go through the door first. She swooshed down the stairs on Martin's arm, to the gushing sound of her silk skirt.

'Who's Pruddle's guest?' she whispered.

'No idea.'

'Hope I'm sitting next to him. I like his face.'

'No such luck. I've checked. You've got Timothy and PPE. I've got the gold.'

'Ah well,' said Ursula. But she did not mind because, unlike Rachel, she had no expectations.

One of the rewards of anticipation is the enchantment it lends to any scene. As Rachel followed Pruddle's furfuraceous shoulders into the Hall, she felt as if she was entering a magical place, very different from the bleak Hall she remembered from her own undergraduate days. She glanced up at the husky arch of the high ceiling, the dark portraits of former Wardens united in their sombre reflections, the spears of late sun slanting from each window into the brown light. She listened to the chorus of squawks as the undergraduates rose from their seats, uninterested in the grand guests who gushed up to the High Table, and was back as one of them – nothing but grim young women, in those days: no wine on their tables. And now she stood, curiously excited, by Pruddle's side, as he mumbled a Latin grace. As she sat down, Rachel's gold skirt plumped out at the sides, leaping to join the grubby black folds of Pruddle's gown.

'I'm so sorry,' she said, pushing it away as if it was a dog.

But Pruddle did not hear. He was dipping a huge spoon into a bowl of thin gruel, chasing after the few grains of pearl barley. Rachel picked up her own spoon. She looked at the woman opposite her. White hair cowered close to her head in a ripple of waves. The pale surfaces of her face were jarred by scarlet lipstick that ripped across her mouth. Municipal make-up, Rachel thought: the splash-of-colour school much admired in city parks. The woman's knobbled eyes were on Rachel's cleavage. Rachel smiled, returned her giant spoon to its place. She was unable to attempt the gruel.

In a moment, she thought, luxuriously, she would turn to the beautiful man on her left, whom she had noticed at once in the Common Room and prayed she might be placed beside him. But while he listened to a woman with rimless glasses and bloodless mouth on his left, and Pruddle continued to prod in abstracted silence at his soup, she looked more carefully at the High Table and observed how bleak it was, and felt the illusions of a few moments ago slipping away.

The dark stretches of oak were curiously unadorned: just four islands of salt and pepper, she counted, on the whole length of the vast table, within reach only of a privileged few. Two silver candelabras stood far apart as telegraph poles. No flowers. No side plates. No napkins. Nothing to deflect from the huddle of glasses at each place, awaiting their important wine.

Rachel picked at the plaster-hard sides of her cold bread roll, and marvelled at the fact that the great and wise men at the table apparently did not notice its imperfections. She leaned a little to her left to read the name on the card in front of the exquisite don. Dr Martin Knox, it said. He turned to her immediately.

'Mrs T. Arkwright? Pruddle's guest?'

Rachel nodded. In a flash she saw him standing at one end of a punt, guiding the boat into a tangle of willow, laughing at the cliché but enjoying it all the same.

'Pruddle has quite a line in exotic guests,' Martin said. 'They come from everywhere but Oxford.'

Rachel blushed. Once again she patted at her brilliant leaping skirts. This time they pawed at Dr Knox's thighs, and he noticed.

'You'd never get the wives daring to wear such gold,' he added, smiling. 'They're mice where clothes are concerned. You should hear my wife on the subject.'

My wife. The words ran off Rachel with as little effect as warm water. After all, she was not in search of infidelity. She wanted merely to be rewarded by some small response to her signals.

'Which is your wife?' she asked.

Martin nodded towards Ursula, at the far end of the table. 'The one in blue.'

149

Rachel took in the grave face, the wild hair, the look of dutiful attention on her attractive face as the woman listened to the Fellow on her left, a crumpled man with mushroom-coloured skin.

'I'd call that sea green,' said Rachel. 'It's lovely.'

She might have guessed no man so handsome as Dr Knox would be without a wife. She took a sip of pale sherry. But his unavailability, even for lunch in a punt, somehow spurred her on. She could afford to be outrageous. Quite by chance, not really caring, she might even win him that way.

'It's funny, isn't it, about colour?' she said. 'How we can never prove what anyone else's colour is to us? I mean, your rust might be my brown. I can never understand why people always refer to an olive skin, can you? Olive is green. People don't have olive skins. And yet it's become an established cliché, hasn't it? People don't question it any more, they just think they know what each other means. And then there's the curious thing of peach pink – nothing like a peach. And apricot – a terrible insult to anything but a tinned apricot, don't you think? People go on using such descriptions because they're too lazy, or too unimaginative, to be more precise. Though I suppose perhaps it isn't possible to be absolutely precise, because colour's such a subjective thing. . . .' She could hear herself babbling, the words spewing out, in order to stop herself asking the unavailable doctor what she really wanted to know.

'I dare say you're right,' said Martin gently. He did not give the impression he thought her outrageous, or mad – or irresistible. 'I don't think I've ever thought about the matter before. It's the kind of thing my wife gets worked up about.' He smiled at the thought. Rachel finished her sherry in one swoop.

The untouched soup was taken away – small frown above the white sleeve of the server, she noticed. It was replaced by a large and cold white plate. In its centre lay a fillet of opalescent fish, wrapped round itself like a bandage. It was scantly covered by a dollop of pudgy white sauce. This in turn was decorated

150

with a single button of carrot whose edges had been serrated by a cutter, reminding Rachel of one of those plastic tools the children used for geometry. She drank her glass of white wine very fast, and wondered about the sous chef, whose possibly illustrious career began designing fancy bits of carrot in a College kitchen.

'And another funny thing,' she heard herself going on, the words rolling out like wobbly coins, 'have you noticed how children use their eyes, moving them from side to side when they want to look at something, without moving their heads? Whereas grown-ups peer round with their whole head as if their eyes were static. Part of the whole stiffening-up process, I suppose.'

This time she was rewarded with a smile for herself rather than in response to the thought of his wife. Martin moved his head just far enough towards her for her to see his exaggeratedly swerving eyes. Rachel laughed.

'Now, that is something I've observed, I admit. In fact, I find myself making a conscious effort to move my eyes, exercise them. I'm a great believer in exercising all the different bits so that they shan't seize up.'

The possible double entendre in this remark caused goose pimples down Rachel's arms.

'Then we do have something in common,' she whispered giddily, and drank a second glass of white wine.

'Two things: we don't like the fish.'

Martin had taken a single bite and pushed his plate away. Rachel had not bothered even to try it.

'No.'

'It's not renowned, St Crispin's, I'm afraid, for its food.'

'In my day, Merton and Balliol were the four-star places.'

'You were here as an undergraduate?'

'Some years ago.'

She had no intention of slipping into that sort of mundane conversation. The disapproving arm took away her fish. It was replaced by a plate with something humped in the middle – from the shape it was impossible to tell if it was meat or game.

151

The sight of its ruddy sauce forced Rachel to begin on her red wine – which she never normally drank – for courage. Silver-plated vegetable dishes were dumped at spaces down the length of the table. Rachel observed lumps of potatoes, leeks with all the life cooked out of them, afloat in water, and peas of livid green, all a little blurred at the edges. The reshuffling of courses had caused a break in communications with the good doctor. Rachel felt a surge of panic. Time was running out: Pruddle would be turning to her, any moment. She prodded at the hump of food, spoke without looking up.

'Is the whole tricky business of marriage made more difficult by being a don?' she asked.

She felt Martin's curious eyes upon her. She could feel him weighing up the tone of her question, guessed he would try to ignore its seriousness and treat it lightly.

'I don't think I know what you mean,' he said.

'Such obsessive pursuing of your subject, such conscientiousness when it comes to lectures, seminars, tutorials – the pupils. It must mean a wife is so deserted. And then a lot of academics I know never seem to switch off when they do come home. It's dash in, cup of tea, up to the word processor for the rest of the evening. Are you guilty?'

'No,' said Martin.

'That's rare,' she said. 'Your wife must be one of the lucky ones.'

She watched him glance towards Ursula with another swivel of his eyes.

'It's very difficult to get it completely right,' he answered, apparently thinking about her observations quite hard. 'You have to settle for a cocktail of guilt, compromise, sacrifice to some extent, fluctuating priorities, don't you? Not perfect, but a balancing act, I suppose, that both parties must contribute to –'

'– You're talking in such abstracts,' Rachel said, hearing the words emerge crushed, furred. 'What do you mean, in practical terms?'

Her hand slurred on her knife as she tried to cut the meat,

or whatever it was. Martin sighed, and she knew she had lost him. He was not really interested in the subject. Like most men, he did not like to talk about the finer points of marriage. There was no chance he was going to confide details. He had no need of her sympathy. Smug, complacent, irritatingly charming – she was wasting her time.

'I'm sorry,' he said. 'I'm not much good at domestic analysis. I'm very lucky in having Ursula. We don't work things out. We just feel our way. It seems to suit us.'

Rachel finished her second glass of red wine, smeared her plate with congealed gravy to look as if she had eaten something, and decided to play her last card – flattery.

'You seem to me to be a very good man,' she murmured.

Almost imperceptibly, Martin retracted from her. Her cheeks burned.

'Rubbish,' he said sharply.

And then came the moment that Rachel, next morning in the privacy of her dark room, relived a dozen times with horror and tears.

Martin turned to her, eyes steady, impatience shadowing his expression.

'It seems to me, Mrs Arkwright, there's something on your mind that you would like to say, and you're having trouble saying it. Why don't you just tell me what's the matter?'

Rachel looked at him in frozen horror. She felt waves of blood scorch her cheeks, tears cut across her eyes. She hated him for his perception and his insensitivity, for his cruel slaying of her hopes, and for his polite indifference.

'I couldn't possibly,' she whispered, and the white arm, with perfect timing, came between them to snatch away a third uneaten course.

Eyes down, hands clenched on her knees, Rachel saw Pruddle's knotty fingers scramble into her skirt, grasp kindly at her knuckles.

'My dear Rachel,' he said, 'I hope you're enjoying yourself. I've been deserting you. Tell me how you are, and how dear Thomas is.'

153

Rachel turned, savaged, to concentrate on Pruddle and news of his fossil collection. Tinned strawberries under a cover of snowy meringue passed before her, as did vols-au-vent stuffed with prunes and bacon, and still she found herself unable to eat a thing. She kept drinking, though: many glasses of claret and exquisite Chateau Yquem. The chant of voices, the guttering candles, the stone floor beneath her swelling feet became the diffuse stuff of dreams, unable to hurt any more. There was only one more incident left, before she and Dr Martin Knox went their separate ways, and that she would remember always.

It was time for Pruddle to rise to his feet, say another grace. As Rachel moved to copy him, the independent spirit of her gold skirt betrayed her again. It bulbed up over Martin's thighs like a small parachute. In her dazed state Rachel put out a happy hand to quell it, and found herself grasping the Fellow's hand. For an infinitesimal second she felt the warmth of his fingers, then wrenched her own away. Martin was kind enough to smile, but she recognised his look. It was one of pity.

'*Benedicto benedicatur,*' murmured Pruddle.

At the opposite end of the long table, Thomas crossed his hands over his stomach and bowed his head. It had been a long dinner. Disgusting food, as usual. Wine pretty good but oddly, he had had little desire to drink. He had made adequate conversation to the two etiolated women on either side of him, both keen to talk about their children's progress in school, and had occasionally allowed himself a glance at the glorious woman almost opposite, in a dress of peacock blue. Not that, in his present blissful state of love for Rosie Cotterman, he would have been interested in making any approach. Simply, she had the look of a woman who would not have been offended by his preoccupation, and he would have liked to be beside her. She could only be, he guessed, wife of the handsome man at Pruddle's end of the table, with whom Rachel seemed to be having a lively conversation.

Grace over, Thomas gave a dutiful glance towards his wife.

154

He wondered if she would be as eager as he to leave early. The events of the day were beginning to press upon him. He stifled a yawn, discreetly pawed the ground with a cramped foot. Rachel, he could see from here, was scarlet in the face and unsmiling. In fact, he noticed, as she moved away from the table, she stumbled, and the gallant Pruddle offered his arm. Somewhere beneath his own overwhelming sense of happiness Thomas felt a small tremor of concern. Rachel, who rarely drank more than a glass of wine, might have judged it impolite to refuse the splendid choice provided. She was altogether in a funny mood, tonight: the unusual hair, the unseasonal dress, earrings out of the bank. All most peculiar. He hurried after her.

But he was detained by the slow shuffling crowd, in particular the woman in blue, just ahead of him, who had stopped to wait for the handsome Fellow, Rachel's companion at dinner. When they met, the man put an arm briefly round his wife's shoulders, bent his head to whisper something in her hair. They both laughed, moved unhurriedly together. Their discreet private moment in a public place reminded Thomas of such times in the early days of his own marriage, and he envied them.

By the time he had caught up with Pruddle and Rachel, they were halfway across the quad, on the way back to the Common Room. Rachel was listing slightly, despite the support of Pruddle's arm. Her golden skirt, bright under a full moon, billowed in a small breeze.

'Everything all right?'

'Oh, my dear Thomas.' A trace element of relief crossed Pruddle's old face. He came to a halt, Rachel clutched to his arm. 'Very good to see you. Trust you're coming up for coffee and so on.'

Thomas scanned Rachel's face. She seemed not to see him.

'You're looking pretty good, old thing,' he said. He patted her vaguely on the bottom. The gold skirt raised its hackles under his hand, silently snorting in protest.

'Isn't she?' agreed Pruddle.

Rachel aimed a wisp of a smile somewhere between the two of them. Thomas took her other arm.

'Get some coffee into you,' he said.

Alone by now in the courtyard, the wavering trio made their way to the door that led to the Common Room. As they moved in uneasy silence, Thomas was aware that his mind had become a split screen. On the one side, the here and now, he was definitely not enjoying himself. Due to Rachel's untoward behaviour he would have to concentrate hard for the next hour or so, put on a good show for Pruddle's sake, a task for which he had little heart. But on the other side of the screen, huge and shining and private, was the thought of Rosie Cotterman, whom he loved with a terrifying suddenness and force. The fact of her existence, miles away, gave him strength to manoeuvre his drunken wife up the stairs with affectionate skill.

'Good old Thomas,' muttered Pruddle. He was bent almost double as they pushed towards the top of the stairs. Thomas, who had the advantage of the bannister for support, tugged at his wife so that Pruddle should be relieved of the greater part of her considerable weight.

'Brace up,' he hissed, too quietly for Pruddle to hear.

'Up,' whispered Rachel obediently, missing a step.

On the lonely staircase her skirt, earrings and eyes all glinted with a certain defiance. Rather magnificent, in all her absurdity, thought Thomas, and fancied that the portraits of Pruddle's predecessors looked down upon them in agreement.

*   *   *

In the place where Toby Farthingoe camped in the woods, not far from the vicarage, the brightness of the moon was of little avail. Branches of the trees, dense with new leaves, allowed the merest scattering of light on the undergrowth. But Toby's eyes, accustomed to the chequered darkness, missed nothing.

It had been a good night. He had arrived at ten-thirty, settled himself, warm in a waterproof jacket, on a groundsheet.

156

The Italian cook, who believed his nightly sojourns in the woods were to meet a more companionable creature than a badger, had made him enough sandwiches for two – prosciutto in French bread – and a thermos of strong black coffee. These were packed in a basket beside him but, absorbed by the sounds and smells of the night, he felt no hunger.

Away from his machine, he had intended to think about a complicated part of the new computer programme he was devising. Having struggled with the problem all day, his tired mind had turned instead to the time his interest in badgers had begun. It was a day – he must have been about ten – when he heard his father, a keen amateur naturalist, ask his mother for a fine new shaving brush for Christmas. It must be badger hair, he said: he could only shave with badger hair. When the brush arrived, Toby examined it closely. His father had pointed out the delicate design of each hair – white at the bottom, black in the middle, and white again at the tip. Overall, he had explained, a badger's hair looks grey. But when it moves, the hair ruffles into changing shades of darkness, making a perfect night-time camouflage. Toby, intrigued, went with his father on his next badger-watching expedition. It had been one of the most exciting nights of his boyhood – that first experience of night out of doors, far from the safety of houses, exposed to alien rustlings in the bushes, the hoot of owls and screech of pheasant, soughing of trees, rasping of branches, clawing of bramble, occasional thorns lit with a crumb of moonlight between the shadows. Fear sharpened his anticipation. He had sat close to his father on a tree trunk, one foot squirming in a mysterious mush of leaves, sucking peppermints, not speaking.

'Listen. Listen to the night, boy,' his father had whispered just once. 'And keep your eyes about you.'

Toby obeyed, and was rewarded. An old boar appeared not a yard from them, lifted its head and sniffed the air. For a few seconds, Toby was able to observe every detail of its black and white head: the knowing eye that buttoned the wide black stripe, the white-tipped ears, the quivering jet nose. . . . Toby held his breath. The animal looked at him, then moved back into denser shadow, calm, unafraid. Toby, trembling, grasped his father's hand. He remembered envying the badger's oneness with the night. He remembered admiring its caution, but lack of fear, in the strange dark world of the wood, and how his own fear had left him.

After that first night in the woods, badger watching became his passion. Gradually, he realised that he, too, was a nocturnal creature, happiest, most at peace, in darkness. While others sought salvation in God, or art, or sun, or the company of family and friends, his hunting ground was the countryside at night. He felt no fear, no haunting, even in storms or rain, or silent freezing snow. But the excitement – the excitement on seeing yet another badger, never left him. He had felt it tonight. A sow had appeared out of the bushes – Toby knew her sett was not far away – followed by three young ones. She settled herself, resting from the journey with the resigned air of a mother who has come to a playground to watch over her children. The babies gambolled round her like kittens, cuffing one another, rolling over to expose their silvery underbellies, then daring themselves to leap a couple of feet away from their mother's side. Their small striped faces were sometimes clearly lighted by a scrap of moonlight. Toby regretted, as he often did, that he had been deflected by computers from his first ambition to make wildlife films. If you had the patience, he had discovered, the opportunities were extraordinary.

Tonight, when the babies followed their mother away, obedient to some unseen signal, Toby turned to the coffee and sandwiches. It had been an exceptional performance, but he knew there would be no more. He ate and drank, and lay back on the groundsheet waiting for the usual sleepiness that came to him in the early hours before dawn. But tonight his mind was sharp, awake. He watched the clouds rummaging through a small patch of visible sky, and thought of Frances. The thoughts provoked guilt, as they always did. For the last week or so, he had been wholly occupied with his new programme by day, and the delights of his solitary excursions to the woods by night. He had deserted her. The fact that she, too, had much on her mind with all the organising of the party, was no excuse. He knew, from the look in her eyes every night after dinner when he kissed her goodbye, she was puzzled he wanted to go. She had not complained or even responded to the terrible suggestion that she should come with him; but he knew that his leaving hurt her.

Now, the part of him that Frances could never begin to satisfy, was sated by half a glorious night, and he was left with a base desire for her. While he would not ever want her to be here with him, sharing his secret place, he still sometimes very much fancied being in bed with her. It was one of those moments. With uncomfortable urgency he gathered up groundsheet and basket, and made his way fast along the small, familiar path. Once out of the woods he saw that both moon and sky were paling.

Toby opened the bedroom door quietly. Frances was deeply asleep. He stood by the bed looking down at her. One long arm was thrown out over the bedclothes, the rather sharp profile softened by long hair scraped, as always, behind her wounded ear: the silver thread of the scar glinted on the lobe. Gently, Toby pulled back the sheet. Frances was naked – had given up, perhaps, the pathetic idea that a satin nightdress might tempt him. He looked at the roundness of a breast, squashed into an imperfect shape by the arm, and the childlike neck.

Toby ripped off his shirt, undid the belt of his trousers. In his violent haste he did not bother to take them off, but threw himself with hampered feet on to his wife, plundering her sleep, forcing her into surprised and confused wakefulness.

In the morning, Frances found the bed empty again. Under the sheets, she came upon his crumpled trousers, and wondered whether to laugh or cry.

*   *   *

Rachel was wakened next morning, most unusually, by Thomas bringing her a cup of coffee.

'Are you all right?' he asked.

Painful fronds undulated through her head. She felt sick. Through half-closed eyes she saw that Thomas looked anxious.

'I'm all right. Why?'

'You seemed a bit under the weather last night.'

'I just couldn't eat anything. That food. . . .'

'Ah. That must have been it.'

Thomas half drew the curtains, making sure the sun was shielded from his wife's sore eyes. Such consideration, she thought, dabbing about the bedside table for a packet of aspirin. What had come over him?

'Thanks for the coffee, anyway. Are you off?'

'Not just yet. Got a few papers to see to upstairs.'

Rachel felt a stab of irritation that exacerbated the pain in her head. She ached to be alone in the dark, to know the house was empty, so that she could go over the events of last night, and thus try to exorcise her degradation. For this she needed absolute privacy. Thomas stood by the door.

'Anything else you want? I'll look in to say goodbye.'

'No. Don't. I think I'll go back to sleep.'

'Very well. See you this evening.'

Thomas blew her a kiss, keen to be gone. There was a sort of inner bounciness about him, Rachel observed, before closing her eyes. Perhaps it was due to some kind of uncontainable moral superiority. He had drunk little, uncharacteristically. She had drunk too much, equally out of character. He was triumphant. She was weighed by invisible stones to the bottom of a dark pit.

Overhead she could hear Thomas's heavy tread: backwards and forwards, backwards and forwards. What was he doing? Further irritated, Rachel swallowed three aspirins and drank the cup of coffee. Then, falling back into the protection of her pillow, she allowed the tears. She wept quietly for a long time, whimpering with shame, humiliation, self-scorn. Had she been less exhausted, she realised, she might have seen some humour in the foolishness of the situation. Signalling availability, indeed – what a preposterous idea! How could she ever have kidded herself that she had a chance in hell of a man responding to those signals, particularly among such a desiccation of dons? She must have been off her head, allowing herself to be carried away by stupid fantasies spending all that time and money only to end up making herself a laughing stock. There was at this moment nothing funny about any of it. In years to come, perhaps, she could look back, privately reflect and remember, and allow herself a small smile. But for now she could only live through, and try to shake off, the terrible abjection.

Thomas's footsteps stopped at last. In the silence, her weeping over, Rachel forced herself to confront the worst thought of all. This was it: her hand, restraining her skirt, had brushed Dr Martin Knox's hand by mistake. He, she knew, did not imagine the gesture was a mistake. For the timeless moment that their fingers had been accidentally intertwined, Rachel had been charged with a blissful electric shock. Even through the dullness caused by wine, she had felt it clearly. And she had wanted to go on grasping his fingers. More than anything she had felt for years and years she wanted to go on holding the hand of the handsome tutor.

Those were the facts.

Confronted, stated, they should now be buried. Sleep would best exhume.

Warm, comfortable, headache fading, Rachel slept.

When she woke, at midday, she felt surprisingly energetic. She dressed quickly, then took the gold and black dress from its hanger. Its skirt, which had proved so treacherous, ballooned about her as she carried it downstairs. The gold was horrible in the morning sun, the gold of cheap paint. She went to the grate in the sitting room where, occasionally on winter nights, authority was defied and wood fires were lighted. She took up yesterday's evening paper from the sofa, twisted its pages one by one. In the empty grate lay a few black petals of torn-up paper or card, too thick to crumble into finer ash. When she had made the twisted newspaper into a base for the fire, she stuffed the dress on top of it, pushing it into as small a bundle as possible. The velvet bodice responded placidly. But the gold skirt, recalcitrant to the last, billowed up at her, bubbling over the edges of the grate. As she punched one bit back, another puffed up. Rachel and the skirt fought hard for several moments. Rachel screamed obscenities as the engorged skirt defied her over and over again. Then suddenly all the fight went from it. Deflated, it panted against the sides of the fireplace, waiting.

Trembling, Rachel struck a match, put it to the paper. Flames rose quickly. With no wood to crackle, their silence was alarming. So was their height. Some of them escaped the chimney, spurted up towards the mantelpiece. Rachel moved back. She watched fascinated, as fingers of orange flame and golden skirt entwined, parted, entwined again, the one consuming the other.

She had no idea for how long she watched the fire. When eventually it subsided a large pile of charred mess was left in the grate. Minuscule edges of gold still glinted among powdery worms of material. A wisp of chemical-smelling smoke floated into the room. Later, she would sweep the grate, throw the cold remains in the dustbin. But now she was empty, hungry, in need of food at last.

Rachel boiled herself an egg, buttered thick slices of home-made bread and sliced them into fingers. She settled down to enjoy her lunch. When she had eaten she would go back to bed for her usual afternoon sleep: the break in the routine, yesterday, was the beginning of disaster.

Happy in her silent kitchen, she felt the warm return of normality.

*　　*　　*

Thomas was well acquainted with the feeling of peculiar excitement when engaged in some act linked to a woman in his life. This time the feeling was all the more powerful because the

162

woman was so very different from all the others: she was no minor affair, he had fallen in love with her. The extraordinary realisation had kept him awake most of the night as Rachel, snoring, slept deeply beside him. He had risen at dawn and undergone the rare experience of making his own breakfast. In fact, he had rather enjoyed it. He ate quite competent eggs and bacon in the kitchen long before the papers were delivered, and usefully employed his time by trying to compose a postcard to Rosie. The wording was very important, as would be all his future overtures. He was most anxious not to alarm her, or burden her with his feelings. Restraining his natural impetuosity would be a hard battle which he was determined to win. Caution, slowness, understatement: that would be his way, until the right moment came to declare his hand.

At eight o'clock, he took Rachel a cup of coffee. As making fresh coffee would have been an unnecessary extravagance of gesture, on this of all mornings, he heated up what was left in the pot.

Pleased with himself, he entered the bedroom quietly. Rachel looked a bit rough, he thought. But there was no point in chiding the old thing. She didn't often make public mistakes. Her rum performance last night had not affected him. In all but body he had been far away from St Crispin's, the Fellows, their dreadful spouses, and his inebriated wife in a dress that flashed like lightning.

Coffee delivered, he hurried up to the studio. There, for inspiration, he walked up and down for a while, and studied the three new watercolours propped up on his desk. These, he thought, would never go downstairs. These were his, from Rosie. The ones she had said she would most like him to have. He looked at each in turn, letting himself be sucked into the view of light sky and distant ethereal sand, until his present surroundings ceased to exist. He was still conscious, though, that his heart pounded unnaturally loudly, and his hands sweated and trembled as adrenalin charged through his body. Eventually he sat down at the desk, further disturbed by the pungent smell of his own sweat, and the damp armpits of his clean shirt. He longed for the nursery sofa of his boyhood, for arms around him, for comfort. But with the object of his love so far away, innocent of his need, there was no comfort. He put his head in his hands, rubbed his eyes, groaned out loud to ease the esurient feelings that had reduced him to this pathetic state so early in the morning – a time he was usually at his strongest.

At last, with a great effort of will, he took a pile of postcards from a drawer, cards he had collected from art galleries all over the world. As he flipped through them, the old excitement of committing a private act connected with the loved one rose within him, giving him strength. *Solitude*, he chose first: Serusier's pained peasant girl on a mountainside. He wrote a message, but his hand shook so much that the result was as full of mistakes and smudges as the work of a young child. Never mind, he thought, Serusier was wrong for Rosie anyway. Not her kind of solitude. She would be impatient of loneliness, might even take the card as a sign of misguided sympathy. He tore it into small pieces.

An hour later, six other cards had joned the pile of destroyed rejects. But the finished product, the one he was going to send, was also there. Finally, he had chosen a Van Gogh self-portrait, where the artist's look of anguish exactly portrayed all Thomas himself was feeling: with any luck Rosie might get the message. His economy of actual words, he felt, was admirable: *Please could I come for more pictures*, he had written, *and to see you again? Thank you for yesterday, Thomas.*

He stamped the card, put it in his wallet, intending to post it at the box on the corner. The deed done, he felt calmer. What would happen next – whether Rosie would contact him, or he would give in to his impatience and ring her – he did not know. He would have to think carefully about the next move. But for the moment there was the evidence to be disposed of: the pile of torn cards. It was not the kind of thing a man should leave in his wastepaper basket, no matter how unlikely it was that his wife would go nosing through the rubbish. He could, of course, hide the scraps in his jacket pocket, take them to the office and throw the confetti of his guilt into the wastepaper basket when his secretary was not looking– but even that would be a risk not worth taking. Burning was the only safe answer. Well, there should be no problem. Rachel was obviously asleep. He would be undisturbed. The fire would be a matter of a moment.

Thomas crept silently downstairs, the pile of torn cards in the cup of his palm. He scattered it in the empty hearth, lit it with a trembling match. Unaided by newspaper, the glossy surfaces of the cards burned uneasily. Thomas watched the slow process impatiently. He looked at his watch: he had a meeting at twelve. It was eleven-thirty. There were footsteps overhead. Rachel must be getting up at last.

Thomas poked desperately at the burning cards, urging them to disintegrate into fine ash. But the flames were too feeble. They died completely, leaving suspicious-looking blackened curls. There was no time to try again. Thomas propped the guard in front of the fire, and made a mental note to be the first one to lay it in October. But deception has its revenges: he left the house in a state of unreasonable panic.

Two minutes later, at the postbox on the corner, Thomas was able to smile at himself. For the thought that now over-whelmed him was that he would like to *be* the postcard. Here I am this sunny morning, he said to himself, a middle-aged, hard-working, reasonably intelligent man, generally con-sidered sane, whose greatest wish is to be a postcard. . . . I long to travel in the darkness of canvas bags, whirl through sorting machines, be snapped into the local postman's elastic band, and at last be dropped through that door, to be picked up, held, read, studied by *her*. . . . He slipped the card into the box, the envy of its journey a physical pain.

*   *   *

Frances Farthingoe stood in the ash-coloured front room of her dressmaker's house, contemplating her reflection in the long mirror.

She had been so busy with the party that there had been little time to think about her own dress. She had devoted just one day to shopping in London, and quickly decided that shopping was a hopeless waste of time. The dress she knew she would recognise as the right thing when she saw it did not materialise. She tried on a dozen expensive things in electric colours, either too stiff or too supple, beaded, embroidered and even feathered, but all lacking in charm. Depressed, she was then inspired. On the drive home a picture came to her of exactly what she wanted: a mermaid look.

For her own party, after all, she calculated, the hostess should turn up in something memorable. The design she had in mind was exactly that – strapless, silver sequins would be tight to her knees (she had privately to admit her curvaceous figure would thus be seen to maximum advantage), then flare out with a tail effect, a frou-frou of speckled, pleated organza. . . . The vision brought her much relief.

When Toby had gone off to the woods one night she drew a sketch, and went to London again in search of material. This time she was lucky. The stuff she found was embroidered not only with sequins but mother of pearl beads, and crystal drops were sewn across it in definite ripples. To the close observer there would be a sense of water, waves. . . . As for the Italian organza – she found some with a tiny pattern of shells etched on to a background of misty grey. To celebrate the gods being on her side, Frances had allowed herself a chocolate milk-shake in Selfridges. She sat alone, straw prodding the milky bubbles, happy as a child, thinking of the sensation her dress would cause.

Now, she looked at herself critically. Noon was not the ideal time to judge the development of an evening dress but, even in the gloomy light that pressed through the net curtains, she saw its potential.

Miss Hubbard, a seamstress who had once worked for a grand couturier in Berkeley Square, but had now retired to Northamptonshire, knelt at her feet. She was stabbing pins at the curved hem, from which eventually the froth of chiffon would emerge. Some twenty pins were stored between Miss Hubbard's bony lips. This arrangement was no impediment to a torrent of opinions when she felt in the mood, though for the moment she worked in silence.

Frances noiselessly sniffed the thick air: smells of marigolds and boiling cabbage mingled with a fustiness that was hard to define. On the wall over the gas fire hung a clock whose face beamed from a bonnet of oak sunrays. A cabinet of glass animals hung on another wall beside a calendar whose rural scene was stuck at March 1987, the time of Miss Hubbard's proud retirement. Frances liked the minimal decoration which conveyed the dressmaker's positive tastes. She felt safe in this room, which she had been visiting for three years in all weathers and lights, watching the satisfying progress of her sketches turning into beautiful dresses. There was something reassuring about the large table with its muddle of machines, materials, tape measures, reels of many coloured cottons, from which the clothes mysteriously emerged. There was no reason to feel pity for the solitary Miss Hubbard. She loved her work. It was her life.

'My word, we're living through an interesting time in history if you ask me, Mrs Farthingoe, not that I catch it all on my wireless, we get a lot of interference with Radio Four here, but I like to keep in touch. . . .' Like a ventriloquist, her lips did not move as she spoke, but the pins swayed slightly, a spiked fan round her mouth. 'I'll nip this up just a bit higher in front, I think, and then there's this ozone business, isn't there? If I had grandchildren I'd be worried. I'm buying environment-friendly cleaning things now, but, my, what a price, don't you find, fifteen shillings for a roll of kitchen paper, I don't know.'

The voice lapped peacefully over Frances, not disturbing her own thoughts. She was remembering that at her last fitting she had still been in love with Ralph Cotterman and it was for him, really, this dress was being made. Now, that useless passion finally exorcised, she could concentrate her love, as well as her duty, on Toby.

It was not easy to feel encouraged by Toby, but she was determined to do her best, to make up for the years when her energies had been dissipated. But his polite distance was hard to penetrate. Now that the old days of his jealousy were over, she sometimes felt quite helpess trying to get through to him. Still, it was evident that at least he still desired her, even if she failed him in other areas. Last night, when she had least expected it – indeed, she had resigned herself to his preference for badgers continuing through the summer – he had returned, wild, impatient, passionate. It had been something of a smudged occasion, she was forced to acknowledge: taken by surprise, deeply asleep, her response was not as rapturous as it might have been. And it was saddening to find him gone so early in the morning – but work, of course. Toby liked to start early. . . . Frances fingered a slight mark on her neck. Perhaps he would return again tonight. Perhaps he had had enough of badgers.

'There.' Miss Hubbard moved back on her knees. She spat the remaining pins on to the carpet. 'What do you think?'

Frances shifted her weight, put one hand on her hip. She saw herself gliding down the stairs on the night of the party to give Toby a private view before the guests arrived. The dress was now for him, a message.

'Marvellous,' she said.

'You'll be the belle of your own ball, if you ask me.'

'Oh, no.'

'You've still got the figure. Others couldn't get away with this sort of thing.'

Frances winced slightly at the word 'still'. How old did she look? The shadows under her eyes were not often there. It had been an unusual night.

'I hope so,' she said.

'You mark my words. Have you told Mr Farthingoe what we're working on?' Miss Hubbard tugged the skirt, making the sequins flash like bells in frost.

'It's going to be a surprise,' said Frances.

'His eyes'll be all over his head,' assured the dressmaker, taking out pins.

The dress fell twinkling to the ground. For a moment Frances saw in the mirror the pale replacement of her own skin and bare breasts, and wondered, and hoped.

*　　*　　*

The morning after Rosie Cotterman had visited Bill and Mary Lutchins and given them details of her good news, Bill's watch stopped. So, by chance, did the kitchen clock. It wasn't until he switched on the radio to hear the news, only to find it over, that he realised he was behind schedule. Indeed, half-an-hour behind schedule, because he had planned to be at work by eight-forty-five.

As he hurried across the field to the fallen tree, the distress he felt at being late was soon dissipated by a mild sun in the blue sky, and a temperate westerly breeze which would ease his work. On the back of this breeze came the familiar smell of the balsam leaves – a sweet, grey, Eastern smell, always most potent in May. The slain tree was not yet dead, and were he not to chop it up it would take a long time dying, Bill thought.

He reached the pile of logs from the larger branches, and sat on them to plan his day: first, he must strip leaves from the small branches and put them aside for kindling. Light work, and a break from the noise of the saw. By next week, Bill reckoned, he would be ready to begin on the trunk. To saw up the whole tree would be a long job, and he worked slowly. But he had time, as much time as he wanted.

He looked at the great trunk-corpse, some twenty metres long, helpless in a slash of long grass made by its falling. He remembered the day he and Mary had planted it, not ten years ago, and secured it with a rubber belt to a tough wooden stake. 'Take an alarming gale to blow her down,' Bill had said at the time. But this recent gale had been of peculiar force, and there was warning of similar storms to follow. Bill glanced at the group of other trees he had so carefully planted and nurtured, and felt afraid.

He stood, bent to pluck a leaf, and rubbed it in his fingers. Its scent came powerfully to him, and with it the memory of the tree's seasons. First came the long, pointed bronze buds of the early spring, which only smelt if you squeezed out the sticky yellow wax. Dull brown catkins followed (the tree was a male), and then the surprisingly yellow-green leaves of May. By September the scent was waning, the leaves turned a deeper yellow with rusted veins, while their undersides were white, as if covered by a permanent frost. In a late autumn wind, the flickering of the yellow-white leaves made a splendid light show against an evening sky. Bill could not remember how many times he had stood, just looking at this private view, smell of the bonfire coming from the orchard. In winter, the disorder of the thin high branches was exposed as they scratched against hard skies, fretful, cold. But no more seasons for the poor old tree. Bill kicked at the trunk, and threw the leaf from his scented hand.

'How're you getting on, then?'

Bill turned. Mr Yacksley, the postman, stood there, bagless, bicycleless.

'Morning, Jack. It's a long job.'

'That it is, I can see. I could give you a few hours help some evenings, perhaps, though the wife's got this trouble with her joints.'

'That would be kind. I'm not as fast as I was with a saw.'

'We're all slowing up, Mr Lutchins. My bike's an elephant to push some mornings. We've been married thirty-seven years.'

'I hope Mrs Yacksley . . .'

'She'll pull through.'

'Still, I enjoy it. Mary and I have been married a good many years, too.'

'I was leader of the choir at your wedding, remember? That was a grand day, that was.'

Both men looked at the tree, silent for a while. Then Mr Yacksley transferred his gaze to the logs, and smiled.

'That's a neat pile you've made there. Shipshape.'

Bill smiled, too. Jack Yacksley was probably the only man he knew who would appreciate the fine architecture of his pile.

'Thanks.'

'I came over to say we've a regular fight on our hands again at the meeting tonight.'

'Oh?'

'Vicar's wanting to take a vote this time. I said to him yesterday: I said, Vicar, you've lost all the old folk for miles around with all your new fiddle-dee-faddle. They're not the words we know, Vicar, I said. He didn't seem to care.'

'No.'

'He said he's got this guitarist lined up for Sunday evening in place of the sermon. Said people will flock.'

'I won't be there.'

'Nor me. So we can rely on you for some of your strong words this evening, Mr Lutchins?'

'You can. Of course.'

'I must be back on the round, then.' Mr Yacksley's grey eyes, under a tough thatch of white eyebrow, tipped up to the sky. 'That'll be a good day you've got for sawing. . . .'

The old postman trundled back the way he had come. Bill watched until he disappeared. He and Jack Yacksley, fellow sidesmen, had much in common. They were united in their fight for the preservation of traditional services in their church, their abhorrence of the rapid desecration that was taking place at the hands of the young vicar, whose wife had been known to organise tequila parties in the graveyard. Sunday after Sunday, when urged to shake hands with their neighbours, Bill and Jack Yacksley kept their arms rigid as guardsmen by their sides, gleefully defying the order. When, this last Christmas Eve, the vicar had urged everyone to kiss during the Peace, the two rebels had left, noisily, in disgust. In truth, they made little headway, as the vicar had lined up several like-thinking young people on the church council, leaving the few remaining older members in an uncomfortable minority. But they persevered, and insisted on the rights of one 1662 service a month when – the vicar seemed not to notice – the church doubled its congregation.

Jack Yacksley also shared Bill's love of trees. He had followed with interest the development of Bill's arboretum, and had been the first to bring sympathy after the storm.

Bill bent down to snap off the first thin branch. The luxury of retirement, he thought, was that the fate of a cluster of trees, and the fate of a single old church, could occupy most of your waking hours. With perhaps less than a decade left to him, the future of the wider world was too large to think about most of the time. Priorities changed. Visions narrowed. The sawing of a tree, and the loving of a wife, could occupy you wholly.

*   *   *

Toby Farthingoe's office, converted from two attics, was very different from every other room in the house. Minimalism, here, he had insisted upon. White walls, silent grey rubber tiles on the floor. A roof window looked on to a high black branch of one of the cedar trees: even on bright days natural light was poor and the down lights were switched on constantly. Bookshelves held software manuals and dictionaries. A fax machine, photocopier, and two telephones were arranged in precise spaces on top of a row of white metal filing cabinets. The only curvaceous object in the room was a soft leather sofa: Toby's favourite place to sit and think, or scribble some calculation. No photographs, pictures, ornaments, or unnecessary distractions.

The huge working table was furnished only with Toby's recent acquisition – an expensive and elaborate new Spark work station, on which he had just installed the MACSYMA symbolic manipulation programme. Taking thirty million characters on the Spark hard disk memory – good thing he had another seventy million left – this system, of incalculable sophistication, finally freed his creative mind from the pedantry and laborious drudgery of conventional programming. He was able to confide his innermost thoughts to the Spark, using its electronic circuitry as an extension of his own brain, and its tremendous power and speed as intellectual slaves to his own mind, whose imagination was forever thwarted by the slow and uncertain meanderings of his meagre powers of calculation. Each side of the machine were long spaces of laminated table which – his peculiar working quirk – Toby liked to keep empty. When he had to write he would go to the sofa with a block of paper, rather than sit at one of the pristine lengths of tabletop.

Toby found the lure of this room, light worlds in feeling from the rest of the house, as irresistible as his visits to the night woods. The white silence, the sensation of enclosure in a private capsule (in which no-one else was ever allowed) was his escape, his solace. He spent eight or nine hours a day there, and sometimes much of the night. Often – as he would admit to anyone interested in enquiring about his working methods – not achieving very much. While more conventional software engineers would learn about a new system by studying the complex manual, Toby preferred to discover how it worked by trial and error. He enjoyed playing around, throwing disparate problems at the system to see how it reacted – experimenting. For the moment the MACSYMA was still a stranger to him, and it was a daily pleasure to find and marvel at its complexities. Previously, he had been happy for a decade with a more modest piece of software. On this it had been his good fortune (Frances said his genius) to invent a new algorithm for automating the complexities of airline booking. He had come upon it by chance, really. Reminiscing one day about his earlier work on semi-simple Lie groups, which he had always hoped would unveil the mysteries of symmetry, he had seen the light: some new, simple geometric ideas, which distilled all he had learned about groups by drawing funny diagrams describing the weight systems of finite dimensional representations, would finally render linear programming manageable. Gone would be the days when Crays and other supercomputers would churn away

173

for days doing the simplex method. He had seen a way of literally cutting through the interior of the simplex, going straight at the solution, rather than meandering aimlessly along the boundary, searching for better and better vertices, like an English tourist on the coast of Malaga looking for a free spot on the beach. This moment had been his triumph. In that first moment of discovery, it was not greed that assailed him but, rather, a sort of triumphant and lonely joy. The greed came later. The next morning – when he realised that he could sell his discovery to the world's major airlines. He knew then he would be rich. The subsequent annual royalties never ceased to astound him.

Since that discovery, Toby's mind had darted in many different directions. He had worked on a programme which provided a revolutionary diagnosis of childhood diseases – as yet not ubiquitous, but already in use at an Oxford hospital. His current preoccupation was to devise a programme that could accurately predict the stockmarket. Did the stockmarket contain an internal dynamic which would reveal itself to his mind? Could he ever distil the confusing, feverish data in the *Financial Times* into a coherent pattern? Would they finally emerge and reveal themselves as having some simple structure, some predictability behind the noise, which he would one day understand? He thought of his discovery of the pattern of weight multiplicities, years ago, and he felt that anything was possible, nothing was incomprehensible. And now, with this extraordinary new instrument in front of him, he was convinced, suddenly, that it was much more likely. What's more, if he did succeed, there was another fortune to be made, besides an historical change in the world's finances. . . .

On the morning that his wife glowed at herself in the dressmaker's mirror, Toby sat at the barren table tapping at his machine, transforming the flow chart he had written on his sofa into lines of programming code. He sat back, waiting for the computer to race through the billions of instructions he had coded in by the squiggles and formulae which he had jotted down in a few minutes. At ten millions of instructions per second, the machine would go through its motions in a matter of minutes. He liked to think of the hundreds of human calculators who would have to work a lifetime in order to perform what he had willed his slave to do in minutes. This thought Toby never took for granted. The wonder of technology impressed him every day – a fact he would be loath to admit to colleagues, to whom the writing of software was as pedestrian a part of life, these days, as the telephone.

He sat back, enjoying listening to the soft ticks of the electronic brain, mesmerised by the small flashing light that revealed its keen 'thinking' process. In a state of excited anticipation he waited for the computer, his slave, to type the answer he wanted on the screen. This moment, experienced dozens of times a day, was always a thrilling one. But on this occasion the machine did not like what he had asked it to do.

'Unhappy, unhappy,' he muttered out loud, typing out 'C 13' and thus restoring the matrix he had created earlier. How pedantic are computers, he often thought – how over-allergic to the slightest mistake and therefore, despite their wondrous sophistication, how irritating. Stupid, even. . . . He intended one day to design a new kind of chip that would produce a computer system with a fault-tolerant memory. And even, most useful of all, a system able to perform pattern recognition. . . .

But this morning Toby's mind was full of curves and the geometric paths between them. In the optimisation problem he was working upon, if he could achieve one small brick towards the vast wall of the solution, he would consider it a good morning. He tapped the keys, trying to define a certain transcendental curve in terms of a parameter. . . . A moment later, at the flick of a button, the figures had leapt into a series of elongated loops, sharp as a geometric flower, much as he had imagined they would.

Toby was satisfied with the image on the screen. And yet, as he looked at it, intently, it disconcerted him. He recognised one of those moments, which unnervingly came upon him from time to time, when an answer on the screen reminded him of real life, and the thought struck him that it must be

175

conveying a message. When such notions descended, Toby despised himself for his suspicions. But nonetheless, they would cause him to pause, to think, to calculate in human terms.

The flower on the screen spelt warning. Reluctantly, diverting his mind from the sophisticated language of the software to the inarticulate strugglings of the conscious, it occurred to him he had tried his wife's patience far enough. His lack of interest in the party, his lack of support concerning her problems, and his absence at night, had been unforgivable and must cease. Silly, trivial woman though she was in many respects, she was tolerant of his shortcomings and he loved her in a way (though since the old days of jealousy that way was not very exciting). He did not want to hurt her, or lose her. She could never be many things he had discovered, too late, he would ideally like in a wife. But there were compensations in his work, the pleasure of his daughter, and the higher delight of the peace in the woods. One day, perhaps, he would meet someone whose silence conveyed understanding rather than lack of interest: but he doubted it. Meantime, he must make amends. In the last couple of months before the ball he would attempt some show of appreciation by day, come to bed by night. After all, he believed in the continuation of marriage once the rash embarkation had been made.

So, warning taken. White silence a comfort. Intricate shadow of cedar branch on floor. The familiar pattern of things, shapes, spaces, all contained in one room, were permanences that reassured. Toby touched a button, firm of purpose. The mendacious curves vanished at once, to be stored as a long sequence of *O's* and *I's* in the computer's hard disk for as long as he cared to keep them. Their dual purpose, this morning, had been achieved.

'How are you getting on, darling?' asked Toby. 'How's it all going?'

Frances glanced surreptitiously down the table to calculate the depth of her husband's interest. She knew by the quality of the wine that there was some contrition in his heart. But it was important not to take advantage of his mood, or tax his interest too far.

'Oh, marvellous. Very well. One or two hitches, but I've sorted them out. Very small amount of refusals. Everything going pretty smoothly.'

'Good.'

'I won't bore you with details.'

'Oh, you wouldn't bore me.'

'I might, despite your good intentions. I won't take the risk.'

Toby smiled. 'You'll be pleased to know I've done my bit. Drink all ordered.'

'Wonderful.'

'Better champagne than I intended, somehow.'

'Tobes: you're so extravagant. How lovely.'

She watched his face as Luigi brought in a perfect chocolate soufflé: her silent remonstration had been no soufflés for some time.

'I say, look at that.'

'There hasn't been one for a while.' She hoped he would understand what she was really saying.

'Perfection.' Toby spooned a large slice of the sugar-coated crust on to his plate, followed by a mass of soft and airy chocolate bubbles. 'My last meal on earth would be two chocolate soufflés.'

Frances sat back, smiling. She had not seen her husband so happy for ages. He was economical about his enthusiasms. It was an unusual joy to see him excited about something, even if it was only a chocolate soufflé. Frances took very little herself, so that later he could be persuaded to finish what was left.

'I thought that along with the Perrier we should have gallons of iced coffee. So many people like soft drinks these days,' she ventured.

'Good idea.'

'Do you really mean that?'

'Of course I do.' Toby looked up from his empty plate.

177

'There've been dozens of parties where I would have given anything for iced coffee,' he lied.

'Now you've gone too far.'

'What do you mean?'

'You're lying. You've never given iced coffee a thought at a party.'

Toby sighed. 'Well, perhaps I exaggerate. I was only trying to encourage. You have such good ideas.'

'Thanks,' said Frances. She recognised they had come to a dangerous impasse. The subject of the party should be changed at once. 'Why don't you finish the soufflé?'

Toby scarcely bothered to hesitate. 'If you're sure. . . .'

'Go on.'

As he scraped at the bowl on the sideboard, silver spoon against white bone china, Frances was aware of the oppression of the dining room. Sometimes she wished they had no servants and supper was in the kitchen, Toby mixing the salad while she stood at the stove. Sometimes she hated the formality of their dinners here among the shadows from the cedars outside, in the stuffy air that smelt of pepper and polish.

What could they talk about now? What did people who had been married for fifteen years talk about night after night if they dined alone? The children, the mortgage, practicalities, plans, work? Never, in their case, work. Frances had once claimed that anything to do with computers was beyond her, so Toby – not wanting to bore her, perhaps – kept that part of his life to himself.

'I must show you the letter from Fiona that came this morning,' said Frances, knowing she sounded drab.

'Oh yes?'

'She's apparently top in English, bottom in maths.'

'No need to worry about her. She's pretty middle of the road all round.' Toby scraped the last morsels of chocolate from his plate. 'What about the party? Is she coming?'

'Of course. She'd hate to miss it. I've said there's only one condition, she absolutely can't wear her jeans.'

Toby laughed. He liked his daughter's tomboy phase.

'Shouldn't think she'll enjoy it much. All us old things.'

'Well, she wants to come and I've said she can.'

'Fine, then.'

They both stood, paused at their different ends of the long table.

'I'm going to watch the news,' said Frances. 'Your sleeping bag was washed today. You'll find it in the laundry room.'

Toby looked at his wife as if she was someone he had only just met. 'I won't be using it tonight,' he said at last. 'I've been lucky: so many badgers these past few nights, I can afford to give them a miss.'

Frances, though expecting this decision, was confused by his announcement. She felt suddenly soft, malleable, accommodating.

'Oh, Tobes, you mustn't ever think I mind you badger watching. . . .'

'I don't think you do mind very much. Come on, I'll watch the news with you.'

He left the room ahead of her. In the study he poured her a drink, sat close to her on the sofa, one hand dormant on her knee.

Tonight, thought Frances, would be a small gain for them both, then Toby would retract again. In her new mood, freed of Ralph, she longed to stop his habit of ebbing away. But she knew she never could. And besides, a changing tide in marriage is a healthier thing than static waters. So, she was resigned to meeting, parting, meeting, parting, on their small, equable scale. It was their way of dealing with the gulf that divides all human souls, and it worked quite well.

Frances kept both hands round her glass of whisky, intent on the news. She imagined Toby had no idea how impatient she was for it to end.

*　　*　　*

On the first morning of half-term, in early June, Ursula drove the children to Martin's mother in Dorset. She hated to be

179

without them, even for a few days. But they shared her love of the country, and for them a long summer's weekend on their grandmother's farm was infinitely preferable to staying in Oxford. Sarah's only reluctance had been to leave the cat, but in the end she had agreed that cats like to stay in one place. Taking it away would make it unhappy, Ursula explained, an argument which found Sarah's sympathy immediately. And so the cat was left behind, the fur of its chest clotted with her tears. It licked itself clean, bored by her histrionics.

Since its return the night of the dinner in St Crispin's, the animal had behaved in a docile but aloof manner. It was capable of ignoring almost all life that went on around it. Untouched by events, uneager for food or milk, it was a loveless, self-contained creature, entirely preoccupied by its own private thoughts. It would sit immobile for hours, staring into space, upright in its china-cat position on the dresser. Or curled on the window-ledge, eye on the birds, but disdainful of them now. It made no indication it was intent on further killings. Apparently immune to temptation, there was no perceptible twitch of whiskers when provocative pigeons strutted the lawn.

The cat was polite to Sarah, allowing itself to be held and stroked, but never responding with any gesture of pleasure or affection. When Ursula returned to the house alone, it gave no sign of welcome. On many occasions it simply left the room, tail rigid with animosity, high in the air, and it would not appear again until the children came back from school. The dislike and distrust between Ursula and the animal, recognised on both sides, flourished daily. But Ursula kept her uncomfortable feelings to herself. She had always believed a husband's attention should be reserved for things of some importance, and to burden Martin with the trivial worries of every-day would be the quickest way to corrode his sympathy. In the broad scope of their marriage, the cat was not of major importance. So she said nothing. Besides, she could not bear to upset Sarah. The cat was established in the house, now. Ursula could only try to make the best of it.

Today, the cat was far from her mind. She had planned a good day for herself to make up for parting with the children. When she had left them, happy with their grandmother, she drove to Marlborough to shop in the market. This was always a pleasure: the cheapness and freshness of the vegetables, fruit and fish; the friendliness of the stallkeepers; and her especial relationship with the butcher, who would carry her heavy bags of meat to the car and give her presents of homemade sausages. In contrast, shopping in Oxford was an act of misery – surly, unhelpful shopkeepers, over-priced, poor quality food, dozens of perfectly ordinary things unavailable. She had long ago given up trying. The bargains she found in nearby market towns were perhaps cancelled out by the price of the petrol, but were worth the journey for the pleasure of finding delicious things and agreeable country people. Today she bought fresh monkfish, and Somerset Brie, and Jersey cream to go with early strawberries. Tonight would be the first time she and Martin had been alone for a long time, and she was determined to make a special effort with dinner.

But before returning to Oxford she had an appointment at a farm near Pewsey. In response to one of her advertisements in a country magazine, a farmer's wife had written to say she had a 'lot of old junk jewellery in the attic', which she would be willing to sell if Ursula liked to come and make her choice. Such an invitation inspired the thrill of the chase: tracking down beautiful things in unlikely places, to Ursula, was irresistible.

She found the farmhouse at the end of a long track that led into a cleavage between soaring downs. There were some dozen cars parked in the drive. It was an unkempt place set in a neglected garden. But the basic structure of the house, once handsome Regency, was pleasing, simple. Its potential, so far from her grasp, struck Ursula with a weakness of longing. She paused at the door for a moment before ringing the bell, trying to restrain the thoughts of what, given the chance, she could do. . . . She looked down, then, to see she was standing in a sprinkling of pink and blue paper petals – very superior confetti, she thought at once, picking up a perfectly formed paper rose petal – very different from the commercial rubbish that passes for confetti today. What was going on?

The door opened before Ursula knocked. Mrs Green, the farmer's wife, smiled up at her. Mrs Green wore a cotton dress ablaze with cabbage roses, and a pink plastic comb in her curly hair.

'I'm afraid we're in the middle of a wedding reception,' she said, 'but I didn't like to put off our appointment. It was rather a sudden wedding, actually, though not for the usual reasons.' She laughed.

Ursula stepped into a hall that smelt strongly of dog. Strings of silver horseshoes had been hung across mud-stiff mackintoshes that bulged on a row of hooks. The horseshoes swooped merrily across immemorial wallpaper, old framed photographs of prize bulls and rams and faded football teams. Yet other horseshoes secured to bannisters and hatstands, hung in inverted arches to meet at the central overhead light, where they were joined in a bow of blue tinsel ribbon. From down the passage came voices and laughter, and *Danny Boy* picked out in single notes on an accordion.

'I've put the stuff out in the spare room, if that's all right,' said Mrs Green, leading the way upstairs. 'Take what you like, no hurry. Then come on down for a drink and a piece of cake. Horace and June would like to see you.'

She showed Ursula into the room, and left with apologies, shutting the door behind her.

Ursula stood still for a few moments. Up here, the wedding reception was reduced to a muted ruffle of sound, singing and laughter. More clear was the bleating of sheep which came through the open window.

It was a neat, bare room: polished wooden floor that smelt faintly of lavender, white walls, cambric curtains, a single brass bed with a candlewick cover of fluorescent pink. On a table beside it were a Bible and old copies of *Woman's Own* and *Farmer's Weekly*.

There was a small chest-of-drawers under the window. On

this Mrs Green had put two opened cardboard boxes, both sprouting aged tissue paper. Ursula went over to them, peculiarly excited. But before she would let herself explore the treasure, she looked out of the window to the sweep of Downs, a huddle of sheep, corn-rippling distances, trees no clearer than smudged fingerprints on the horizon. Her excitement, she then knew, was more to do with where she was than the unopened boxes before her. She felt that she knew this land, had known it for ever. It was at once recognisable, the place she should have found long ago, the place she would like to be for the rest of her life.

She unwrapped a twist of paper to find a French paste crescent moon set in blackened silver. She laid it on her palm and its fine stones doubly sparkled through the tears that had come to her eyes. Then she sniffed, smiling to herself, pulling herself together: Ralph would laugh when she confessed she had gone through another 'earth crisis', as he called them, but with understanding. This time, though, it would not be just to Ralph she would try to describe the powerful sentiments that had accosted her so unexpectedly: she would explain to Martin, too. There was the perfect, rare chance, this evening. Perhaps, very gently, she could persuade him just to consider . . . leaving the alien city for somewhere like this.

Half-an-hour later, Ursula had made her choice – handfuls of necklaces and stars and moons, bracelets and brooches in marcasite and paste, jet, ebony, moonstones, garnets – all things redolent of a quieter age, when old craftsmen spent a lifetime in spartan workrooms turning slithers of coloured glass into birds and flowers and stars to be worn on stiff Sunday bosoms of virginal grosgrain. . . . The buying and selling of such things was a small sideline in Ursula's life, though of late she realised her business sense was waning as she found herself unable to part with more and more of her beautiful finds.

Downstairs, she peered round the kitchen door. It was a large dark room, unmodernised, but for a black glass oven and a microwave that were fixed, incongruously, on the dun walls. Strings of yet more silver horseshoes frilled over cupboards, dresser and fridge. Food and drink covered the large wooden table: huge pork pies, sausage rolls, salads, home-made bread, sponge cakes and trifles. There was beer, cider in basket-covered jars, and ginger wine. The smell of pipe smoke mingled with the smell of sweet chutney. An old man sat by the fire playing *Daisy, Daisy* on the accordion. Some of the guests were singing, others laughing at their attempts. Judging by their colourful faces, the celebrations had been going on for some time.

Mrs Green caught Ursula's eye and beckoned her in.

'June and Horace would like to meet you now,' she said. 'Over here.' She led the way to the window, where the bridal couple sat side by side on upright chairs. They were well into their eighties. 'Both married over fifty years, both widowed,' whispered Mrs Green. 'This is my great aunt June; Auntie, this is Mrs Knox, come to buy the trinkets in the attic.'

'Very nice,' said the bride to Ursula, not at all confused by the idea of commercial transactions taking place during her wedding reception. 'My mother used to collect all that stuff. Nice to think it's going to someone young and pretty again.'

She gave Ursula her hand. It felt like a small pouch of antique satin embroidered with blue silk veins. Their blue matched the wool of her dress, crocheted with scallops at neck and hem, the kind of dress that might be worn by a very young child. On her head was a beret of blue cornflowers, and a small silver horseshoe dangled from a chain round her neck.

Her hand slid from Ursula's: she waggled her wedding-ring finger, smiling mischievously. 'This is the ring the other one gave me,' she said. 'Couldn't get it off for the life of me. So it saved Horace a ring, didn't it Horace?' She tugged at her new husband's sleeve.

'Horace, this is Mrs Knox,' said Mrs Green, and turned to Ursula. 'You'll not say no to a piece of cake and a glass of my home-made wine, will you?'

'I'd love some. Thank you.'

Horace put out a hand to shake Ursula's. It was large-boned, ruddy-knuckled.

'Very nice, too,' he said. 'Come and sit down with us a moment. We've spoken to all the others.'

Horace was upright as a soldier in pinstripe suit, waistcoat, fob watch, and a yellow carnation in his buttonhole. White hair stood straight up from his magnificent temples. Sprightly eyes blinked fast to rid themselves of constantly returning tears. He pointed to a chair with his stick. Ursula pulled it up and sat beside him.

'Now, dear,' June smiled at Horace with the air of one who is resigned to a future of restraining a husband to whom flirting is second nature. 'He's my husband,' she giggled to Ursula, incredulous.

'She knows that, silly.' Horace patted his wife's hand. 'She's a wedding guest.'

'Lovely wedding,' said June, looking round.

Horace bent his head towards Ursula. 'Truth of the matter is, we were both so used to the married life we wanted to carry on. She and Jack were forty-nine years. I'd run along with Edith for fifty-two. All friends for life, we were. So when our partners passed on and we were put out to graze in his Home place, we thought why not? Jack and Edith would have been pleased.'

'Quite,' agreed June. 'Jack and Edith would have done the same if they'd been left.'

'You get used to being married, see,' added Horace. 'You find you miss it if it's not there.'

'That's just it,' said June.

Mrs Green returned with a large slab of wedding cake and a tankard of ginger wine. The cake was damp and fiery with brandy, the wine sweet and sharp. It made Ursula sneeze.

'Shotgun wedding, actually.' Horace threw back his head in merry laughter. 'I said to June, if you don't marry me next week, old girl, you'll miss your chance.'

June blushed. 'I wouldn't have wanted to miss my chance,' she said.

'So there we were, weren't we? My great-niece Dora, here,

arranged all this knees-up in a trice, and we had a lovely Blessing in the church besides.'

'We couldn't wait,' added his wife. 'Horace, this music is going through my head. Ask Andy to play a lullaby.'

'You can't hear anything against this music, that's it,' agreed Horace, waving his stick towards the accordion player, who took no notice. 'Blots out the linnets.' He shut his eyes for a while. His wife patted his hand. 'Nothing like the linnets round here, this time of year,' he murmured, eyes still shut.

Later, having been pressed to more food and drink by Mrs Green and her husband, Ursula slipped away from the reception. In the hall, Mrs Green said she wasn't interested in what Ursula had taken: if she hadn't come, it would have gone to a jumble sale. Ursula tried to convince her that some of the pieces were worth thirty or forty pounds.

'Give me a hundred, if you like,' Mrs Green conceded in the end, smiling. 'That'll pay for the wedding.'

Ursula wrote a cheque. She liked the idea of paying for a party she had so enjoyed. Mrs Green followed her to the car.

'You're very lucky, living here,' Ursula said.

'Oh, I don't know. Been here all my life but it's hard work in winter. Still, we're packing it all in, in a few years' time. Selling up. My husband wants to end his days in Spain, near our daughter.'

'Would you let me know when you're thinking of leaving? We'd love . . . first offer.'

Ursula spent the journey home wondering how she could ever hope to convey to Martin the extraordinary delight of her day: the strange feeling that she had been part of that house, those people, for ever. When Mrs Green had gone back inside, Ursula had turned slowly round, imprinting every aspect of the landscape on her memory. Then she had heard the linnet, whose song had been drowned for Horace by the wedding music, and she had shivered slightly, despite the warmth of the sun.

The sadness in marriage is that you can never quite perceive each other's experiences, she thought: on the other hand, they might not have happened had you been together. Often they are treats (from God? from somewhere) provided for one person to bestow upon another – to enlighten, perhaps, or to entertain. Had Martin been there, it would not have been the same. He would have been impatient of her slow choosing of the jewellery. Horace and June might have found it more difficult to talk to both of them than to just Ursula. Total immersion into a sudden, strange new world is easier by one than by two. But you are left with the difficulty of reporting: in this case it would be particularly hard to make sure Martin would understand the significance of the unexpected wedding, and to make sure her account was not embellished with sentiment, or the wrong kind of humour. She was determined to choose her words carefully. Depending on his reaction, she would produce the trump card at the end – Mrs Green's plans to sell.

Home, Ursula carried her bags of heavy shopping into the silent house. The kitchen, which she had not had time to clear properly that morning, was full of reminders of her departed children: an odd shoe, a ruler, a small navy bomber-jacket curled round a pot of cold tea. She longed for Martin's return, but that would not be for some hours. Still, there was plenty to occupy that time: tidying up, ringing the children, preparing the especial dinner, having a bath.

The kitchen was warm and stuffy, the smell of summer jasmine almost too strong. Ursula opened the window over the sink, glad of the fresh air that blew in. Outside on the lawn she saw the cat, belly flat on the ground, hindquarters hunched, tail flicking slightly. Its eyes were intent on a blackbird which pecked the earth in the shade of a lilac tree.

'No!' she shouted, and ran from the room to the garden.

She saw the cat briefly turn its head, sneer at her, then flee. The blackbird, a squawk of black-fanned feathers, rose into the air and flew crying away. Ursula stood still, shocked and relieved. Then she saw the cat slink along the terrace. It

187

jumped up on to the window ledge and slid back into the kitchen.

She returned to the house, heart as flummoxed as the blackbird's wings, unsure what to do. She found herself creeping cautiously through the kitchen door, tense, eyes all about her.

The cat was on the dresser – not in its normal place, but on the top shelf, static between two glass jars of dried beans. They looked at each other. Ursula found the rare eye contact unnerving.

'You loathsome horrible animal,' she said out loud, and felt better.

The cat tipped back its head, looked down at her unblinking. Ignore it, thought Ursula. That was the best thing – ignore it. Make it realise. . . . She moved, back to it now, to unload a basket on the table. A moment later she felt a weight on her shoulder, the scrabbling of bony limbs as it fought to keep its balance, the drag of claws on her skin.

Ursula screamed and turned her head. For a second, she had a close-up view of creamy points of teeth exposed by a snarling lip, a small flash of pink tongue. It hissed at her, eyes flat, cold, livid. As Ursula struggled wildly to remove the animal from her, its claws tore the flesh of her bare arm. Rubies of blood darted along the skin, some smeared into feathery marks by writhing fur. Then suddenly it dropped on to the table, still spitting, hackles raised. Ursula backed away, terrified, fingers of one hand running through the streams of blood on the other arm.

She thought too fast to be conscious of the plan: picked up an empty wine box from the table. The cat arched its back, waved its tail in the air. Ursula crashed the box down over it. The animal gave a piercing yowl, moved frantically inside the darkness of its cage, scratching at the cardboard sides. Ursula kept her weight on the box so that the cat could not upturn it and attack her again, all the time trying to decide how to secure it until she could get to the telephone. . . . Martin. With a sudden inspiration she picked up one of the shopping baskets,

188

put it on top of the box. The two other baskets she jammed close to its sides. Now, although the cat continued to scratch and yowl, and the box moved very slightly, there was no longer any danger it could escape.

Ursula backed away and surveyed the ungainly prison she had made. She looked down to see blood on her skirt and on the floor. The cat's voice changed to a kind of moaning, a horrible noise.

'Oh, Martin,' she cried out loud, and tears, before she could control them, jerked down her cheeks. At that moment she heard the bang of the front door and hurried footsteps.

She turned to see Ralph, an expression of stupefied horror on his face.

'What on earth –'

'The cat.'

'The cat?'

Even in her ungrounded state, Ursula saw that a wisp of Ralph's thin, dry hair had been disarranged by a breeze or his hurry. She had never noticed, before, quite how thin –

'It attacked you?'

Ursula nodded. The blood was sticky between her fingers.

'Go away, darling. I'll deal with it.'

She had never heard him so stern. She registered liking sternness in a crisis. With no further word she ran from the room. Ralph banged the door behind her.

Martin, as much as Ursula, felt the loss of the children on the rare occasions they stayed away. But today, knowing they would be happy, there was little room in his crowded mind to think about them. His own research work constantly suffered the mundane interruptions of university life: it was essential to make up for lost time if he was to finish by the appointed deadline his paper on Human Resources and Economic Development, commissioned by the World Bank. He looked forward to a rare day free of both pupils and the administrative business that fell upon him as Senior Tutor, so that he could concentrate on the formidable pile of journals waiting his attention. This evening, with no fatherly duties to divert him, he planned to continue reading in peace at home.

Some days, Martin found the copious study of dry matter essential to his research so tedious that only an act of supreme will would keep him at it. To achieve the sustainability of empirical conclusions, he found – as does every economist early in his career – is a long, hard slog. Short cuts cannot be risked for fear of destroying a whole edifice. The bulk of his work, to establish the validity of conclusions, was the endless reading of scholarly reports with their assessment of data gathered in the field. What kept Martin's adrenalin going, even on the toughest days, was the knowledge that suddenly from other scholars' findings would come an idea of his own that was so exciting that he would be obliged to pause for a while, sit back and take in its implications before settling down to prove its worth. When such inspirations came to other academics, Martin was always swift in his acknowledgement. His first duty this morning was to write a note of congratulation to a colleague whose recently published econometric study proved that cognitive skills 'explain' more of earning capacity than any other variable. As he walked across the quad, Martin felt an almost tangible sense of pleasure in his friend's brilliance. The man had come up with remarkable data sets whose analysis definitively blasted the sociologists' screening hypothesis: and proving that the best predictor of earnings was not the number of years spent in school, nor the child's innate ability, but, without a doubt, cognitive skills learned in school. . . .

Martin installed himself at the familiar muddle of his desk, and wrote a letter of enthusiastic congratulation. Then, the luxury of time being on his side, he did something he had been meaning to do for a week or so: he searched through a book titled *African Educational Development* to see if there was any reference to an early paper of his own – *Schooling and Age-Earnings Profiles in Zimbabwe*. There was. That was a good start to the day. The rewards of an economist are to find his published papers referred to in learned journals, discussed at conferences. Martin knew the occasional joy of such acknowledgements. They revived impetus, boosted determination to face the next quest.

He made himself a cup of coffee, stood for a few moments in the quiet untidiness of the room which may have seemed chaotic to others, but to him was a place of absolute orderliness: he could lay his hands on any paper in a moment. He returned to the desk, every object sharp with sunlight, the light coating of dust brilliant as frost. There could be few more perfect places to work than a mellowed room in an Oxford College, he thought, as he often did, and would not let himself linger on the idea of leaving one day, in accordance with Ursula's wishes.

He flipped through some journals – *World Development*, *Economic Development and Cultural Change*, *Population and Development Review*, making a mental note of which articles he would return to read. His sense of excited eagerness to get going was due to the fact that yesterday he had found a paper in the *Journal of Development Studies* that produced some evidence of maternal and child health relationships with a sibling control . . . the outcome of his own work would depend as much as possible on studies employing that very concept. Research into this subject had meant reading almost sixty scholarly papers so far, and a long list still remained.

Martin took up his pen. Beneath the veneer of enthusiasm for the present project, other thoughts spun their delaying tactics. He was impatient to receive the print-out of the new data he had brought back from Kenya – would it confirm his hypothesis? He was fascinated by a study on age earnings profiles recently carried out in Brazil by the distinguished W. Rosenberg – the paper sat tantalisingly before him. But he was also determined nothing would deter him from his own human resources theory, and he forced himself to take up the paper that had caused him so much interest yesterday.

Seven hours later, having been so absorbed in his note making he had forgotten to break for lunch, Martin closed his books at last. He stood up and stretched stiffly. It had been a good day's work, and there was no reason to hurry home: he could carry on till evening. But such concerted concentration had tired him just enough to make the thought of leaving now, for a quiet tea with Ursula, irresistible. Further pursuit of optimal solutions could wait till tomorrow, he decided, with the slightly guilty smugness of one who knows his day's work has contributed a small but positive link in the vast whole. He ran a finger through the dust on the only uncluttered space of desk, thinking he could never decide which light he preferred to work by, morning or afternoon, and piled the journals in private order. He was a man well pleased.

When Ursula had washed the blood from her hands and arms (the scratches were not deep) and changed into clean clothes, she returned to the kitchen. Ralph was sitting at the table reading the newspaper. Box and cat had gone. Shopping bags and baskets had been placed in a neat row on the floor.

'What did you do?' she asked.

'That's absolutely no concern of yours.'

'It didn't hurt you?'

'No. It had spent all its fury on you.'

'Where is it?'

'Safely in the back of my car. Look, I'll find it a new owner in the village, a cat lover. I'm sorry I ever brought it, but it's gone now. Don't let's talk about it any more.' He was still being unusually firm.

'Sarah will be devastated.'

'Tell her what happened and she'll understand. I'll try a puppy next time.' He smiled, got up. 'Tea? I'll put the kettle on.'

Ursula nodded. She watched him in silence as he efficiently made a pot of tea, chose her two favourite mugs from the dresser, familiar with everything as if the place was his.

'You all right? How are those scratches?'

Ralph came towards her, lifted her arm. He studied the long pink marks. They were slightly swollen.

'I'm fine.' In truth, Ursula felt shaken. 'It was the fright

192

more than anything. I don't know what I'd have done if you hadn't come. How did you manage to appear at precisely the crucial moment?'

'You know me. Always turning up here.' He was stroking the scratches with a light finger.

'You haven't been for ages, come to think of it.'

'Over a week. You noticed?' He laughed slightly. 'Still, I was thinking about you.'

'Oh Ralph, you're always thinking about us. Anyhow, thank you.'

Ursula found herself in his arms, deliquescent with relief, grateful for his comfort and protection. She thought guiltily of her dismissiveness to him on occasions – her unconcealed impatience and irritation. Strange how he never seemed to mind. Nothing shook his devotion and, for her part, despite her moments of wishing he would turn up less often, he remained her closest friend. She felt him back away from her. Post trauma had made her curiously sleepy – she would not quite let go. Head against his shoulder, arms loose round his neck, she was aware that her own comfortable calm was not mutual. His hand was anxious, or afraid, on her neck. His cheek, brushing against her forehead, was hot.

'What's the matter?' she asked.

'Nothing, nothing.'

They continued in their uneasy position for some moments without speaking.

Martin came quietly through the half-open door to see his wife splayed up against Ralph, and Ralph's hand muzzling through her hair. He paused for no more than a second. Ralph, facing him, broke gently away from Ursula.

'Seducing a man's wife, I see?' said Martin, in the kind of voice that believed the impossibility of any such thing. He smiled.

'Comforting, rather,' said Ralph. 'I arrived to find . . .'

'The cat, Martin,' Ursula interrupted. She whirled round, threw herself against her husband.

Ralph watched painfully as she transferred her previous position, in his arms, to Martin's.

'It attacked me, the horrible thing. Look!' She held up her arm.

'I'm sorry, I'm sorry.' Martin kissed her forehead, unknowingly repeating Ralph's gesture of a few moments ago, but with a different kind of anxiety. 'But you're not badly hurt?'

'Not really. And Ralph has dealt with it. It's gone for good. Well, I couldn't have stood it much longer anyway, our mutual animosity. I knew that in the end either the cat or I would have our revenge. . . .'

Martin ignored Ralph's pot of cooling tea and took a bottle of wine from the fridge. The three of them sat at the table. Ursula told the story of the attack from the beginning. Safe now, she reflected on the absurdity of the event, the gallant rescue, and the assurance of the cat's non-return. Soon the mood of her happy day was restored. Within ten minutes she was laughing. Martin suggested that Ralph should stay for supper. Ursula hesitated for an imperceptible moment before agreeing. She had so looked forward to the evening on their own, pleasing Martin with an unusual dinner. But she realised this was a selfish wish: Ralph's great kindness and help must, of course, be rewarded. He, feeble in his protests at intruding on their evening, was easily persuaded.

Ursula, distracted by her appreciative audience, cooked the monkfish in a much simpler way than she had planned, and the three of them settled down to a lively supper. Over prolonged strawberries, the story of the wedding guest in Wiltshire emerged. Martin and Ralph, enchanted by her account, urged her for more and more detail, and it was not till long after midnight that Ralph finally left, sympathising with the bridegroom who had missed a day of the linnet's song.

By the time he had gone, Ursula felt, it was too late to mention the matter of the farmhouse. . . . To win Martin's consideration of the possibility, let alone approval, it was imperative to choose the right moment. The chance of this evening had been missed. Still, in compensation, Ursula could

194

store the thought within her. She would ponder upon it at great length, and in the weeks to come it would occur to her how best to break the idea to Martin.

Martin insisted they left the clearing up till next morning. He had no intention of hurrying to work next day, he said, and hugged his wife, firm of purpose, as, late into the night, they went upstairs.

Ralph drove slowly home. The cat protested in its covered box on the back seat. Impervious to its complaints, he relived the long-short moments when Ursula was crushed against him. He tried not to think of the pleasure in her eyes when Martin returned, or of the evident happiness of their marriage. He tried not to think what they would be doing at this moment.

Somewhere on the road between Oxford and his cottage, Ralph resigned himself to the fact that he would never find another woman he would love as much as Ursula. As he could not bear the thought of a second-best wife, he also resigned himself to the idea that he must remain unmarried, and come to terms with his solitary life.

*   *   *

It was not often these days that Bill's thoughts turned to the part of his life that had been spent running the museum in Yorkshire. Although he had enjoyed those years, they had always been backed with the idea of this, a return to the country, in old age. Now he was here, doing what he wanted in happily unadventurous retirement, he wasted little time looking back.

But on a morning in early June, the morning he was at last to begin sawing the trunk of the balsam poplar, memories of the aimlessness of the place came back to him. His first duty every morning, long before the staff had arrived, had been to go round opening a window in every gallery in the hope that the smell of central heating and strong polish would evaporate by midday. It never did, but he enjoyed the various shafts of air that blew in to shake the deposits of the night. He liked the silence at this time, too: the feeling that he was the only human being in the building. He would pad round the glass cases checking the disparate collection: flintstones, old coins, fragments of pottery, arrowheads, scraps of leather shoes, a few undistinguished remnants of the Iron Age and so on. It was a mish-mash of a collection, really, but popular because it was local. Tourists and schoolchildren from neighbouring towns seemed to enjoy the thought that the stuff came from fields and ruins nearby, proving history had touched their own territory, and putting time into perspective.

One of Bill's innovations had been the collection of farm machinery. He was proud of the gallery in which early milk churns, ploughshares, and immensely heavy sets of harness had been displayed. On his early morning round it was always this gallery he left till last. Here, in the polished silence of every morning, he would allow himself the indulgence of imagining the plight of the farm labourers whose job it was to clean the tack or wipe down the vast scythes. He would pick up a pair of old wooden butter pats, engraved with four-leaf clovers, and try to imagine the thoughts of the raw-fingered milkmaid as she slapped gleaming pats into shape, and lined them up on the slate shelves in the buttery. Such imaginings often left him hopelessly stuck: what *would* a milkmaid be thinking, for heaven's sake? But on some mornings, touching objects of daily use from the past filled him with a curious sense of knowing what life must have been like, and he regretted having given up the idea of becoming a historian when he went into the Navy.

Bill's final stopping place, before the day's work in his office began, was the small room (once Domestic and Farming Accounts Books: fascinating) that he had reluctantly agreed must be given over to a coffee shop. There was no doubt that the postcards and refreshments attracted far more interest than the previous old books. School parties squeezed round the formica-topped tables with their cans of fizzy drinks and bags of crisps, and the turnover in postcards (particularly those in sepia) and plastic models of a nineteenth-century horse and plough (complete with brawny-armed plastic ploughman) was remarkable. Profits were high every week. Mrs Ludd, who ran the place, did very well on her twenty per cent of the takings, and was a wizard at keeping the rowdiest children in order.

Bill would sit alone at a pristine table of duck-egg blue speckled formica, plastic beaker of coffee from the machine in his hand (later, for elevenses, Mrs Ludd made him the real stuff) considering how his life in the museum was spent. He wondered what more he could do, on very limited funds, to be competitive with 'Stories of the Past' which was currently the big tourist attraction. He knew the time would come when the museum would have to succumb to modern marketing if it was to survive: and knew that he would go at that time. Waxworks and light shows, 'authentic' smells from aerosols, and headphones which provided history in the deadly voice of a coach-tour guide were not for him. One morning in the empty coffee shop, he remembered, he took up one of Mrs Ludd's paper napkins (bought in bulk from an economy range) and, inspired, wrote 'red felt'. It occurred to him that if the smaller artefacts were arranged on a bright red background, instead of their sand-coloured one, they might be more appealing. Bright colours were apparently what the public liked. But later in the day the idea waned. He was not so sure an investment in red felt would be an infallible solution. . . .

As Bill lowered his buzzing saw into the trunk of the balsam poplar, he was grateful that worries of that sort were over. By the time the first disc of wood (pale as a slice of lemon) lay on the grass, all thoughts of the museum had left him.

But at lunch, briefly, they returned.

'I was thinking,' he said to Mary, 'don't know why – about that time I thought red felt would be the solution to our problems. Remember?'

Mary laughed. She gave him a second helping of cauliflower cheese. He liked hot food even on a hot day.

'Course I do. It was one of your dafter plans.'

'Wonder what they've done to the old place.'

197

'Too awful to think about.'

'Too awful indeed.'

They both kept a moment's silence, trying not to imagine.

'Rhubarb pie,' said Mary eventually, going to the Aga.

'Rhubarb pie? Darling girl. You spoil me. Listen: come and join me before tea. I want to impress you with the logs. I worked full speed ahead this morning. Quite a pile.'

'Right. I'd love to come.'

Eager to return to his work, Bill refused a second cup of coffee. He stood and hugged his wife – a daily ritual after lunch, though not after breakfast.

When Mary stood back from him she saw that several pieces of stuff from her pink cardigan clung like burrs to the coarse Arran wool of his jersey.

'I'm coming off on you,' she said, picking them from his chest.

Bill smiled, and asked how she was going to spend her afternoon.

'It's too hot to weed,' she said. 'Read my book, I think, in the shade. Might even fall asleep.'

'Good idea. You go to sleep, then come and fetch me.'

Bill strode away then, the picture of his wife's sweet face as bright in his mind as the real thing. He thought – as he had thought a million times in their long life together – how he regretted being unable to release her from the chaff of anxieties that almost drowned her at times: he had never been able to find the right words to tell her he understood her plight. And how, also, in their mutual silence, he shared her suffering. He could only hope that she instinctively knew of his helpless sympathy, for to say anything now would be to risk intrusion and destruction. He liked to think the silence on such matters was a mutual acknowledgement, one which they would keep for the rest of their lives.

As Bill crossed the field, he plucked another piece of pink wool from his jersey and flicked it from his fingers. It sailed down to the ground hesitant as swansdown. Then he pulled off his jersey and threw it, from afar, to the trunk of the tree.

He was pleased to see it land in exactly the place he had aimed for – the schoolboy in me, he thought. He often aimed for pointless targets: pebble to a distant wave, stick (for Trust) to a particular place on the lawn.

Bill chose the thickest part of the trunk to begin working. He reckoned he could get through a yard or so by teatime. Mary would be proud of him.

He picked up the saw, switched it on. By now he had grown accustomed to its whine, sympathetic to its extra straining when the wood was particularly hard. The sun was hot on his shoulders, the smell of the few remaining balsam leaves very powerful in the heat. Bill wished he did not have to bend over so far to saw, but there was no way he could raise the trunk. It would be a back-breaking job, but not beyond him.

Before he positioned himself to make the first incision, Bill looked up to see a skylark quivering in the sky of untrammelled blue. He could not hear its song for the noise of the saw, but wondered how he must look, from up there, to the bird: old man sawing a fallen tree.

He leaned forward, felt the thrust of voracious blade against bark. Then, an almighty pain in his chest. Sweet-smelling grass, tall as a forest about him, tickled his face, and his cry, against the saw, went unheard.

Mary woke slowly from a dreamless sleep. The points of light through the straw brim of her hat, pulled down over her eyes, were no longer dazzling, indicating the lateness of the afternoon. She threw the hat off on to the ground. It lay beside *Love in the Time of Cholera*, which she had been reading before she fell asleep. Its pink ribbons undulated on the grass in a slight breeze.

The sun had lowered. Mary sat up, chilled. She pulled her pink cardigan round her shoulders and looked at her watch. Shocked, she saw it was just after five. She had slept, most unusually, for two hours, and was late for Bill. He must be wondering where she was, why she hadn't come as promised. A small wing of anxiety fluttering within her: he should not work so long in the heat of the afternoon. On the other hand, he was strong, he was fit, and he was enjoying the job on the tree so much that she feared there would be a sense of anti-climax when it was finally completed.

Mary hurried to the end of the garden and through the gate that led to the field. As she shut the gate – mossy wood beneath her hand, next job for Bill, perhaps – a swarm of Red Admiral butterflies dazzled out from the buddleia tree. She watched them till they were too high to see, small flames snuffed out like daytime fireworks, and wished Bill had been there to see them too. The buddleia was the first tree they had planted, to ensure the garden was always host to butterflies.

Once in the field, she could hear the saw, a minuscule whine drilling the silence. She would have found its buzzing all day an annoyance, but Bill did not seem to mind. Mary turned the corner and saw the various piles of logs, and Bill slumped bridge-like over the trunk of the tree, face down. She ran.

At first, she thought he was alive but unconscious. His shoulders, as she tried to pull him up, were very warm from the sun. But he was a deadweight. She could not move him. She tried to push her hand under his heart, but his chest was clamped to the tree, blocking her frantic fingers. She shouted his name over and over again, longing for silence, but the saw kept up its perpetual buzz and she did not know how to turn it off. As if from afar, she saw her own actions contained in a small crystal of immeasurable time – time that is judged by some as the conscious present. The last action, there by the tree, aflutter with hope, was to look at Bill's face. To do this, she had to kneel and part the soft long grass which obscured his profile. Then she saw that it was he who had died first.

An hour later, Mr Yacksley, in gardening clothes and carrying an axe, saw Mrs Lutchins wave at him from the kitchen window. Something odd in the stiffness of her gesture, he thought. A moment later he was close enough to see the shocked white of her face, the fallen arch of her mouth.

'Bill's dead,' she said.

'God in heaven. Where?'

'Tree.'

'And I was coming up to lend a hand.'

'Doctor's on his way. Ambulance, I suppose.'

'I'll stay with you. You ought to sit down, Mrs Lutchins.'

'I'm all right. But please go and be with him.'

Mr Yacksley took in the dullness smeared across her pretty eyes.

'Very well,' he said.

He propped up his axe and set out for the field. On his reluctant journey it occurred to him he now had a real job on his hands: finishing the tree and carting the wood to the house for the winter. It was the last thing he could do for his old friend. He had no doubt that what would please Bill Lutchins best, looking down from his place in heaven, would be to see another old man sawing the tree, so there would still be logs for the winter.

*　　*　　*

The funeral, a week later, was on a fine day. 'Ruddy blue sky,' as Mr Yacksley said to his wife that morning. She was not able to come with him, her arthritis had taken force over the last few weeks, making her almost immobile. But quite a gathering of parishioners and local friends turned up, and Mr Yacksley was able to report that floral tributes, some very grand, banked the entire length of the path to the church.

He and Mrs Lutchins – who to date had comported herself with amazing calm – worked hard on arranging the kind of funeral service Mr Lutchins would have liked best. They quashed all the vicar's suggestions for modern alternatives, and insisted there should be no sermon: Mr Lutchins had always ridiculed the vicar's mundane attempts at preaching. The vicar's revenge was a deprived look on his way up the aisle. He read the magnificent old prayers in a pinched voice more suitable for a council agenda. But then he had never been a man who knew how to cope with fine words, and most of the

201

congregation knew that he must be thinking how much easier life would be now that Mr Lutchins had gone to his rest.

Mrs Lutchins was very upright between her daughter and son-in-law, and did not shed a visible tear.

Now, in the graveyard, uncomfortably hot after the stone-cool of the church, friends and relations gathered round the newly dug hole in the ground into which an oak coffin had just been lowered. Mr Yacksley found himself between the two grandchildren. The young lad, in grey flannel trousers and a navy school blazer, tugged the postman's sleeve.

'Never knew Grandpa was so long, lying down,' he said.

'It can give you a turn, that's right,' Mr Yacksley whispered back. The little girl, on his right, was restless, shifting her weight from foot to foot. 'Not long,' he assured her.

'Hope not. I've left my puppy in the car and she'll be lonely. She's a Cavalier King Charles spaniel,' she added, and a sudden tear sped down her cheek. Whether caused by the thought of her imprisoned puppy, or her grandfather, Mr Yacksley could not be sure.

There was a strong smell of the sea. Also, the smells of warm daisied earth, and chemical gardenia. This last came, overpoweringly, from Rosie Cotterman. She, Ursula realised, glancing at her across the grave, was enjoying the part of mourner. She was dressed in a black velvet coat with a matching black velvet meringue of a hat, more suitable for a State funeral at St Paul's Cathedral than this simple village affair. Always something of an actress – Ursula had heard she had had a short, undistinguished career on the stage before she turned to painting – she was now taking centre-stage as the strong friend and neighbour, mouth turned down but beautiful eyes quite dry. But perhaps that's mean, Ursula then thought – perhaps I'm just clinging to any old thought that will blot out the picture of Father turned into an effigy in the coffin –

'Derst to derst,' intoned the vicar, and she winced.

Martin, feeling her anger and knowing its cause, took her arm. He looked across the grave at the children, and was proud of them. They had insisted on coming – providing she could bring the puppy, Sarah had said– and perhaps it was no bad thing to witness the mechanics of death when young. There had been copious tears at the news of their grandfather's death, but spirits had soon been resumed. Now, Martin could tell, Sarah's slight wriggling was due to some anxiety about her dog, while Ben's fidgeting among sweets in his pocket indicated he was eager to get back to the house for tea. As for the old postman, gravely handsome in Sunday suit and black tie, he displayed all the discipline of an old soldier. He stood very upright, war medals twinkling on his jacket, clenched knuckles by his sides. A small tic in his cheek indicated the measure of control he was presently keeping, while a peak of white handkerchief pointing from his pocket showed the wisdom of precaution. Curiously, it was the sight of Mr Yacksley's dignity, rather than the unbelievable view of the coffin, that brought tears to Martin's own eyes.

Mary Lutchins saw none of these things. In a whorl of calm, eyes fixed on the ugly coffin, she could only think of the strangeness of Bill dying first. This, within moments of finding him, had given her great strength, which had not left her. She knew it never would. For the rest of her life she would be relieved of the worry that had tormented her for so many years. In the future she saw lightness, as well as the dark of loss – relief within her grieving.

She was glad it was such a fine, warm day. Bill would have liked that. He would have enjoyed Rosie Cotterman's dramatic funeral clothes, and been infuriated as always by the vicar's unfortunate pronunciation. But . . . silly, pointless thoughts. For the moment she must concentrate on the prayers, trying to blot out the voice: then she would allow herself to wonder if she had made enough cucumber sandwiches. (Oh, the luxury of such small worries.) Eighty mourners were invited back to the house for tea.

'Lord have mercy upon us,' simpered the vicar, pushing back the sleeve of his cassock for a surreptitious glance at his watch.

'Christ have mercy upon us,' Mary answered, with the rest, in a voice firm and strong.

*　　*　　*

When ten days had gone by and still Thomas received no reply to his postcard to Rosie Cotterman, his agitation became almost beyond control. He saw the summer stretching ahead, Rosie-less, and felt near panic. There were plans for the annual family holiday: an expensive villa in Portugal with the children and their impossible friends. Helen threatened to bring her new boyfriend from Durham, apparently 'into social sciences'. Last year, in Porto Ercole, she and her jazz drummer, when they weren't complaining about the expensive heat, spent the day by the pool communicating in coded grunts about Milton – whom they were both into. This time-consuming occupation meant they were unable to be of any help to Rachel. She, uncomplaining, worked so hard that on return to England the doctor declared her suffering from exhaustion. Jeremy, as usual, had grumbled daily about the lack of beer, and kept his own inconvenient hours – up mid-afternoon, bed at dawn, so they saw little of him. This year, he announced he was bringing a girl called Aida, about whom Thomas knew nothing but could imagine all too well.

He dreaded the three weeks in Portugal profoundly. The thought of being physically so far away from Rosie, and having no notion of her feelings, was making him ill. He felt a dull sickness all the time, and ate little. To keep himself going he returned to his old habit of drinking at lunchtime and consuming a whole bottle of wine every evening.

Pride, he supposed it was, kept him from writing a second postcard, or telephoning Rosie. He was determined to stick to his intention of acting slowly this time: none of the disastrous haste of the past. Ravaged by the canker of impatience, he suffered for ten days. Then he could endure no more. He decided simply to go to her, surprise her.

His second journey brought him peace mixed with excited

anticipation. Whatever happened, he would buy more pictures, and have a few hours in Rosie's company. Gently, he would make some suggestion for the future that might appeal to her: a trip to Aldeburgh, perhaps, in the autumn – nothing that would alarm her, but something that would furnish him with an event to look forward to while suffering in Portugal. Above all, he ached for time with her.

Thomas had dressed more suitably this time. In open-necked shirt and corduroy trousers, he was warm and comfortable in the Mercedes, zooming along the motorway in the enclosed capsule of his thoughts. Dismay was caused only when he glanced down at his stomach. He kept his eyes on the road.

He arrived, as before, at about noon. He let himself in and found the place empty. Nothing had changed. The confusion of objects and paints and pictures was wonderfully familiar – again, the sensation of being home, in the place he was born to be, was almost overwhelming. More boldly this time, he picked his way through the furniture to the window, and stood looking out at the unblemished sky and expanses of feather-headed reeds of the marsh. Any moment, he imagined, she would come pottering down the path in her yellowhammer oilskin, see him, and look surprised and pleased again. But half-an-hour went by and there was no sign of her. Perhaps she had taken sandwiches for lunch, Thomas thought with regret. He would have to wait until the light began to fail. Ah well, no matter. Surrounded by her things, he was happy to wait for her all day.

He began to examine new pictures, some pinned carelessly to the wall, a stack of them piled on the table. One in particular he knew he must have – he would pay any price for it: the merest swoop of pale colour indicated the beach, while a single curve of deliquescent blue made the sky. Just sea and sky: no distant figure, no promontory, nor ship nor dune to disturb the awe of emptiness. Rosie Cotterman understands, he thought, the essence of aloneness.

Thomas returned the picture to the pile and felt the kind of shiver down his spine that precedes a major decision. And then

205

it came to him. He, Thomas Arkwright, Sunday painter of no talent, would never try again.

The pleasure of trying, or aspiring, was a thin pleasure without the aid of talent. His own attempts were pathetic, always had been. Dry, frizzled, pernickety, spiritless things. What had he been doing, frustrating himself all these years, wasting his time? His motive, of course, had been escape. But while hours in his studio had afforded him one kind of escape, it had also produced another kind of prison – his own limitations. There is no escape from those.

Such truths, sweeping relentlessly upon the confused Thomas that fine Norfolk morning, caused him a profound sense of melancholy. The happiness of only moments ago, anticipating Rosie's arrival, seemed to have drained away. His private decision, of no interest to anyone else on earth, left him feeling physically clumsy, cold. He sat heavily in the largest chair, and listened to the silence.

After a while, he picked up the bottle of red wine from the table and studied its impressive label. He had been waiting almost two hours, now, and needed a drink. Rosie, he felt sure, would not mind if he helped himself. He filled Rosie's unwashed glass with the dark wine. He sniffed, swished, sipped appreciatively. But he was hungry, too. Almost faint. The fridge, he found, was empty but for a small corner of wizened Camembert on a saucer. This he nibbled slowly, alternating the nasty taste with swigs of the wine. After a second glass – the bottle was almost empty now, he made a mental note to replace it – the familiar strands of indigestion began to lace through his chest. Thomas groaned out loud, tipped back his head and shut his eyes. Soon he fell asleep.

He was woken mid-afternoon by the noise of the front door. Confused, he saw the glass of wine in his hand and was aware of the pungency of his own sweat. He quickly returned the glass to its place, and turned. A woman in black stood looking at him.

For a moment, dazed, Thomas felt he was in the presence of an Edwardian ghost. The figure wore a droopy sort of coat, and a large, squashy velvet hat on whose brim meagre ostrich feathers lay exhausted. Then she smiled with one side of her mouth, and he knew it was no phantom.

'Mr Arkwright?'

'Thomas.'

'Thomas, to be sure. I wasn't expecting you, was I?'

'No, I just came, I'm afraid.'

'Ah. People do turn up here out of the blue. It's how things are, I've noticed.'

'I hope you don't mind –'

'Not at all, not at all. It's good you're here.'

'I was impatient to buy more pictures.'

'Were you, indeed?' She took off the hat, punched its mushy crown. 'I've just been to a funeral. Bill Lutchins. Old friend. Very old friend, as a matter of fact. We danced together.' She paused to undo the huge mother-of-pearl buttons of the coat. 'But he loved Mary more, and married her.'

'Ah. I'm so sorry.'

'Mary was the woman you met on the beach.'

'I remember.'

'Fascinated by the buyer from London, she was. Poor Mary.'

Thomas took the coat and laid it on a chair. He now saw that the top layer of clothes only had been in deference to the funeral. The coat had concealed an old blue T-shirt and black jeans.

'I should have let you know I was coming,' he said. 'But it was a sudden decision.'

'Never mind about that. Now, shall we be opening a bottle of wine?'

'Why not?' Thomas's head was still unclear. Another drink might help. 'Did you get my postcard?'

'Your card? Why, I believe I did. I'm not much of a writer, myself.'

The thought of a one-sided correspondence with the woman he loved added a brick of gloom to the melancholy structure within him.

'But you didn't mind my writing?' he asked.

207

'Of course not! I like to hear from friends. You could write again, perhaps.'

In that case, thought Thomas, Portugal might be bearable after all.

He bought the picture he particularly wanted, and two others besides – and stayed for just over an hour. Rosie was friendly, sympathetic, warm, but distracted. Thomas assumed she was affected by the death of her friend. He cursed himself for having come on this of all days, and decided that, if he was to act with the unselfishness of true love, then he must leave her shortly. He had no wish to intrude on her grief.

'Mary organised funeral meats,' Rosie was saying, 'but I couldn't bear to go. I'm no good at parties. I'm not one for funeral wakes. I like to be alone when someone dies.'

Thomas stood up. 'I'm on my way,' he said. 'I'm so sorry today was . . .'

'Oh, think nothing of it.' Rosie's face, swept with relief, seemed to be dusted with invisible gold. Thomas dared not kiss her on the cheek for fear the touch would cause a conflagration he could not control. 'Come again, and buy some more. How can I refuse so good a client?'

She laughed. Thomas tried to smile. Client to Rosie Cotterman, then, was his position so far: by winter things would have changed. One way or another, he would make sure of that.

They shook hands. Thomas drove away. He told himself he had made some progress, but there was no conviction. The heaviness of waiting once again – how long, this time? – came upon him, and he fell to wondering about her friend who had died. What had they been to each other, she and this Bill Lutchins, in their youth? And how far had they danced?

*   *   *

Rachel woke slowly from a glorious afternoon's sleep. The margins of sun round the drawn curtains told her it was late afternoon, and she did not care. Usually she was up by

208

four-thirty, sitting at the kitchen table with a mug of pepper-mint tea and her book. But since the dinner in Oxford her energy had flagged, somehow. Her afternoons in bed, mostly asleep, had lengthened.

As the disappointment of that evening – a deeply private thing – began to wane, the humour of it appealed more strongly to Rachel. Sometimes, in bed, she found herself smiling at the absurdity of the whole catastrophe. Signalling her availability – the vanity of the idea! Still, she had learned sharply and quickly. There would be no more signals. No more humiliating availability. A return to the containing of self. Easier, that. It brought small rewards, sometimes. Nothing to do with men, or sex, or passion, but happinesses that, in love, are clouded by exhilaration. Out of love, they become more clear. They compensate. Rachel recognised this, and was grateful.

Her thoughts were broken by the bang of the front door: Thomas. What was he doing? Rachel realised she had no time to dress and make the bed before he came looking for her. She dreaded his finding her, and his disapprobation. She heard him hurry up the stairs, past the door, and on up to the studio. (Relief.) Bang of another door. Then, impatient steps, a curious crashing and thumping. What was going on?

Rachel took her chance. She quickly dressed, drew back the curtains, straightened the bed. Then she just stood, listening to her husband's puzzling antics overhead.

When at last she heard him on the stairs again she opened the bedroom door. Thomas was making his way down, slowly, hampered by a huge cardboard box.

'What are you doing?' she asked.

'Throwing away the painting things,' he said.

In the moment that he paused to answer, head peering round the box, Rachel saw a desperate tiredness in his eyes. Sweat poured from his temples. She had never seen him look so sad.

'I'll get you a drink,' she said.

The relief that he had not discovered her in bed turned easily to benevolence. She poured him a large glass of malt whisky and waited for him to join her in the kitchen after his journeys up and down to the studio. She would keep her silence, Rachel decided, and Thomas, goaded by her lack of curiosity, might explain.

She took great care preparing dinner, and noticed that Thomas, though obviously hungry, ate little. He told her briefly about his day in Norfolk, and his purchase of more pictures. But he made no further mention of his strange earlier statement about his painting things, and Rachel, knowing her husband, deemed it wise still not to ask.

At breakfast next day, Thomas observed another Bonnard morning: backlit wife in grubby bathrobe, half-dead Mermaid roses slumped over vase. Again, the butter hurt his eyes and the newsprint, even with his glasses, was unclear. He had had another restless night and risen at dawn to pace his studio. There, he had made another decision, almost as momentous as the one yesterday. Now he was exhausted by decisions, but kept his faith in strong coffee. When he had finished the third cup, he put down his paper and looked Rachel in the eye.

'I've been thinking: perhaps we should go our separate ways,' he said.

He saw the slight lift of his wife's shoulders as she sighed. There was a moment's silence.

'I've no separate way to go,' said Rachel.

It was Thomas's turn to pause. Her unexpected answer relieved him of explanations.

'Very well, then,' he heard himself reply. 'It was just an idea.'

He picked up the paper, folded it untidily as always, and left the room.

The idea of a separation scarcely touched Rachel before it vanished from her mind. She thought only how tired Thomas looked, how unusually grim. Thank God the holiday in Portugal was only a few weeks off. For her part she dreaded it, but knew how the children, for all their perversity, seemed to inspire Thomas with a certain joviality when they were abroad. He needed the sun: he worked too hard, all the dashing up

210

and down to Nottingham, and now Norfolk seemed to be becoming a regular visiting place. Ridiculous.

Rachel continued to sit at the table. Her thoughts turned to the day ahead. Nothing much to do. Perhaps she would take Thomas's dinner jacket to the cleaners. The Farthingoes' ball wasn't that far away – the Farthingoes' ball where she would be quite, quite unavailable, and give not the smallest signal.

Smiling to herself, Rachel then thought of the luxury to follow. After her mission to the cleaners, she would shut herself in her room, draw the curtains, burrow into the cool darkness of linen sheets, and sleep away the afternoon.

PART TWO
THE
PARTY

ON AN evening in September, Toby Farthingoe walked in the garden clutching at his last hours of peace. In the sky above swifts gathered in ponderous flight, wondering when to leave. The shadows of the cedars, he fancied, were a little deeper than a week ago, and some of the roses had scattered their petals on the ground. Intimations of autumn were visible. It was the time of year he most loved, and he wished he could have the first few days of tentative change to himself. Instead, they were to be blasted by the party.

Tomorrow at dawn lorries would begin to arrive, and for the next two days havoc was expected. Toby knew Frances's elaborate plans – he had avoided hearing too much detail – meant elaborate preparations. She had warned him there would be a certain amount of men 'doing things'. 'And to be honest,' she had added, 'a certain amount of upheaval.' Toby dreaded the very thought of this upheaval, longed for it all to be over. Why, he wondered for the hundredth time, had he ever agreed to pay out a fortune to entertain three hundred middle-aged guests, only half a dozen of whom were real friends? The answer, he supposed, had been to furnish Frances with an occupation for the summer – to keep her happy so that he could concentrate with an easier heart on his computers and badgers. Never again would he agree to such folly. His indulgence, he realised, had been inspired by self-protection rather

215

than love. Not only was it a high price to pay for a quiet summer, but, in the present economic climate, an extravagant party was morally suspect. To be host to such profligacy was embarrassing. In future, Frances would have to devote her energies to more worthwhile and less expensive projects. She was constantly in need of activities to fulfil her days, and each of her whims had cost him a great deal of money. He would be a richer man, he reflected with a grim little smile, if she were to take a lover.

That thought, it struck Toby this evening, caused him no jealousy. How curious! How very curious. Here he was, actually contemplating the idea of his wife taking a lover, and feeling no jealousy. Instead, he was suffused with a certain longing for that to happen. A well-mannered lover (who knew his place, of course) would free him of his obligations concerning Frances's tedious chatter, her well-meant but silly observations. A lover who took over the part of Frances's life that held no interest to Toby would be of great service. Funny he had not thought of it before. For his own part, it was inconceivable that he should desire another woman – look for one, or find one. Work was his lover. Apart from work, he needed nothing except the comfort of his dark house, the privacy of the garden and woods and – the new thought – someone to satisfy Frances in a way he found impossible.

Toby sat on a garden bench. The party, he now realised, held real promise. The guests must surely include some suitable man. . . . Warm with the thought, he tipped back his head to watch the swifts again as their curves scythed gently across the sky.

Frances stood in Fiona's room, arms crossed, trying to control her increasing irritation. She had enough on her mind without the ungrateful child kicking up a ridiculous fuss at the last moment. Fiona sat on the bed, arms crossed also, staring sulkily at the floor. A plain child, Frances thought, guilty at the meanness of the admission. A heavier version of Toby's face. Absolutely nothing of her own. The outline might fine down in a few years, but nothing would ever improve the closeness of her eyes.

'Fiona: I took a great deal of trouble to find you the right dress,' she said – the third time she had made this observation in a variety of ways.

'You shouldn't have bothered.'

'I tell you, it's lovely.'

'Well, I'm not going to wear it, so there. It's babyish.'

'Don't be so ridiculous.' Frances patted the bunchy skirt: graded frills of spotted organza. 'It's the sort of thing Spanish gypsies wear. Grown-up Spanish gypsies.'

'Well, I'm not a Spanish gypsy, am I? I'll just look a real prat.'

'You won't.'

'I will.'

'You won't. And, anyway, I'm not going to argue with you any more. I've a million more important things to do –'

'I might have known getting me something decent to wear wouldn't be on that list –'

'Fiona! You're behaving like a monstrous, spoilt child. That dress cost a fortune. It's very pretty, and there's no time to get anything else. So you either stop grumbling and wear it, or don't come to the party.'

There was a long silence. Fiona continued to look at the floor. Finally she shrugged.

'I don't care if I don't come to your stupid old party. And, anyhow, even if I did, what would I do? Who would I talk to? Everyone will be about a hundred.'

What her daughter would actually *do* at the party was not a problem, Frances had to admit, to which she had given much attention. She had some vague picture in mind of the child wandering about with plates of mini-éclairs, being polite to godparents.

'Darling: how do I know what you'd do? You'd know lots of people. One or two might dance with you –'

'Very funny.'

217

'Well, I mean, it might not be that much fun for you. But it was your decision to come, and I think it'd be an experience worth not missing. Just seeing it all.'

Frances glanced at her watch. She had to ring the caterers before dinner, and check that Luigi had bought enough cloak-room tickets.

'Huh.'

'Well, it's up to you. But Papa and I will be sad if you don't come. We'd like you to be there.'

Fiona looked up. 'You won't have a single moment for me. You should have let me ask a friend. May I ask a friend?'

'For heaven's sake: it's a bit late to arrange anything now. I haven't time to start ringing round –'

'Don't worry. I'll ring Jess.'

'Jess lives fifty miles away, you idiot.' Frances's voice was rising, her exasperation almost beyond control. 'If you think I've got time to start worrying about how Jess gets here –'

'I'll ring her.'

'You won't! I forbid you to ring her. Besides, I need the telephone non-stop.'

'Oh, go away, Mum, and get on with your telephoning. Leave me alone.' Fiona's voice had risen, too. She was on the verge of tears. Her glasses were steamed up.

'Right! Sometimes you're the most inconsiderate child I ever –'

Frances, shouting, left the room, slamming the door behind her.

She hurried away, not wanting to hear the chord of tears. Up until half-an-hour ago she had been excited, in control, happy knowing that all her plans, her work of months, were about to crystallise beautifully. . . . Now she was inflicted with the irritation of a spoilt child. Toby would have to deal with her.

Frances snapped open a window. Toby was at the far end of the garden, slumped on a bench, back to her, head in the air, probably asleep. She shouted at him. He did not stir, probably could not hear. Further annoyed, and time running out, Frances stomped across the grass to wake him. He was always good with Fiona, patient. He could bloody well hurry up to her room, and make her see sense before dinner. It would be one of his practical contributions to the party.

*　　*　　*

Despite the warmth of the evening, Mary Lutchins had lit a fire. The balsam logs – Jack Yacksley had finished sawing and had carted them to the shed – burned merrily, and she looked forward to another conversation, from the comfort of her chair, with Rosie Cotterman. Rosie had promised many times to come to the party with her: they had made elaborate plans for the journey, and Mary believed Rosie would not let her down. But you could never be sure: Rosie sometimes suffered radical changes of mind, and many an arrangement had been known to collapse. Before going to bed tonight, Mary wanted to reassure herself: if Rosie refused to come there would have to be hurried new plans. Mary did not want to drive all that way alone.

'Rosie?'

'Mary, my darling.'

'I was just ringing to make sure.'

'What about?'

'The party. Your coming. I just wanted to make sure you're not changing your mind at the last moment.'

'What an idea! Of course I'm not.'

'Good. I'll pick you up at eleven, then, as arranged.'

'Wonderful. Ralph's just rung. Seemed doubtful of me as you, the silly man.' She laughed. 'We'll have fun, the journey together. Two old things.'

'Two old things, indeed,' said Mary gaily. 'I'm going to bring a wonderful picnic.'

'Now, there is a change of plan, I think. We won't have a picnic, it occurred to me. We'll stop at some delicious road-

219

house, have a good bottle of wine for our lunch, then potter along slowly.'

'I'm not sure there are many such places between Norfolk and Oxford,' answered Mary, as she had done several times before. The tussle of picnic versus 'roadhouse' had been going on for days.

'And we'll arrive at Ralphie's in time for tea. I've told him to get in scones and Lapsang. He's such a vague house-keeper – needs a wife. After that, you can be going off in your own time to the children. All lovely plans, don't you think?'

The lovely plans had been gone over so many times that repetition was causing them to sag, thought Mary. But she was reluctant to let Rosie go. She could hear a barn owl outside. Trust growled, half asleep. She still did not like going up to bed alone.

'Another thing, Rosie,' she said. 'I've been meaning to ask: what are you going to wear?'

There was a long silence.

'To be honest,' said Rosie at last, 'I hadn't given the matter a moment's thought. But I do believe I still have my old pansies in the back of the cupboard.'

'Pansies?'

'You'll see. Exquisite they were, once. Thank you for re-minding me. Ralphie would've been furious if I turned up with nothing to wear. "You're so hopeless, Mother," he says, when I forget the sort of things he minds about.'

Both women laughed. They wished each other goodnight. Mary, curled up in the chair, returned to listening to the barn owl, and the twitching of the fire. She knew Rosie was coming to the ball only for her sake, and was grateful. Mary would have gone anyhow, to please Bill ('Death needn't change old plans and habits') but with less enthusiasm. As it was, she was quite looking forward to it: Martin and Ralph would give her a polite whirl round the floor no doubt, and she had always enjoyed the role of spectator. It would be odd not to have Bill by her side, but people were kind to new widows. She would find herself a corner, pull her shawl round her shoulders – mustn't forget her shawl. . . .

Mary fell asleep in the chair.

*   *   *

At breakfast Thomas told Rachel of his plan to be away for the night: late meetings in Nottingham, early meetings the following morning. No point in coming back.

In truth, he had decided he could bear Rosie's curious silence no longer. He had sent her a light and witty postcard every other day from Portugal (acts which required devious planning but were necessary to his sanity) and was finally demolished by her complete lack of response. His plan was to ring her at lunchtime today, when she returned from painting, and to propose a visit in the afternoon. He would book into a nearby hotel as a precaution, but had an instinctive feeling there would be no need to use it.

'As long as you're back in time for us to leave for the Farthingoes.'

'Goddammit! Their bloody ball. I'd forgotten all about it. I'll be back by seven, I promise.' In which case there would be but one evening and one whole morning with Rosie. 'Are the children coming with us?'

'I don't know yet.'

'What do you mean, you don't know yet?'

'I'm not sure they've made up their minds. Helen says she thinks she'll come. Frances said it was fine to bring Jasper. Jeremy said it was unlikely he'd show up.'

'Bloody marvellous!' Thomas slammed down his paper. 'The manners of my children are deplorable, do you realise? Why didn't you force them into some decision, get them to write, get them to commit themselves one way or another like any civilised person invited to a party?'

'Thomas, please. They're grown-up. I can't dictate to them.'

'You could have brought them up to have better manners.'

'Do stop shouting. You could have shared the responsibility.'

221

Thomas stood up, banging and crumpling the paper as if he was preparing to light a fire.

'I can tell you this: if they condescend to come, and are wanting us to give them a lift, I shall tell them in no uncertain terms what I think of their appalling rudeness –'

'That should make for a very merry journey.'

Rachel reached across the table for the mess of paper and patiently began to smooth it out. Thomas barged out of the room, sweating heavily.

In a small show of contrition, he made a great effort to shout goodbye from the front door in a normal, friendly voice. Rachel, reading the crumpled paper at the table, did not bother to reply.

*　　*　　*

The marquee men arrived first. Frances heard the clatter of their poles on the drive soon after seven. She looked out of the bedroom window to see them carrying huge slabs of neatly folded canvas across the lawn. She was impatient for the tent to be up, to see the hundreds of yards of grey and white stuff she had triumphantly procured in place. Toby was asleep, unaware of the excitements. She shouted to him to come and look. His response was to burrow further down the bed, pulling the sheets well over his ears. For a moment, Frances looked sadly at the impervious huddle. She was almost, but not quite, used to surviving his lack of enthusiasm.

At breakfast, she consulted her list of prospective arrival times. Today, the marquee, the floor, the bandstand and filigree partitions (designed by her, made by the local carpenter) were all to be established, and the electricians had promised to be through by the evening. Frances had ordered an extravagance of lights both for the marquee and the garden: hundreds of minuscule bulbs would trail through trees and over hedges outside, and round pillars inside. Her idea was that it would look as if the place had been invaded by a million fireflies. Bloody nightmare to organise, the electrician had warned her,

222

but not impossible, and yes, he wouldn't mind the challenge. Apart from checking that everything was put in the right place, and organising a constant supply of tea for the workmen, Frances realised there was little else she could do today. Tomorrow, with the arrival of the flowers, food and drink, tables and chairs, she could be of more practical help.

By mid-morning, the roof of the marquee was up. Frances wandered beneath it, looking up at its high, unadorned spine. In her impatience, she thought: how slow is transformation. It then occurred to her she was being unreasonable – the men were working very fast, the marquee had become a reality with astonishing speed. She stood among them, listening to their shorthand instructions, their sarcastic exchanges, their blunt humour. She felt like a producer, a designer, excited by the thought that these skilled men were now executing what had been in her imagination for so long. It then occurred to her that perhaps production of some kind was what she would enjoy as a job. When this party was over, there was an empty autumn ahead – she had been thinking for some time that she would like a regular job. Television, perhaps? The theatre? A wheel of ideas now began to spin. She could feel it gathering pace. . . . Well, she had friends in the kind of world she would like to work in. Next week she would begin to make enquiries. She had no qualifications, of course, but that did not always matter. Ideas were what were needed. And she had ideas. Dozens of ideas. A job! That would be something to look forward to, give cohesion to her life.

Frances walked out into the garden, possible long-term prospects adding to her excitement. A butterfly flew across her path, weighted by the dull air. Omen, she thought, and frowned at the sallow clouds. She had not let herself think of rain. For months, in her mind's eye, guests had filtered about the garden on a warm, clear night, cloudless moon shining down upon them. Now, a small note of worry struck within her: the entire plan would be ruined if it were to rain.

Toby and Fiona were playing croquet on the far lawn. Toby was stooped over the mallet, eye seriously concentrated on a red ball. Frances waited impatiently for the click. It came eventually: the ball shot along the grass, just missing the hoop.

'Blast.' Toby straightened, rubbing his back.

'It's not going to rain, is it?' Frances asked.

'Shouldn't think so.' He didn't seem much interested in the possibility. 'Come on, Fi. Take your time lining up the shot.'

The ungainly Fiona stooped over the mallet in imitation of her father.

'I think it'd be quite funny if it rained and everybody got wet,' she said, head down so that Frances could not see her face.

Frances turned and left them. On her way back to the house she was met by a frantic Luigi. His rolled-up shirtsleeves revealed huge biceps and thickly haired arms, always concealed until this moment by his neat striped jacket.

'Madam come quickly please: a lorry has arrived full of trees.'

The two dozen bay trees, each one carefully selected by Frances at a tree centre, had been ordered to arrive tomorrow morning. But premature bay trees were just the sort of problem Frances needed – anything to take her mind off the inspirational new idea that was making her restless.

She ran ahead of the panting Luigi. In her speed, further inspiration descended. She knew what she must do – the first, the most sensible move to make in quest of her job, was to ask Ant's advice. Ant, to date, had been her greatest ally over the party.

*   *   *

I'm going to pieces, thought Thomas, on his drive to the office. If I don't see Rosie soon, I may finally tip over the edge.

His hands shook on the steering wheel, sweat made huge melon-shaped slices under the arms of his fresh shirt, and the bones of his temples battered against skin that felt bruised. The physical discomforts of impatience, he had discovered, are as odious as those of jealousy, and he could not bear them any longer. He had been a model of reticence for so many weeks. Friendly postcards were hardly the stuff of bullying – but, no more. He now had a simple choice before him: action or madness.

Once in the office – coffee and the air-conditioning slightly restored his equilibrium – he did not wait for midday, but dialled Rosie's number at once. He let the telephone ring for a long time but there was no answer. Right: he'd be on his way. No point hanging about. He was incapable of work in this agitated state of mind.

The almost empty motorway was soothing. As the mental and physical torments of the morning began to recede, the slow, inward burn of anticipation took their place. Soon after passing Newmarket, Thomas realised he was hungry. He decided to stop at the next decent-looking eating place, have a sandwich and ring Rosie once more.

He found a pseudo-Tudor hostelry at the edge of a minor roundabout. He parked, was briefly oppressed by the humidity of the air as he crossed to the entrance. With a steady hand he dialled Rosie's number, but again there was no reply. No matter, he told himself over a gin and tonic and a tuna sandwich: she would definitely be back for tea, when the light had changed. He would surprise her once more, thrust the carefully chosen bottle of claret into her hand, and suggest taking her to dinner in Wells-on-Sea. (Highly recommended restaurant, table already booked.) Happily imagining the scene, he was back in the Mercedes within half-an-hour.

As Thomas waited at the exit of the carpark to move into the road, he watched a small brown car nosing hesitantly past him. It paused at the entrance to the carpark, then continued jumpily on its way, a van hooting behind it. In the moment that it passed before Thomas's bonnet, he saw that the driver was an old lady with white hair and vaguely familiar face. The passenger was Rosie.

Heart thrashing within him, Thomas remained where he was, eyes on the car as it edged its way round the central circle of grass once more. Then it cut rashly across the path of a lorry to enter the carpark. Again, for a moment, Thomas had a clear view of the old lady – the one he'd met on the beach, surely – and Rosie. He looked in his wing mirror, but the car disappeared round the corner. Unable to turn off the ignition, or to make any kind of movement, he sat listening to the familiar idling of the engine. He stared at his useless hands slumped on the sweaty leather of the steering wheel. A driver behind him was blasting his horn, someone was shouting abuse. It did not occur to Thomas he was blocking the exit, or that he was the reason for such far-off, ugly noises. Nothing occurred to him. The shouting and hooting increased. Then a gloved hand thumped on the windscreen. It was an expensive glove of tanned leather, holes punched over the knuckles. Thomas did not move.

'I've brought chicken and watercress sandwiches in rye bread,' said Mary. 'I know you like rye. And bacon and tomato and a little pot of brown shrimps. Two peaches and apricots, some wild strawberries, a nice ripe Brie and a thermos of coffee. If you see anywhere nice to stop. . . .'

'Good heavens.' Rosie had been concentrating on the weird dark trees that lined the road, wishing she had brought her sketch book. 'It's nearly Newmarket.'

'Quite near lunchtime.'

'I believe I remember rather an agreeable posthouse not far from here. We might come across it, mightn't we, darling?'

'We might,' said Mary, patiently, 'but never mind if we don't, because I've a half bottle of champagne in the cold bag so we'll have a drink, come what may. I rather like champagne in the open.'

They puttered along for a while in silence. It had taken a long time to get this far. Mary's extreme caution forced her to brake every time she saw a car on the horizon, and she would only risk accelerating on the rare occasions the road was absolutely clear.

'I agree I haven't been this way for a good many years,' Rosie said at last. 'Maybe the place I'm thinking of has gone. Still, there's bound to be somewhere else.'

Mary pursed her lips. She was determined her picnic was not going to be wasted. In the end, she knew, there would have to be a compromise: but that compromise must include a *déjeuner sur l'herbe*. She had been looking forward so much to that part of their journey. If Bill had been here, he would have stood no nonsense from Rosie, and she would have conceded to his wishes with an enchanted flutter of her pretty eyes. But Rosie's ways with her men friends and her women friends had always been different.

'Hope the dresses are all right,' Rosie said at last, once it was plain Mary was not going to respond to her previous suggestion.

She swivelled round to look at them lying on the back seat. Pansied satin on top of ruby velvet. Mary, Rosie observed with gratitude, had taken the precaution of putting her own dress underneath, to protect Rosie's from Trust's hairs.

'Why shouldn't they be?'

Mary sniffed. Rosie was prevaricating now. Maddening. She would just have to be firm.

'We seem to be a little swervy now and then, don't we? I mean, not your fault, darling. Just avoiding all this awful traffic.'

'Nonsense,' scoffed Mary, jamming on the brake. A few miles later, she drew up in the gateway of a cornfield. 'As we haven't seen your place, we're stopping here,' she said. 'If we find it later on, we'll stop there too.'

'Anything you like,' agreed Rosie, who was hungry and battle-weary by now, and longing for champagne.

They laid out a tartan rug and ate and drank unhurriedly. The suffused sun was just strong enough to keep them warm, skylarks sang above them. Rosie, who had enjoyed herself, despite defeat, was now determined that her part of the compromise should be executed. To her delight, they had not been back in the car for more than a mile – Mary even more cautious after a beaker of champagne – when she saw the roadhouse she had had in mind.

'Tarted up a bit, but definitely the place,' she said.

'Are you sure?' By now Mary had passed the entrance to its carpark.

'Quite, quite sure. It's got a lovely bar with a real mahogany counter. Go round again.'

'Very well.'

Mary hoped Rosie had no idea the trauma the roundabout was causing her – thoughtless cars darting every which way, cutting across her, impatient, threatening. But somehow she managed it, and on the second attempt darted finally into the entrance.

'Look!' shrieked Rosie, suddenly, dangerously snapping the last threads of Mary's concentration. 'Look, there at the exit – a huge great Mercedes just like the one my client comes down in. Mr Arkwright.'

'Really.' Mary knew it would be fatal to glance anywhere but straight ahead. 'That means the place'll be wickedly expensive.'

'But I'm paying,' said Rosie magnanimously. 'Of course I'm paying. Mind that tub of geraniums.'

The car came to a crunching halt on the gravel. With great reluctance, Mary followed Rosie towards the entrance of the pretentious-looking hotel. To sit in a darkened bar – albeit mahogany – on a bright afternoon was the last thing she wanted. But of course she had to stick to her part of the bargain, and she would do her best to look as if she was enjoying herself. If Bill had been here, he would have diverted Rosie from her plan in his usual, tactful way. But Bill, as Mary kept having to remind herself, was not here, and never would be again.

*   *   *

The sky grew darker all day. By evening, thunderous clouds shunted back and forth. Sometimes they crashed silently, then split apart again to show greenish sky above them. A few large, heavy drops of rain began to fall: a storm, and thicker rain, seemed inevitable. At least the air would be cleared, thought Frances. But what would happen to the party?

She stood in the empty marquee. It was filled with a low, cathedral light. The lining of broken grey and white stripes had been designed to look like moving shadows when the firefly bulbs were lighted. But for the moment, unadorned, the effect was sombre. Pillars that soared into arches, awaiting their flowers and garlands of ivy, were glaringly white, as was the intricately designed woodwork of the partitions that divided the dance floor from the supper tables. The bandstand, undecorated, was a bleak stage at one end of the tent, overlooking the expanse of parquet floor, as yet unpolished. A huge, gloomy space, about to be rain-battered all night. Was there any chance that by this time tomorrow the transformation would be complete?

In her nervous state, Frances paced the dance floor, arms crossed beneath her breasts. Through the opening at one side of the marquee, she saw that the lawn was menacing green-yellow, and in the silence she could hear the sparse knocking of raindrops on the roof of the tent. Then, unexpectedly, Antony Cellar, whose band was to play tomorrow night, appeared. He carried a small tape recorder.

Frances had heard Cellar Music on the radio some time ago, thought it the perfect band for the party, and had tracked down its leader. They had met in a meagre Soho office in early spring, and negotiated the contract. Since then, Antony – 'Call me Ant, everybody does,' he had insisted at their first meeting – had sent her several tapes and they had talked occasionally on the telephone. These conversations were mostly about music, though on occasions Ant required sympathy for the nefarious activities of his ex-wife. One of the joys about the Farthingoe ball, he had explained to Frances, was that his old mum, as he referred to her, lived not ten miles away. He and the boys in the band would be able to spend whatever was left of the night with her.

Ant Cellar was in his late twenties. He had a Roman profile and long, thickly curling hair. Apart from his penchant for 1920s and 1930s music (the band owed much to the inspiration of Roy Fox) he had a weakness for fancy dress. At the meeting in Soho he had been dressed like a character from *South Pacific*. This evening he wore a pink and cream striped cricketing jacket and cream flannels. His handsomeness was faintly ludicrous, but impossible to deny.

'Hello, Frances. Thought I might find you here.' He strode across the dance floor. It squeaked beneath his cream leather shoes. 'I just dumped my stuff with my old mum, ready to set up in the morning. How are you?' He put an arm round her shoulder, kissed her on the cheek.

'Ant! What a surprise.'

'Brought you another tape. Few new old numbers we been working on. Like to hear it?' He snapped the tape into the recorder. Before turning it on, he looked round the marquee in extravagant wonder. 'I say: this is quite something. Fab-u-lous. Terrific, Frances.'

'It's nothing like finished. All the flowers –'

'I can imagine. Terrific.'

'I'm terrified it's going to pour with rain and everything'll be ruined.'

'It won't rain, believe you me.'

'How do you know?'

'I just do.' He gave her a look of such profound significance Frances almost laughed. 'Here, listen to this.' He switched on the machine. A sweet, nostalgic tune piped forth, so thin Frances could still hear the rain, heavier now, behind it. 'You can imagine what it'll be like. Get all the old things crying for their youth.'

'I can, I can.'

Frances moved away from him with a few little old-fashioned dance steps. Ant stood back, appraising.

'Terrific,' he said.

The lawn had lost its dazzling yellow, and turned the sour green of pond weed. Here inside, the tent was husky as a barn. To Frances, dancing faster, Ant appeared like a man under water. His silhouette trembled. He was coming towards her, insubstantial as sea fronds. Frances stood still, dizzy. He put a hand on her arm. The music played on.

'Tell you what: do you think it would be okay for the leader of the band to have a dance with the hostess? At the very end of the shindig, of course. Nothing improper. It's something I sometimes do.'

Frances felt herself blushing. 'Of course,' she said.

Then Toby came striding into the tent and across the floor, which squeaked more loudly than under Ant's tread.

'Darling,' said Frances, 'this is Ant Cellar, leader of the band.'

'How do you do.'

Ant switched off the music. The men shook hands.

'I was just bringing along one of our new tapes,' said Ant.

Toby's look scorched up and down him like a blow-lamp.

'Good, good,' he said.

There was a crash of thunder, rumbles of eerie applause among the clouds.

'It's going to pour,' wailed Frances.

'I was just telling your wife, it'll be all right on the night.'

'Hope you're right,' answered Toby.

'Well, I must be toddling. See you guys tomorrow.'

Antony Cellar hurried out of the tent the way he had come, waving.

Frances looked at Toby and laughed.

'The point is, his music is wonderful,' she said.

'Good,' said Toby, again. 'You know I trust your judgement in such matters. Dinner's been ready for ten minutes.'

'Sorry, Tobes.'

Frances skittered ahead of him, up the steps of the terrace – all under cover of the tent – and through the French windows of the drawing room.

Toby followed more slowly. He felt the wrench of normality stripped away: his house, his garden, were unrecognisable. The intrusion was monstrous. He longed to go to the woods. There was another roar of thunder, a slash of flinty rain against

231

the sides of the tent. Bloody party, he thought, and envied the badgers taking cover in their setts.

*   *   *

The thunder, which swept across the country, woke Thomas from a deep sleep in a layby near Newmarket.

He had slept with his head on his arms, his arms crossed on the steering wheel. He woke to see a moving cloth of rain on the windscreen, and to feel the painful clench of a headache. As the ghastly picture of some hours earlier began to re-enter his mind, he knew that he must somehow get back to London and check in at his club. All he wanted was food, drink, silence in which to take his bearings. Lying to Rachel about cancelled meetings was out of the question. He must sleep alone, he must sleep until a solution came into his dreams. And somehow he had to muster enough energy to put on a good face for the Farthingoes tomorrow night. Bloody party on top of all this, he thought, and switched on the engine with a desolate hand.

*   *   *

The storm had spent itself by midnight. In the morning, grass not covered by the marquee glistened in an opaline light that promised later sun, and drifts of fallen petals made tidemarks on the dark wet earth of the rose beds. Frances's hopes of a fine night returned.

She found herself much busier today. Orchestrating a party of this size, ensuring each element was perfect, meant dizzying mental somersaults in the unravelling of disparate last-minute problems. The woman in charge of the flowers needed Disprin for a nervous headache. Miss Hubbard, the dressmaker, who had obligingly made four dozen pink cloths for the tables, spilt a cup of coffee over one of them in her excitement, and became uncharacteristically helpless in the finding of cold water and an iron. There was a panic about ice: had enough been ordered? Where was the ribbon that had been bought to tie bows round

232

the skinny trunks of the bay trees? More ladders were needed if lights were to be flung over the whole garden. Mrs Farthingoe? Mrs Farthingoe, a moment please. . . .

At some point Toby flashed by saying he and Fiona were off to lunch at the pub – the most helpful thing they could do would be to keep out of the way. Ant Cellar, in purple satin shirt and chamois leather jeans, arrived early afternoon with two helpers to set up seats and microphones. The girl prettifying the bandstand with pots of hydrangeas found herself in immediate conflict with the bandleader. Her flowers were taking up too much space, he said. She'd had her orders, she said. Mrs Farthingoe to arbitrate, please. . . .

Frances had no idea what time it was – sun high and hot – when she and Ant took a break in the shade of one of the cedars. They shared a can of Coke.

'Looks like it's going to be a proper event,' observed the musician, lying back on his elbows, charming tendrils of hair falling over his eyes. 'Fixed it all yourself, did you? Or did you get one of those party planning people in? We get a lot of hassle with some of them.'

'I did it all.' Frances tried to sound modest.

'Terrific. Like I said, last night: terrific. You've obviously got a good eye, plenty of ideas.'

'Oh, I don't know about that.'

'Believe me.' Ant gave her ankle an encouraging squeeze.

'But I'm glad you think so, because there's something I wanted to ask you.' Frances did not move her foot. 'I've this idea I'd like to be some sort of designer, producer, whatever: in films, perhaps. I was wondering if you knew anybody in that world.'

Ant gave a deep sigh. He thought for a long time in silence.

'Well, I do, and I don't,' he said. 'My territory's parties, as you know, and a few recordings. But, like, here's an idea.' He banged her knee. 'Why not design parties professionally? Extravagance at someone else's expense, and the more you charge the better they think you are, believe me.'

Frances kept quiet for a while, internally dealing with a small disappointment. She would have preferred Ant to consider her capable of designing greater things than parties.

'That's not a bad idea – it would be a start,' she said at last.

'Then of course there's always the chance Spielberg or someone will be a guest, be knocked out by what you've done, and hey presto there's a commission for a feature film.' He was endearingly convincing. 'You've got a lot going for you, Frances,' Ant added. He sat up, dented the empty Coke can with his thumb. 'Anyway, I think we should talk about this more. I could put you in touch with a lot of people who give expensive parties. I could flash your name about, say we liked working together.'

Frances smiled and felt herself blushing. She was glad of the shade.

'That would be very kind,' she said.

'I could give you a buzz next week.'

'Fine. Thanks.'

Then she heard her name being urgently called from within the marquee. She saw Ant's visible sigh. But he leapt instantly to his feet and held out a hand to pull her up.

'Be back later,' he said with an intense look she could not quite define. 'Looking forward to it.'

* * *

'I've brought the works, darling,' Rosie Cotterman told her son as she walked behind him up the garden path to his cottage. 'I've brought Arnold's emerald bracelet, Philip's diamond necklace and Michael's sapphire earrings.'

'Good heavens, Mother. Where's your bodyguard? It's only a country dance, you know.'

'Probably the last one I'll ever go to. Then I'll flog the lot. Serena doesn't care a damn about jewellery.' In Ralph's forlorn kitchen she laid her dress of pansied satin over one end of the table, was pleased to see a pot of tea and two cups at the other end. 'Oh, what a kind boy you are. The journey took so long, Mary's anxious driving, and then her tiresome idea of having to stop for a picnic.' She sat down, poured tea. 'Unless – I'm back on to the jewellery now, you understand – unless you find a wife pretty quickly, while I can still afford the insurance, I'll have to sell it, Ralphie. Any hope?'

'Mother, please don't let's have this conversation again. As I keep telling you, I'm not getting married.'

'Is that a final decision? You sound horribly final, Ralphie.'

'Unless something unimaginable happens, yes.'

'I'll never get used to the idea. I so fancy half a dozen grandchildren.'

'I'm sorry. You'll have to rely on Serena.'

'Serena! Thirty-one and not a steady man in sight, as far as I know.'

'That's how it is these days.'

'Poor old you – all of your generation, darling. We seemed to have much more fun. So many men to open doors, and give one a good time. . . .'

'In your case –'

'I wasn't particularly –'

'I have it on very good evidence that you were. Irresistible and irrepressible.'

'You always say that, Ralphie!' Rosie laughed with great pleasure. 'Well, tonight I've decided I shall make my last effort. I shall pull out all stops, be charming to any young men I may meet, then go back home for ever.'

Rosie flurried up from the table, swept her dress over her arm and dashed a tea-breath kiss on her son's temple.

'There's enough water in the tank for one large bath. Why don't you? I had mine this morning,' he said.

'Ralphie, you're an angel.'

An hour later Ralph found her pulling up weeds from the roots of his hollyhocks. She stood up, dry earth on her hands, satin pansies lustrously clinging to her tiny body, stars bouncing blindly from the various diamonds, topaz tilted eyes unusually defined with mascara. Ralph was speechless for a moment, unnerved by the confusions of time. She looked just as he remembered as a child, when she would glide into his nursery before going out, to say goodnight: the most beautiful woman he knew.

'Will I pass?' she asked.

'You look amazing.'

'Just this side of sixty, Ralphie, you realise?'

'Unbelievable. What about washing your hands?'

Rosie looked down at her earth-stained fingers and shrugged. She wiped them on the sides of her dress.

'Let's be off,' she said, taking her son's arm. 'Now I'm here, I'm looking forward to it.'

He led her down the lavender-tangled path. When they reached his car, he opened the passenger door with a flourish of exaggerated gallantry, the sort of gesture she had been accustomed to in her wild youth, and which the prospects of this evening had encouraged her to remember.

*   *   *

In the Arkwrights' bedroom, Thomas and Rachel stood looking at each other in the faintly amazed way of married couples who have watched each other dressing for a party. Thomas did up the jacket of his pristine dinner jacket, disliked the tightness round the stomach, and undid it again.

'Shrunk at the cleaners,' he said.

He fiddled with his cufflinks and bow tie.

He had surprised himself by surviving the traumas of yesterday. After a twelve-hour sleep last night at his club, a fragile calm had been restored. His present thought was simply that he must put on a good face this evening, despite his reluctance to go, and return to Norfolk again next week.

'The funny thing is,' Rachel was saying, 'I remember the morning the Farthingoes' invitation came, and I felt really keen to go. Now, I don't want to at all.'

'Nor me,' agreed Thomas. 'I'd do anything for a quiet night.'

'You do look quite tired.'

'All the driving.'

Rachel surveyed her reflection in the mirror with scant

interest. In her determination to abandon all signals of availability this evening – and for ever more – she had made little effort with her appearance. There was no new dress – she could trust her comfortable old black not to embarrass her with its independent life – and she had washed her own hair. She did put on the ruby earrings, because she had forgotten to return them to the bank, but no other jewellery.

'We better be off.'

She stood, reluctantly. Thomas patted her shoulder.

'You look rather good, old thing,' he said.

Rachel touched the lustreless black stuff of her skirt. 'Must be fifteen years old.'

'I like it better than that gold.'

'That was a mistake.' They both smiled. 'Come on.'

Thomas followed her downstairs, drifting in the slipstream of her hyacinth scent. She had worn it ever since he had known her. Its acute familiarity was comforting. He was lucky, he thought, that she had dismissed his silly suggestion to go her own way. . . . In the difficult months that lay ahead, securing Rosie, he would be glad of Rachel to return to. The truth was that he could not imagine ever being quite without his wife.

*   *   *

Mary Lutchins – with no notion of vanity, and to whom changing for a party was a tiresome business which should be executed in the least possible time – was ready long before Ursula and Martin. In their kitchen she washed up the tea things, careless of her old ruby velvet dress, and played with Sarah's King Charles spaniel, Flapper, whose white hair soon made an ermine scattering over her skirt. When Martin came into the room, she rose from her position on the floor, where she had been tickling the puppy's stomach, and made her pronouncement.

'I've decided to take my own car,' she said.

'What?' Martin was horrified at his mother-in-law's suggestion. He was well acquainted with her driving.

237

'I want to be absolutely independent, if you don't mind. I may want to leave early. I want to know I can leave whenever I like without being a nuisance to anyone.'

'We won't stay late.'

'You might. It might be a wonderful party. Anyhow, I insist.'

'Well, if you insist. But at least let me drive you there. Ursula can follow in your car.'

'All right. I'll settle for that. In which case I could have a tiny drink now, nothing later.'

Martin fetched her a small glass of weak whisky. He thought how pretty she looked in the pinkish light of the kitchen: soft, smudged eyes, dimples, curly white hair. In a curious way, since Bill's death, she seemed younger. The fine web of inexplicable strain, which for years had meshed her features, had vanished. Ursula said it was because she was released from her old, neurotic worry about dying before Bill, leaving him to fend hopelessly for himself. Martin had never been aware of any such preoccupation. Mary would naturally never talk about such things, even to Ursula.

'Hope it'll be fun,' Mary said, taking the drink. 'I almost backed out, you know. It was only because the Farthingoes' party was one of the things we'd agreed about, and Bill believed plans should be stuck to . . . that I decided in the end to come with Rosie. I think it's the last of the engagements we'd accepted together. After this, if there are any invitations, I'll have to make up my own mind, no consultation. Quite odd, getting used to that.' She laughed, glanced out of the window. 'Look: there's Ursula.'

Ursula was drifting back and forth across the garden, picking up cushions and books from the grass. Her white organza dress, dotted with large black spots, had a skirt of three tiered frills. When she turned, Martin and Mary, watching, saw the back was done up with huge black pom-pom buttons, in the fashion of a clown.

'I shouldn't say it about my own daughter,' said Mary, 'but, well. . . .'

238

'I've reason to be a conceited husband,' agreed Martin.

Ursula waved at them with her free hand. The sun dazzled behind her, fuzzying the clown dress and her rumbustious hair.

'Coming,' she shouted, and moved, shimmering, towards them.

'I wish Bill could have been here to see her,' said Mary. She finished her drink with swift distaste, like one who is obliged to take medicine.

*　　*　　*

In the end, despite her meticulous planning, Frances was called upon for so many last-minute decisions that she almost missed the moment she had been most eagerly awaiting: her entrance at the top of the stairs. She had to hurry more than she would have liked over her dressing, and the slight trembling of her fingers made her clumsy. At the dressing-table, stabbing an earring at each ear in turn, she felt grateful for Toby's absence and for his tactful behaviour. He had kept out of the way, all day, had occupied Fiona. After changing early, he had left the bathroom unusually tidy, and was now downstairs 'checking the drink' with Luigi. She hoped that he would be in the hall as she came downstairs.

At last the earrings were in place – two waterfalls of glitter which, the observant eye might perceive, were faintly trout-shaped. (Such a lucky find: Frances had not been able to resist them.) She tossed back her hair, allowed herself a moment to appreciate the reflection. Then she crossed the peach carpet with tiny, hobbled steps forced by the tightness of the mermaid skirt. Last private moment before her last spectacular. . . .

Frances shimmied on to the landing, leaned over the bannisters to peer down into the hall. She had an aerial view of the enormous bowl of flowers on the table, daisy-centred spray chrysanthemums of the exact dusky pink she had wanted, finally located at a grower in Somerset. But nothing else. No Toby. Damn, damn. Where was he? Frances had not wanted to call. She had wanted him just to be there. But the grand-father clock said five-to-eight – call she must if they were to do a private tour before the guests arrived.

Toby appeared instantly, from the drawing room, holding Fiona's hand. Frances had not reckoned on her daughter's presence at this crucial moment: she tried to swallow her irritation.

'Yes?' Toby looked up.

Frances made her way down, negotiating each polished step with an elegant caution she hoped might disguise the diffi-culty of moving at all. She kept one hand on the bannister. Her skirt would not survive the slightest mistake in her footing. Halfway down the flight of stairs, she paused.

'Well?' she said.

Toby arranged his face. Backlit by the evening sky that dazzled through the intricacies of the half-landing windows, he saw his wife transformed into an absurd-looking fish. She seemed to be dressed in a skin of glittering scales, sequins, pearly stuff spattered over a chiffony froth of hem in the shape of a tail . . . could it be?

'Mum, what on earth?' Fiona asked.

Toby quickly squeezed her hand.

'Darling,' he said to Frances, searching for an adjective. 'Amazing. Come on down. I want to be sure my eyes are not deceiving me.'

Frances smiled. Having held her breath so long, she let it expire in an uncomfortable shudder. She felt she had passed the test. Toby, of the understatement, man of few declarations except when fired by jealousy, approved. She thought: he really does. I can tell by his astounded face.

At the bottom of the stairs, eye to eye with his wife at last and not allowing himself to glance lower than her neck, Toby was affected by her wily, sharp-chinned beauty: the simple structure of her face set against the too-long hair which she refused to cut, the extraordinarily vulgar earrings that struck her cheek bones with tiny reflections, the ever-visible scar on the pale lobe. . . . He kissed her briefly on the forehead, guilty at his weeks of inward sneering, his lack of enthusiasm, his dread of this moment.

'Think everything's under control,' he said.

Frances, exuberant, felt a small finger poking her hip, digging between the fragile sequins.

'Don't!' she snapped. 'Fiona!'

Fiona whipped back her hand. Her milky cheeks turned scarlet.

'Sorry,' she said. 'I was just going to say I suppose my dress isn't *too* bad after all.'

'Good.'

Frances was brusque. After all the fuss, she had no intention of telling her daughter she looked lovely when she did not. Gloom had plainly set in the child's bones, and would harden throughout the evening. Frances bent down to kiss her on the cheek – the stilted action of a bride whose gesture combines the preservation of her make-up with dutiful affection.

'Let's go and see everything before everyone arrives,' she said, and took Toby's arm.

The Farthingoes made their way into the drawing room – armchairs and sofas pushed back against the walls, *longi florum* lilies in stately clusters on every table, the precision of their stems softened by ruffles of old man's beard – and through the open French windows to the covered terrace. There, white wicker chairs were placed among the rose beds (Maidens Blush and Felicité Perpetué had miraculously survived last night's storm, only a few fallen petals decorated the flagstones). The bay trees, alert in their pristine white boxes and with pink bows tied round their skinny necks, stood like prim sentinels in various corners. This was the grandstand, the place, in the night to come, best to observe the scene below.

'Look,' urged Frances, squeezing Toby's arm.

'I am looking,' said Toby.

'It's brill, Mum,' said Fiona. 'Though I can't see everything terribly well without my glasses.'

Frances hobbled to the edge of the terrace and studied the culmination of her summer's work. The polished lake of parquet floor, at her insistence and at great extra expense, had been made with various gaps, like beds in a lawn, so that columns could be rooted. These fine pillars soared to the high roof of the tent. They were almost completely garlanded with a density of small ivy leaves whose flowers were the bright nostalgic green of spring – within days they would turn black. At the top of the pillars, huge baskets overflowed with branches of blackberry (fruits purply gleaming) that trailed, with other greenery, on loops of pink ribbon to the next pillar. It had worked, thought Frances: the flower ceiling had been her most rash and ambitious plan. She had had to fight rampant pessimism among the florists: they had declared the idea impractical, impossible. But she had been right, as they admitted in the end. The guests at the Farthingoe ball would dance under a ceiling of ribboned foliage. Frances hoped some of them might notice.

Her eyes lingered over further triumphs: the grey and white striped material that skirted the sides of the tent made exactly the impression she had wanted – a background of flickering shadows to the huge swathes of roses, lilies and chrysanthemums looped like millionaire paperchains, or plumped with artful carelessness into cream china urns (job lot from a country house sale in Derbyshire, another lucky find). Funny how no one would ever know the miles she had driven, the often desperate hunts necessary to find exactly what she envisaged, the hundreds of hours engaged in manifesting the smallest detail. . . .

'Only the tinest bit over budget, Tobes,' she said, eyes on the magnificence but feeling him next to her.

'Never mind. It's wonderful.'

On the bandstand, transformed by so much greenery and so many pink flowers that it reminded Toby of some Shakespearean bank, a couple of Ant Cellar's bandsmen were tuning up.

The odd squawk of trombone and clarinet thrilled Frances like the sound of a hunting horn when she was a child: goose pimples rose on her arms. She longed for the music.

Toby had preceded her down the steps to inspect the other half of the tent, where supper was laid at two dozen round tables. Frances, missing the support of his arm, clutched at Fiona's shoulder and wobbled after him. For a wild moment, she wondered if she should dash upstairs and change into one of the old dresses in which she had always felt comfortable: maybe the mermaid was her only mistake. But even as the thought occurred, she knew there was no time. People would expect her to be in something new and extraordinary and, most important of all, Miss Hubbard, who had taken such trouble making the beastly dress, was helping in the cloakroom. She would be irreparably hurt were Frances to change.

Clutching her daughter's shoulder, Frances skittered across a corner of parquet and followed Toby through the arch in the lattice partition that divided the supper room from the dance floor. There, the profusion of scents from the flowers flung over her – almost visible, almost tangible, warm, creamy smells of gardenias, roses, summer jasmine.

Toby, Frances saw with pleasure, stood in a kind of trance among the tables. For a moment, she thought he looked like a small frog confused by a pond overcrowded with water lilies, and the idea made her smile.

'Each of the tables, Mum, they said took an hour to lay,' said Fiona, by now holding her mother's hand.

It was no wonder.

The cloths of dusk pink could scarcely be seen under their encrustations. At the centre of each table stood a glass bowl of gardenias and pink roses, guarded at four corners by cream candles in silver holders. Each place was laid with a regiment of silver knives and forks and spoons and thin-stemmed glasses. There were cream porcelain side plates with a pink key pattern (eventually found in Edinburgh) and cream damask napkins. Name places were written on parchment cards in sepia ink. To achieve perfection in this part of her plan Frances had taken six lessons in calligraphy.

She and Fiona reached Toby.

'The detail,' he said. In some awe, thought Frances.

243

'It's what matters,' she said, in a modest voice.

From the other side of the lattice partition a clarinet skittered up to a high note and down again.

'We must go,' she added.

The three of them began to edge their way back to the arch that opened on to the dance floor. The lacy wood of the partition was so thickly decorated with leaves and flowers that a clear view of the band, except through the arch, was not possible. Forethought, here: guests must be able to carry on a conversation easily, despite the music and dancing so near. Frances had noticed, through gaps in the foliage, comings and goings on the bandstand. Now, back on the empty dance floor, she saw every member was in place, all in white dinner jackets, minor versions of their leader. Mr Cellar himself, a master of public relations, gave a small bow at Frances's entrance and raised his baton. With a great swoosh, the huge plush sound of *The Very Thought of You* filled the empty tent, and Frances, nervous tension suddenly flown, burst out laughing.

The creep, thought Toby, glaring at Cellar's servile little smile. Marvellous music, though. Had to admit that.

Ant Cellar kept his eyes on Frances, smiling at her laughter. She moved away from Fiona and Toby, gave a few sinuous wiggles. This caused the sequins to dazzle so brightly their glare seeped into Toby's reluctant vision. Then, to his embarrassment, he saw that his wife, alone on the floor, shuffled her feet expertly beneath the frothy tail and waved her arms like a ballet dancer who has not learned the art of restraint. The sight certainly amused the repulsive Mr Cellar. Laughing, he increased the tempo, thus encouraging Frances to speed up her ghastly performance.

Fortunately, at that moment, Luigi – dressed at his own insistence as a gondolier, to denote his position as captain of the staff – came running on to the terrace, arms flailing wildly, his face stricken. Frances stopped at once. Ant Cellar, ever sensitive, hushed the band to a mere pianissimo.

'What is it, Luigi?' The sudden halt of her movements,

Frances found, was unbalancing. She skidded about, was saved by support from one of the enfoliaged pillars.

'Mrs Farthingoe! Guests!' shouted the suddenly unnerved Luigi. 'They are come —'

And indeed, behind him, rolled an anticipatory pair: a large woman in mayoral satin, who had chosen not to disguise her arms with any form of covering, and her limpid husband.

Trust the bloody neighbours to arrive first, thought Toby. He hurried over to them, calculating that Frances's constricted journey across the empty dance floor would take some time. Ant Cellar switched key into *The Lady is a Tramp*. Fiona remained where her father had left her by the arch. She watched her mermaid mother, slightly out of focus, slithering luxuriously across the polished floor. She wondered why on earth she had decided to come, and how on earth she was going to spend the long night ahead.

* * *

By the time they sat down to dinner, the three hundred guests had been drinking excellent champagne for three-quarters of an hour. Thomas was among those whose policy was to drink quickly at an early stage, knowing some effort was required to ease himself into an appreciative state of mind. Having found his place at a corner table near the partition that divided the supper room from the dance floor, he closely observed his fellow guests. Awful trap, dinner, at these sort of occasions. If your host had placed you badly, you were stuck for a couple of hours. No chance to be free till after the coffee.

Across the table, he saw with slightly rising spirits, was the woman he recognised from dinner at Oxford — Rachel had sat next to her husband. Unfortunately, the table was too wide to talk across, but he might manage to shift nearer to her later. Not that he had the least desire to pay any attention to any new woman, his heart being so completely occupied by Rosie. It just happened that she was the most attractive woman at the table by far. . . . What mischief had been in Frances's heart

245

when she had chosen to place him between the two who were settling on each side of him?

Thomas shifted slightly to his right, scrutinised the place card: Marina Folks. Mrs Folks, presumably, judging by a garnet ring in a 1950s setting on her finger. Thomas's eyes rose slowly. Mrs Folks had chosen to wear a multi-coloured Indian dress covered with a quilted waistcoat of the same material – the kind of thing very popular in the early 1970s, which even Rachel had abandoned some years ago. He turned to the white orb of her face, the clenched hair, the flash of a cherry lipstick smile.

'I come from Wendover,' she said.

Thomas occupied himself in taking two long sips at the very good white wine while he reflected on this fact. Launching into conversation with a complete stranger was never an easy matter, and Mrs Folks, along with hundreds of others at these ridiculous middle-aged balls, scored zilch in the art of Striking Up. It would be much easier, less trying, altogether more agreeable, if, at this very moment, they voted that her comment should be both the beginning and the end. They should call a truce, agree there was absolutely no point in speaking to each other for the rest of dinner, and they could enjoy their food in silence.

As it was, Thomas took a spoonful of delicious iced mint consommé, and said: 'Do you.'

His graceless lack of response – she had expected in return a similar piece of information – flummoxed Mrs Folks completely. A rash of pink spots flashed on her neck, clashing with the fuchsia pattern of her quilting.

'I mean, I suppose it's a long way to come, but I'd travel any amount of miles to one of Frances's parties, wouldn't you?'

Thomas looked across at the pretty woman from Oxford. The rotten luck of it was, she seemed to be poorly placed, too. They exchanged a small, secret smile. He'd definitely move, later.

'I'd travel about sixty-two miles,' he said. 'Possibly sixty-three.'

The Folks woman tittered, further unnerved.

'Such fun,' she may have murmured.

But Thomas was not listening. He glanced to his left: hulk of emerald satin. He sighed. A setting such as this – delicious music, flowers so powerful they almost knocked you out – emphasised imperfection as much as beauty. With his entire being he longed for the impossible: Rosie Cotterman to be beside him, her fragile Irish beauty mesmeric in the candlelight. Oh God, Rosie. . . .

'Do you come from round here?' asked the satin.

*   *   *

Fiona hadn't realised she would be so in the way. Everywhere she went ladies in lacy aprons carrying five plates had to duck and swerve to avoid her. When she had refused to have a place at any of the tables, not wanting to be stuck all through dinner with a lot of boring old grown-ups, she had not realised how conspicuous she would feel, the only non-helper standing up. It was awful, really awful. If only Jessica had been allowed to have come they could have gone off somewhere, had quite a good time. As it was, it took her at least twenty minutes to persuade one of the bossy ladies to give her a plate of food – some sort of salmon stuff falling out of pastry, parsley everywhere, which she hated – and then she had to spend ages trying to find a free fork. . . . In the end she slipped along the edge of the dance floor, observed only by Ant Cellar's bandsmen, and sat on the floor at the foot of their stage. She had a curious feeling of wanting to be near Ant. He was so cool, with his smashing hair and white suit. His music was all right, too: a bit sad. She looked up at him: couldn't see him very clearly without her glasses, but realised he smiled at her. Actually smiled. Perhaps she would stay here all night. She smiled back. But he was concentrating on his conducting, didn't see her. Never mind. She'd have another go, later. She dug her fork into the pink fish, pushing away the revolting parsley. The smell of the million lilies made her feel sick. Or maybe it was the salmon. Still, if she was lucky she'd get Ant's autograph. Somehow.

*　*　*

Frances's own place at her table was as skilfully calculated as every other detail. To her right was her father, a retired colonel: to her left, his best friend, a deaf old boy of equal rank. Their pleasure was to reminisce about the last war together: Frances's constant forays from the table would afford them many opportunities.

She deserted them first as their spoons slithered about the brilliant jade of their jellied consommé. She herself, devoid of appetite, had sipped at half a teaspoon, and left the rest. She patted both old men on the shoulders, whispering she would return soon: they neither heard nor cared.

Frances made her way through the tables. She found it hard not actually to dance, as she had earlier, in time to Ant's heavenly music. But she restrained herself, fearing a return of Toby's disapproving look. She merely tossed her head instead, shining hair swinging like an advertisement, diamanté trout earrings speckling her cheeks with diamond stars. On the tide of gardenia scent and nostalgic music, she glided above the heads of her guests stopping here and there to clutch a bunch of raised fingers which squeezed her own in congratulation. Sometimes she was pulled briefly down to brush a cheek, to feel a wet mouth, and to register a small chip of expensive scent behind an ear – no match for the overpowering smell of the party flowers. Single words were exchanged: party shorthand.

'Frances!'
'Amazing!'
'Thanks!'
'Dress!'
'Like it?'
'Stunning!'
'Mermaid!'

248

'Mermaid?'

'This salmon –'

'Koulibiak –'

'Triumph!'

'Thank you! Thanks –'

On, on, through the swell of praise, awe, congratulation. All worth it, then, the trouble. All worth it. *Night and Day*, Ant was playing. So appropriate. It had been a struggle, night and day, for months.

At the last table, Frances saw Thomas Arkwright. Poor old Thomas: he was fatter, flushed, hot. She had chosen Marina Folks very carefully for him: her husband, too, was a brewer. She thought they might have had something in common. But by the looks of things she had miscalculated. Frances decided to cheer him up with the whispered promise of a dance: Thomas had always given her the encouraging eye. But meantime, Ralph, on the other side of the Folks woman, was beckoning.

'Frances, my darling, you've done it again.'

Slightly drunk, the confused thought struggled in Ralph's mind that, now he was free of her affection, it was in order to address her thus at her own party. She would see it meant nothing beyond admiration for her party skills. He kissed her hair.

'Ralphie! Enjoying yourself?'

'Wonderful!'

'Marina! Lovely to see you –'

'Frances! This is fun –'

'And Thomas!' Frances stretched out an arm. She felt her left bosom rise slightly from the sequin bodice. 'Thomas, have you met Ralphie?'

'I haven't, no.'

Things were a little out of focus, Thomas found. The sequins on Frances's flank hurt his eyes. He was conscious of sweat running down the back of his neck. His underthighs itched against the wicker seat of his chair. His shirt strained against his stomach.

249

'Ralph Cotterman,' said Frances.

The two men looked at each other, shook hands across Marina Folks.

Thomas swallowed. There was something faintly familiar – top lip, set of head on neck.

'Promise me a dance later, Thomas.' Frances glided away.

'Lots of dances,' promised Thomas, too late.

Useless as an underwater fish, his mouth moved silently. Heart in a turmoil, he tried very hard, then, to summon a calm voice.

'Cotterman? Any relation to Rosie Cotterman, the painter?'

The man smiled. Weakish face.

'My mother,' he said.

'Good heavens.' Thomas felt the blood fleeing his own cheeks, leaving cold skin flaccid against the bone. 'I've bought several of her paintings. . . .' He was aware that Ralph Cotterman was straining to see his place card. Frances, in her hurry, had not completed the introduction. 'Thomas Arkwright, the name.'

'You're Mr Arkwright? She told me.'

'Told you what?'

'That you were a very generous client.'

'Ah.'

Thomas registered that Mrs Folks, unable to contribute to this exchange, had taken out a silver compact and was powdering her nose with a matted piece of cotton wool.

'She's here, as a matter of fact,' Ralph Cotterman was saying, voice on one level as if it were a perfectly ordinary piece of news.

'Here?' Thomas felt so weak that he thought he might faint. 'All the way from. . . .'

'In the old days she'd go any distance for a party, my mother. Quite a girl in her time.'

Mrs Folks smiled noisily, snapping shut the beastly little tortoiseshell lid.

'When I was younger,' she offered.

'Where is she?'

Thomas's head was swivelling about. Myriad diners floated, scarf-like, unclear, before his eyes. Dizzying.

'Somewhere,' said Ralph. 'I'm not sure.'

Thomas crashed his spoon down into a pink mousse that twinkled with fraises du bois. He must eat, stop drinking, gather strength, retain composure . . .

'I'll be off in a moment to do the filial duty,' Rosie's son was saying. 'First dance and all that. She'll be very tickled to discover you're here.'

Tickled. . . .

'Could you pass the cream, please?' Marina Folks' huffy little voice came from some far-off horizon.

. . . my darling beloved Rosie, I'm going to dance with you all night. . . .

Somehow, Thomas passed the cream.

*   *   *

Frances's thoughts for Toby's *place à table* was no less calculated than for that of her own. He should have Rosie Cotterman and Mary Lutchins. Thus, if he, too, wanted to wander round the tables before dinner was over, they would have a good time talking to each other across the gap.

It had not occurred to her that Toby would have no intention of wandering about. His idea of an enjoyable dinner was to stay where he was, relishing the conversation, the wine, the food. And this he did. His companions were two game old girls: Mary, sweet and brave; Rosie, the wild, dotty Rosie, sharp and funny. Toby, despite all predictions to the contrary, positively enjoyed himself.

'Lovely, lovely music,' Rosie was saying. Since her third glass of his superb claret, Toby noticed, her adjectives had begun to multiply. 'Takes me back.'

'Also, you can talk against it,' observed Mary. 'Very clever of Frances to have found this Cellar Music.'

'Very, very clever,' agreed Rosie.

Toby's mood of easy contentment was then jarred by the

251

view of his wife filtering, once again, through the tables. It was the third time during dinner she had set out on a solo peregrination. Surely there wasn't a guest in the room she had not greeted by now, not a guest who had not observed and wondered at her dress . . . ? Attention-seeking, as usual. He longed for her to sit down, stay put till the dancing began. But then he felt the meanness of his sentiment: it was her party, her evening of glory. She surely deserved the rewards of approbation she so desperately sought.

This time, Frances's journey brought her to Toby's table, which previously she had resisted visiting. She slunk straight over to him, blowing kisses and smiles to others on the way.

'Tobes . . .'

'Everything all right?'

'Think so, don't you?'

Toby put a hand on her hip: public recognition, that's what she wanted. That's what she should have. The sequins grated his hand.

'Wonderful. Fine. Marvellous dinner.'

'Oh, Tobes. I'm in such a spin.'

At that moment, Ant Cellar's rendering of *You're the Cream in my Coffee* came to an end. Nothing followed. Suddenly, without music, the tent was left uneasy with the ruffle of voices. There was a surprised hesitation – why had the band stopped? Then the murmur settled back into place. People shifted. Coffee was stirred.

Frances peered anxiously through the arch. Far away on his podium, she saw that the handsome leader of the band was signalling to her: eyebrows raised, he made an encouraging movement with his baton. Time for dancing, he seemed to be saying. Why don't you take the floor?

Frances put a hand on her husband's shoulder. 'Ant thinks we should start dancing,' she said, and immediately regretted her mistake. Shouldn't have mentioned Ant. Some small instinct told her Toby did not share her enthusiasm for him. But at least Toby was standing. Perhaps he hadn't heard.

'Good idea.' He said it lightly. Frances could have no notion of the irritation that stabbed him. Why should that creep of a bandleader take it upon himself to orchestrate things? Besides, he had no intention of dancing.

'Come on, then. Please. Just for once.' Frances watched his face. 'Just for *once*, Tobes,' she pleaded.

Even as Toby stood rigid in his intention not to dance, he realised he could not humiliate his wife in public. It would have been indefensible to ruin her evening by refusing to dance with her merely to keep to a rule of a lifetime. He followed her to the empty floor with hands clenched hard as iron, face grimly pale. Cellar Music broke into *The Nearness of You*. Toby put an arm round Frances's waist, aware of the eyes of their guests. She was trembling.

'See if I can remember,' he managed to say, smiling.

In the whoosh of sweet music, he felt himself unbend a little. His feet moved in some kind of instinctive pattern, steps he had learned at twelve years old. Their lone act lasted a very short time – signal for release from the tables. A dozen couples quickly joined them.

'Thank you, Tobes.' Frances leaned her cheek against his for a moment. He quickly drew back, with no wish to acknowledge her gratitude.

'Where's Fiona?' he asked, letting go of her and leaving the floor.

'I don't know.' Frances struggled to follow him. She didn't care where Fiona was: all she knew was that for half a minute she had had the exquisite pleasure of dancing with her husband for the first time in fifteen years, and that was some kind of triumph whose implications she could think about later. Toby's acquiescence, which must have cost him so much, gave her hope: from now on, no more parties, but better marriage. The object of her sudden happiness (the feeling of deep contentment, previously missing beneath the mere thrill of the party) had disappeared into the crowd. But Frances swung her long hair provocatively, smiling, knowing she was safe: newly bound to Toby, she could flirt with an easy conscience. She would be no one's prey, just an exuberant hostess generous with her pleasure.

How quickly are moods transposed!

Almost at once, her smile was returned. Ralph, standing alone by the arch, held out his arms.

'Dance with me,' he said, 'I want to be first in the queue.'

Frances inclined herself into his arms. She did not care whom she danced with now: dear Ralph was a good enough beginning. Funny how only months ago she would have longed for this invitation. Now, shuffling as skilfully as she could in the wretched dress, she felt nothing. Her eyes searched for Toby.

*   *   *

When Toby had left the table, Mary and Rosie bent towards each other just as Frances knew they would.

'I think I'll take myself off for a little potter,' Rosie said. 'Want to look around. Take it all in. It's all so marvellous, marvellous.'

'Very well. Shall I come with you?'

'No, no. You go and find a nice corner on the terrace, where we can look down on it all, and I'll join you later.'

'Very well,' Mary said, 'but I shan't expect you. You'll be off dancing.'

Rosie stood. She refilled her glass from a bottle on the table. 'Who on earth would want to dance with me? Ralphie'll give me a little twirl, perhaps, and your nice son-in-law, if I'm lucky. But that'll be it. Dancing days over.'

'Nonsense!'

Rosie stood, sipping her wine, eyes on the dancers.

'All this trouble Frances has gone to,' she said. 'Pity about the women. English women's party dresses. . . .'

'Some of them have tried quite hard.'

'Most of them look as if they're dressed for an afternoon's dead-heading.' Rosie sniffed, then smiled. 'I say, you know who I can see? Dancing with Ursula? Mr Arkwright. Thomas

Arkwright, my client you met on the beach. What a coincidence. He's very rich, you know. Must be. Keeps buying and buying my pictures. Well, I'm off. Ralph said there's a good vegetable garden. I'm off for a look at the fruit cages, my darling. See you later.'

Rosie moved away from the table, very upright, cooling herself with a small silk fan. Mary noticed that, with a slight inclination of her head, and a distant smile, her friend managed to swathe a path for herself through the crowds. People moved back from her as if she was a member of the royal family, someone for whom the way should automatically be cleared. Their eyes followed the small upright figure with curiosity.

Mary waited until she could see Rosie no longer, then pulled her shawl round her shoulders. There was no one left at the table. The bottles of wine were empty. She got up, moved towards the terrace, determined not to think about how Bill would have taken her arm, guided her through the narrow spaces, the scattered empty chairs. Instead, she hummed along with the band: lovely nostalgic tunes, words she would never forget. *They ask me how I feel.* . . . She pressed on, pushing through a clump of women whose glances were so brief it was as if they did not like what they saw – a single old lady on her own.

No-one moved out of her way, but in the end she reached her destination in a corner of the terrace.

*　　*　　*

Rachel, who had drunk three glasses of champagne before dinner, found herself sailing towards her table in an ungrounded fashion, the delights of the scene all a-tremble before her eyes. Once installed in her wicker chair, she drank two glasses of water, determined to drink no wine: the memory of the night at Oxford still stung in her mind. To counteract the effects of the champagne, she ate an unusual amount: two helpings of each delicious course, and enjoyed (in a way, she thought, that only other women do) thinking of all the imagination and care that must have gone into planning each perfect detail. (Hot rolls studded with olives were an inspiration.) Her old black dress was still comfortable by the end of dinner, and conversation with Toby's brother, now peacefully petering out on both sides, had bobbed along quite easily. He was a taciturn Somerset farmer with a scientific approach. His answers to Rachel's questions about the rotation of crops were of enormous length and seriousness. She was forced to concentrate so hard that the charming music, cooing from the other end of the marquee, became a mere backdrop, fragile as lace, to her attention.

Now the floor was crowded. Through the leaves and flowers of the trellis partition, Rachel watched jigsaw pieces of the dancers – the tiny movements that indicated politeness, boredom, pleasure. She saw that Thomas, dreadfully red in the face, was dancing with the woman who had been at Pruddle's dinner: trust him to have secured the belle of the ball at an early stage. Rachel smiled to herself. Sometimes, she was quite proud of Thomas's audacity. He would never hesitate to ask an unknown woman to dance if she was beautiful and, curiously, he never seemed to be refused. These dances, in many years of Rachel's experience of party-going with her husband, never lasted long, were rarely repeated, and there was never the slightest hint that, after the party was over, Thomas gave a moment's thought to the girl who had obliged him with a waltz.

Frances, Rachel could not fail to notice, was wiggling, rather than dancing, a few feet from a tall, pale-looking man whose vacant look might have been a cover to embarrassment. The only mistake of the party, Rachel judged, was Frances's ludicrous dress – a signal of availability, if ever there was one, but also a serious impediment to enjoyment. It was plain that poor Frances had difficulty with every step: perhaps hip wriggling was the only comfortable thing she could do. Rachel felt sorry for her, remembered her own mistake with the badly behaved gold skirt. She saw that Frances was swaying towards her, waving with one hand: the other, behind her back, was clasping her partner.

'Rachel! We've not spoken a word. I want you to meet Ralph Cotterman. Ralphie, this is Rachel Arkwright, very old friend. . . .' She wafted away.

Rachel stood up. The man she was left with looked reluctant to begin. But he smiled politely.

'I sat near your husband at dinner, I think. He buys a lot of my mother's pictures.

'That's right.'

'Would you like to dance?'

'Why not?'

In the old days, when she enjoyed parties, Rachel always loved this moment – this stepping on to the floor with a new man wondering what, if anything, would happen. She bunched up her black skirt, pushed a bit of stray hair from her eyes. Everything was clear now: champagne effects waned, spirits rising. She stepped through the archway, felt the slide of parquet under her shoe, the intoxicating cocoon of the scent of lilies and jasmine. She turned to Ralph Cotterman, found herself secured in his stiff, sad arms. She hoped he could dance, because nothing else was going to happen.

Ralph, looking down on Rachel's tawny hair, arm comfortable round her sturdy waist, saw his partner as a sweet, old-fashioned creature. She had the wistful look of a woman who is happily married but for whom something indefinable is still missing. As they moved at a stately pace around the floor, it occurred to him she was the sort of woman he would have liked to sit in a summerhouse with, reading books in amiable silence, sipping Lapsang, distant wood pigeons ruffling the silence – the kind of dotty fanciful thing he had never experienced, but still hoped for with some magical girl who might then become his wife. But no such thing would ever come about because of Ursula's existence. While he loved her, there was no hope of loving anyone else: that was the brutal fact.

Nonetheless, this Rachel lady danced very nimbly. He liked

257

the feel of the thick warm flesh round her ribs, and her apparent lack of worry at his lack of conversation. They shuffled round through the whole of *Blue Moon*, nicely in time but politely distant. There was no spark to lift them further: together they made the shell of a sad, pointless husk: two people linked only by good manners.

'I see your husband's dancing with Ursula Knox,' said Ralph at last.

'So he is.'

She did not seem much interested. Ralph's plans, uninterrupted by the movements of his dull body, spun on: he must dance with his mother next, perhaps give dear old Mary a go. Then he would be free for Ursula any time she was free for him. Cellar Music moved into a Charleston. Ralph led Rachel towards the terrace.

'Time to find my mother,' he muttered. 'Goodness knows what she's up to. Thanks very much.'

He was off, knowing that Thomas and Ursula were also making for the terrace, so Rachel would not be stranded. The evening was far too young to ask Ursula for his first dance. He had managed to avoid talking to her at dinner, and did not wish to be near her just yet. It was an opportune moment to do his duty by his mother.

*   *   *

Thomas, completely preoccupied by the thought of finding Rosie, was making a feeble attempt to behave normally. He had moved beside Ursula Knox as soon as dinner was over, and managed to talk to her in a perfectly sane way about their mutual friend, Pruddle. They had then had an agreeable dance. She was of the lively, flinging about school of movement which he chose to watch from a shuffling distance rather than join, having little faith in the stamina of his strained shirt and trousers. And now it was time for the obligatory go with Rachel. Once that was out of the way, he would be at liberty to go in search of Rosie with a free conscience. He found his

258

wife standing at the bottom step of the terrace glancing vaguely about her, unexpectant. She looked rather handsome, he thought, in a disorderly sort of way. For a moment he remembered the first time he saw her at a Commem Ball at Magdalen, Oxford's Zuleika of her year. She had been standing among battered lupins pulling on a velvet glove.

'Care for a quick twirl, old thing?'

Rachel smiled at her husband, straightened his bow tie with a wifely tweak. 'Please.'

They merged into the crowd of dancers. Thomas leaned heavily on Rachel's shoulder as if she was a familiar mantelpiece. His eyes swilled back and forth in search of Rosie. Rachel looked at other husbands and wives dancing lustrelessly together, alone in their preoccupations. Like them, she and Thomas did not bother to speak. Perhaps it was a common habit of married life to save snippets of observation for the journey home.

Home! Rachel closed her eyes. She longed to be in bed at home.

Their single turn round the floor complete, Thomas said he would go to the bar, fetch drinks. Rachel sensed his impatience to be off. She called after him not to bother with anything for her, doubting his intention of returning now his duty dance was over. What to do next? All she wanted was to sit and look, undisturbed. Not have to talk. But even as she started to climb the stone steps she felt a tap on her shoulder. She turned.

'We sat next to each other at St Crispin's some time ago, you may remember.'

Rachel looked up into Martin Knox's handsome face and blushed like a child.

'Oh, we did, yes. Of course I remember.' Earlier, through her champagne haze, Rachel had seen a distant glimpse of Martin, and had determined to avoid him. How could she have been so careless?

'Dance?' he asked.

No, not for anything in the world. It would remind me

259

of stupid fantasies concerning punts and picnic lunches and innocent possibilities. . . .

'Love to,' she said.

Tea for Two was playing now.

They moved so easily together that after a while Rachel supposed Martin could not feel the heat of her embarrassment, or guess at the spinning of her shame.

'I'm so sorry,' she said at last, 'about that evening.'

'Sorry? Why?' He seemed genuinely puzzled.

'I was experimenting. It went wrong.'

'I wasn't aware –'

'And then I was dressed all wrong for Oxford. That awful skirt bouncing about all over you. . . .' Did he remember the untoward brushing of their hands?

'Oh, that. All unimportant.' Martin smiled, friendly. 'To be honest, I got the impression there was something on your mind that I couldn't possibly guess at. Whatever it was got in the way of your enjoying the evening. But I could have been wrong.'

'No,' said Rachel. 'You were right. Thank you for being so . . .'

She felt herself blushing once more. There was a pricking behind her eyes: the kind of self-scorning tears that fill the chasm left by a quickly destroyed fantasy. Martin's kindness made her wretched. She was sick of polite dances – Ralph, Thomas, now him. How many more partners would make her their duty before the evening was over?

'I must find Ursula,' Martin was saying as they regained the terrace. 'Thank you so much.'

'Of course. Thank you.'

Rachel managed a smile of complete understanding. He must find his wife because only towards her were his singular love and energy directed. What, as a wife, must that be like?

Rachel set off once more for the empty chair. From this vantage point she saw that Martin had quickly found the only woman he wished to be with, and that they danced brilliantly together. Ursula would spin away – white frills and black pom-pom buttons bobbing – only to be recaptured for a moment, clasped as closely as two people can be on a dance floor. As for Thomas, he was nowhere to be seen. Rachel looked at her watch: eleven-thirty. But the hours that had to be endured suddenly did not depress her: she was blessed with an idea.

* * *

Toby found Fiona in the library. She was drinking a carton of orange juice, watching a film on television.

'Been looking for you everywhere,' said Toby. 'You all right?'

'Fine. D'you think I can get Ant Cellar's autograph?'

'Don't see why not, when he has a break.'

'I think he's amazing. Are you enjoying yourself, Papa?'

'It's a wonderful party,' Toby said. 'Be back later.'

'Don't bother about me. I'll just wait around for Ant.'

Toby left the room and went upstairs.

* * *

'I can't remember,' whispered Ursula, during one of the moments she came close to Martin, 'what it's like to go to a party without a husband.'

'Mutual safety.'

'Better than that.'

She flitted away, making funny, limpid clown movements that made Martin smile. *Ain't She Sweet*, the band was playing. They whooshed together again.

'Saw you dancing with Thomas Arkwright's wife.'

'She seems a bit sad.'

'He seems a bit frantic. Look: he's over there, barging about. He must be escaping from something or someone.'

'Or searching,' said Martin. 'He looks like a man in a panic.'

* * *

261

Thomas was in a panic. Rosie was nowhere to be found. Nowhere. He'd searched the supper room, dance floor, bar, terrace, and downstairs sitting-out rooms in the house. How on earth could he have missed her? In his desperation, on his third visit to the bar, Thomas's earlier resolve disappeared: he had two quick glasses of champagne. Energy restored, his plan was now the garden. He knew it was a large one, very confusing with hedges and corners and secret places, but he was determined to search every inch till he found her. Very hot, shirt damp, steps a little unsteady, he blundered round the edge of the dance floor aiming for one of the French windows that was let into the side of the marquee. These structures – first observed while Marina Folks was droning on about her husband's uncanny knowledge of hops – intrigued him: for all their solid structure, they appeared not quite authentic, like stage scenery. On reaching one of the open glass doors he could not refrain from testing the wooden frame with a finger. As he had supposed, the wood was of poor quality, thin. It was not a door that would give any support in a crisis. In the event of the guy ropes snapping, and the whole elaborate edifice of the marquee toppling, then these bloody doors would smash down, useless as matchwood. . . . Surely a symbol of something there, somewhere. Where, oh where was Rosie? Thomas tripped over the low step and plunged into the garden.

*   *   *

Mary Lutchins sat in a corner at the back of the terrace. As promised, she had secured a small table with two chairs. The unoccupied one awaited Rosie, who had been gone for some time now. Mary sipped a glass of iced coffee. (Such a good idea.) People filtered past her, in and out of the house, backwards and forwards across the terrace on the way to the dance floor. Some gave a vague smile. Most did not notice her. So this is what it's like to be old, she thought. You can become almost invisible at a party, when you're old, and peacefully enjoy your part as a spectator. She was enjoying her uninterrup-

ted observations: such glorious flowers, such a beautiful marquee, such nostalgic music. She was glad she had come. It
would have been much better, of course, if Bill had been there,
but Mary was surprisingly happy on her own. She saw Martin
climbing the steps, hands outstretched towards her. So
thoughtful, Martin, always: she could not have asked for more
in a son-in-law. And yes, well, as there was still no sign of
Rosie, of course she would love just one little dance, next time
there was something not too fast. Then she would go in search
of Rosie. She had a feeling she knew exactly where she would
find her.

'Yes, I'd love to, just a short one,' she said to Martin, taking
his hand.

*   *   *

Toby shut the door of his room, switched on a single light.
Up here, windows shut, he could hear nothing. The party
below did not exist. Blessed white silence. Half-moon in the
centre of only skylight, clean-edged in its bed of darkness.

Toby sat at his desk. The familiar leather seat of his chair
was cool beneath his thighs. He switched on his machine,
pressed a button. The accounts for the party, if it existed,
leapt on to the screen. The ridiculous figure of the total was
underlined twice. Toby stared at it: preposterous figures. But
they did not matter. They made no sense.

He pressed another button. A familiar geometric flower
replaced the accounts. It had occurred to him – suddenly,
amazingly. . . . He pressed more buttons. Figures danced.
Excited now, his fingers moved fast over the keyboard. Inspiration had to be acted upon – matter of moments, ten minutes,
perhaps. Imperative. Besides, he would not be missed.

*   *   *

Thomas was glad of the air. He gasped, patted his chest,
stumbled towards the low, spreading branches of a bloody

263

great black cedar tree. On reaching its trunk, he paused and looked back: he was aware of a faint, resinous smell – tremendous relief, its freshness, after all that cloying lily and jasmine and whatnot. Before him spread a daft kind of fairyland: minuscule Christmas lights flung over hedges and branches, flaming torches at the corners of paths, small braziers placed beside garden seats. Frances had thought of bloody everything, he'd grant her that. Must have cost Toby an absolute fortune, but then Toby was a very rich man.

The marquee itself, from here, was a vast glowing hump of prehistoric size from which the music, thank goodness, expired very quickly. A few couples – always blooming couples – oozed out of the pretend French windows. None was drawn by the lugubrious shadows of the cedar tree. Thomas kept his place to himself. He struggled to make a coherent plan, but was overcome by renewed panic. There was a chance Rosie would actually leave before he had found her. He decided to continue in his search.

After a while, he found himself on a cinder path lit only by the moon. Here, the hedges were unadorned by fairy lights, indicating this was not a visitable part of the corner. Turning the corner, Thomas saw why: he was in the vegetable garden. It was surrounded on three sides by a high brick wall.

He hurried about between rows of cabbages and pale lettuces, admiring the neatness of the knee-high box hedges and the weedless earth. Some instinct urged him towards fruit cages at the far end of the garden. Voices?

He stopped, listened. Cool air, soft as kid gloves, stroked his forehead. The music was still audible, but just a thin murmur miles away. Voices, indeed! Oh Lord: had he stumbled upon some middle-aged coupling?

'Rosie?' he called.

Silence.

Then there was movement in the raspberry canes: a thrashing and bulging, and the noise of laughter. Girlish giggles, to be precise. What on earth – ?

Thomas watched the flimsy door of the cage open. Rosie

came out first, fan in one hand, small cluster of raspberries in the other. She was followed by the white-haired woman Thomas had met on the beach, and seen in the car at the roundabout – Rosie's friend.

'I do believe it's Mr Arkwright,' cried Rosie. 'Thomas, my darling, you've caught us in the act. Just one or two left, and we found them. Mary, here: this is Thomas the picture man. We've been discovered.'

More sweet laughter, two pretty faces in the moonlight. Thomas felt short of breath.

'Have a raspberry, won't you?'

Rosie was right beside him now, tipping one into his mouth, kissing him on the ear, or was it the neck – he couldn't be sure, the small damp moment was so fast – laughing all the time.

'There, now. You'll like that, that's for sure. You won't tell on us, will you? You won't tell the Farthingoes? Now, why don't we make our way to the alcove and sit ourselves down on the bench?'

'Not me, if you don't mind, Rosie,' said Mary. 'It's getting a little chilly. I'll go back to the terrace, keep you a chair.'

'Then, very well, Mary, you do that. Mr Arkwright – Thomas, here – and I will perhaps have a word about business matters, then I'll be right behind you.'

Mary glanced up at the unmoving form of Thomas, smiled. Released by her look from his state of strange rigidity, he found himself giving her a small bow like an awed courtier. Then he watched her hurry back the way he himself had so recently come, clutching at her shawl.

Rosie reached for Thomas's hand. 'We'll be sitting down for just a moment, I promise you that. Isn't this a nice place I've found, so secret? Say it's a good place, if you like to be away from the crowd?'

She darted away from him, a few paces ahead, whirled about like a young child. Her satin skirts flashed with stained glass colours, a pattern of flowers Thomas could not name.

'And do you like my dress, Mr Arkwright? Do you like my

265

pansies? It's so old you'd never believe, but who knows? It may well be my last party.'

She was back again, clinging to his arm, fanning her face. The path made sugary noises beneath their feet: there was a smell of peach and lavender, and the raspberries on Rosie's breath. Thomas, helpless, weightless, allowed himself to be guided to the upright shell of stone carved into the wall. He allowed himself to be lowered on to the stone seat, whose grittiness pressed through his trousers, itching his thighs. He allowed his useless hand to be lifted on to the satin thigh, and the beautiful head to rest against his shoulder.

'Glory be to God, Mr Arkwright – Thomas, why, you're so silent tonight.'

Thomas made the effort of a lifetime. He must speak before he cried.

'There's so much to say,' he replied after a while. 'Where can I begin?'

*   *   *

Frances found herself dancing without cease. No sooner had she left the floor with one partner, than another came to claim her hand. From the warmth of her body, she supposed, her dress had stretched a little, and movement became easier. She was able to wiggle her hips with more abandon, inspiring laughter, admiration. Well: she must take all that was offered in these few last hours, for she could never go through such efforts again. It was definitely the last party.

Ralph's turn again: he was waiting for her. She fancied his look was one of admiration mixed with regret. Poor old Ralphie. For all his claims, earlier in the summer, that she meant nothing to him, she knew that was not the whole truth. He had loved her, loved her still, would probably always regret he had not married her.

As the two of them moved towards the bandstand, Frances became aware for the hundredth time that Ant's eyes were on her. There was something cheap, almost frightening, in his glance. Several times he had winked at her, and given a small secret nod of his head: signal that he was looking forward to the promised dance. Frances waved and smiled in return. The thought of the dance with him was strangely disturbing. Anticipating it as she danced with others, the thoughts of her better marriage with Toby, so recently overwhelming, seemed slightly to fade. An exciting ache gripped her stomach that had nothing to do with the closeness of Ralph. She sensed a madness in the air, this extravagant night, and dreaded its ending.

*   *   *

Ralph's time had come. He had seen, in his lone wandering between dancing with his mother, Mary, and the sweet Rachel, that breakfast was being laid. Ursula, always hungry at parties, would be bound for eggs and bacon with Martin soon, and would not want to be disturbed.

When he had finished this second dance with Frances – who seemed to be gripped by some kind of dotty exuberance that is the privilege of a hostess – he would find Ursula. He slowed his pace, stopped. Frances kissed him on the cheek. She had distributed dozens of such prize kisses on her partners, he had noticed, and he did not kiss her back. Once again, he carefully set his expression so that she would think it one of admiration. Concealed behind this mask was the incredulous horror that was his true reaction to her appearance.

'Did you realise, Ralphie? I'm a mermaid.'

'I didn't.' Further disbelief to be concealed.

'Promise another dance before the end?'

She was gone before he could make any such promise. Turning in the opposite direction, to leave the floor, he found a familiar arm was flung round his neck.

'Ralph, you've been positively avoiding me!'

Ursula did not sound at all cross. They hurled themselves into a wild Charleston. The wonderful clown-like dress, flipping about as Ursula bounced expertly, seemed the essence of humour in clothes. Its owner had never looked so irresistible.

The Charleston turned into *Dancing on the Ceiling*. They flung themselves together like old friends hugging at a station. Split-second of wild hair in Ralph's face, hay smell of skin, echo of heart that beat as fast as his for different reasons – then Ursula pulled cruelly back with some comment about the party.

'I'm famished,' she said suddenly. 'Let's join Martin for breakfast. He's at a table over there.'

'Don't think I will for the moment. Not hungry, really. Think I'll explore the garden.'

'We'll keep you a place. Come over later.'

All over so fast, the dance might never have been. She would be with Martin for the rest of the evening, now. What was the point in staying? Who else was there to dance with? Where was his mother?

Ralph, longing to go home, made his way into the garden.

* * *

'I'm in love with you, Rosie, that's the crux of the matter,' Thomas heard himself saying. She gave him a slight tap on the nose with her fan.

'Nonsense, my darling man. It's my painting you're in love with. Admit it, now. I saw that the moment we met.'

'I admire your painting, it's you I'm in love with. Hopelessly, helplessly, in love with – tortured for weeks, you know, not seeing you, not knowing what to do.'

'Now, now. Calm down.' Rose spoke patiently as a nurse to a child. 'It's the moon, you know. I do believe that. People say mad things under a half moon.'

'It's not the moon, my love.'

'Very well, then, I'll believe you if you like. It may be the truth in your heart, but there's not very much we can do about it, is there?'

'Not very much,' said Thomas, 'no.' He looked straight ahead at the cabbages, silver globes of matched size. There

268

was another tap of the fan on his nose. 'We could just . . .'

'No,' said Rosie. 'We could not act recklessly. I'm over all that. That's all in the past.'

'You're right,' said Thomas.

They were silent for a while.

'You can keep on visiting me, though,' said Rosie, at last. 'Of course you can.'

'Of course I can.'

'Buy more pictures.'

'Buy more pictures.'

'But I'd never change my life, now, Thomas. Not for anyone. Besides, you've got a very good wife, I'm thinking.'

Thomas stiffened. 'How do you know? But yes, you're right. She's a good woman.'

'You'd be foolish to leave a good wife.'

'Oh, Rosie, you can't possibly know how much I love you, how much I can't bear being away from you.'

He turned from the cabbages to look at her. She was regarding him curiously, kindly. He felt a choking in his chest, tears pouring from his eyes. Then a soft mouth was on his cheeks, curbing their course: a gentle palm on his temples.

'You're a good man, Thomas,' Rosie observed in a smudged whisper. 'You must never love a woman flighty as a butterfly, now, who would never change. . . . Here, don't be crying.'

There was a confusion of handkerchiefs, dabbing. Mouths met for an infinitesimal kiss. Thomas feared a heart attack, death. *Now more than ever . . . time ripe to die, to cease upon the midnight with no pain* and all that.

'I don't believe you,' he groaned. 'I love you, Rosie. I love you, I love you, woman.'

Having kissed her, he would gladly die. He opened his eyes to tell her this and saw, at the far end of the secret garden, a spectre-like figure with long amber hair.

'My daughter,' cried Rosie, suddenly bright. 'Serena! I've been looking for you everywhere.'

Mother and daughter waved. Thomas closed his eyes again, unable to face such interruption. He heard the scrunch of

Rosie standing up, preparing to leave him. But she would not succeed, she would not succeed. He would pursue her for ever, chase her to the ends of . . .

'Come on, Mr Arkwright, my darling Thomas,' she was saying. 'I can't be waiting for you all night, now, can I?'

*   *   *

Soothed by her inspiration, Rachel lingered for a while longer in her place on the terrace. She looked down on the dancers with a mixture of sympathy, scorn, amusement. She found herself wondering, as did Thomas the day the Farthingoes' invitation had arrived, why the middle-aged go to all the bother and expense to give such parties. What were they for? In Frances's case, perhaps, the months of brilliant planning were rewarding occupation in an empty life. But there was a certain pointlessness, was there not, in the end result?

In youth, Rachel reflected, the unspoken plan of every guest was to search for – perhaps to find – a partner. Thus the meanest gathering of party-goers was endowed with a certain excitement, anticipation. In middle age, though cheap wine and scant food may have given way to the sort of extravagance of tonight, the days of the hunt were mostly over. Guests were now married, remarried, divorced. The point of such gatherings was to be reunited with old friends rather than to meet new ones: there is wistfulness in such an occasion, rather than expectancy. As for the idea of signalling availability at a party like this . . . it was laughable. No-one to notice, no-one Rachel would care to be noticed by.

She smiled to herself, observing the dancers. They included a scattering of people she had known vaguely for years, contemporaries at Oxford, the odd school friend. Their various ways had parted, their common interests divided, probably floundered. Rachel had no desire to restrike up acquaintance with any of them: bridging wide gaps is a tiring business – better just to wave in friendly fashion from opposite banks, as she did to a few people who passed her by. She was struck by their general metamorphosis. The unkind truth is that, in middle age, if you don't see your contemporaries with strict regularity, you are faced by the shock of change after even a short space of time. These old acquaintances were all balder, fatter, greyer, saggier and, judging by much cupping of hands round ears, deafer. Their style of dancing, in the intervening years, had changed too. No matter how wildly they had rocked and rolled in their youth, now, with few exceptions, they plumped for just two basic movements: the piston arms, and, just off the beat, a kind of yanking up of one leg in the manner of an undecided dog. Sometimes, to be fair, the men did provide a little variation by arching their backs and twinkling down their double chins at another man's wife. And the women sportingly jiggled about like lampshades in a breeze, careless of their shape and size. A love of puffy skirts was almost ubiquitous among them, while gold edging ran amok round milkmaid bodices and sleeves. Rachel smiled to herself again, enjoying the Englishwoman's complete indifference to the superficial- ities of fashion: she was one of their band. She, too, had different priorities: she understood the familiar comfort of an old dress.

After a while she gathered up the black skirt which had served her for fifteen summers, and decided her moment had come. One final look at the melancholy sight of the Farthingoes' friends bumbling ungainly on the dance floor, and she turned into the house.

Rachel knew its geography well. Firm of purpose, she moved swiftly up the stairs, across the landing past Frances's room – glimpse of women with gold shoes thrown off, dabbing at their hair – and on to the wing destined one day for Toby's aged mother. She came to a door on which a *No Entry* notice had been pinned: a command which had plainly taken Fiona many hours to accomplish, decorated with a border of poppies and ice creams – the pathos of unacknowledged effort, Rachel thought. She would remember to congratulate Fiona if she saw her again.

She pushed through the door into an unlit passage, turned

271

into the first door on the right. The room, Frances had once told her, was sometimes used for an overspill of guests: its decoration reflected its status. Rachel went straight to the window, opened it in the hope that the night air, quite cool by now, would soon dispel the stuffy smell of unaired cotton and lavender bags. She looked at the bright half moon balanced on the crest of a giant cedar, and listened to the faint soughing Cellar Music playing *Lullaby of Broadway*. Excited by her distance from the party, and her absolute privacy, she pulled back the bramble-printed cover of one of the twin beds: it was made up with clean pink sheets. She then unzipped her dress and let it fall to the ground. By the dim light of the moon it looked like the soft ashy mound of the remains of a bonfire. Shoes off, next: the relief of stretching the toes – and into the strange bed.

The pillows were of the prim kind that are often designated for visitors. They did not cave protectively about her head, nor did the sheets have the cool stroke of linen. But it was escape, escape. The mossiness that precedes oblivion lapped over her body. Within moments she slept.

*   *   *

Ant Cellar, bearing in mind his reputation of value for money, did not leave the bandstand during the first short break: he squatted on the floor drinking a can of beer, his pose out of keeping with his white dinner jacket. But it was only fucking human, as he said so often, to let the act slide for a moment or two after hours of non-stop fantastic playing. The rest of the boys had gone off for fifteen minutes – not a moment more, mind – rest and refreshment. To fulfil Frances's wish for 'never a moment without music', Ant had employed his old uncle (his old mum's brother), once a cocktail-bar player who had made quite a reputation at a pub in Marlow, to fill the gap. Uncle Bill couldn't run to the white gear, but had turned up neat enough in a black dinner jacket and red bow tie, and was plunking very nicely through a lot of old tunes on the piano.

So the lovely Frances ought to be pleased. Where was she?

Ant, looking about, saw her daughter – wretched-looking little mite – offering him a piece of paper and a pencil. He kew what she wanted. With the weariness of one who has suffered many years of autograph-fatigue – but with a lovely smile to cheer her up – he wrote his signature with a flourish, and added 'with love'. The child seemed pleased, thanked him.

'Enjoying it?' asked Ant.

Fionia struggled between loyalty and honesty.

'Quite.'

'Some spectacle. Terrific, I'd say. Where's your mum?'

'Don't know.'

'If you see her, tell her I'd like a word. Promise. There's a darling.' Another friendly smile.

Fiona backed away, unable to speak, clutching her precious piece of paper. She began to run: over the empty dance floor, up the steps of the terrace, into the heavy-lily air of the drawing room, scurrying between guests, some of whom tried to clutch at her dress and called her name. But she would not stop. She did not care what happened to the rest of the party now, and she did not want to be part of it. She had Ant Cellar's autograph, her most precious possession in the world, and all she wanted to do was to lock her bedroom door, and think about his kindness.

It wasn't until she was in bed, autograph under the pillow, that she remembered his request. Well, she had not seen her mother or, for that matter, her father, for ages. She wondered whether to get up again and keep her sort-of-promise, but she couldn't bear the thought. Besides, Ant, if he ever found out, would be bound to forgive her. He was a forgiving sort of man, she could tell.

*   *   *

Thomas had always prided himself on his ability quickly to resume dignity if, at some unfortunate moment, it eluded him. Within a few moments of his sobbing declarations of love to

Rosie, he was walking with her calmly over a moon-bleached lawn as if nothing untoward had taken place. She held his arm, they walked in step. With her free hand she held both her fan and the skirt of her dress. Thomas could see a regular flash of pretty velvet shoes buckled with glass jewels. They were supposed to be following Serena, but she had hurried ahead of them and was nowhere to be seen. Thomas sensed that Rosie's enthusiasm for the meeting with her daughter had waned. Rather, she seemed preoccupied and entranced by every aspect of the summer night.

'I have a notion, Thomas, sometimes, that on nights like this the world is tipped upside down. What do you think, now?'

'Quite,' said Thomas, able in truth to agree. Never had his own world been so completely turned upside down.

'What I mean is, the night sky could be a daisied lawn, while we could be walking on a sky of stars.'

'Quite,' said Thomas again. He found his own perception of the earth's turnabout lagging a little behind Rosie's, but wished to convey an understanding of her fancies at all cost. 'Not many daisies,' he added.

'No, but you know what I mean.'

'I do, of course I do.' Flushed with agreement, he squeezed her small hand.

'Marvellous, marvellous party,' said Rosie. 'I'm glad I came. Such surprises.'

Thomas's instinct was to agree most heartedly with this sentiment, too, but he knew he should be cautious from now in his declarations. Nothing too soppy, or she'd be off like a bird. He chose another tack.

'Very glad, though, my children chose not to come. Wouldn't have been their sort of thing at all.'

'No, they were wise. I doubt if Serena's enjoyed it.' Rosie paused for a moment, head cocked on one side. Moonlight becomes you, Thomas said to himself. The potency of old lyrics is as powerful as Keats when a man in love has had a certain amount to drink.

'Listen,' Rosie was saying. 'I hear music, Mr Arkwright. Different music from the band.'

They listened. From behind a thick bay hedge came the melancholy combination of saxophone and bass guitar playing *Michelle*. They rounded a corner and found themselves in a garden thick with white roses, many of their petals scattered on the ground. In the space in the centre of the rose beds a small dance floor had been laid. Here, two couples danced like statues loosely soldered to their base – not, Thomas quickly realised, husbands partnering their own wives, but some kind of slightly nefarious mixture which he hoped he and Rosie were about to join. The musicians, dressed approximately as gypsies, eased their way into another yearning Beatles' song.

'Shall we be dancing a while?' whispered Rosie. 'I'd like to dance again, just this once.'

Thomas led her through the white roses, heart scattered as their petals, moon swinging wildly in the sky, limbs deliquescent with joy.

'Rosie,' was all he could say, and they danced.

*   *   *

Ralph, in his impatience, paid little attention to Frances's transformation of the garden. He was bent on finding his mother and taking her home. Soon as possible.

He passed couples in conversation on the scattered garden seats, faces a kaleidoscope of pink lights reflected from the braziers' flames. Their apparent contentment depressed him: why was there no available woman for him to sit with before a brazier, too? Only his sister, it seemed, shared his aloneness. He found her in the densest shadows of a cedar tree, sitting on the ground. He joined her. They both lit cigarettes.

'Seen Mum?'

'Just came across her in the vegetable garden.'

'Alone?'

'Course not.' Serena gave the faintest snigger.

'Oh God. She's incorrigible.'

'Making up for lost time, perhaps. She's been in Norfolk, what, six years? Long time for her in one place.'

'Who knows what goes on there? Who was the man?'

'No idea. Fat. Vaguely familiar.'

Ralph sighed, got up. 'Enjoying yourself?'

'No.'

'Want to come with me?'

'I'm fine here.'

'Can't think why you agreed to come.'

'Mum's sake. Not that she's shown any signs of wanting actually to be with her children, as per usual.'

'I'd better find her, take her home.'

'You'll be lucky.'

Ralph wandered away to continue his search. This time he came upon the hedge that guarded the more private dancers from the rest of the party. He stood for a while listening to the music, thinking there could be no sadder sound than a saxophonist and a bass guitar plucking away at the darkness. Then, dreading the moment, he turned into the rose garden and saw his mother dancing with the man who bought so many of her pictures. For a moment he felt the illusion of looking at old photographs. This scene was the top one: behind it shuffled dozens of similar images from his childhood, Rosie forever dancing with some new man.

He left quickly, not wanting to be seen. Back in the marquee – its warm, plush lily smell a sudden comfort – less people were on the dance floor, but many of the supper tables were occupied by breakfasters. Martin and Ursula sat together in a corner – Ursula, endearingly, eating a large pile of scrambled eggs very fast. They seemed preoccupied. Ralph had no wish to take up their invitation to join them. But he knew his mother was unlikely to be available for some time yet. Perhaps, he thought, the best way to pass the time would be to sleep. Well-acquainted with the upstairs of the house, he would find an unoccupied bedroom and doze for an hour or so. Perfect solution. He hurried inside and up the stairs he had climbed so often on days in the recent past, at Frances's request.

* * *

Ursula finished her second plate of eggs and bacon, energy restored. This was the part of the evening she had most looked forward to: she and Martin had danced with everyone they were obliged to dance with, now they could remain together until the band stopped playing. Martin drank black coffee.

'You know that evening –?' Ursula said.

'Evening of the cat?' He always read her thoughts so quickly.

'Yes. I never had a chance to tell you.'

'About the place?'

'Quite.'

'You told me about the wedding. You've been biding your time about the place.' They both smiled. Martin often teased his wife for not choosing the right moment.

'It just so happens,' said Ursula, pushing away her empty plate and helping herself to a peach, 'the farmer's wife said this . . . perfect farmhouse would one day soon be up for sale.'

Martin felt a coil of annoyance squirm within him. Why here, of all places, did Ursula have to bring up the old subject once again? She had been wise enough not to mention it for months now. But he gave himself time to regain his calm, still looking at her lively, luminescent eyes so full of hope. She was more beautiful now than when he had married her. His eyes still on her face, he began at last to respond: uncalculated, not quite truthful words.

'What I haven't had the chance to tell *you*,' he said, 'is that . . . I've come round to agreeing with you almost completely.' (To be honest, he had not given the matter much thought, as usual, though of late the irritations of Oxford, caused mostly by extreme quantities of tourists, had occurred to him.)

Ursula held her breath, watched Martin's fine eyes stare now into some invisible depths of the pink tablecloth.

277

'I've come to realise the terrible decline of the place, these days,' he went on. 'My room is the only part I like any more. So it seemed to me that you're probably right, and perhaps in a year or so we should begin to think in terms of a change. . . .'

The stilted words of his declaration amazed himself as much as his wife. As she grasped his hand, incredulous, he then felt an overwhelming sense of relief. It was a strain, defying your spouse year after year: now, the geat unspoken restraint between them would surely begin to fade. Perhaps he should have conceded years ago. . . . As it was, there was no *hurry*. He would not be able to abide sudden change, of course – Ursula would understand that. But his promise was there. Enough for the moment.

Ursula continued to grasp his hand. Trying to contain herself, she knew she must quickly repay this concession with a show of anxiety about Martin's own worries.

'What about your work?' she asked.

'Oh, that.' He shrugged. 'Shouldn't be impossible to arrange something.' He finished his coffee, tugged at his wife's jumbled hair. 'You've waited so long,' he said, 'so patiently.'

At that moment, Ant Cellar and his refreshed bandsmen struck up again. Martin and Ursula were unable to resist the empty dance floor. They swept together like a couple who have enjoyed dancing together for a long time, and whose every movement signified a deep, elusive accord. Other guests, slower to make up their mind, seemed hesitant to join them. They found themselves dancing alone for quite a while, whirling between the flowered pillars, faithful to every change of rhythm. Ursula knew there would still be some waiting, but she also knew they danced in private celebration.

*　　*　　*

Mary Lutchins watched her daughter and son-in-law for a few moments: there was no chance of their leaving for a long while yet. For her own part, it was time to go home. She had had a thoroughly good time, dancing and watching, enjoying the food and the flowers, but now it was time to leave. She worried slightly about Rosie, whom she had not seen return to the marquee since their escapade among the raspberries. Then she dismissed the worry. Rosie was capable of looking after herself. No doubt some romantic adventure had befallen her, and there would be a good story on the long journey back tomorrow.

Mary made her way to the garden. Just one last look, she thought, before going to the car. She would probably never come to such a party again.

She found the sky paling at the edges, and the air damp with approaching dawn. She clutched her shawl tightly about her. If Bill had been here they could have sat beside a brazier for a while to warm themselves before the journey home. She looked up at the vast black silhouettes of the cedars: they dwarfed the smaller trees whose cobwebs of lights were woven among real cobwebs now, which sparkled more brightly with dew. Mary walked with a brisk stride to the stableyard, where her privileged car was parked. 'At Mary's age, she can't go tramping across to the field on her own,' the ever-thoughtful Frances had probably said, and Mary was grateful.

In the stableyard the clock tower said five-past-three. How the night had flown! A barn owl rose from a roof and clapped its way over to some distant tree, hooting its protest at Mary's interruption. Ant Cellar's music was just loud enough to step in time to over the cobblestones – Mary gave a few small skips she would never have dared in public, in memory of her youth. She found herself thinking of the unexpected strength that had come to her since Bill's death, and the relief at no longer having to worry about his aloneness. In fact, though she could hardly bear to admit it to herself, that relief was so great she had found she had spent hours – even a whole day or two – without missing Bill. At such times hideous doubts had come upon her – doubts as to whether she had been right to hide from him the depths of her private anxieties. They might have loomed so thunderously between them that the lightness of their marriage would have been obscured. Now, she would never know. As it was, beneath the protection of the quiet, cosy life

279

they had mutely agreed upon, the pretence of perfection had been able to thrive.

But oh, the disloyalty of such thoughts! Mary slowed her step, appalled. The death of a loved spouse, she told herself in an attempt at justification, brings questions as well as regrets. It is futile to listen to such questions, for they can never be answered. For a while, at least, confusions must be endured, even the confusion of being *perfectly all right* most of the time: often, even, *enjoying* the new, solitary state. But when she reached the car and imagined the journey back to Oxford on her own, she felt her courage waver for a moment. The division between life and death was smaller than she had previously supposed, but the haunting thing was the space between memory and reality. Sometimes she would put out a hand, convinced of Bill's presence, only to grasp air. Alone in the dawn, she wondered for the umpteenth time where he was. Then she gathered her resolve to stop tormenting herself, and to concentrate, as Bill would have insisted – on driving very slowly, very carefully, mind only on the road.

* * *

Ralph quietly pushed open the door of what he knew was a little-used bedroom. At once he realised his mistake. By the light of a greying sky, he saw someone was asleep. A black dress lay expired on the floor.

He found himself closing the door behind him, curious to see a guest who had drunk too much and needed help. But for all his care, he disturbed the sleeper. She raised herself from the pillow, pulling the sheet across her front: quick shadow-picture of large breasts. It was Rachel Arkwright, the sad lady he had danced with earlier.

'Oh my God,' he said, 'I'm sorry. I was looking for somewhere to sleep.'

'Don't worry.' Rachel was dazed, but smiling. 'You haven't disturbed me, honestly. I had the same idea, got here first.'

They both quietly laughed.

'I'll go,' said Ralph.

'No! Please don't.' Rachel raised herself a little higher, letting the sheet slip lower. She was amazed at her own request even as she heard the words. 'Please come here,' she said.

You cannot be responsible if your actions are faster than your thoughts, she reflected much later. Then, anything, anything can happen.

Ralph, also with no time for thought, found himself beside her. She was warm, huge, soft, smelling faintly of hyacinth, so utterly desirable that he had to be firm with himself to control his haste. Strange thing was, Rachel seemed to feel the same. He had never known a woman so eager and sweet in her responses. Mouth clamped to her strawberry-tasting lips, the despair that had lacerated Ralph's evening vanished, and some vague amorphous shape, that he dared call hope, struggled for life in his mind.

'This is all very . . . peculiar,' Rachel whispered at some indefinable moment. 'Between two people who have scarcely met.'

'Don't you think Frances would be very pleased, after all her trouble, to know that at least one extraordinary thing had happened between two guests?' he answered. 'Now, if you could move over just a few inches, I can get in too.'

Rachel threw back the bedclothes. The opal light of almost full dawn drenched her pale skin. Ralph, full of awe, took her slowly.

*   *   *

Frances stopped dancing at last. Skilfully shedding her latest partner, she shook her head at the next one and left the marquee. She wanted a single moment on her own, before it was all over, to store in her memory. Outside she found the sky, whose paleness had been pushing through the sides of the marquee, was striped with quicksilver clouds that dulled flames and lights that had been so bright in the darkness. Still, she thought, the effect of an invasion of fireflies was still there.

She wondered if this had occurred to anyone else. Probably not. People were so unobservant, so uninspired by connections. She had had to tell many friends her dress was based on a mermaid: not one of them had had the vision to guess. Very odd.

Still, it had been a good party. An unforgettable party, actually. And still was. At least two dozen couples continued to dance, showing no signs of fatigue. Frances returned through the French window to the tent, her picture of the garden intact. She had a feeling the moment had come.

Her instinct was right. As soon as he saw her, Ant, who had been so wonderfully patient, came down from the bandstand and hurried towards her.

'Bandleader's perks,' he said. 'Time for. No?'

'Yes.' She smiled, a little afraid. He took her hand. His skin was curiously rough.

'Any special tune you want?'

'No.'

'Dare say I could arrange it, you know.' They both laughed. 'Enjoying your own party?' Frances nodded. 'I'd say it's been one of the great parties of the summer,' said Ant. He held her a little away from him, eyes faintly intrusive on her body. She gave a shy wiggle, thinking it was what he waited for.

'Ant,' she said, 'could you really help me? Put me on to people, like you said? I want serious employment. I mean, I think I could organise this sort of thing quite well, don't you?'

Ant nodded briefly. His keenness to help her, so apparent yesterday under the tree, seemed a little faded.

'Do my best, I promise,' he said. 'Let's get together next week, go through my contacts. You ever free to come up to London? We could, I dunno, have a bite of dinner, something . . .' His voice petered out; he seemed slightly breathless. Then he pulled her towards him, quite roughly. 'No more talking,' he said. 'I want to concentrate.'

Frances obeyed. What is it, she thought, that causes such havoc with my desires? I loved Ralphie, I love Toby – I will always love Toby. And, yet, here I am now, desperately

282

wanting this awful, irresistible musician. . . . What will happen when the party's over?

No answer came to mind. Frances felt Ant Cellar crush her sequins so tightly to him she knew many of them would rip from their fragile backing of silk, and leave a trail of guilt sparkling on the floor behind her.

*   *   *

Toby, pleased by his couple of hours' work – another important brick in place – returned to the marquee to assess how things were progressing. Among the dozen couples moving slowly to *Dancing Cheek to Cheek*, he saw his wife and the rotten little sod of the bandleader clasped more closely together than it might be thought prudent in public, and he did not care. Far from wanting to tear her ridiculous earrings down through her lobes tonight, it occurred to him that Mr Cellar's dubious help over 'a job' might be just the answer for Frances's future occupation.

He hurried out into the garden, surveyed the guests who braved the clammy mists of early morning. Dresses that had benefited from candlelight, he noticed, were now unkindly lit by dawn. Hems were deeply coloured from their trail through the grass. Dinner jackets were flung over pale shoulders. Women's faces were in need of repair: men's jowls were darkening.

Toby reached an unoccupied seat, sat down, rubbed his own cold hands over the brazier's dying flames. Frances had indeed thought of everything. He appreciated that, would tell her properly one day. And it was almost over. This time tomorrow, things would be more or less back to normal. Then it would be back to work, routine. . . . What else? Toby looked about him. By now, he observed, most husbands and wives were reunited, if only bound by the practicalities of getting home together. He supposed he should claim Frances, suggest they have breakfast, stand about together so that people could say goodbye to both of them at once. But his desire not to break up her dance with the appalling Mr Cellar was stronger than his feeling of social practicality, and he stayed where he was.

*　　*　　*

For Ralph and Rachel the last hours of the party went so swiftly they had no time to plot an innocent return. They crossed the terrace together, amazed that no-one looked surprised that they should be walking side by side, to the almost empty dance floor. Neither had any inclination to join the couples clutching their way through *The Nearness of You*. There was no need.

There was dew on the lawns, and indeterminate ground mist. It rose high enough to obscure the holders of the fiery torches, so their flames appeared to rise straight from the mist. They stood looking about for a while, silent, stranded in their reluctance to face searching for Rosie and Thomas, saying goodbye, parting.

'I live not far from Oxford,' Ralph said at last. 'Would you ever come down one day and see me?'

Rachel, holding her skirt above the dew, turned a little from him so that he should not see her face.

'I could,' she said. 'I could come down for lunch. Day return.'

Ralph smiled. 'I think we should make our way over there. That's where I saw my mother dancing with your husband.'

They began to walk, a few feet apart, towards the rose garden.

In the silvery light, Rachel could see the thin electric wires that joined the lights in trees and bushes: illusion of fireflies over. She hurried to keep up with the man who, having begun by disturbing her sleep, was likely in future to disturb her life.

'I've this nostalgic longing to go for a picnic on the Cherwell one day,' she said. 'Silly, I know. All commercial and spoilt these days, I expect. But I'd like to try.'

'We could do anything,' said Ralph. 'Anything.' He saw that a frill of dew had stained her satin shoes, and there was a panda-like smudge of mascara round one eye. 'Look,' he said. 'There they are at last. God, I don't want you to go.'

'I'll come on Monday, promise,' she said.

*   *   *

'My wife must be looking everywhere,' said Thomas, who had not spoken for a very long time. 'Perhaps we should. . . .'

'Ralphie, too. He'll be wanting to go home,' said Rosie.

They unclasped themselves. Thomas had no idea for how much time they had been dancing. (Dancing! Scarcely moving, pressed so closely together Thomas had been able to feel the brush of satin on his stomach, where his shirt had finally come apart.) Soft tunes had come and gone, miles away from outer space. They may have been alone, there may have been other dancers. He did not know or care. And now it was only his ruddy sense of duty that forced him, at last, to break away from the woman he loved with a passion so great that it felt almost like humility.

Rosie tapped him on the nose with her fan once more. In the increasing light he saw her topaz eyes were mischievous.

'I do believe I'm slightly intrigued, after all, Mr Arkwright. Thomas,' she said. 'My darling man, we've had a lovely evening. Will you come to Norfolk again one day, perhaps? Buy some more pictures?'

'I'll buy everything you paint from now on. Everything.'

The idea seemed to please Rosie, whose commercial instincts were no less keen than her romantic ones.

'There's an extravagant promise! But I'll keep you to it.'

'You won't keep me away,' Thomas assured her.

'And now, my darling, we must go in search of Ralphie. I don't suppose he's enjoyed the evening one bit. He's not at all a party man.'

Thomas took her arm. In a moment of swift calculation, he felt it quite in order to do so. If they came upon Rachel and Ralph, both would naturally think he was being polite to an

285

older lady. Nothing else would cross their minds. Deception is so easy.

They left the sanctuary of the rose garden, and the soft thump of the music that had engaged them for so long. In the cool wide spaces of the lawn, no longer pressed to Thomas's fiery body, Rosie shivered.

'I do believe I see Serena,' she said, 'sitting under the cedar. What on earth has she been doing all night, the silly girl? My children. . . .'

Thomas followed her gaze. He, too, saw the scraggy little shape of the girl with the amber hair, huddled on the earth beneath a vast black bough. He smiled to himself, wondering what madness had once induced him to mind so much when a glass door had come between them. Very strange, the acute lack of interest you feel when looking on a woman you once, but no longer, desired. His eyes progressed to the marquee, its glamour in the darkness now dispelled in near-daylight. Music still thumped forth, a sound nostalgic as the scent of flowers. Thomas found it almost unbearably evocative, moving. Or were his feelings inspired by the fact that within moments Rosie Cotterman would be gone?

'Why, there's Ralphie,' she was saying, 'my devoted son.'

'With my wife, as a matter of fact.'

'What a coincidence, isn't that, now, Mr Arkwright – Thomas?'

Rosie stopped fanning herself and waved.

*   *   *

Toby, from his half-obscured garden seat, watched the two couples approaching each other. All four stopped, as if obeying some unseen signal, a couple of yards apart. Thomas gave a sort of half bow, a vague attempt at comedy, perhaps, towards Rachel. She stood holding up her skirt over slightly parted legs. Rosie fanned her face very fast, as if suffering from a hot afternoon. Ralph just stood, arms dangling, hands heavy at their ends. What different kinds of evening had they come from, Toby wondered, without much interest. He rose, intending to join their tense quadrangle. Strange how even after a long night's dancing the act of leaving made people awkward again. He would say goodbye. Encourage them on their way.

*   *   *

Thomas looked at Rachel. The familiarity of her stance seared him inexplicably: toes turned in, make-up rather battered – a bit skew-whiff, somehow. Well, she'd probably had a jolly good time dancing away the night with Rosie's son, various people. He was glad.

Rachel's eyes flicked from Thomas's dishevelled hair, to his bow tie (askew again) to the shirt that had finally shed two buttons. She could see the skin of his stomach through the gap, and was surprised by her lack of irritation or shame. Poor old Thomas: he didn't have enough fun, really. She'd seen him dancing with Mary, and now obviously he'd been doing his bit for Ralph's wild-looking mother. Kind-hearted, Thomas: hopeless, but kind. And in no condition to drive.

Ralph inwardly sighed. He knew so well his mother's end-of-a-party look: she'd been flattered, as always, no doubt, by Rachel's husband and other men much younger than herself. Flattery and wine always raised her adrenalin to fever pitch. But now she seemed a trifle bored, impatient. He need not have feared her dancing with the wretched-looking Thomas: absolutely not her type. Nice of him, though, to have looked after her. Ralph found his gaze attracted to the large slice of Thomas's stomach, and wondered, if, in time to come, Rachel would explain. . . .

Rosie prickled with impatience. Once again, silly Ralphie had not found even a possibility of a wife among the guests. He'd plainly wasted his time on Mr Arkwright's motherly wife, doing his duty as always. She'd have plenty to say on the journey back. . . . As for Serena, what was the girl up to? Breaking the silence between the four of them, Rosie called to her daughter under the tree. Thomas moved to stand by Rachel.

287

'Time to go, old thing?' He patted her cold shoulder.

'Right.'

Ralph stepped over to take his mother's arm. 'We're going, too,' he said.

'Of course we are, Ralphie. Couldn't find you anywhere. Where've you been?'

'Looking for you.'

'Is Serena coming with us?'

'No, she's got her own car.'

*　　*　　*

Toby watched the muted movements of this strange minuet in the dew. When he reached them, they all shuffled about again, making way for him, crowding him with thanks and compliments, and apologies for leaving. He turned, from kissing Rachel's cheek, to Rosie. A thin, pale girl with long amber hair was suddenly standing by her. Where had she come from, and when?

'My daughter, Toby darling,' Rosie was saying. 'I don't think you've met.'

'We haven't, no.'

Serena gave him a limp, cold hand to shake. She turned her eyes to Thomas.

'Er, we . . .' he said. 'The Gallery?'

Serena nodded. 'Hello,' she said quietly to everyone in general.

'Come on, Rachel, home.'

Thomas bedded a hand in his wife's arm, turned her towards the house.

Rosie and Ralph followed them.

'You're hopeless, darling,' Rosie whispered, unable to wait until they were out of earshot. 'You've gone and missed your chance again.'

In the field that had been made into a carpark, Thomas and Rachel made their way towards their marital Mercedes, one of the few cars left, covered in a sheen of dew. Rachel, forgetting she had intended to drive, allowed Thomas to open the passenger door for her, sank back into the familiar support of the seat. Her feet were icy, her shoes ruined. Thomas switched on the engine, began to turn the leather steering wheel.

'Pretty good thrash, that,' he said. 'Didn't you think?'

'Pretty good,' Rachel agreed, after some thought. 'I'm glad we decided to go.'

*　　*　　*

Toby was left a few paces from Serena on the lawn. She wore a very simple silk chemise, much the same colour as the sky. A navy wool cardigan hung over one arm, and she carried an empty wine glass. Toby saw that its side was stamped with a small fan of fractured lipstick. He moved his eyes from its reddish imprint to the girl's pale, unmade-up lips, and felt curious. Her amber hair hung down over her shoulders, but did not hide her fragile collarbones, underlined with shadows.

'Would you like,' he asked, 'to see the garden?'

Serena shrugged. 'Not really. I've been wandering round most of the night.'

Toby turned towards the marquee. Frances and her bandleader, in a close meeting of sequins and white flannel, moved across the dance floor by the French windows to a slow Gershwin tune.

'Breakfast, then? Are you hungry?'

Serena shook her head. 'Not really. Slightly cold.'

She handed him the empty glass, and he helped her pull on the cardigan. Its sleeves all but covered her hands.

'I was thinking,' said Toby, who had not been thinking at all, 'of going up to the woods to see the badgers. Would you like to come?'

Serena nodded. Politeness or interest? He could not tell.

They made their way through trails that crossed in the dew, past the last of the torches that flamed through the ground mist, to the end of the garden. Toby opened a gate into the field that rose up to the distant woods.

In silence they reached the path that led to the place he had visited so often this summer, not far from the badgers' sett. When they arrived at his especial oak tree, he took off his dinner jacket, laid it on the ground. Serena sat on it without a word. She curved her arms round her legs, placed her chin on raised knees. Small points of white fingers just showed beneath the long navy sleeves. Toby chose his own place, the flattened root of a nearby tree, half-covered in moss and last year's leaves. Despite the luminous sky, here in the woods it was still semi-dark. Shadows fluttered.

They waited a long time, listening to the distant thread of music from the party, the occasional crackle of branches. Toby had never known a girl who sat so still. He thought there was little chance of seeing a badger – too late, now, but he could not bring himself to spoil Serena's hope. She seemed happy in her expectation. He decided to say nothing, and to remain unmoving.